Goodbye, Burger City

a novel

Kevin Quigley

for Steve Spignesi

who knows a little about shaping the identity of writers

Part One
Oklahoma City

Chapter 1: The Hole in the Wall

There was a hole in her bedroom wall, and when Karen Luck was six, she found it, and looked through.

Her parents' bedroom was right next to hers. Sometimes she heard sounds coming from the other side of her wall, and made up stories as to what could be going on in there. Were her parents watching a particularly good movie with the sound down – perhaps that was why all the *ooo*s and *oh God*s were so distinct. Maybe they were fighting. She could imagine that: Mom on one side of the room, near the bookshelves, Dad on the other, by the window. They would be trying to keep their voices down, but they could not mask the grunts and other guttural sounds that kept escaping their anger. Karen had to work harder at the story of her parents fighting – she had never even seen them having an argument. It was so hard to picture Dad, who read to her at night and made breakfast every morning, saying a cross word against Mom, whom they both adored. And Mom, who sometimes took her to book signings if she promised to behave, and who would let Karen sit on her lap and read some of her writing out loud when she was done for the day, could no more hurl insults at her Dad than she could fly.

It was those *ooo* sounds when reading that the sounds behind her wall most resembled, but out of context, it was hard to tell. Maybe they were just reading in there, reading at a level and an intensity that dinner-table books were too polite to engender. Then she found the hole. It was behind a framed picture that Mom had hung up when she was born – three strawberries, painted in a folk style. She had only wanted a closer look at the painting; she wanted to write a story about it, about a different girl in a different room who had the same picture hung up. She had begun writing stories the year before, and both parents had discussed whether it was time Karen got her own typewriter instead of using Mom or Dad's. So she took the painting off the wall and there was the hole, eye-height if she stood on her tiptoes and big enough to see the entirety of the room. And here some of her questions were answered.

The image that came most naturally to Karen when she thought of her parents were of the two of them sitting at the dinner table, each with a fork in one hand and a book in the other, sometimes making gentle *ooo* sounds when the language was particularly good. Mom would *ooo* and Dad would look up, testing the weather on Mom's face to see if it was an *ooo* she wanted to explain and discuss or one she wanted to keep to herself. Or Dad would do it and Mom wouldn't look up from her book, but a small smile would pass over her lips. Karen would watch these silent exchanges from behind her own book; by the time she was six, she was reading books that would be assigned to her in high school. Sometimes, she would *ooo* too, and Mom and Dad would both stop reading and look over at her, indulgently. Part of her hated that, because she didn't want to be put on the spot. Part of her loved their attention.

Her father was lying on the bed, crouched and on his belly with his butt in the air. His face – red with exertion and scrunched up as if in concentration – smooshed the pillows down against the bed. He was naked. She had seen him naked before, coming out of the shower or peeing with the door open, and earlier this year, the three of them had had a very frank discussion about the penises boys had and the vaginas girls had. They'd put down their books at the kitchen table and halted passing beans around and laid it all out for Karen, the gist of which was that boys had something hanging outside and girls had something tucked inside. What she saw now seemed to contradict most of the things she'd learned over the course of that conversation. Mom stood up at the foot of the bed, almost as naked as Dad, wearing some sort of belt. And *Mom* had a penis. Different from Dad's – longer and stiffer than the one that sometimes flopped out in front of her father when he didn't bother to put on a robe or a towel coming out of the bath – but, by the parameters her parents had given her, most definitely a penis. And she was sticking inside her father, over and over. Into his butt, over and over. Was it painful? Was that why her father was making that face?

Just then, Dad made that *ooo* sound, and Karen decided that he wasn't in pain. That *ooo* sound wasn't a pain sound. Slowly, quietly, Karen replaced the strawberry painting and retreated to her bed, which was strewn with books and two notepads and a mechanical pencil she had filched from her Dad's desk. For the moment, she didn't want to read or write. She only wanted to think.

At six, Karen Luck was already a contemplative child. She would finish a book during recess and spend the rest of her time outside in the shade of the school, wondering what the ending meant, if it was fair to the rest of the book, whether she knew enough about the characters to like them or hate them. Math gave her trouble, so she would sit during solving time and stare dreamily – to Mrs. Chastain, at least – out the window, turning over the concepts in her head over and over until she understood it as completely as she could. And when faced with an all-new situation, something outside her purview, she would think on it as long as she needed to before acting.

It was this quality that would later propel her into a slightly successful career as a novelist. Even later, it was this quality that would change her career from slightly successful to rampantly successful, with her third novel, *Where'd She Go?*, not to mention the ensuing shitstorm that followed.

Now, she drew on her nature to consider what she'd seen. Boys had penises. Girls had vaginas. Mom had a penis. But that wasn't exactly right, was it? She'd also seen her mother naked. She slept in the nude, and sometimes when Karen had a nightmare and needed comfort, she would sneak into her parents' room and nestle between them for safety. In the morning, Mom would get out of bed and Karen thought if Mom had had a penis then, she would have noticed. Her first conclusion, then, was that Mom had a penis, but not *all* the time. Maybe not even *most* of the time. Maybe *only* when she wanted to put it into Dad's butt.

Her second conclusion was that she shouldn't talk about this with either of them. As parents, they'd always been very supportive of her curiosity, but even at six, Karen suspected that this went beyond curiosity. This was a *private* thing. If she hadn't found the hole in the wall, she never would have seen what her parents were up to, and if she had come through their bedroom door in the normal way, she thought they would have stopped and looked embarrassed. Otherwise, she would have seen them doing it in front of her. For whatever reason, this was a thing they didn't want to do in front of her. And that meant it was *very* private; they didn't usually shut their office doors when they were writing, and writing, Mom told her, was the most private thing a person can do.

Could she talk to anyone about the thing she had seen through the hole in the wall? Henry Dear, maybe? Henry lived next door and sometimes Karen went over to have dinner at their house. Henry's Mom was the best cook in the world and sometimes made desserts like pineapple upside-down cake. Her own Mom might be a writer who'd been on television, but she couldn't cook to save her life. Dad was the cook in the family, and his food was just okay. Maybe he was better because *he* hadn't been on television. He wrote his books but no one knew he was the writer. He wrote his books under the name Doreen Daley and no one could interview her because she wasn't real. Would Henry know why Mom would only have a penis when she wanted to put it inside her Dad?

Karen Luck thought for awhile and came up with no solutions. The situation was too new and had too many variables that she didn't understand. Nothing in real life or in the books she'd read had prepared her. Instead, she relegated the problem of the hole in the wall to the back of her mind, picked up the book she was reading – *Anne of Green Gables* – and fell back inside.

Over the next year and a half, Karen would peek through that hole often. Mom didn't always have a penis. Sometimes she sat astride her father and bounced up and down on him. Often during these moments, her Dad would be in a dress and lipstick, wearing a wig whose long brown hair draped over the pillows on the bed. Sometimes Dad would wear stockings like Mom did – dark and sheer, all the way up to his knees. When Mom did have a penis, Dad would occasionally lie on his back with his feet on Mom's shoulders, and he would touch his own penis while she went in and out of his butt. Karen saw all these things before she was eight years old; she questioned none of them, asked about none of them. They all went into the growing repository holding the specifics of this unexplained phenomenon down at the back of her brain.

She finally managed to ask about it the day after her ninth birthday, and of course by then her mother was dead, so it didn't have to be a secret anymore.

Chapter 2: Carried Away

Oklahoma City was founded by a group of settlers who stood outside the Unassigned Lands (well, except by the native people) until noon on April 22, 1889. Then they rushed, en masse, into the lands and claimed whatever land they stopped at. Before the end of the day, skeletons of houses and farms were erected. Some settlers had actually come early, sneaking onto land and claiming it before the Land Run even began. Those people were called Sooners. It was a baffling and chaotic way to start a city, and that was only the beginning of its chaos. A little under a century later, when the city was larger and modern, developers constructed an amusement park called Sooner City. The Home of the Sonic Boom, was its tagline, and that was where Karen was going for her ninth birthday.

"Did you know," Mom said from the front seat of the car, "that when I was your age, they used to fly supersonic jets over the city?"

"Like rocket ships?" Henry Dear asked. Henry was the only one Karen had asked to her birthday. She had friends at school, but none of them were close enough to be brought into the world of her family. Her family was *weird*, and it didn't take some girl in her class to come over and see how they lived to know that. Most parents didn't stay home all day and write. That alone was enough to label them *weird*, but there were other things, stuff Karen couldn't quite put her finger on. Intangibles, a word she didn't know but understood. Take the way Mom was dressed right now. She was wearing what she wore to write: namely, jeans, a T-shirt with Garfield on it, and a baseball hat into which she tucked her hair before it had even begun to dry. Mom was messy when she wrote and that was all right, because writing was private. But Karen always hated seeing Mom outside like that. It was like showing the whole world your hidden self. Karen intended to never let the world see her hidden self.

Her father had his own hidden self. Sometimes when he was writing, Karen would poke her head into his office and find him wearing that wig, the same wig he wore when Mom put her penis into him. Was he trying to *become* Doreen Daley, trying to understand who she was, sitting at his typewriter and creating another mystery novel that she, Karen, wasn't allowed to read yet? Did her Dad want to be a girl? And if so, how come he didn't sometimes have a vagina? If her Mom could grow a penis sometimes, why couldn't her father grow a vagina?

These questions were too vague and too unsettling to bring anyone inside. Henry Dear, at least, understood her family to almost the same degree as Karen did. He'd been around them since the day he was born. Maybe he didn't know everything – he didn't know about the hole in the wall, or what her parents did behind it – but he knew *them*, and had always accepted them because they were just a part of his world. Mom could wear Garfield T-shirts every day and Henry wouldn't have questioned it, even though his own mother wore beautiful clothes all the time, and did her hair and nails and makeup even when she was just vacuuming the rug or reading a novel at the kitchen table. Sometimes she wished that her mother would dress like Mrs. Dear all the time.

Sometimes she wished, even though the wish confused her, that her *father* would dress like Mrs. Dear all the time. And sometimes – only sometimes, in the dark when she knew her parents were fully asleep – she wished Mrs. Dear *was* her Mom. It was an awful thought to have. She loved her own mother very, very much, and if she was also sometimes embarrassed by her, maybe that was okay. Like the stuff she saw though the hole in the wall, these were things she would never voice out loud. She suspected she was a bad person to even *have* these thoughts, and if she gave voice to them, she would probably go straight to hell.

"Not quite like rockets," Mom was saying. "Like regular planes, but they went overhead very fast. Do either of you know what the sound barrier is?"

Karen said, "It's the speed of sound. It's not as fast as the speed of light, but it's pretty fast." She didn't say it smugly, like she was smarter than Henry. Mom liked to say, "Be endlessly curious, and be generous with what you learn." You could talk about the stuff you knew, in other words, but you didn't have to be a smarty-pants about it. She'd learned about the speed of sound in science class. Henry wasn't in the same science class as she was.

Mom glanced at her in the rearview mirror. "That's right. And these were planes that *broke* the sound barrier. And for whatever reason, they decided to do it over our city."

"Did it make a sound?" Henry asked.

"Oh, it made sounds, all right. The biggest booms you'd ever heard! Some of the booms were so strong that they broke windows in town. They knocked stuff off of shelves. My Mom – your grandma – once had these amazing porcelain figurines on a high shelf in the front room. They fell to the floor and all of them shattered into pieces. It was madness."

Karen settled back into her seat, glad to listen to her mother orate. This was the voice she used when she read at night, and the voice she used when she read to people at book signings and media events. Mom didn't write mysteries like Dad did, and she didn't write under a different name. Hers was right there on the cover, more prominent than the illustration: Elaine Luck, novelist. Her books were more complicated than Karen's Dad's – lighter on plot and far more concerned with character and situation. She'd written her first novel, *The Absence of Sure Things*, three years before Karen was born. It sold well. While struggling through the final months of her ten-month pregnancy, she saw her second book, *An Unexpected Island*, come out to tepid reviews and even more tepid sales. Two years passed before the book that made her name, a thick, sexually-charged novel called *No One Knows Where Sarah Goes*, was released and immediately sold out its print run. Karen was two and didn't remember the hoopla surrounding the release of *Sarah*, but she *almost* remembered it. They started telling her the story a year after Karen had discovered the hole in the wall, when they were both feeling mellow and there wasn't anything good on TV. Maybe they thought she was finally old enough to understand some things.

"We weren't poor," Dad would say. "My books were selling well. Steadily. Steadily is good when you have diapers and formula and baby clothes to buy, not to mention keeping a roof over your head."

At this point, Mom would smile indulgently and touch his hand. "You don't need to apologize for being a successful novelist, Gary."

And Dad would chuckle and say he knew, but that he'd grown up hoping to be a bestselling writer and settling for merely *good*-selling was something he was adjusting to.

"No one was really pushing *Sarah*," Mom would say, squeezing Dad's hand harder. "Denton didn't really believe in it, even when *Publisher's Weekly* said it was the best of my three."

"Well that's not saying much, given your second book." And then Dad would wink and Mom would slap him playfully and Karen would smile because she loved this story.

"*An Unexpected Island* has its fans," she said, but not defensively. She was merely explaining. "But nothing like the fans that came on board with *Sarah*. I had no idea there were that many readers in the world! Cynthia called early. *Sarah* wasn't originally planned for a paperback run at all. They were only doing it in hardcover to fulfill the three-book contract and then they were going to quietly drop me. At least, that's what

I'd heard. Then Cynthia called to tell me there had been a bidding war – a *bidding war!* – for paperback and foreign rights. High Hopes won. And suddenly we were millionaires."

No One Knows Where Sarah Goes went back for three exponentially larger printings and still they didn't sate the desire for this book. Much of the excitement circled around a scene in which Sarah is dragged to her friend Stacy's book club, only to discover that Stacy and her husband are swingers, and so is everyone else there. In the sequence that follows, Sarah revels in carnality as-yet undreamt of by either her or her dull suburban husband, Chip, who only sometimes wanted a blowjob and who would never go down on her. Sixteen orgasms later, Sarah leaves the book club with a whole new understanding of her own sexual liberation, and she is determined to teach Chip something new. The sequence is so powerful – packed with sex but managing to avoid lasciviousness or objectification – that Karen's Mom had considered calling the book *Sixteen Orgasms*. "Maybe," Cynthia Auburn – both hers and her husband's agent – had cautioned, "that *would* be vulgar."

"Always listen to Cynthia," Mom would interject here, and both she and Dad would laugh. Karen had only met Cynthia a few times, but she didn't have to be told twice. Cynthia was a commanding presence, large and smart and stern, with a big head of dark red hair that flowed over her shoulders like a crimson waterfall. Mom thought that her name – the *Auburn* part – was as made up as Doreen Daley, but Dad swore up and down that it was real. "The *color*, Elaine, came from the woman, not the other way around." Karen could believe it. If someone had told Karen that Cynthia had simply willed that shade to happen, Karen could believe that, too. Most of her parents' other friends were dull and mediocre. When Cynthia was over for coffee or dinner (which she always brought with her; she was as sure of the Lucks' lack of cooking expertise as she was about their ability to write popular novels), Karen would sometimes sit off in a corner and watch her talk. It didn't matter what she talked about. Contracts. Character motivations. The weather, even. All of it was fascinating, accompanied as it was by that loud, full voice and that hair moving back and forth as if it were waves on a red sea.

"Anyway, the second I hung up with Cynthia, I was so overwhelmed that I could barely think. Your father was out shopping with you..."

"I was out at Chuck E. Cheese with Karen, you'll remember."

"That's right, Chuck E. Cheese. And I didn't know how to reach you or how to call you. So I ran out into the street, laughing and unable to wrap my mind around how much money *Sarah* had made us. And that was before the royalties. My advances for the first two books had been pretty high, but for *Sarah* it was miniscule. Your Dad thinks that I made the advance back in a week. I was thinking about all of that when I ran out into the street, screaming with joy. I wanted to *do* something. I wanted to commemorate this moment. So I ran into the first store I came across. It was called..."

"Hair by Claire!" Karen jumped in. She always loved this part best, because it rhymed.

"That's right!" Mom said, and tousled her hair. "I asked for the best, most expensive wig they had. I had them put it in a big round box with polka dots on it."

"I was home when your Mom got back," Dad said, picking up the story easily and effortlessly. "You were tuckered out and asleep in your crib. That was the *only* reason I didn't shout out loud when she gave it to me. I wanted to. It was such an extravagance, but she knew I wanted it. She *knew*. It was just right."

The look Mom would give him then was so enrapt, so in love, that Karen would often want to turn away from it. It was like looking in through the hole in the wall in some way that she didn't quite understand. But it was good to see them in love, and it was good to know how happy they always wanted to make one another. She could picture the whole story in her mind's eye, and before long would write it out into a story she showed them both. The name of the story was "Polka Dot Box," and after the success of her third novel, Karen Luck would find the story in a box in her father's attic. She would re-write it in her current style and bookend her fourth book – a short story collection titled *The Things She Left Behind* – with both versions. The *New York Times* would refer to this as "a glimpse into the evolutionary magic of Ms. Luck's writing."

Why the story worked – and why it still had potency years later, as she read it in a shaft of dusty sunlight on the floor of the attic – was because she understood now how one thing could have multiple purposes. The thought had never occurred to her before. A doll was the same doll no matter what. A plate didn't change what it was given its circumstance. But Dad's wig had meant one thing when Mom bought it for him, and it meant another thing when he wore it to write, and still a third thing when he wore it when Mom put her penis into him. At seven, Karen grasped all this, even if she didn't yet grasp exactly *what* those multiple meanings were. After writing "Polka Dot Box," she would stop seeing Dad's wearing it to write as *weird*; she only wanted to know *why* he did it, what it meant to him. But she didn't ask. She feared if she asked, he would somehow find out she'd found the hole in the wall, and she wasn't ready to give that up yet.

Now, in the car, Henry Dear asked, "If it was so bad, why did they name the roller coaster Sonic Boom?" That was the difference between Henry and Karen; Karen preferred to keep her questions inside, biding her time until the answers revealed themselves naturally. Henry didn't care about any of that. Knowing things wasn't a waiting game for him. Sometimes Karen thought that made him look dumber. Sometimes Karen thought that it made him smarter. Either way, it was good to have him around; she got the answers she needed more quickly when Henry was with her, and she didn't have to betray herself. Once or twice, she came close to bringing him into her room to peek through the hole in the wall; in the end, it just seemed too private to show anyone else.

"Well," Mom said, "when enough time passes, sometimes the confusing and bad things of the past turn out to be the things we celebrate. You know that song 'Okie from Muskogee'? A lot of people think that's a song about being proud of being from here. It's not, but it sort of made people use the word with pride. But just sixty years ago, being an Okie was the worst thing you could be. It meant you were dirty and poor. Sometimes things just change over time. Sonic booms were terrible if you had to live through them. Now they're an exciting thing that happened in the past."

"I don't get it," Henry said, but Karen did. She knew how things could have multiple meanings.

"Imagine, Henry, if..." Then Mom stopped abruptly. Karen sat up. Henry didn't – not yet. Mom was looking up at the sky.

"Oh. Oh no."

Now it was Karen's turn to look. The sky ahead of them – brilliant and blue when they'd left the house – had gone a sickly shade of dark green. It reminded Karen of sick days and throw up and coughing and phlegm. Mom switched on the radio. The urgent yet restrained voice of Gary England, the weatherman out of KWTV, commanded out of the speakers:

"Do not – I repeat, *do not* – attempt to leave your house or drive over the next few hours. The weather today is extremely dangerous. Stay in your homes. Get into your basement, or a bathtub if you don't have a basement. Children, if you are listening and an adult is not home, go to your basement and stay there."

Mom flicked off the radio and slowed the car to a crawl, craning her neck to look at the sky, now turning black. Stormclouds were stacking up on top of one another like obsidian blocks. "Kids, I'm sorry, but I don't think we're going to Frontier City today."

Tears immediately pricked Karen's eyes, but she blinked them away furiously. Yes it was her birthday, and *yes*, she had been looking forward to Frontier City all week ... but those clouds scared her. To Karen, it looked like a giant black hole had opened in the sky, one from which no light would ever escape.

"Aw, *man*," Henry grumbled in the seat beside her. "But we're tall enough to ride the Sonic Boom for the first time."

"Henry, shut up," Karen said, absently. She unclicked her seatbelt and leaned between the front seats to stare out the windshield, as Mom slowed the car to a stop. Other cars on the road were also stopped, their drivers seemingly transfixed by what was happening in the sky. One short man with a flapping combover actually got out of his car, putting his hand up to block the glare from a sun that had disappeared. "Mom, is it going to storm?"

"I think it's going to…" Then the hail started, all at once, like someone had twisted the dial on a celestial showerhead. Hailstones plummeted toward earth, smashing against the asphalt, against the cars. When they hit the roof of the Lucks' Ford, they made a hollow, insistent *bonk-bonk-bonk* sound. Henry looked up at the sound, his eyes wide and his mouth hanging open.

"Get back in the seat, Karen," Mom said. "Put on your seatbelt."

She did as instructed immediately. Mom's easygoing way of talking had vanished. Neither she nor Dad were much on giving punishment or yelling, but occasionally, if Karen needed to take some very specific direction, this was the tone both of them used. It was a tone not to be trifled with – the voice of absolute authority. She snapped on her seatbelt and looked over to make sure Henry had done the same. He was still staring up at those sounds on the roof, like angry punches from a tiny creature. Now he craned his neck and looked at Karen out of the corner of his eye.

"Something bad's going to happen, Karen," he said, and his voice wasn't shaky or worried or panicked. It was as calm as if he was asking her if he could borrow one of her books. "Something terrible. It's a good thing you have your sneakers on."

"What?" Karen asked him. "Wait, what does that mean?"

Then the car lurched backward, and their back bumper collided with something. Karen jolted forward, then back against the seat. She barely noticed. She was still staring at Henry, who was still staring at the roof of the car. Was the hail going to break through the roof? It began to fall on the windshield now ... though "fall" wasn't the right word. "Fall" implied gravity was working in the normal way. Hail smashed against the windshield. It hurtled. It dove. Mom managed to get the car turned around just as a barrage of hailstones, each the size of golf balls, bulleted against the glass. Suddenly, a small, almost infinitesimal crack appeared in the glass, just above the rearview mirror.

It's going to break the glass, Karen thought. *The glass is going to shatter into our faces, into our eyes, and then the hail will come in and fill up the places where our eyes used to be.* Years later, this horrifying image would recur to her at her writing-desk in the new house, and she would use it, grimacing the whole time. One of the curses of being a writer is that your memories are rarely far from you; Karen Luck would always remember every second of her ninth birthday.

Mom's eyes were in the rearview, wide and startled. At first, Karen thought she was looking at the crack, wondering sickly how long hail would take to melt in a dying person's eye socket. Then she heard the sound, muffled only slightly by the sound of the hail pelleting the earth all around them. Like a freight train, hurtling down the tracks. Distant at first, then coming closer. Were they near train tracks? Were they stopped on train tracks?

"*Move!*" Mom screamed, and Karen craned her neck to see what Mom was seeing out the front window. It was traffic, if traffic was chaos. The whole road was crammed with cars: some pointed toward them, some pointed away, some sideways, blocking anyone from moving. When had it gotten like this? Now Karen saw that almost all the cars were trying to do what Mom was doing: turn back toward town and drive away from that awful sound. That sound was everywhere now, all around them. Mom pressed the heel of her palm against the horn and held it there. The honk was a small, lost thing in the consuming, deafening sound of that oncoming train. "Fuck this," Mom said, which was crazy because Mom very rarely swore. She turned her steering wheel and pitched forward, slipping shakily between two cars trying to do the same as she was. Another opening appeared diagonally to their right and Mom swerved the car that way, jumping forward once again. Karen could see clear road ahead, and not that far. From her line of sight, she could see cars breaking out of the jam and speeding away onto the empty road that would eventually get back to her house. But there were too many cars, like Mom's, that had been going the other way and were now trying desperately to turn around and drive back the way they came. That was why they couldn't move. That was why they were stuck.

Mom managed to get the Ford out a little more, the front end eking toward the side of the road, which had no breakdown lane and which dropped off slightly to form a divot. Sometimes when Mom or Dad were driving her along this road, Karen thought it looked like the world's biggest bowling lane, with deep gutters on each side. Now a new sound rode in, louder than the hail, not as deafening as the train. A car engine, moving fast, also coming close. Mom's eyes flicked to the passenger's-side mirror so Karen looked there too. Not a car but a truck. A Dodge 4x4 rushing down the cut in the shoulder like a horse on fire. It was moving side to side erratically, unable to keep its tires straight; the cut was deep but the width wasn't, and the truck weaved drunkenly from side to side as it headed toward them. Once, it weaved just a little too far to the right, and Karen saw something else in the mirror, far back and mammoth. It came down from the clouds, black and furious and consuming. To Karen Luck at nine years old, it was what a scream would look like, if it had a shape.

"Mom," Karen said, turning to her mother as sweat broke out all over her head and face. "Mom, we have to go."

"You thought it was a train," Henry said. He was no longer staring up at the roof of the car. He had his eyes closed. "But it's not."

Mom glanced back, her hair coming out of its loose plait. Her eyes went wide. In later years, Karen would swear that she saw the shape of the tornado doubled in her mother's eyes. Her rational brain would tell her no, that was impossible, that was something hack fiction writers throw into a story to seem profound. But rationality and belief lay in a vast gulf apart from one another, and when Karen thought back to her ninth birthday, she could see that twisted, massive shape, winding its way up the road toward them, reflected in the irises of her mother's pale blue eyes.

Before Mom could say anything, the truck speeding erratically through the gutter at the side of the road suddenly heaved to the left. Karen only got a momentary glimpse of the driver, a portly man wearing a cowboy hat and an expression of raw panic. His hands were off the wheel. There was a companion with him, a woman leaning across the wide front seat toward the wheel, her hands outstretched. It was easy enough to piece together what had happened: they were speeding away through the ditch at the side of the road, something caused the driver to lose control of the car, his girlfriend or wife tried to reach out to steady it. And that was when the front of the truck barreled into the front of the Lucks' Ford, going nearly sixty. The front seat accordioned inward. The impact drove the car into another to Mom's left ... and crushed Mom's body between the seat and the steering wheel. The wheel drove up and in, so that the bottom curve lodged into her belly and the top slammed into her sternum. Karen could very easily hear the crack as it – and likely several ribs – snapped. That was no novelistic flourish. She remembered those sounds quite well.

The woman in the truck began to scream. It was a distant sound, almost lost in the screaming, hurtling sound of the train – which Karen Luck knew wasn't a train at all. The man driving the truck had been thrown against the windshield; his head had collided with the glass, and a thin network of cracks spun out from the point of impact. Blood, bright and plentiful, gushed from the man's head, filling some of those cracks, making it look like a scarlet spider-web. There was no blood on her mother's face or shirt, but she could find no comfort in that. Just because she couldn't see her mother's injuries didn't mean Mom wasn't hurt. She had heard those cracking sounds. Mom's eyes were wide open and staring, her head tilted up toward the rearview mirror.

"Karen," she murmured. "Karen, listen to me. Listen now." It was her stern voice, the one that had to absolutely be listened to, but Karen didn't want to listen. She wanted to scream like the woman in the truck. She wanted to scream and scream because she was more terrified than she'd ever been in her life. What nine-year-old wouldn't want to scream at a moment like this? But she knew she couldn't. Even at nine, Karen Luck knew that sometimes you had to save your screaming for later, when it was more convenient.

She scooched closer. "Time is short," Mom said, "and I can't move. I'm stuck, kiddo. I'm sorry about that. But you're not. And you're responsible for Henry. You're responsible for your Dad, too. You understand that?"

Karen didn't, but she nodded. The sound of the train was everywhere.

"You're responsible for *each other*," Mom said, and now she sounded tired, like when she was at the end of an especially long day of writing and she wanted only to go to sleep, but she couldn't stop. When the words got hold of her and she just couldn't force herself to stop typing. Sometimes, Karen would lie awake in bed and hear the sound of her Mom's typewriter echoing down the hall, imagining her staring down at the paper as it filled with ink, Mom's eyes wide and glazed, almost painful, and still pushing, and still pushing, to make those people inside her head live. The image didn't scare her. It excited her. Mom's motto seemed to be, "give until you can't give any more, and then give a little more. Maybe a lot more." Now, in the car, it seemed as if Mom was on the verge of giving all she had.

"Karen, honey. You have to run now. Run as far as you can. Don't stop running. You got that?"

"Mom," Karen said, her eyes now welling with tears, even as she tried to will them away. "Mom, you can—"

"*Run*," Mom said. Karen could see in her eyes that she wanted to elaborate, wanted to explain, wanted to be eloquent and smart and comforting. But in the end, there was only that one word. "*Run!*"

Karen threw the backseat door open and turned, at last, to Henry Dear. He was sitting in the backseat, his hands on his lap, his eyes glazed and straight ahead. He was like a lump of clay in the shape of a boy. The hail had stopped. Henry seemed to have stopped, too. She reached out and grabbed his hand. For a moment, the boy wouldn't move. Karen thought, *I'll leave him here if I have to.* Then the wind shrieked around her, and the backseat door squealed against its hinges, metal upon metal. Not more than a minute later, Karen knew, the wind would be so forceful that it would rip the metal door out of its frame, like pulling a perforated stamp off of a sheet.

"*Henry!*" she shouted and yanked again. It was as if hearing his name brought him to life. He turned to the girl in the yellow dress, and his eyes went as wide as Mom's. He looked like someone who was coming out of a deep sleep.

He murmured something Karen couldn't hear. It didn't matter. Her last tug was enough to jar him from whatever stillness had infected him. Henry scrambled across the seat and a moment later he was on the road with Karen. It felt solid beneath their feet. It wasn't. Karen understood that, too. Still holding Henry's hand, she ran, weaving between the parked cars and gaining speed. Horns around her shrieked and blared. It was as if the unseen train behind her was blowing its whistle, urging her to move or get out of the way. Her eyes darted left and she found an opening between two cars, and dragged Henry through it. Then there was an opening to the left and she slammed that way. She wished she was strong enough to simply throw Henry on her back and simply run. The boy was trying his best, but she was faster. Not stronger, not yet, but a lot faster. He felt like an anchor, dragging her back, toward that awful sound. How easy would it be to just let his hand go? Let him go and sprint, fast as she could. But her mother had been emphatic on what she was responsible for now. It was that word more than anything: *responsible*, four hard-won syllables that her mother had managed before sending her daughter away. She wouldn't let Henry's hand go. She couldn't.

She passed a station wagon diagonal across the road. There was no driver in it; whoever had been behind the wheel had simply gotten out and run. For a brief moment, Karen entertained the notion of jumping in and trying to steer the vehicle away. There were no cars ahead; only empty road, and beyond the road, the city. The thing behind them couldn't hurt them in the city, Karen was convinced. Karen had never sat behind the wheel of a car aside from the Kid Kars at Sooner City, but the mechanics couldn't be that hard. She'd watched her parents drive hundreds of times. But a cursory glance inside the car revealed two problems: it was a manual shift car ... and there were no keys anywhere that she could see. Her parents had only ever driven automatics. This car had probably stalled when the driver was trying to turn around. That's why it was here, blocking traffic. Only later did Karen wish she could have figured out who had gotten out of the stalled station wagon and left it there to barricade the traffic. If she'd found them, she would try to kill them. For years, Karen would fantasize about murdering the driver of that station wagon. Now, though, her only thought was getting past the stalled vehicle, and saving herself and Henry Dear.

"*There!*" Henry shouted behind her. Karen chanced a look around and saw that he was pointing. Beyond the road, standing by itself in the middle of a field, stood a small red barn. Its better days had been in some decade past – some of the slats had fallen off the roof, giving it a sinister pirate-grin look – but it was still shelter. It would do.

She tugged at his arm, her feet pounding at the dirt. He pulled at her, moving slowly, too slowly. Wanting to scream but not wanting to spare the breath, she looked back at him, meaning to command him with her eyes. It was then she saw one of his feet leave the ground, and take too long to come back down. He wasn't trying to hold her back. It was the wind. Its sinister, invisible hands clutched at her, grabbed at Henry. That train sound now surrounded everything, but it wasn't the sound of a train as it rumbled past on fine tracks to destinations west. It was the sound of a train when you were tied to the tracks by some sinister evildoer. Your eyes are closed. You can feel the vibration in the steel to which your wrists and ankles are secured. Will your hands and feet be severed when the train finally reaches you? Will you bleed slowly? Or will it be quick? Bam, out like a light? A sound like that isn't the sound of a train anymore. It's the sound of the end of the world.

They reached the barn and Karen threw open the door. The hinges, rusted from years of storms and scorch, tried to resist. With one move, Karen yanked open the door and yanked Henry in front of her, and inside. She was about to head in herself and pull the heavy door behind her, but a sudden, unholy compulsion came over her, and she looked back to the road.

The Ford was rising in the cyclone like people in alien tractor beams in movies. The tornado was black as hell must be, endlessly shrieking and crying, endlessly destroying. From where she stood, she could see her mother in the car through the driver's-side window. She was still moving. Karen saw

Mom's shoulder hit the window; the pattern of her shirtsleeve flattened against the glass. Mom was trying to force the door open. She was still trying to get out of the car.

"But she'll fall." Karen's voice came out in a choked, meager whisper. The wind stole it away at once, tearing it to shreds.

But Henry was right behind her then, holding onto the door handle and looking out at what Mrs. Luck was doing. "No she won't," he said, and that was when the car door opened. The tornado sucked Mom out into itself, devouring her like a starving child will devour grapes. It took less than a second.

Now Henry was grabbing Karen's arm, pulling her into the barn. Her eyes were wide and wouldn't close against the image. Her mouth hung open. Was she screaming? She couldn't tell if she was screaming.

The barn smelled of long-departed horses and rot and turpentine. Henry dragged her to an old horse stall at the back, where ancient, desiccated hay sighed under their feet. They got into a corner and hunched down on the floor. Karen thought she might be crying, but couldn't feel her tears. The sound, now apocalyptic, rent and screamed, like thick steel bending. Karen thought she could hear her mother in there, shrieking for her life. She clapped her hands over her ears and shut her eyes and tried to think about anything but the sound, and the way her mother had opened the door and simply been dragged away. It would be a very long time before those things ever completely left Karen Luck's mind.

An unknown time later, Karen realized that the sound was gone. The eerie green cast of the day that had choked the sunlight away before the coming of the tornado was also gone. The light that shone through the slats in the roof was bright and cheery: a springtime light. An Easter light. Her hands were no longer over her ears, Henry was sprawled out on the floor of the barn a few feet away, bathed in one of those shafts of light. *He's dead*, was her first thought. Somehow, after ripping her mother away, the tornado had gotten its grasping hands in here and somehow throttled the life out of her best friend. Maybe it forced air into Henry's nose and into his open mouth and simply exploded his lungs, like a balloon if it's been overinflated. Could that really happen? Karen Luck wondered if her mother's lungs had exploded. At the thought, she wanted to scream. It locked in her throat, which felt too thin, too obstructed. Maybe the wind was in there, too.

Then Henry's chest rose, just a little, and a crunchy little snore escaped his nose. Remarkably, he had fallen asleep. Wait, had *she* fallen asleep, too? After everything she'd seen and been through today, how could she have possibly fallen asleep?

No answers came. No revelations.

Then she saw the ant. It crawled out from under the shelf of Henry's bangs and across the pale, smooth skin of his forehead. The light coming in from the holes in the roof cast in in a horrifically angelic glow. Its carapace seemed lit from within, red and fiery. As the creature trundled down Henry's creamy white cheek, it seemed to raise its terrible, alien head and regard Karen as she regarded it. Then, as if it had made a decision, turned from her and toward Henry's open mouth.

No, and that was the only word she had inside her. *No. No. No.*

Then her own mouth was open and though her throat was raw and her head ached and she was exhausted, she screamed the word into the still barn. She screamed it, and again. Henry sat up, sucking in air. He sucked the ant in, too; it flew into Henry's mouth as easily as her mother had flown from the Ford. Henry coughed once. Twice. And then was still.

Karen stopped screaming. The absence of sound in the barn was as deafening as the sound of the tornado had been. Almost.

"We have to go, Henry. Right now, we have to go."

Getting to her feet, she held out a hand for him again, wondering only momentarily if the ant was still alive inside of him. Maybe it would take him over, like in *Invasion of the Body Snatchers* she and Mom had watched last winter. Maybe Henry would start to *become* an ant. A big red fire ant with gleaming eyes. Its antennae would burst from the top of his head and scabrous ant-legs would tear from his boy-arms. One night, he would be at her bedroom window, looking in at her, *regarding* her. And it would say in its clacking alien tongue, "It's time, Karen. It's finally time."

I will not scream again. I will not. I will not scream again. These words repeated in a mantra, a chant, as she and Henry left the barn together. And she didn't scream. She wanted to, but it was all suddenly too much to diminish with her own negation. All the cars were gone. Most of the street was gone. Big chunks of the shoulder had been ripped from the earth, as if a giant child had been digging up worms with her fingers. They had been right there, the two of them. They had escaped. They had been the only ones.

Karen thought suddenly, *it's a good thing I was wearing sneakers.* When she looked at Henry, he was staring out across the wreckage, same as her. She remembered his face staring up at the roof as the hail pelted down, how transfixed he had been, how haunted. His eyes had none of that glassy intensity now. Now Henry just looked like a sad, tired little boy who wanted to go home.

The first house they came to was small and yellow, with flowery white curtains in the window that reminded Karen, forcibly, of the pattern of her mother's shirt. When she blinked, she saw it flatten against the car window glass, seconds before ... before...

A woman with her silver hair in a tight bun at the top of her head answered Henry's insistent knocks. She leaned out of her door cautiously, looking out toward the place where the road had been. Had this woman been afraid that the tornado hadn't gone away, but had merely taken the form of two small children who'd had the bravado and cunning to knock at her door. Karen could have told her that the tornado doesn't actually go away, not really, not ever.

"Can we use your phone?" Henry asked. "Please, can we use your phone?"

"Did you two come from ... there?"

"Yes, ma'am. Please can we use your phone?"

"I know you two. You're Henry Dear and Karen Luck. Where are your parents?"

They both only looked at her, unblinking. Then Karen said quietly, "Ma'am, please let us use your phone. Please."

The woman looked from them to the destruction and back to them. Her hand went to her mouth and she stepped aside. The woman's parlor was dark and claustrophobic. Now that the storm had cleared, the day was bright and sunny and cheery, but this woman's house was anything but. Maroon velveteen wallpaper dominated every wall. Karen wanted to reach out to touch it, wondering if it might feel like the skin of a peach. A small glass case held a variety of miniature tea sets, in a rainbow of pastel colors, designed only for dolls. It should have been a whimsical touch in this oppressive room, but instead it struck Karen as creepy. She imagined what sort of hands would grasp those teacups. In high school, she would write a short story called "Their Little Knuckles"; at one point, the tiny creatures that invade the old woman's house find her tiny tea set and drink the woman's blood from the intricate porcelain. Karen's teacher, Ms. Dorian, would ask her to read the story aloud in class for the Halloween Storytelling Round. Hers would be the only student story read. "Their Tiny Knuckles" would have a long future. Later, it would be included in an anthology edited by Graveyard Waltz, a niche horror publisher that specialized in limited editions and collections showcasing lesser-known horror talent. Karen's story would be nominated for a Stoker award. She'd lose to Stephen King, which was an honor in itself. But she could never quite enjoy "Their Tiny Knuckles'" success; writing it had brought her back to this parlor, on the day her mother died, staring at those somehow horrifying teacups.

A single lamp by the squat couch threw insufficient light across the room, and Karen noted with little surprise that there was a Doreen Daley novel on the coffee table. A cat-shaped bookmark jutted out of the width of pages; the woman was almost done with her Dad's latest book, a slender volume called *The Dead Never Stay*. The cover showed a lush garden of flowers that had grown in such a way that it looked like they were forming the shape of a skull. Most of Dad's books had those covers where a skull emerged from the illustration. Karen never understood those covers. Were there really skulls like that all over the world, or just in her Dad's novels? This was the year she was going to find out. She'd been reading at a high school level since she was six; there was no reason she couldn't read her parents' books.

The telephone sat on its own table on the other side of the couch. Henry went to it, dialed a number from memory, and talked into the phone excitedly. Karen barely heard him. The old woman stood in the doorway that communicated from the parlor to a small unseen kitchen. It was brighter in there, Karen thought, but this woman was blocking the light. Karen studied the woman for a moment, looking at her frankly and without guile. She didn't know she was saving up her details for the story that would later get her a Stoker nomination; she didn't know that simply noting this woman's hair was coming loose from her bun, as if the storm had knocked some of its severity out of whack, would get her in a room where Stephen King accepted an award she'd been nominated for. She was only nine, and her first short story publication was still a decade away.

"I've read a few of your mother's books," the woman said to Karen, as Henry shouted into the phone. "I don't like them much, but I think she's a good writer."

"Why do you keep reading them, then? If you don't like them."

"I don't know," the woman said, seemingly lost. "It seemed like the neighborly thing to do."

"I haven't read any of my Mom's books."

"Well, you're young yet."

"I'm going to, though."

"Of course you are, honey. I just wish I liked them more."

"You don't have to. It's okay. You like my Dad's books."

"Your Dad's a writer?" the woman asked, suddenly confused. "I don't know if I've read a Gary Luck novel."

"You have," Karen said, but would not elucidate. Henry had hung up and ran over to them. "My Mom is on her way."

"Is my Dad coming with her?"

"She said she'd get him."

"Thank you, Henry." She reached out and he took her hand. Together they looked up at the old woman and she looked down at them. No one spoke for what seemed like forever. "It's my birthday," Karen eventually said.

"Oh! I have cake, I think."

What she had were powdered circles of dough she called Russian Tea Cakes. They were at the back of her refrigerator in an empty glass coffee container, and when Karen bit into one, she found they were stale. It didn't matter. She put the whole thing in her mouth and was still chewing when Henry's mom pulled up outside and banged on the door and bust into the house without waiting for a response. Karen watched as Mrs. Dear swept Henry up off the floor and squeezed him in a hug so violent that it knocked the wind out of him. *She's her own cyclone*, Karen thought, and moments before her father barreled in with his own hug, Karen looked into the woman's eyes, trying to see the fury behind them. She thought she caught it. It swirled and whirled and danced in the wilds behind Mrs. Dear's eyes.

"Karen," her Dad murmured. "Oh Karen, Karen." He didn't lift her up, as Mrs. Dear had done with Henry. Instead, the novelist crouched down on one knee and took her gently by the shoulders. He searched her face as she searched his. A smear of lipstick screamed against his cheek. Another kid might have thought her father was kissing someone other than her mother; maybe Mrs. Dear, and maybe that wouldn't be the worst thing to contemplate. But Karen knew better: her Dad had been writing as Doreen Daley, and today the wig hadn't been enough for him to get into Doreen's mind. He'd needed more help.

The question that rose to her lips was so bad that she almost didn't ask it, but in the end it was too powerful and too huge to hold inside. "Did you finish your writing for the day?" she asked her novelist father.

For a long, long time, he just stared at her. The streak of lipstick was very red against his pale cheek, like an exclamation point laid on its side. "Not quite," he said finally. "I probably had another five hundred words. A thousand, maybe."

"Will you finish when you get home?"

"Oh God, you're in shock," he said.

"You need to finish," Karen said. The new parameters of her life were only beginning to sink in; maybe she was in shock, maybe that was true, but two absolute certainties gripped her nonetheless: her mother was not coming back, and her father had to write better than ever. Better and faster. His writing was now the most important thing in both their lives. Karen Luck, at nine, knew this as truth.

"Okay, honey," he said, and then he hugged her, as always lacing his hands behind her back and squeezing. As he pulled her close, she was enveloped by the sudden, unexpected scent of her mother. It wasn't just her lipstick; he'd put on her perfume, too. Karen closed her eyes and inhaled deeply, not thinking of her mother's final moments, not thinking of the blood after the crash, but instead of her explaining how sonic booms came to Oklahoma City long before the roller coaster did. That throttled her in a way that the tragic stuff didn't, and that was when she started to cry in earnest. She squeezed her father's neck in a death grip, as if letting him go meant that he was subject to the whims of the wind, too.

The wind wasn't through with Karen Luck's life, not just yet. Her mother was officially missing for two weeks. Dad was in his office, writing, when they got the call. Later, Karen would recall the tragic, lost look in his eyes when he held that phone to his ear. She would write about that look in at least three of her own novels. Some critics would accuse her of repeating herself, but Karen could have told them that so much of her writing was exorcism. That look, right before Karen knew what had happened, would haunt her for the rest of her life.

"In Texas?" Dad asked. No makeup today, and no wig either. He didn't wear either in his office anymore. "In *Texas*?" This was the point Dad couldn't get past. The part Karen couldn't get past, after she learned everything, was not the state but the place: her mother had been found in the top of a tree. One of her shoes had come off, as had that pretty flower-patterned shirt she had flattened against the glass as she forced the door open. For a very long time after, Karen would wonder when her mother had actually died. Had it been when the tornado had first taken her? Had it been sometime on its journey to Texas? Or had it been when the wind hurled her at the tree? Had the *impact* been the thing to kill her, finally? Karen hoped not. Her mother could stand a tragic death, Karen Luck would think later, but not an ignominious one.

When Karen would invent deaths for her mother in her novels, none of them would involve ending up shirtless at the top of a tree. Her misplaced mothers, as some critics would call them, were allowed to die in gruesome and sometimes shocking ways, but never shameful ones. Mothers deserved better than that, Karen thought. Most mothers, at least.

Chapter 3: Mrs. Luck

Cynthia Auburn sat across from Gary Luck at a restaurant called Jambon on the outskirts of Oklahoma City ... although Cynthia, who lived in New York, thought all of Oklahoma City was outskirts. Jambon served semi-fancy French cuisine, and the food was far better than it had any right to be: peasant stews and patisserie made in the classic French way. Cynthia didn't think she'd had French food this good in New York, which likely meant Jambon was destined to fail. Cynthia wasn't a cynic by nature, but the town Gary lived in always made her just a little cynical.

1992: eight years after Elaine Luck had been found at the top of a tree in Texas. The manuscript on the table between her and Gary was a brand-new Elaine Luck novel, the fourth since her awful death. Cynthia had read it front to back and then had read it again. It was Elaine Luck's best novel yet, but the problem was of course obvious: it was not an Elaine Luck novel.

She, like the purchasing public, had been able to fool herself for a good long time. The first post-tornado novel had been called *Chaos Logic*. She'd sat at a table across from Gary, Elaine's husband, in a different restaurant, and in a different time. Despite Elaine being dead for four months, this new book, *Chaos Logic,* had arrived just in time. As her agent, Cynthia loved Elaine because she *always* delivered on time, turned in clean manuscripts, and of course because she brought in vast shitloads of cash. But she'd also just loved Elaine. She and Gary would sometimes host dinner parties at the house in OKC, and even though it was a tragic backwater in the middle of nowhere, people would show up. Writers, for the most part, but some civilians. Cynthia was the only agent there. "Most of the others would try to network all night," Elaine slurred out in the kitchen during one of these parties. Karen was over at her friend Henry's house for a sleepover and wouldn't have to see her Mom soused. Cynthia, who had seen her own Mom soused more than once, appreciated this.

"But Elaine," Karen had slurred right back. "*I'm* networking."

"Yeah, but it's you. It's okay if it's you."

Sometimes Elaine would fly to New York and they'd explore the city, Elaine never knowing where to look next. Elaine's characters were so often cosmopolitan – at least until they had to reckon with their family's inconvenient past – so it was always so amusing to see Elaine terrified of buildings taller than ten stories in real life. Once, a grizzled man with a patchy beard and eyes looking in opposite directions approached them as they walked down Broadway. "You ladies want any *white*?" he grunted at them. Cynthia had nearly thrown back her head and laughed at the *white* word; she was familiar enough with drug street names to know that wasn't one. But Elaine had cowered next to her, clutching her arm in a grip so tight that Cynthia had small, finger-shaped bruises the next day. Such was the conflicting nature of Elaine Luck.

Grief over Elaine's death had overwhelmed her. It wasn't the circumstances of how she died; it was simply the fact. Elaine hadn't yet been thirty when she'd died; Cynthia, five years older, had never been prepared for a world without Elaine Luck in it. The shock she had seen in Gary and Karen's faces when she'd first flown down to OKC was the shock that she felt during the funeral, when they were able to break down and let the tears come, let the ratcheting sobs hitch out of them until they were empty, until they were ready for what came next. She had told herself that holding it together for the two of them was her primary concern ... but later, in the Lucks' guest bedroom, where she couldn't sleep, she wondered if she just hadn't been willing to share her anguish. It still felt raw, like someone had cut her open and stuffed her full of it. Until that night, she had never dared to ask herself exactly how *much* she loved Elaine Luck. Reckoning with her death might mean reckoning with her life, and lying sleepless in that cozy bed in that cozy room where Elaine would never be again, she knew she wasn't quite prepared.

So when, a month later, Gary Luck called her and told her that Elaine had left some writing behind, she didn't even bother to ask details before she booked her flight. That day had been much like this day, only Gary had selected the Outback for their dinner. Cynthia, who was a sometimes vegetarian and who abhorred chain restaurants, found herself agreeing simply so she could get a look at this writing. The greed with which she wanted to devour those words frightened her a little bit; she'd always enjoyed Elaine's writing, but now she was ravenous for them. Gary had set the manuscript on the table between them after they'd ordered their drinks, and said nothing while she lifted the title page and the dedication – *To my daughter, Karen* – and began on the first chapter. The first sentence was an all-time keeper, an Elaine Luck fastball:

I killed my husband on a hot August night in 1958, and I wasn't even trying.

From there, it seemed boilerplate Elaine Luck: a woman trapped in a marriage in which she doesn't belong in a bygone era, whose own parents were neglectful and who had never prepared her for a life outside their home. No more mention of her husband or the fact that she killed him. The writing itself was sumptuous, but Cynthia found herself racing through to try to pick that thread up. It came at the end of the chapter, and it was a doozy. As it turned out, all of chapter one was a diary entry, being read by the woman's daughter in

1990, who had never known her father had been killed. And her mother, very much still alive, had just walked into her bedroom to find the girl holding her book.

"Goddamn, Gary," Cynthia murmured as she reluctantly placed the chapter back on top of the manuscript and then slid the whole stack into her briefcase.

"It's good, right?" Gary asked. "She was always so good."

Cynthia was about to pick up her water glass, her mind still hooked into the story, when instead she put her hand on Gary's and looked him in the eye. She and he had never been what you would call close. She liked him well enough; he was a nice guy, a great father, and not bad as a writer. He had a dedicated following and each of his mysteries managed to pick up a few more readers. They were good books, all of them ... they just weren't what Cynthia would call *distinct*. She represented a few mystery writers and most of their books demanded to be remembered. Gary Luck's seemed to demand to be read quickly, enjoyed, and then forgotten about entirely. Maybe that was part of the appeal, even. Create something that gives you a burst of mild joy on a regular basis, and people will remember that joy, and crave it like they crave chocolate or coffee.

But despite the lack of distinction in his novels, the writer part of Gary Luck had been the part Cynthia knew best. She'd signed him first – had even named his pseudonym for him, after two girls she'd known in middle school – and had agreed to read his wife's first novel as sort of a favor to him. Eclipsing Gary in her life had not been difficult for someone of Elaine's talent, Elaine's verve for life. And, in her quieter moments, Cynthia found it was possible to admit, if only to herself, that there had of course been other reasons. Sometimes in the dark, lying in bed alone, she could still feel that soft touch of Elaine's hand on her arm, still smell that light perfume she sometimes wore, still see the way that the sun would shine through her hair, piled high on her head, and the effect would make it seem like a halo hovered over her. She'd never dreamed of saying anything of this to Elaine, although she sometimes suspected Elaine knew. And now she was sitting across from her husband at the Outback, his dead wife's manuscript between them. How much had Gary known? How much did he know now?

"We have to talk, you and I," he now said, picking up his glass of beer and draining it. Was Gary drinking too much lately? Crying at the funeral was a doorway to healing, but it wasn't a panacea. It had only been months. "About Elaine's work. About my own."

"Your own?"

"I need to make a change, Cynthia," he said. He was smiling, but that smile hadn't traveled upwards. His eyes looked scared. No; his eyes looked *terrified*. Maybe that was the reason for the beer. "I need to start being myself."

For a moment, she merely looked at him. "In writing, you mean? You want to write books under your own name?"

Gary shifted in his chair a moment and looked down at the table. Appetizers had come – the Bloomin' Onion, Cynthia, had been a favorite of Gary and Elaine's – but he hadn't touched a bite. "That's the short version of it. Do you think the publisher would be willing to release a few of my older titles with my actual name on them, too? Maybe boost interest in a new book?"

Cynthia studied his face. "Do you have a new book?"

"Almost. Three chapters away from the end. I think you're going to like it. I wrote it as me." Cynthia had questions. She had known everything about Elaine's writing process: her schedule, her quirks, the little dance she did in her office when she passed a hundred manuscript pages. She knew nothing at all about Gary's. What did he mean *I wrote it as me*? The pseudonym had been a split second decision they'd made at one of their first lunches together; he'd been teaching history at the time and didn't want the book's success – or failure – to distract students or excite his colleagues. Of course, the book had been a big enough hit for him to quit his teaching job, but the name had hung on all the years since. But it was just a *name*, right? A name with a reader base and a bit of a following, but in the end, it *was* just a name.

But she didn't have time for those questions now.

"You have a new novel but you wanted to show me Elaine's first."

"Of course I did," he said, and leaned closer. "She was the bigger seller, after all."

Cynthia nodded and wouldn't look at him. "And a posthumous novel would be ... I mean, it has the potential to be even bigger. Her name was all over the news. Curiosity will drive people to it." She paused. "God, that sounds ghoulish. I'm so sorry, Gary."

He waited a long time to speak. "I can't be angry at you seeming ghoulish when I want to publish my books as the husband of the woman who died, can I?"

That startled her. "Gary, that's not the *reason*..."

"It's *a* reason. Not the main one. Not one of the important ones, I hope. Mostly, I just don't want to be Doreen anymore."

After a long while, Cynthia nodded. If there was any adult person who loved Elaine Luck more than her, it was Gary. She knew that, had known that even those few drunken nights in New York, when they'd stayed at the Waldorf on the publisher's dime, and had lain in bed across from one another, and the night had pulsed with possibility. Looking into her eyes made it just possible to believe in fiction. Gary was her reality, though. Gary and Karen. There was no use in resenting it, or him. And there was no part of her that believed he would capitalize on his wife's death just to make a few bucks.

"She left a few books behind," he now said. "Most of them were fully complete. 'Insurance against writer's block,' she called them. Some of them were most of the way complete. And there were a few that she started and stopped fairly early on."

"How many fully complete books are we talking about?" Cynthia asked, almost unable to breathe.

Gary looked up, as if he were calculating in his head. "Including *Chaos Logic* – and the two she wrote in high school – fourteen."

Cynthia's eyes widened. "*Fourteen?* How is that *possible*? She's only ever published six!"

Picking at the Bloomin' Onion, Gary said, "She wrote fast. And she'd been writing a lot longer than *The Absence of Sure Things*. Her high school books weren't her best, but they were remarkably good for juvenile writing. And then she kept writing. College and ever after. I would say that *Sure Things* was her sixth adult novel."

It was a crux moment, Cynthia realized later. She had a decision to make, looking into Gary's still-grieving eyes, and it was a decision that didn't have to even touch her subconscious, if she didn't want it to. She could keep it away from any deeper scrutiny by pretending she wasn't making a decision at all.

Believe this man, or don't. That was it. That was all. But it meant everything. Because the agent knew that if she believed him now, she would have to go on believing him. That belief would become bedrock within her, the foundation on which so much else could be built.

Cynthia Auburn said, "That's incredible, Gary. It's like not having to say goodbye all at once."

A slow, sad smile crossed Gary's face. "It is like that, isn't it?" He stopped picking at the Bloomin' Onion. He met her eyes and for a second – just for the barest second – Cynthia thought she could see Elaine in his eyes. That was absurd, of course. They'd been husband and wife but they hadn't been *related*. And yet that gleam had been there, some essential bit of Elaine Luck that Cynthia would have been able to recognize immediately in her old friend's face. When she laughed, or was melancholy. When the writing wasn't going well. When...

She would have told me if there were more novels, her brain tried to assert. Cynthia slammed down on that as hard as she could. *Chaos Logic*, this new Elaine Luck book – this *new Elaine Luck book!* – was called, and she found she couldn't wait to take it back to her hotel and devour it, as slowly and as reverently as she could.

The publisher agreed to Gary's terms, almost at once. The news that Elaine Luck had had a cache of novels in reserve shook the publishing world, if not to its foundations, at least enough to cause some major aftershocks. *Publisher's Weekly* did a whole cover story on her, including reviews of each of her novels. That was when the cultural re-evaluation of *An Unexpected Island* really began, and the reading world at large decided it had been too harsh on that sophomore slump novel. After that *Publisher's Weekly* retrospective, Denton brought *An Unexpected Island* back into print as a hardcover, and it immediately shot to #1 on the *New York Times* list. They tried a similar trick with *The Absence of Sure Things*, with a new foreword by her husband, and while it sold well, it didn't climb back to the top of the charts. "It's not surprising," Gary told Cynthia over drinks. "Everyone already has it."

What *was* surprising was how thoroughly the Gary gambit had worked. In that same issue of *Publisher's Weekly*, a long interview with the grieving widower also appeared. He talked about the Doreen Daley pseudonym – how it had begun and how it stuck around, tenaciously – and why it was time to retire it. "I have to figure out who I am without Elaine in my life," he said, "and it's a hell of a lot harder to do when I'm hiding behind someone else's name." It was a good pull quote, something the trades got to pick up and run with. Part of it even appeared on the front covers of the initial three paperbacks Denton decided to republish with the name Gary Luck on them: "I have to figure out who I am," appeared across the top, with Gary's name right beneath it. His name, Cynthia noticed, was a lot bigger than Doreen Daley's had been. The three books – *Jane St. Clair Is Dead*, *The Long Way Back Home*, and *Something You'll Never Find,* his three featuring Detective KJ Sprouse and Cole Apa – had sold better under the Gary Luck moniker, well enough to justify a million-copy printing of *his* new book in hardcover. It was called *For You*, and though there was nothing explicitly in the text about dead wives or tornadoes, most agreed that those things suffused every page.

"A remarkably mature work from mystery writer Gary Luck, née Doreen Daley," *Time* Magazine said of *For You*. It wasn't an unusual sentiment. Even Cynthia had to admit that, after a decade and similar number of novels, Gary had finally figured out how to make himself *distinct*. The novel opened on a scene of a dead chef lying on the counter in his kitchen. He's missing his arms and legs. Detective Sprouse and Detective Apa spend the entire first scene trying to figure out if his limbs are *actually* missing, or if they'd been served at the restaurant the night before. It's a grisly scene, but there's an undercurrent of humor to Sprouse and Apa's discussion; no one had ever come to a Doreen Daley novel expecting laughs, especially not this sort of gallows humor. Then again, no one had ever come to a Doreen Daley novel knowing who its true author was, and now everyone knew the man behind the words, and that he was probably in a grisly state of mind.

Readers loved it. Maybe some had come to the first new Gary Luck book – the only book published with his name on the first printing – out of some morbid curiosity. Seeing how the husband of the dead novelist Elaine Luck held up inside grief, perhaps, or just because the timing of Gary Luck's reveal coincided with his wife's death. Those readers stayed because the book was simply fantastic. The pairing of detectives Sprouse and Apa had always felt a little generic, with neither revealing too much of himself and both existing as mere functionaries of plots that moved them where it wanted. Suddenly – but not incongruously – they had an actual relationship. They regarded their work more deeply, as well as themselves, and each other. In the prior Sprouse and Apa novels, there was a sense that these guys were timeless, that they would never age. Some characters in book series are like that, especially in mysteries that can go on indefinitely. Some are allowed to age with the progress of the books. And some age, but do it slowly. Cynthia thought of Robert B. Parker's

Spenser, who had been in the Korean War in his twenties in the first book of the series, and by the time the 1980s rolled around, he was a young and hale thirtysomething.

Cynthia wasn't sure where Sprouse and Apa would end up, temporally, but realized that for the first time, she cared. If they were in something of a stasis in the first three books, they didn't seem to be now. *For You* had been released to the general public six months after she'd read the manuscript, and she'd picked the novel up in hardcover – the cheesy skull collage motif that had marked so many of his novels had been replaced by a more moody and stylized series of disappearing dots – and read it again. She hadn't done that since reading *Chaos Logic*. In the mid-1990s, the Lucks had some of publishing's best re-read values, despite one of them being dead and the other writing under his own name for the first time.

Dead. Now, sitting across from Gary Luck in Jambon, the new manuscript in between them, the word swam up from the depths of Cynthia's mind and clanged there in the center. Another word followed it: *fourteen.* As in *Eileen Luck is dead and she has fourteen novels left in her.* It was sort of a ridiculous thought, wasn't it? Sort of an alarmingly silly thought. Because no one writes fourteen novels – in addition to the six she'd already published – and simply sits them aside for a rainy day, like a squirrel saving its acorns for winter. You'd have to be really dumb to believe something as bizarre as that. Dumb or lonely. So lonely that you'd be desperately willing to keep someone you love alive, even if it means staring logic in the face and screaming it down.

The title on the cover of the manuscript was *There's Something Wrong with Betsy.* A good title. A great title, maybe, one that fit right in with everything Eileen Luck had ever published, posthumously and before. Only this manuscript had not been typed with a typewriter, not even a fancy electric one. It had been printed out on dot-matrix paper, the perforated sides neatly torn away, the ink a shade or two greener than true black. Eileen hadn't ever written a novel on a computer or a word processor. They hadn't had one in 1984, Cynthia was quite sure of that. They had one now, did the Lucks. Gary's most recent novel, *You Run Away*, had been printed on dot matrix paper. Cynthia had even commented on it. "The Lucks are moving up in the world," something like that, and they'd clinked glasses.

"Gary," she said quietly, looking from the manuscript to his eyes. There were delicate age-lines around them, and less delicate bags under them.

"Read the first paragraph," he said quietly. Reluctantly, she did, turning over the title page and picking up the first page of Chapter One.

Elizabeth Dardenelle – known to her mother as Betsy – was born without empathy, and by the time this was discovered, the little boy was already dead. Betsy's mother found him washed up on the beach by their summer house. She had wanted to scream. His arms and legs had been weighted down with stones on strings. He must have struggled mightily. His skin was pale, almost translucent, from his time under the surging salt water. His head lolled back, as if looking up at the blameless blue sky, as if marking his own place in heaven. He could no longer see, of course. The fish had eaten the eyes out of his head. He stared up at her with sockets that looked out on infinite darkness. When Betsy's mother turned back to the small clapboard house, she saw Betsy on the back porch, leafing through Uncle George's crossword magazines. Sensing her mother looking, she raised a hand and waved a big, cheery wave, accompanied by a child's innocent smile. Only then did Betsy's mother scream.

Cynthia put the page down, but the imagery wouldn't escape her. It wasn't Eileen's most gruesome scene – there was a sequence in *Four Summers at Eastlington* in which a woman ties her daughter down and tries to straighten her spinal curvature with a rolling pin – but it was the first time an Eileen Luck novel had been so front-loaded with one. Even if she read no further, Cynthia knew that this scene would accompany her to bed tonight; she would be staring down into those eyeless sockets, very aware that a psychopath in the form of a little girl was sitting behind her, unable to understand why I was so scared.

"Is it good?" Gary asked her.

"You know it is," Cynthia said.

Gary looked her in the eye, hesitated, and said, "I don't, actually. I'm not sure if I'm working the way she would anymore, or if I'm just writing my own stuff and slapping her name on the book."

Okay. Wow, okay, that's where we were suddenly. Only there was nothing sudden about it. This printed manuscript had been the final statement, the last confirmation. Gary voicing it was simply his way of not treating Cynthia like a blathering idiot.

Still, she had questions that needed answers. If the delicate play of pretending was over, it was time to get real. "How much of this was hers? Any of it?"

Gary put his hands over his eyes and rubbed them. Not in negation, she thought. *The man is exhausted.* "In bed, once. Before Karen turned six. She'd started reading early and that excited us. We loved how smart she was. Eileen woke me up in the middle of the night. I wasn't getting a lot of sleep then – I was on one of the early Sprouse and Apa books, and it was fighting me – and at first I didn't want to talk. Then she said, 'What if she gets *too* smart?' That woke me all the way up.

'What if she gets so smart that she stops caring about other people?' And I told her that was ridiculous, that's not something that happens. And she started going on about how many psychopaths start young. I don't know if she'd been reading something about that or if it was just something she was making up. Eileen liked to make up facts and then go back through in the rewrite and either confirm them or remove them. She wrote with such passion, Cynthia."

"I know she did," Cynthia said. She wanted to say more.

"I'm trying to honor her. That's the most of it. I'm trying to ... *extrapolate*. I've read her books – the ones that were *all* her – dozens of times. It's not enough to copy her style. I have to get better. I have to *keep* getting better, but I also have to make sure that there's a stylistic through-line."

"You can't be Eileen in 1984. You have to be Eileen in 1992."

Slowly he nodded. "And I can't get lost in her. I *want* to. God knows I want to sometimes. Sometimes I think it would be easier. But easy isn't why I do this."

The question was out there on the table now, alive and flopping like a goldfish outside its bowl. She leaned toward him and took both his hands in hers, noticing for the first time how soft his hands were, how very soft. "Then why, Gary? Why do you do this?"

He looked down at her hands and grasped them tightly for a moment. "You of all people should know that, Cynthia."

Slowly, she nodded. It was the question that had plagued her subconscious this whole time, ever since *Chaos Logic* and that lunch at the Outback, when she'd decided to accept Gary's lie. The *why* question had loomed so heavily between them that Cynthia never once considered that the simplest answer was the correct one. He didn't want her to be dead.

"I loved her," Cynthia said. Then, in a much softer voice: "I love her."

"I know," he told the agent. "I know you do."

"Gary," she started, thinking about the last time she went to confession. Six years ago that had been, and the priest had told her to pray the sinful feelings out of her. She couldn't tell him that she'd been trying, especially since Eileen died. She'd thought, perversely, ever since they found her old friend in that tree, that those feelings would simply dissipate. Eileen, it was logical to reason, was the only thing standing between her and a normal life. But nothing had changed in her since that terrible day, nothing about the way she was and nothing about how she'd thought about Eileen. If anything, both of those things strengthened. And had there been instances? Dalliances? Yes, and she worked hard not to feel terrible about them. She worked very hard indeed, because it wasn't just the *fact* of them. It was that in some perverse way, she felt as if she were cheating on Eileen Luck, even though Eileen had never known and wouldn't have reciprocated if she had. "I don't think you understand."

But Gary Luck was already nodding. "I do, though. I do. You couldn't know her and not love her. All the way love her. She was irrepressible." He tapped the manuscript. "I wrote this whole book, but it's *not* my book. Eileen is in every page. She *suffused* it. Every time I sit down to write as her, she is in me. I don't think she'll ever leave. I don't *want* her to leave."

"I don't either," Cynthia said, and now her tears, eight years too late, finally started to come.

Cynthia Auburn submitted *There's Something Wrong with Betsy* to Denton a week later. Two weeks after that, she moved into the Lucks' house in Oklahoma City.

Chapter 4: Burger City

The day after the funeral, Gary Luck had stood in his wife's writing room, looking down at her typewriter. Her gray cover was over it, and it seemed to Gary like too much of a shroud for his liking. He removed it and laid his fingers on the keys. It was impossible, of course, but he thought he could still feel the warmth of Eileen's fingers on the home row. He closed his eyes and inhaled, and there on the air was her perfume. It was called Cloud Dreams, and it never quite left her skin or the air in her office. He'd gone to the mall the day after Karen's birthday and bought as many bottles of the stuff that he could find. It was unthinkable to ever stop smelling her smell.

Sitting down at Eileen's desk felt alien and frightening, but not *wrong*. He was willing to listen to his gut if it felt *wrong*. Never in their years of marriage had he sat in this chair, at this desk, in front of this typewriter. Loading a sheet of paper in, he took a deep breath – Cloud Dreams – and typed:

My name is Eileen Luck. My daughter is Karen. My husband is Gary. I am a famous writer. I did not die. I will not die. My name is Eileen Luck.

Gary looked at that piece of paper for a long, long time before setting it aside. Beside the typewriter, in a neat little pile, was a stack of maybe two hundred and fifty pages. You couldn't see the typing on them because they were all face down, obscured. But not gone. Not dead.

Turning the manuscript over, he came face to face with the title page Cynthia would see three months from now, turning it over in the Outback and reading that amazing first sentence. If for whatever reason Cynthia hated it, or figured out what he was doing, that would be fate telling Gary that this whole ridiculous idea was absurd.

"But it's not," he said, and thought of Karen in her room, crying long into the night, unable to get more than two hours' sleep at a stretch. "She can't be dead, Daddy. I saw her die and I know she is but she *can't* be. She just *can't* be. I *need* her."

"I need her, too," he'd said, and that was probably why he was down here, thinking the worst thoughts, hatching the worst plans.

Chaos Logic, that was the title. A short title for Eileen, immediately intriguing. He placed the title page on top of his miniature manifesto of identity and read the first sentence:

I killed my husband on a hot August night in 1958, and I wasn't even trying.

Immediate tears pricked the backs of his eyes and he blinked them away. Clashing storms of doubt battened his brain. *I don't know how to do this*, he thought. *She writes at a different level. She's so good and I'm just a guy who writes these dumb mysteries.*

They're not just dumb mysteries, one of those clashing storms in his head murmured. But if you think they are, why are you writing them?

It was a question he'd heard more than once in interviews, from fans who seemed to like his first three books better than anything that had come later, from reviewers who posited the question as a rebuke to either his style or his story or his choice of genre itself. Light thriller with a soupcon of characterization. The type of book they could put in the mystery section of the store or the fiction section, but which the publisher decided to have the cover artist make a series of skull collages on the cover, so they *feel* like dumb mysteries, they *feel* like secondary stories, they *feel* like piffle when his wife was creating art. Maybe there's nothing wrong with piffle. Maybe there's nothing inherently the matter with writing novels for masses and not challenging them. But what Eileen did was so elegant, so masterful. Even if he hadn't been married to her, she would have been one of his writing heroes.

Why do you write these? Why do you keep writing them?

Because they're fun. Because I like writing them.

It was an answer he hadn't given before. He'd talked about journeying along a path trodden by great mystery writers of the past and present. He'd invoked Sherlock Holmes. The only time he ever talked about Eileen in interviews about his books was when he told them to come to him for dessert once you get through the meal of an Eileen Luck novel. And why not? Dessert's delicious.

But it's not fully satisfying, is it? Especially not when sleeping next to one of the world's greatest writers. Of course she didn't see it like that. She thought *his* books were better than hers. "I don't have plots," she would say to him. "I have situations. Families in situations. I couldn't tell you the first thing about a plot, and you write those every day."

Gary knew she was just saying it to make him feel better. And it worked, most of the time. Because he loved writing. He was good at it. It was the first thing he thought of when he thought of himself. It hadn't started off as love. It had started off as desperation. From the time he was twelve until the time he was nineteen, he wrote primarily so he didn't have to think about the things he did in the dark. The things he *wanted* to do. It was easier not to ruminate on the pair of panties he'd stolen from Sears at the bottom of a box in his closet when he was just starting to get whiskers on his cheeks. It was easier not to think about Mrs. Bishbaum from AP Bio lying him down in her bed at her house and somehow putting something into him. Her fingers, maybe. Or a candle. She'd touch his head and run her fingers down his scrawny body and something would be inside him, and then she would rub her lips with the tip of her finger until it was coated with her lipstick, and smear it on his mouth and whisper that he needed to be a good little girl, a good girl for her, and then he would come, he would come so hard and do it into that pair of pilfered panties, and then hid it deep in the box in his closet.

So he wrote stories. Ones that everyone would like. His teachers liked them. His parents liked them. His friends at school all wanted to read them. In 1970, he was awarded Best Short Story at Magellan Middle School for his story, "One Week," which was about a woman who has a vision that she's going to die in a week's time. She does everything in her power to stay out of harm's way, even going so far as to lock herself in her father's old fallout shelter in the back yard, planning to wait out the vision, and disprove it. She doesn't die. The week passes and she's fine. When she emerges from the shelter, however, she enters a nuclear wasteland. She's very much alive ... but the rest of the world is dead.

It was derivative of so many science fiction stories Gary had been reading at the time, not to mention the old *Twilight Zone* shows he'd watch with his dad before bed every night. But *they* didn't know that, the people who'd read it. They only knew how effective it was. How it reached past the page and made them care. Made them a little bit scared. And it wasn't a copy, either. Inspiration he'd take; stories, he'd make. Even now he could think back on "One Week," and remember the stuff he'd put in to make it a Gary Luck story and not Asimov or Bradbury or one of those guys. The woman in the story was young, but she'd had an old-timey name: Gladys. How many twenty-two year old women were named Gladys? He *loved* giving young people old names, or weird names. He loved naming streets after birds. Gladys lived on Heron Lane. Detective Sprouse lived on Robin Way. And so on, and so on. Only Elaine had ever picked that up, at least through 1984. They were Easter eggs. Moments of whimsy. More reasons to love writing, and more reasons to keep doing it.

"I am Eileen Luck," he whispered, and read what his wife had written. He didn't move from her chair. He didn't go to the bathroom or get a glass of water. He read straight through, and when he looked up, his eyes were dry and red and it had gotten dark outside. Eileen's last paragraph read

She'd always told me she'd never meant to kill my father. I'd believed her. What choice had I had? If I were to go on loving my mother, I'd had to believe everything she'd told me. How he hit her. How he hurt her. How there'd been no recourse if she'd wanted to live. If she'd wanted me *to live.*

Not being able to remember anything about the abuse had always worried me, but I'd grown to accept it over the years. I'd been so young. I barely remembered my father at all. But I remembered the woman I now saw in my mother's bed. Remembered her full lips and straight hair. Remembered – all at once – that she'd been in the house sometimes when my mother was out ... and my father was not.

"Oh no," the woman said, looking scared, gathering the blankets around her so I wouldn't have to keep seeing her laid

bare. When had she started coming to this bed? Why hadn't she stopped? "Kiddo, please, you have to understand."

"She understands, all right," my mother said, striding into the bedroom from the en suite, in a flowing silken robe and a sour look on her face. "You were fucking her father, and then when he was out of the picture, you started fucking me."

"That's not how it was, kiddo. You have to believe me. I..."

My mother had gone to her vanity and I turned my attention away a moment too long, focusing solely on the naked woman in my mother's bed. When I looked back up, she had the gun in hand. Seconds before she

That was it. In the cruelest of all worlds, that is where Eileen Luck's newest novel would have ended. Gary rested his fingers on the home keys and slowly typed

opened fire, the woman in the bed screamed. The distraction was long enough to get my mother looking away. I took the opportunity to knock the gun from her hand. It flew across the room, skittered on the floor, and came to rest against the brass vanity in the corner.

"You shouldn't have done that," my mother spat. I tried desperately to reconcile this woman with the one who had helped me ride a bicycle, who put bandages on my knees when I scraped them, who read me fairy tales at night before bed and convinced me everything was going to turn out all right. I couldn't do it. I was seeing the woman my father had seen the night she had murdered him.

"You shouldn't have killed my father," I spat back.

Both of us had forgotten about the woman on the bed.

Gary Luck fell into the story as if he were reading it, not writing it. She'd laid the bones out for him – all he had to do was follow where it led. Eileen had done him a favor, in a way, as if she'd known he was going to have to finish this in her name: it was undoubtedly an Eileen Luck novel, with its dark family dynamics and secrets bubbling up from the past to smear the present ... but it was also something of a potboiler. It was as if Eileen had sat down to say, "What would happen if Jim Thompson decided to write an Eileen Luck novel? Or what if Colleen McCullough decided to dabble in

James McCain territory? I think that would be interesting. Let's see how it goes."

As it turned out, pretty brilliant. It also gave Gary an in. Could he have picked up in the middle of *No One Knows Where Sarah Goes,* and made it into the type of novel capable of carrying the Eileen Luck name? Gary wasn't so sure. But this? *Chaos Logic* was at least putting a toe through the door of his own wheelhouse. He found his way inside the book more easily than he had dared hope, and sat down at his wife's typewriter every day and managed ten or more pages without breaking a sweat.

The day of her funeral, he started wearing his wig when he wrote. The day after, he started putting on her lipstick. When he felt he was in the final week of the first draft, he went to the mall and bought a dress that would have looked fantastic on her. Of course, he'd had to buy it in his size, and there was never any guarantee what looked good on Eileen would look good on him ... but him *looking* good, wasn't really the point. It was more about the feeling. Did it make him happy? Did it make him feel more in touch with his wife? More importantly, did wearing the dress make him write better?

The answer to all these questions was yes.

And sometimes Karen would stand in the doorway and watch him, quietly, serenely. Both adult Lucks had always valued quiet when they wrote – neither played music or kept the TV on in the background – but noise had never been a problem with Karen. She only wanted to watch her father create. She liked seeing him type in clothes her mother would wear, too. Some afternoons, when the light slanted just right through the towering cathedral windows, it cast him in a glittering, slender silhouette. You couldn't see his face at all. In those moments, Dad could actually *be* his mother. He actually leaned over his work the way she had, hunching his shoulders slightly and peering down at the page. Karen could believe, easily, that her memory was faulty and that her mother hadn't been sucked up by that tornado. That had all been some dark dream. Mom was here, of course. She would always be here.

For his part, Gary Luck felt the same way. There were times while writing *Chaos Logic* in which the story felt lugubrious, even as the words flew. Those times, he realized, were when he was trying to impose himself on the story. Use words that came up in Gary Luck – well, Doreen Daley – novels. Gary could have a jerk cop call a female perp a "gal," but Eileen never would. Gary's sometimes abrupt, Hemingwayesque prose threw up stop signs in Eileen's more flowing – but never florid – word pictures. She loved semicolons, did Eileen Luck. Her husband liked to stop sentences and start fresh with a new one. The novel demanded that he write as his wife, that he *become* his wife, at least when he sat down at her typewriter. Gary Luck flourishes could not be tolerated, not if he had any chance of convincing first Cynthia and then the reading public that Eileen Luck had written every word.

Late in the writing of *Chaos Logic*, after Karen had gone to sleep and he sat up long past midnight, Eileen's old robe with the puppies on it draped around his shoulders, he paused, looking out at the dark yard beyond those cathedral windows. A question that hadn't seemed important when he'd started this enterprise now burbled up, fully formed, as if it had just been waiting for the right moment. *You're excising your Gary Luckisms*, his mind clanged, *but what about Gary Luck himself. Are you excising* him, *too?*

He looked down at the typed page in front of him. The estate was going to burn, like DuMaurier's Manderly before it. The other woman – her name was Marisole, a name you would absolutely never find in a Gary Luck crime novel – had become the daughter Andrea's ally against her mother. As it turned out, her father had kidnapped Marisole right out of high school, convincing her that she was in love with him. When her mother, who is never named, found out, she'd intended to kill them both, then herself. Instead, *she* fell for Marisole, and Marisole, desperate to still be close to the husband, clung to the mother. Only Andrea had been able to break her of her parents' terrible spell. Things were coming to a head. If he wanted to, he could press on until morning and finish this novel tonight.

Instead, Gary got up and went to the window overlooking the yard. The twin pine trees that had towered over the house when he and Elaine bought the property dominated the side yard; their gargantuan shapes towered over the house, shapes in the black beyond. Gary's reflection walked toward him, out of the dark. The person looking back at him was not quite a woman, not quite a man. Gary didn't know *what* they were, or *who*. Once upon a time, dressing up like this meant only one thing: that sex was in the offing, and with a woman who understood what he needed, and who was willing to give it. Eileen had been perfect in that way, as in so many others. She had told him early on that she didn't much like being penetrated. It had spilled from her with the import of a church confession, and there had been some tears. She hadn't believed him at first when he'd told her that didn't matter much to him. She'd thought he was just placating her, biding his time when he could leave the girl who hated sex.

    She only believed him when he'd taken her back to his dorm room at college and showed her what was in the box under his bed. That very afternoon, she'd worn a strap-on for the first time, clumsily and with many false starts. Over the years, they'd progressed to better ones, longer, thicker. He was insatiable for it, and she was insatiable for his insatiability. When his wife fucked him, it lit up bright neon lights inside his body and mind. She hit all the happy spots. She knew the right rhythms. She could get him to come with just her thrusts. And when he finished, she would pull out and throw the strap-on across the room, and he would take care of her, burying his face in her public hair so vehemently that *she* usually came within moments, and just kept going until they both fell on their backs, exhausted.

Gary had only penetrated his wife twice: once, on their wedding night, which was when they'd conceived Karen. And the second and final time was when Gary sold his first novel to Denton. "It's momentous," she'd said, tapping her champagne glass against his. Then in the bedroom, he'd entered her slowly, hating the wincing look on her face, the one he'd never seen in their wedding night bed because the lights had been off. He'd pulled out of her quickly and whispered into her ear: "My love, I don't need this. I've never needed this. Now let's reverse this and do it the right way."

Now, at the window, Gary reached out toward his reflection and touched his fingers to the apparition that floated in the darkness. "I miss you so much, Eileen. I miss you more than words can say."

Then these words, in his mind: *Don't lose yourself in me.*

Later, he would tell himself that he jumped, startled at the sound of those words, in his ear, in his head. *Her* words, real as houses, clear as day. They were ridiculous words, of course, ones that Eileen would never say. Of *course* he should lose himself in her. That's what he'd always done, wasn't it? Both he and she had known it. He'd pecked along, workmanlike at his typewriter, selling books but not ascending into the stratosphere like they both knew Eileen would. Was that why he'd chosen a pseudonym, or at least part of the reason why? They were all just biding their time until Eileen took her place in the spotlight. Nothing was going to get in her way, especially not this mediocre man in a wig pounding out mediocre mysteries...

Don't you dare. That voice again, sharp and actual. It was as if she were in the room with him, whispering in his ear.

He waited for the voice to say something further, anything further. It remained silent.

Slowly, he turned away from the window and looked at the sheaf of papers next to Eileen's typewriter. His body echoed with sense-memory. He'd been here before. Not in this room, not with this typewriter, but he'd been here before, over and over. How many pages was he until the end? Thirty, maybe fifty? That sounded right. Had he gotten up at this point during the writing of all of his novels to tell himself how unworthy he was? How he was about to finish the worst piece of hack work the country had ever seen, and that he was going to turn it into Cynthia and watch her face fall, watch her face tumble away, her mouth hanging open in a stunned O of disgust.

This moment had little to do with Eileen, despite the fact that he was wearing her lipstick and perfume and a dress she would have worn had she still been alive. And despite the fact that her name would be on the title page of this book, maybe even the cover if this whole ruse worked out. This moment wasn't about Eileen, and even Eileen knew it.

Now the voice in his head was his own. *You've spent this entire book elevating yourself, Gary.*

"I am Eileen Luck," he murmured.

Tell everyone else that. Be honest with yourself. She started this off for you, and you honored her by doing the best writing of your career. Don't diminish that. Don't fucking make her death part of your self-pity. She's worth more than that. And in case you've forgotten this, so are you.

The novelist had rarely heard such words out of his own head. His pep talks around the brick walls in his writing had tended toward the "let's just get through these last few pages, what do you say?" variety. He'd relied on Eileen to give him the actual boost, to make him feel like he was as worthy as she was to have a career doing the thing he was best at.

I need you, honey, he thought.

You have me, the voice in his head came back immediately. *But you need you, too.*

Sitting in front of the typewriter, Gary put his hand on the home row, and once again was sure he felt the warmth of her fingertips on the keys. Then he got to work.

Dawn was a long time coming.

Three days later, he leaned into Karen's room and knocked on her open bedroom door. She looked up from the book she was reading – a novel by a man named William Sleator; it had a monster on the cover and looked scary – and offered him a wan smile. He wasn't wearing the wig or the dress or the lipstick. He wasn't even wearing Dream Clouds, as much as he'd wanted to spray it on after the shower.

"Hey kiddo," he said. "The book's done."

She slid a bookmark to keep her place and sat up. "Mom's book?" she asked.

"Mom's *and* my book," he corrected gently. "Ours."

"Right, yes," she said, and that wan smile again appeared on her face. "Sorry, Dad."

"I want to ask you a couple favors," he said, haltingly. "I know asking anything is a lot right now, after all you've been through."

Karen watched him expectantly. He only knew some of what she'd gone through. The nightmares started the night

Mom had died and hadn't stopped. Nearly every night, she'd woken up in the dark, tears on her face, screaming. In the dream, the tornado was still out there, sentient. Her mother hadn't been found in a tree. She was still in there, still alive but only barely, kept aware by the tornado's malevolent energy, its furious, psychotic will. And she was in pain. Mom was in so much pain. And the only way for her to die, for her to really die and make sure she'd stop hurting, was to throw herself into the tornado, and take her place. The last thought she always had, seeing the cyclone tearing up the small stone walk her mother had installed a year before she died, watching its approach with paralyzed horror, was *Maybe I'll wake up in Oz.*

But she actually woke up in her bed, and even in her sleep, she knew better than to scream into the dark, empty room. Dad might be writing downstairs, and the last thing she wanted to do was interrupt him as he wrote. In the midst of her dream, she'd turned her face into the pillow and screamed there, over and over. Though she didn't know it yet, all of this would be good practice for a life in which nightmares were almost common. The terror dreams of the man in white were years ahead, and would haunt her into her adulthood as the looming specter of the tornado haunted her youngest years. That tornado was never going to take her to Oz. It was only ever going to take her to Hell.

"I want you to read the book, if you want to."

Now Karen sat up. "I thought I wasn't allowed to read Mom's books." She had, obviously. She'd read *No One Knows Where Sarah Goes* when she was seven, wishing she understood more of what she was reading, loving it anyway. The day of the funeral, she'd smuggled a paperback copy of *The Absence of Sure Things* into her dress pocket, and touched it during the whole service. When she'd approached her mother's coffin – closed-casket, a practice that horrified Karen more than whatever might be inside there – she'd reached one hand in her pocket and gripped the book as tightly as she could. "I'm going to read everything you wrote, Mom. I'm going to be a writer, like you."

Even at nine, Karen was a person who at least intended to keep all of her promises.

"You are now. I need someone to read it to let me know if it's any good."

"What about Cynthia?"

"I want you to be my first reader. Are you up for it?"

"*Yes*, I'm up for it," she said, and now the smile she tried out felt less forced, less deliberate. "What's the other favor?"

He took a deep breath and let it out. "You want lunch? I was thinking burgers."

Two gifts in one day; Dad's idea of weekend lunch usually extended no further than turkey and ham sandwiches with a slather of mayonnaise or Miracle Whip on the bread. Burgers were unheard of.

Oklahoma City is made up of dozens of neighborhoods, some of which extend for blocks, some of which are barely bigger than a street. Bergin was one of those latter, stretching down Walter Bergin Avenue, home of independent shops and restaurants for over seven miles. It was the only place in OKC where you could get an armful of used records, walk next door and get an armful of used books, and walk next door again and get milkshakes at Sock Hop, made up to look like a 1950s diner and playing only early Elvis and The Crystals and their pop contemporaries on the Wurlitzer in the corner. If Karen had had her druthers, she would have asked Dad to take her there ... but she sensed that the favor he was going to ask was going to be a big one, which meant it was up to him where they are. Sock Hop could wait another day. Today was Burger City.

Karen Luck slid into the booth across from him and picked up the paper menu, only to put it down a moment later when she sensed her father simply staring ahead. "Dad?" she asked, reaching across the table and touching his fingers. She could just smell a bit of Mom's perfume on the air. He hadn't put it on today, not yet, but something like that sticks with someone. Maybe it didn't really leave until you stopped using it for weeks or months. The perfume was sticking around awhile. She guessed these memories of her mother were going to stick around, too.

"I have to tell you something," her father said, still staring ahead.

"What?" she asked simply.

"I think I want Doreen Daley to go away," he told her, his eyes shifting to hers. His voice was shaking.

"For good?"

"For good. I think I've written my last Doreen Daley novel."

Slowly, Karen nodded. "You're just going to write books as Mom from now on, then."

Gary let out a breath. "Yes ... and no. I'm going to keep writing books as your Mom as long as I can. That depends on Cynthia more than me."

"Cynthia's always right." It was a reflex. She was barely aware that she was saying it.

"Exactly," he said, looking into her eyes and seeing so much of Eileen in them. "But I also want to be ... I haven't written anything as me in a long, long time, honey."

It was easy to picture her Dad in his writing room, wearing the wig he now wore in her Mom's studio. It was only the wig then, not the lipstick and perfume and clothes. It had been easier to get into the mind of Doreen Daley, Karen thought, because she was made up. Fiction writing fiction,

Mom had called her. But Mom herself wasn't fiction. She was just dead. And writing as her must have worn her Dad out. He sat across from her, his eyes puffy, his body hunched. The book he'd finished had taken so much out of him; it had taken that much to come alive, to be real. It had wrecked him.

Now he was asking for a favor. She knew what it was, had probably known it was coming the second he put on his wife's perfume and sat down at her writing-desk. Something she didn't quite understand was happening to her Dad. Maybe it was like her nightmare about the tornado. He was stuck in something and he wanted permission to get out.

"Well, I think you should," Karen said. "Write as yourself, I mean. I've never read a book by you."

"You've read all the Doreen Daley novels."

"Yeah, and they're good. Maybe they're not *you* though. Like Mom's book isn't *you*, not really."

Dad nodded. "Not really."

Karen Luck said to her father, "I miss Mom, Dad."

"I know, Karen."

"I miss you, too."

They looked at each other for a long, long moment, and then Dad nodded and picked up a menu.

Three days later, he met with Cynthia Auburn to tell her a lie. Eight years after that, Cynthia moved in.

"Is it weird?" Henry Dear asked, picking up a french fry and drenching it in ketchup. They were at Burger City because they were always at Burger City.

"What?" Karen was looking out the window down Burgin Avenue. The story she'd been constructing in her head felt flimsy for the first time all day. Why would the woman try to kill the chef? She had no real motivation. Earlier today, distracted beyond reason in science class, motivation had seemed completely unimportant. The woman in her story, Cassandra Wall, strode into Eggtown, searching for the chef who she hadn't yet bothered to name. What she had in her mind was the confrontation: he was going to deflect her bullet with a frying pan, then hurl it at her and escape. Wall, a trained assassin, was going to follow him, eventually catching up with him in Canada. She chose Canada because it was a lot like the

US, and she wouldn't have to do too much research on foreign countries. Research could be done later, in the rewrite. When you were writing the first draft, it was all about getting it down as quickly and as well as you could. "Is what weird, Henry?"

But he was shaking his head. This was a new aspect of Henry's personality, and it could be infuriating. He picked up another fry and stared out the window.

"Henry, I wish you wouldn't do that."

"Do what?"

"This whole ... being mysterious on purpose." A sudden, unexpected memory occurred to her: *It's a good thing you wore sneakers.* Karen groped for it, but it slid out of her mental fingers before she could hold on.

He shook his head again, and for a moment Karen thought he was going to remain quiet. She liked being quiet in Henry's company, sometimes preferred it, but not when he threw these gambits out. Wanting her to ferret him out. Figure out what he wanted, what he was thinking. Did he know she'd do it every time because curiosity was her dominant personality? Of course he knew. Henry Dear knew her better than any other human ... but he didn't know everything.

"The Cynthia thing," he said finally. "I don't get it."

Karen blinked. "What's not to get?"

"Isn't she your Dad's agent? Why is she living with you guys?"

One of the big things Henry didn't know about was the hole in her bedroom wall. That was the biggest thing he didn't know *external* to her. Over the many, many years she and Henry had been friends, she had often been tempted to show it to him, and to tell him what she used to watch through it. One of the worst things about curiosity was that you wanted to share it with people, if only to see if they were as curious as you were. Somehow, she'd avoided telling him, showing him, even though he'd been in her bedroom more times than she could count, and there were moments when any distraction would have been a welcome one. Henry's had never pushed himself on her, never demanded, never even really asked. But she had known what he wanted the first time he'd followed her to her room when they were both fourteen, and had listened to his stuttering, awkward attempts at conversation only so long before lifting her shirt for him. His hands had been cold, inexpert, and she had wanted him to stop almost as soon as he started, but she let him keep going as long as he'd wanted. Those hands roamed. They felt every inch of her chest and belly, had wandered over her nipples – she wasn't wearing a bra that afternoon, knowing this might happen – and only stopped there, completely baffled by what to do with them. She'd lain there unmoving until he attempted to pinch; only then had he aroused action in her. Karen Luck slapped his hand away.

"You can't do that."

"Girls like that," he's said, yanking his hand away and rubbing it with his other hand. Karen had rolled her eyes and wanted to tell him to stop being such a baby, she hadn't hit him that hard. She didn't, though.

"What girls like that, Henry?" She grinned at him, teasing. Even though her shirt was up and she could still feel his hands on her, all at once she felt on equal ground with him. The thing about Henry was that she actually really liked him.

The best friends designation wasn't one-sided. And, if she wanted to be honest with herself, it wasn't just to placate him that she hadn't worn her bra on the day she'd invited him up to her bedroom. Was it his fault that she hadn't liked what he was doing the second he started doing it? Was it his fault that she'd been curious about this, too?

For a moment, Henry looked at her, dumbfounded, then burst out laughing. "Goddamn it, Karen."

Then she was laughing, too, because Henry Dear was her best friend, and it didn't matter that her breasts were out, or that she had an idea this wouldn't be the last time he'd attempt to touch her in that way ... or the last time she'd let him.

"No, really. What girls like their nipples being yanked out like that?"

"I didn't *yank*."

"You might as well have. How would you like it?" Unprompted, she sat up and ran her hand under his shirt, grabbing his nipple and giving it a twist. *What the hell, Karen?* her brain demanded. She had no answers. Her brain, with whom she'd been warring ever since the ache in her chest had begun and the dark, curly hair had started showing up around her vagina, threw up its hands in horror.

Henry's eyes fluttered closed and he made a sound deep in his throat – animal, guttural. Where had he heard that girls liked their nipples pinched? She saw it clearly now: Henry, after dark, a flashlight clenched under his arm as he leafed through a porno magazine he'd found somewhere. Borrowed from a friend, maybe. She had no idea where boys got porno magazines. And in the pages somewhere, a slutty-looking girl in high heels and nothing else was bending forward, her breasts in her hands, her fingers teasing her giant aureoles, making them hard, making them tight. Or maybe it was one of those spreads where it was two girls. She knew boys liked that for some reason. Two girls, and one of them would be lying back against a satin bedspread and the other one would have her face in the other girl's ... you know, her *crotch*, and her free hand would be sneaking up to squeeze one nipple, and maybe she *did* like it. Maybe she wouldn't like it when a boy would do it, but she didn't mind one bit when a girl did it. Because a girl would know how her body worked, and not just paw at her tits like a cat on catnip, all flailing limbs and claws. A girl would be able to sneak up on it, test it out, read the other girl's eyes to see if what she was doing was okay before going any further.

All of which sounded so amazing that Karen Luck, at fourteen, briefly wished she could be one of those girls. Of course, what she *really* wanted was men, because of course she did. This whole thing with Henry was probably supposed to be a little weird. It wouldn't be this weird with other guys. She'd just known Henry her whole life, and they really were best friends, and that was always going to be strange. Henry wasn't a good litmus test.

And here she was with her hand under his shirt, discovering that, perhaps like those girls in the pictorial that he'd probably looked at, Henry liked *his* nipples yanked. Part of her wanted to roll her eyes. Part of her wanted to make fun of him some more. But most of her was fascinated.

"Karen," he said, struggling with breath. "Would you ... could you keep doing that, please?"

It took nothing of her to do what he'd asked. She sat up, her shirt tumbling down and covering her. "Take off your shirt," she said, and immediately he did it. *Now* something was stirring in her, raw and alive, and she didn't know if it was because Henry was shirtless in front of her or because he did what she told her to do at once, no questions asked.

Except she absolutely knew.

She laid him down across her bed, which should have been awkward because his head hung off one side and his legs off the other, but Henry wasn't complaining. She took both his nipples in her fingers and gave each a tentative pull. Henry groaned, squirming on the bed. Glancing down at his pants, Karen saw the unmistakable outline of his penis pushing against the fabric. He was going to want to pull it out and mess with it, wasn't he? Yes. But wanting didn't mean getting. Henry's eyes were closed, his hands lifting off the bed to drift toward his crotch, then drifting away. More of that violent warmth blossomed in Karen, and she let it happen. She didn't want to see Henry Dear's dick, not today, and she knew suddenly that if she didn't tell him to take it out, he wouldn't.

She yanked his nipples harder, and he lifted up off the bed, his breathing shallow and stunted. His eyes were closed. He bit his lip.

"Harder," he grunted, and something in her turned over. Not nausea, not exactly. This had started as retaliation and turned into something else. Something she could work with. Now it was something else. She was in control here, she had the power ... but did she? Did she really? All at once, she wanted Henry to leave. All at once, she wanted to yank his pants down and turn him over. All at once, she wanted to understand why this weird thing was working for him but not for her, why the thought of doing normal things *also* wasn't working for her, and whether it was Henry's fault or her own. Instead of taking any action, asking any question, she bent down over him and bit his right nipple as hard as she could.

At the same second, she reached up and clamped a hand over his mouth, knowing he would scream, not wanting to alert her father as to what was going on up here. He'd been in his own office today, working on a new Gary Luck book. Those sometimes went slowly. When he wrote as Mom, the words flew. When he'd written as Doreen Daley, they'd flown even faster. Karen didn't know whether Dad was more uncomfortable writing as a man or writing as himself, but something kept the words from pouring out. Still, you couldn't argue with results. Karen thought her Dad's last couple of Gary Luck novels had been the best writing he'd done under any name, but of course, he couldn't believe that. Was it a tragedy that Dad abhorred the work that went into creating his best art? Or that the work *he* thought was best was paying tribute to a woman who had died five years before, work he'd never take credit for?

Either way, today was not the best day to interrupt her father.

Henry screamed behind his hand, and now he bucked away from her, shrinking and squirming. For a moment, Karen only wanted to hold on tighter, to bite down harder, but anticipated the taste of blood squirting into her mouth, warm and coppery, and let go. "Jesus, Karen," Henry had moaned, but he didn't seem as upset as she thought he probably ought to be. He scootched up on the bed so that his head buried itself in her imbroglio of pillows, and closed his eyes.

"Are you okay?" Karen asked, examining his nipple. It was red and puffy but not actually bleeding. She reached for it and grazed a fingertip over its surface. Henry sucked in air through his teeth but didn't move away from her. "Henry, I didn't…"

"I came," he said bluntly. His tone was too complicated to fully investigate – sated and frustrated and confused, all at once.

So what's your damage? she wanted to ask him, a distant part of her furious. *I didn't.* But she couldn't hold onto that fury, even as she sensed that if this is how easily boys came, and if this is how they behaved afterward, the prospect of her *ever* getting off with someone other than herself was pretty close to nil. All at once, she just felt tired, not wanting to argue. She remained silent.

"I just thought…," Henry began, and stopped. She still said nothing. "I thought our first time would be different, that's all."

Karen placed a hand on his chest. That tiredness persisted. She wanted to comfort him because she loved him. She didn't know *how* she loved him, in what capacity, but she did. She'd loved him ever since that day of the tornado, when they'd hidden in the old barn together. Maybe she'd saved his life that day, and wasn't there an old Chinese axiom that said if you saved someone's life, you were responsible for that life? At the same time, her only thought was, *So this was a foregone conclusion, wasn't it? Eventually, Henry Dear and Karen Luck were going to fuck.* Rhyming it didn't make it cuter. She was mad at him for simply expecting that this was going to happen. She was mad at herself for expecting the same thing.

Then a thought occurred to her. "*Our* first time, Henry? Or *your* first time?"

Finally, he opened his eyes. "You're saying it's not your first time?"

"I don't think this can qualify as a first time for me."

An absolutely baffling look passed over Henry's face. Was he *angry*? Was Henry Dear, who'd just gotten off because of something she did *angry* at her? Then that look – whatever it was – evaporated. "I should have done more," he said. "I'm sorry. I didn't know the nipple thing was going to be so…"

"Potent?"

"Yeah. I mean, I thought it would work on you, too. It's always worked on me when I'm … you know, alone."

Henry reddened and she found it fascinating that she'd just bit his nipple hard enough to get him to come in his pants, and he was still squeamish about talking to her about masturbation. Anthropologically, this whole situation was fascinating. *I'm going to write stories about this*, she thought, at the same time wishing she could just be inside it.

"Well, it doesn't," she said. "But you didn't know."

"Karen, I don't know anything about girls."

"I do," she said, and a galvanizing, steel excitement suffused her. For the first time since she'd let him feel her up, Karen felt something akin to arousal. But why? Was talking about sex more exciting to her than actually doing it? "But I don't really know anything about boys. So you're not alone."

Henry got up on his elbows. "I could … you know, do something you want. Not nipples. That's off the table for you. But I could, I don't know, get you off. If you tell me what to do."

Absurdly, tears pricked the backs of her eyes and she blinked rapidly. Whatever emotional cyclone was happening inside her, it needed to stop. There was literally no reason she should feel so lost, so alone, so forlorn. Picturing what he'd suggested just doubled down on all that. "Do something to my vagina," she thought of saying, not knowing what she would want him to do. Put his fingers in it? His face? His penis? The idea of any of that made her cringe. It was like the time when, at the age of seven, her Mom had taken her to the public pool, and she'd been splashing along happily, dog paddling, until she realized she was in the deep end. Knowing it was now *possible* to get in over her head made the *probability* seem likely, seem destined. That was when she started screaming, right before she started sinking.

Only here, in her bedroom with Henry Dear, no statuesque blond lifeguard with sun block on her nose was going to save her.

"I don't know if I'm ready," she told him slowly. "I thought I was."

Henry now sat up and looked her in the eye, putting a hand on her leg. "I don't know if anyone's ready." And that internal cyclone still kept swirling, twirling, rampaging around in her. Maybe she wasn't interpreting anything correctly, but Henry's hand where it was didn't seem to signal anything remotely sexual. And again, she remembered him in that barn on that long-ago day, looking scared, looking helpless. She'd taken his hand that day and had kept taking it almost every day since. Henry was her best friend, the boy she'd told all of her secrets to before they sort of fell into the role of boyfriend and girlfriend, before any of this happened. She wished she could talk to her best friend about how confusing her boyfriend was. Why did they have to be the same person?

Now he stood and put his shirt on. "Can we try again sometime?" he asked, sounding like he knew the answer.

"Maybe," she said. They knew what conversation they were having. Henry nodded, then said something so out of context that she had to ask him to repeat it.

"I said I'm thinking of joining Civil Air Patrol."

Karen blinked at him. "The kiddie Air Force thing at Yeager?" Yeager Air Force Base was at the edge of town, because most things were. Her school bus had passed it every day in middle school, and now the crosstown bus passed it on the way to the mall. Once upon a time, the sight of all those planes on a tarmac behind that massive chain-link fence had excited her beyond reason. How many other towns in the world just had a place with *planes* in it? Huge, sleek machines that hunched on the ground like sleeping scorpions, only to, improbably, take to the air, scaring the birds and chasing the clouds. Every time Karen would see one of those planes take flight, she was reminded of the history lesson Mom had given on her last day on Earth: how, when she was a girl, supersonic jets would fly over OKC, breaking the sound barrier and thunderclapping the city below so hard they would break window and shake foundations. She waited for one of *these* planes to go supersonic. They never did. And eventually, Yeager Air Force Base just faded into the background, other dull thing on another dull bus ride.

So she was aware that Civil Air Patrol existed in her town, but that was where she and the facts parted ways. If she had thought about it at all, she might have thought it was weird that there was an Air Force for kids, like Girl Scouts or Boy Scouts but with planes. The whole thing sounded bizarre.

"Yeah, but it's not kiddie. Okay, well it's for kids. Well, it's for anyone from twelve to twenty-one. I thought you liked planes."

It was almost impossible for Karen to believe she'd been biting on his nipple two minutes before, or that he had *stuff* drying to the inside of his underwear while they spoke.

"Sure, planes are cool," she said, "but I don't want to *fly* them. Do you fly them?"

"I don't know," he said vaguely. "My Dad and I talked about it a little. He was really into the idea. I guess they had it back when he was my age but he never joined."

"Oh." Karen racked her brain. Was this the first time Henry had brought up Welton Dear without immediately cursing his name? She thought it might be.

"Yeah, he bought that movie *Top Gun* on videotape and we just watched it, and then we rewound it and watched it again. Have you seen it? It's a really great movie."

"I've seen *Top Gun*."

"Anyway, I thought it might be fun. Maybe I'll become a fighter pilot."

Karen smiled at him and nodded. "Yeah," she said.

Shifting from foot to foot in front of her bedroom door, Henry said, "Burger City after school tomorrow?"

"I wouldn't miss it."

He'd been looking down at his sneakers. Now he looked up and into her face. "You're not mad or anything, are you?"

"No," she said, maybe too quickly, because she maybe didn't know. "Just figuring out what I want."

"Okay." He opened his mouth to speak again, and instead stole out of her bedroom and down the stairs and, as she watched, saw him striding down her driveway, his hands crammed in his jacket pockets, walking with a slight but noticeable limp. *I did that*, she told herself, then went back to her bed.

His warmth was still in it and she thought that would make it impossible to do what she needed to do. But it didn't. Henry mattered to her in so many ways ... but this wasn't one of them. It wasn't just that she wasn't turned on by him, that she wasn't *harmed* or *upset* by what he'd done, but that she wasn't affected by it all that much at all. That might have changed had things progressed – if she'd allowed him inside her, or if he'd put her mouth on her, but those were what-ifs for future days. As it was now, she could lie against her pillow and close her eyes. Her mind settled on Henry at first, the thought of him, the face and body of him. Then she cast her mind just a little more outward, being careful to put blinders on her mind's eye so that she couldn't *quite* see around her. There was a shower running somewhere in Henry's house, and she followed the sound, throwing up mental roadblocks to prevent herself from analyzing what she was seeing.

Someone was on the other side of that shower curtain, Karen knew. Someone whose nipples were a lot more interesting than Henry's.

Karen slid her hand into the waistband of her jeans.

Later, after her shower and after sitting at the typewriter in her room for an hour or so, struggling to find the threads of the story that had seemed so easy yesterday, she made her way downstairs. The typewriter sounds down there had also quieted. She searched for her father, finding him in the living room, situated between the two writing studios. He wore a Billy Joel T-shirt and faded jeans and Chuck Taylor sneakers and an OKC Dodgers baseball cap. Regular clothes, Dad clothes, but the whole look was every bit as conscious as when he was wearing Mom's perfume and that wig and the dresses he thought she'd like. This is what he wore when he was writing Gary Luck novels. He sat with his feet up on an ottoman; there was something amber in a glass on the coffee table. His eyes were closed.

She sat down across from him, slowly, deliberately. "How long today, Dad?"

He didn't open his eyes. "Ten hours."

"Good work?"

"I think so. I don't have perspective anymore."

"You want me to read what you have so far?"

Dad sighed heavily. "No, better not. I'll be finished this week. Then you can have a crack at it."

Offering her a little smile, he picked up his drink and drained the rest. Karen watched with a frown. Dad wasn't a drinker – not to excess, anyway – but he tended to drink more when he was writing as himself. Was it part of the uniform? Some sort of Hemingway affectation he felt he needed when he was attacking the pages in his masculine persona? And it *was* a persona. Her real Dad was in there somewhere, but she'd learn long ago that there was a world of difference between Novelist Dad and Actual Dad. The more he wrote, the harder it was for him to snap back between the two of them. It was easier on the days when he wore the dress and progressed on whatever the newest Elaine Luck book was. All he needed was a shower and a change of clothes. The stuff he wore to write as himself was already in his closet.

Karen opened her mouth, then snapped it shut. She didn't want to have the same conversation again. He knew how difficult it could be to live with him when he was like this. Of course he knew. He had to do it, too. Besides, talking to him about how he was treating himself right now might upset the balance. It was always worst when he was nearing the end of a novel, so if he was right about his progress, he wouldn't be like this for much longer.

Plus, not to be selfish or anything, but at some point this week or next, she would have a brand-new Gary Luck novel to devour. Even if she weren't her father's daughter, getting the new Gary Luck would be an event in her life. Mom's books were the ones the world loved the most – even now, even with her father making them up out of whole cloth – but Gary's books weren't exactly slouching in obscurity, either. They used to be. When Mom was alive, the Doreen Daley books were some solid midlist titles that only expanded their audience incrementally. In the years since, the books had gotten better, almost astoundingly so, and the reading public had responded. Cynthia tried to keep their publication schedules separate – Karen would never really understand why – but last Christmas, the new Gary Luck and Eileen Luck novels had been released two weeks apart. For one week, her father's book, *I Live With It Every Day*, and her Mom's, *Nothing Stays*, sat at #1 and #2 on the *New York Times* bestseller list. Karen had cut that out of the paper and framed it. It hung in her bedroom; she'd originally hung it in this room, but Dad was so embarrassed by it, she moved it. Years later, Robert James Waller would hit #1 and #2 on the list with *The Bridges of Madison County* and *Slow Waltz in Cedar Bend*, and much was made of it being the first time ever a single author had novels at the top two spots. Karen knew better.

"I'm going to make dinner," she said suddenly. "How do burgers sound?"

"Henry was here," he said quietly now.

Crisp, sudden fire blossomed in her cheeks. "Yeah, Daddy, Henry's always here."

"Yes," he said, now opening his eyes again and meeting hers. "But your door was closed."

She elided his mild, curious gaze. He was a writer, wasn't he? He had to see everything, understand everything. Had she thought that the fact that he was deep into fiction in his office meant that he didn't know what was going on in the rest of the house? Had she really?

"Nothing happened, Dad," she said, then pulled herself up short. "Well, not *nothing*, but really, it was nothing."

Mildly, he said, "A little not nothing can turn into something, Karen."

"I don't like him that way, Dad."

That made him pause. "No?"

"I don't think so."

Slowly, he nodded. "But he likes you that way."

"Yeah. I think so, yeah."

"Well, that's complicated."

"You're telling me."

Dad leaned forward putting his glass down on the table. The ice clinked. "Just be careful, honey."

"I already told you…"

"You like making people happy, Karen. It's a wonderful quality. But it can get you into trouble. I just don't want to see you getting into something you have to reckon with later just because you didn't want to hurt Henry's feelings."

At this point, Karen was pretty sure her cheeks were crimson. They would glow in black light, bright pink maybe. She stood. "I'm going to make dinner, if you want some."

"I was going to order."

"We've ordered every night this week. We need real food."

Now he grinned at her. "Do you want me to cook?"

"You're such a good writer," she said. "Sometimes, people only need one thing."

They laughed a little together – it was an old joke – but he stopped her before she was out of earshot.

"Be careful with writing, too," he said. Karen put a hand on the doorframe leading to the kitchen and gripped it. Her fingers suddenly ached to be back at her typewriter upstairs. She'd thought she was done for the day, but apparently she still had some oomph in her.

"Dad?"

"Don't be like me, Karen. This is killing me."

Her eyes slipped closed. "Don't talk like that."

"But it is."

"When you finish this book, you'll have a different perspective."

"When I start your mother's book, I'll have a different perspective."

Why wouldn't she look at him? "It shouldn't be this hard being you, Dad."

After a very long pause, he said, "It's the writing, Karen. It's the book."

He didn't say anything more. She didn't turn to look at him. Instead, she stole into the kitchen like a thief, and turned on the radio, and lost herself in Bon Jovi. It had been a long day. A tough day. And by the time she and Dad had eaten their burgers and salad and watched *Jeopardy!* and the *M*A*S*H* rerun, her brain was too fried to even consider doing the writing she had planned.

Then she trudged up to bed and brushed her teeth and moisturized her elbows and put on her long T-shirt and boy shorts and very sincerely meant to crawl in bed with a book, and then found herself at her typewriter, bringing her assassin Cassandra Wall to Manitoba, where that chef was hiding out, believing he'd gotten away safe. But if Cassandra Wall is after you, you're never safe.

It was long after midnight and her eyes felt like cracked, dry desert earth when she finally put the cover on her typewriter and slid under her sheets. As she turned the light off and closed her eyes, she could hear – distant, faint, like the clanging of ghosts – another typewriter clacking into the night. "Oh, Dad," she whispered, and then sleep took her like a rogue wave.

Now, two years later, Henry looked at her expectantly across the booth. His Civil Air Patrol buzzcut still looked weird on his head; the day he'd talked to her about joining, his hair had been almost shoulder-length. He still listened to hair metal but he no longer looked like it. She could talk to him about some things. Most things, maybe. She could talk to him about that night after Henry had come in his pants, and how her Dad said writing was killing him. None of that would shock Henry Dear. What would shock him, and the thing that she absolutely couldn't talk about, was the hole in her wall. Not what she saw through it when her mother was alive, and especially not what she had begun to see now that Cynthia moved in.

"I think she's helping him. I think he's been lonely." Of course, it was more than that; with Dad, it was always something more. "He's writing better."

"As who?"

"Whom."

"Don't be pedantic."

"Himself," Karen said. "He always wrote easily as Mom."

"How about you?"

She sipped her Vanilla Coke. "How about me what?"

"What are you writing lately? You used to give me all your stuff to read. It's been awhile."

"I've written some stuff," she said, not looking at him. It was an obvious evasion, and she couldn't evade Henry. Not for long. Not about most stuff, at least. The novella currently hidden inside a floppy disk slid into a folder behind her locker door at school was called "The Transmigration," and as much as she would try to cling to the idea later that "Their Tiny Knuckles" was her only foray into horror, that was because that story had had a long, long life past juvenilia. The idea for "The Transmigration" begun forming after Dad had rented *Child's Play* at Blockbuster one night between books. In the movie, a serial killer puts his soul into the body of a kid's lifelike doll, and that doll ends up coming to life and killing people. Both of them had loved it. But it was kind of funny, the way writing hits you. Karen had been fascinated with the transmigration part; Dad, thinking as Mom, had been far more interested in the story of the single mother raising a somewhat disaffected young boy. Neither of them had written a story like the one *Child's Play* inspired. The difference between them is that when Dad, as Mom, had finished *The Interior World of Andy McLean*, he'd immediately handed it to her to proof. Dad, she was pretty sure, would never read "The Transmigration." No one would.

The story concerned four friends who decide to mess around with a ouija board they'd found in the basement of a school. Sometimes at night, after even the janitors had gone home, they'd sneak back into the school and hang out away from their parents and other lame-os who didn't get them. And nothing bad happens, until one of the kids – who was in ROTC and who bore a striking resemblance to Henry Dear – sneaks back into the school and uses the board himself to try to contact his father, who had been carried away in a tornado years before. But he doesn't find his father. Instead, something finds *him*.

Karen Luck could be objective enough to know that the story was a good one. Something was happening with her writing. It was one thing to be the best writer in her class, or even in her school. Karen wanted more than that. She wanted to be the best writer, period. And all her early stories – even "Their Tiny Knuckles" – weren't hitting what she thought they should be hitting. She thought she was getting closer with this one, and it sucked because she knew it would never get beyond her.

Her mistake was in writing a main character who was gay. God, even typing the word terrified her. Her gay character was this girl with shortish hair who wore these really cute print shirts and jeans and baseball caps for teams she didn't care about it. This character, Sam Barony, was about as far from Cassandra Wall as you could get, but Karen hadn't had any real problem conjuring up a picture of her immediately. All she really had to do was look in a mirror.

She hadn't gone crazy, okay? She hadn't named the girl, like, Sharon Fortune or anything. But Sam Barony was Karen Luck through and through. It wasn't just the looks, although that was probably what her Dad or Henry or Cynthia would pick up on at once. It was the subtle stuff – the exact way she tucked her hair behind her ear, even though she didn't really have long hair anymore. The way she doodled the names of books she liked onto the covers of her textbooks at Haveline Academy, where she went to school. Most of the other kids at school – girls *and* boys – either wrote band names or the names of the person they were in love with. Karen saw a lot of Megan Heart Steve or Jeannie Heart Jason, but nothing in the way of Megan Heart Jeannie.

Or Hartford and Karen, her mind whispered, but she didn't pay attention to it.

Nothing in that way at all. Haveline used to be an all-girls' school, and Karen wondered if things might have been different if she'd enrolled then. Maybe then she'd be able to experiment and get whatever it was out of her system so that she could go forth and be normal.

Except Sam Barony felt normal. She was Karen Luck in all ways but the way in which she was out and gay and it wasn't actually the most important part of her character. All the other characters knew and none of them mentioned it. So it had the trappings of a horror story, but it was really a fantasy story. Life wasn't like this, and the world wasn't like this, and ... fuck, *Karen* wasn't like this.

"Hey, I'm full," Karen suddenly said, signaling the waitress, a new girl with red hair and cat glasses who was pretty in the way Burger City wanted its waitresses to be pretty. 1950s pretty. Her nametag said Enid and Karen found herself wondering, as she paid the bill, if that was her real name or the name Burger City assigned her. "Why don't we go back to your house and maybe play Nintendo or something?"

He blinked at her. "Nintendo? Or something?"

"I'll decide when we get there," she said, hoping her voice sounded seductive, hoping Henry wasn't able to pick up on the slight revulsion crawling in her gut. "Is your Dad home?"

Henry, who had grown red and out of breath – despite everything, seeing Henry horny was always hilarious – laughed. It was a laugh without humor. "Is he ever home?"

Now Karen bit her lip, and the seduction felt more natural. "What about your Mom?"

"I think she's around. It's tax time, so she's been bringing papers and stuff home."

"Well, let's be as quiet as we can." Karen smiled and only dimly noticed her revulsion had vanished. "Let's make sure we can see her, but she can't see us."

Henry Dear never expected that the way he'd spend the sexual moments of his junior year was on all fours, wearing his on-again, off-again girlfriend's underwear and bra, letting her stuff a dildo inside him. It wasn't that it didn't feel *good*, because something about the way it hit his insides made his lower body tingle and tremble in the best ways; and it wasn't that he didn't want to do it, because it was with Karen, and sexual proximity to her meant that he was willing to do literally anything she wanted.

A lot of it had to do with the clothes. The first time they'd done anything like this was a few months after that time in her room, when she'd discovered his nipples and what they did. Moving to his room had seemed to liven her up, excite her in ways that she never seemed to be at home. That was fine. Maybe it was more difficult to be in her house when her father was literally always there, typing away in one office or another. For Henry, it didn't really matter to him if his Mom was home – or, in much rarer circumstances, his Dad. If Karen Luck wanted to come over and spend time in his room, he was going to find a way to make that happen.

She wasn't in love with him; that wasn't the point, probably. He was in love with her, though, and that seemed to matter more. Henry Dear had a pretty good idea that he could live a life without being loved by Karen Luck, just as long as she consented to letting him love her. Henry wasn't dumb, and knew that a life of one-sided love would be a lonely one. He was prepared for that. He was prepared to do anything.

That first time, she'd come over after school to play *Super Mario 3* and do some homework. Mom had been there, atypically making brownies. Mom wasn't what you'd call a June Cleaver housewife. She was an investment planner in the city and while she didn't make as much money as his father – whose job made little to no sense and had to do with shares or loans or something – she held her own. So did Henry. He'd make dinners most night, or order something if homework was daunting or he'd spent too long at the Nintendo. He was never going to be the world's greatest chef, but Mom rarely complained. Those rare complaints came from his wildly ill-advised attempts at baking. Cookies burned. Brownies dried up. Cakes were crumbled ruins. He followed the instructions on the boxes specifically, but the boxes lied. It was the only explanation.

Mom, on the other hand, had a flair for it ... it was just a flair she didn't employ often, because her greater flair was numbers. And she didn't use box mixes. The brownies she made for him and Karen that drizzly afternoon four months after Karen had bit his nipple hard enough to leave a bruise had been homemade, using real cocoa powder and peanut butter chips.

"Hey guys," she'd said, winding up the circular staircase with a plate in one hand and a container of whipped cream in the others. "I thought you might want sustenance."

Karen paused her game and stared at the plate, as if she'd never seen brownies before. A pang hit him around his heart. For the first time, he wondered if it was hard for her, being over here. Was it like he was rubbing it in her face that he had a mom and she didn't? Or was it more like his Mom could sort of be both their Mom, in a limited capacity. That made sense. Half the time, didn't he go over to Karen's house just to be in a place with a Dad? Even if all he was doing was typing in his office, it was good to sort of sit in the living room and study or read or watch TV and know that he was right there, and that he would stop would he was doing if you needed him.

Of course, the other half of the time when he would go over to Karen's house, her Dad would be wearing a wig and a dress and in her Mom's office, writing a whole different novel. Like his own Mom, it was an approximation of Mrs. Luck, who had always been so funny and pretty and smart about things, but it probably wasn't enough for Karen.

So when she stared at those brownies, he could only wonder how weird it was for her here, how strange to have a mother who stereotypically baked brownies and served them hot while you were playing video games. A mom who was usually there, and who hadn't been found in a tree hundreds of miles away.

"These smell really good, Mrs. Dear."

"You know," she said, smoothing out her skirt and sitting down on the loveseat perpendicular to the couch, "You really can call me Sky."

Karen smiled so widely that Henry thought the top of her head might topple off and onto the ground. Then she giggled – Karen Luck! Giggling! – and looked away. "I couldn't do that. Not *that*."

Mom shrugged a shoulder and the strap of her shirt fell down, making Mom's shirt look like it was hanging crookedly off a hanger. "Suit yourself," she said, absently pulling the strap back up. "You want whipped cream?"

"Yes," Karen said, in a small voice. Was she getting ready to cry? Had Mrs. Luck ever made brownies like this? Maybe this was a PTSD moment. He was learning about PTSD in Civil Air Patrol. He knew how you could bury emotions and traumas and then something will happen to you, a *trigger*, and then blammo, you're right back there and dealing with it like it's real. The unsmiling, unemotional staff sergeant who'd run the class, Yates, had told them stories of soldiers who run into a fight, knowing that their side was right and just and true, only to be brought low by the brutality of man. "The things some men see," Yates intoned, never stopping his clipped pace, "the things some men *do* ... they stay with them. They never leave. If you're ever in armed combat, I urge you to remember that." What was Karen remembering now? Seeing her Mom trying to slip out of the car window, only to be wrenched away by the swirling fury of air?

Mom sprayed whipped cream on both brownies and set the canister on a coaster on the table. "Don't eat too much. When's dinner?"

"Seven."

"What is it?"

"Chinese food."

"Hmmm."

"What's hmmm?"

"I thought we'd have something homemade tonight."

He looked to Karen, who was still staring at Mom, the bringer of the brownies. Henry nodded, his eyes flicking back to Mom. "Yeah, okay. I'll rustle something up."

"Thanks, honey. I'll be in my office, but if you need anything…"

"I'll holler."

Both he and Karen watched her walk downstairs. Waited until the door to her office closed and from behind the door came the sound of Rod Stewart, Mom's favorite. Karen was staring at him when he looked around.

"How long will she be?"

Henry blinked. "I don't know. She sometimes ... I mean, usually a couple hours?"

"Let's go into your room."

He blinked again. "Now?"

"Look, Henry," she said, impatiently, "if you don't want—"

"Okay. Now. Okay."

Because of *course* he wanted, and had not expected a thing, never a thing, after that last time when he'd tried to twist her nipple off. In fact, he'd been priding himself on having the maturity and depth of caring for Karen, his best friend, to carry on with their friendship as if nothing had changed. In a way, not much *had*. By the textbook definition and as far as he knew, both he and Karen were still technically virgins. As virgin as you can be, anyway, when the girl you were in love with bit your nipple so hard you came.

But here they were again, she and he, and the door was closed behind them. Karen's back was to it, and she was looking at him with an all-new species of lust in her eyes. It hadn't been there the last time. "I have an idea," she said. "Do you trust me?"

Implicitly, he thought. "Yeah," he said.

"Take off your clothes." He didn't need to be told more than once. When he was naked, Karen simply looked at him a moment, running her eyes up and down his naked body. It would have been easy to interpret this as lust ... but Henry had a feeling it was something less primal than that. The cast of her eyes. The tilt of her chin. This was the way she looked when she was proofreading one of her father's books. Karen was *assessing*.

"Okay," she finally said, and then yanked her shirt off. "Give me your boxers. And put this on." She unhooked her bra and handed it over. These weren't questions. These weren't requests.

"Karen," he said, holding her bra at arm's length. It terrified him. The fabric – smooth and silky and foreign – and the *warmth* of it. How close it had been to Karen's boobs, how it was there all day, holding them, cupping them. She would be in English class and bent over a notebook, maybe comparing and contrasting the sequels *Huckleberry Finn* and *The House on Pooh Corner*, because Mr. Engstrom was weird and gave them weird assignments. But Karen would love it, smiling a little as she made connections, and her breasts would be there, *always* there, even when she took a math test or went back home to write or rode the bus. This bra was with her the whole time. He wanted to pull it close to him. He wanted to bury his face in the shallow cups. He wanted, maybe more than all of that, to comply with what she wanted, to wear her bra, to try to eke some of her warmth and put it into himself.

But he was suddenly scared. He couldn't exactly pin down what was scaring him; only that the last time they'd been together, it had gone weird. This was weirder. Didn't … and he knew this wasn't the time to be thinking this, but didn't her *Dad* wear girls' clothes sometimes? Like half the time?

"Do you not want to do this?" she asked. Her tone was brusque, like a brush-off, but Karen had paused, and seemed to be interested in the answer. Henry had a feeling that if he had told her right now that this was too bizarre for him, she would shrug and laugh it off and they would head back to play Nintendo some more.

Why would he do that, though? Why did it matter how weird this was? Karen Luck was in front of him, fully and completely naked, and he was *waffling*? Jesus, Henry, you're really dense sometimes. "No, I do. I am. Sorry."

Even with his momentary hesitation, he could still feel a little of her body heat in the fabric of the bra. His skin tingled. His brain felt like it was crunching, like when he was eating a bowl of Cocoa Krispies. Plus, it actually *felt* good. He had no kind of chest to fill the cups of the bra out, but the fabric kept brushing against his nipples, sending sparks of joy through his whole body. His penis jutted out from his body, a exclamation.

"Give me your underwear," she said. "Take mine."

At this, he very nearly balked. Maybe it was one thing to wear a bra, but it was entirely another thing to wear *panties*.

Guys didn't wear *panties*. Did Karen's Dad wear panties? And why was he thinking about her Dad again? Stop thinking about her Dad, Henry, Jesus. He thought of the guys in his classes at Civil Air Patrol, none of whom he was especially close to, but still: what if they knew about something like this? Or the kids at school? His best friend was and always would be Karen Luck, but Karen didn't go to Uxbridge High. She was off and away at her fancy private school and all day, he had to navigate his school alone. The trick to high school is to keep your head down, do your work, and not stand out in any way. One kid on the first day at Uxbridge spilled some meatball sauce on his shirt at lunch and it was three years later and everyone was still calling him Meatball. What would they call him? Panties? Panties Dear.

All these thoughts passed through his head in less than a second. The crux of the matter was – and always was – Karen. How many times had he told himself that he would do literally anything for her? How many nights had he lain awake in bed, convincing himself that, if necessary, he would actually die for Karen Luck? Was that just all hyperbole? All she wanted to do was put on her panties ... and, honestly, Henry, have you forgotten that no matter how intimate her bra was, her panties were *way* more intimate? He'd seen her boobs before, but she had never taken off her underwear in front of him. He had never quite considered that he ever would. You get used to ideas, even the ones you don't like. You get used to pining for Karen Luck and knowing that you will never have her, because the pining hurts but it's also kind of good, too. It gives you a kind of purpose. Maybe even a fucked-up sense of nobility.

And now here was Karen Luck, the literal girl of your dreams, asking you to try something sexual with her, and you're *waiting*? Does the pining actually feel *that* good, Henry?

Karen slid her underwear down her legs, and for a moment, Henry could only gasp. Never in his life had he seen a girl completely naked. For a moment, he could only stare at her, his eyes returning over and over to the thin thatch of dirty-blond pubic hair and what was beneath. He'd seen plenty of vaginas in dirty magazines – sometimes guys brought them to school and passed them around – but seeing one up close and in real life was almost too much to handle. *All of this* was almost too much to handle. He wanted to take a step toward her and touch it, feel if her pubic hair was as soft as it looked. His own was rough and kinky and sort of unpleasant. Karen's wouldn't be unpleasant. Karen's *couldn't* be unpleasant.

"Well?" she asked, and now Henry saw that she was holding these out to him, too. He was to put these on, as well, even though they were a lot slimmer than his boxer shorts and he would probably bust the elastics on them. Girls' underwear had elastics, right? Plus there was his penis to consider: hard and intrusive and way too big for this sliver of cloth she was proffering. But he would try. He would absolutely try to comply with everything she wanted, for whatever reason she wanted it.

But:

"Give me a second, okay?" he said. "Just a second. I've never seen you naked before."

Karen looked at him for a moment, then her face softened. "Okay. I'm sorry, okay." She dropped her arm a moment and did a slow turn. When she faced him again, she was smiling, just a little.

"I know this is a weird thing," she said. "What I want, it's a weird thing."

"It's not that weird."

"That's nice of you to say."

"Give me those."

But she didn't. Instead, she came over to where he was, and put a hand on his chest, running it up under the loose bra. Then she squatted down, holding her underwear out for him. "Step inside."

Steadying himself by reaching out and putting the tips of his fingers on her bare shoulder (even as all this other stuff was happening, he still couldn't believe he was being allowed to touch her shoulder), he stepped into the legholes: right, left. Slowly, exquisitely, she pulled them up his legs. The feel of it sent electrical charges throughout his whole body – not just the fabric, but the light touch of Karen Luck's fingers. In comparison, his own boxers were rough and scratchy. As much as he wanted to watch Karen at work, he involuntarily closed his eyes and threw his head back. This was heaven.

The whole process would be more difficult in a couple years, after regular CAP calisthenics and weight training had bulked Henry Dear up significantly, but for now, his legs weren't the difficult part. As he suspected, it was his penis. "I'm sorry," he told her, looking down at it. He'd never thought of his dick as looking ridiculous before, but here it was, sticking more than halfway out and leaking pre-come so much that it might as well have been a faucet. Henry didn't know if he was apologizing for the bad fit or the frankly absurd amount of pre-come. The first time he'd encountered his own pre-ejaculate, four years before, he thought he'd broken something in his penis and he was going to bleed out this odd, sticky, clear liquid until he was dead. It awould serve him right for playing with it so much. Now, the only real issue was that his dick made sounds when he was jerking off in bed at night if he let the pre-come get out of control. That intermittent squelching was the only sound in the whole house when the lights were out and he was ostensibly sleeping. What if his

Mom heard? So he'd gotten good at mopping up in the middle as well as the end.

But this? Doing it in front of a girl? Not just a girl but Karen Luck? This was filth. This was embarrassing filth.

"It's okay," she said, staring at it. Not assessing this time. He couldn't quite figure out *what* the look in her eyes was. She didn't *sound* like it was okay. "Last time, I didn't see it. I'm seeing it now."

"I'm sorry," he said again.

"You don't think it looks weird?"

Karen hesitated, glancing up to look in his eyes before looking back down at the penis. "Yeah, it looks weird. But that's okay right now."

"It is?"

"Lie down, Henry. On your belly."

Eager enough to hide his sloppy erection from her, he moved to his bed and sprawled down on it, prone. Her panties just barely covered his ass, which was still skinny and flat. That would change over the next couple years, too.

Then her hand was on his back, trailing lightly between his shoulder blades. She was wearing some sort of perfume, light and citrusy, that he would forever associate with this moment. Henry's face against the pillow, he closed his eyes and imagined her behind him, above him. Was she smiling? Concentrating? Trying to decide what to do first? Part of him wished that she would turn him over and take off this bra and start squeezing his nipples until he popped. He couldn't get off on his own doing that, and he hoped, desperately, that he could do that again with her. That would give them something that was exclusively theirs, something that was intimate between she and he. No matter what happened with him or her in the future, that would be something he could hold onto for the rest of his life. They would be tied together.

Instead, she unhooked the bra, her fingers tapping against the middle of his back as she worked. His penis throbbed against the mattress. He could feel his pre-cum spouting all over his comforter. Could he hide that from his

Mom? Don't think about Mom. Karen Luck laid the bra out on either side of him.

"Don't move," she said.

"Don't worry."

"And don't talk."

Against the mattress, he offered a barely perceptible nod. His dick was geysering like mad. He wanted her hand on his back again. He wanted her to tell him to do stuff, or not do stuff. For whatever reason, that part of it – the commanding part – was sizzling the back of his brain just as much as her fingertips. He craved more of it. He needed it.

Karen herself couldn't stop staring at that bare back. Her knees were on either side of Henry's butt and...

No. Her. Not Henry; say her.

Slowly, she dragged air in through her nose, letting it stutter out slowly from her mouth. She closed her eyes and tilted her head to the ceiling. Okay. If that's what this was going to be, okay.

Karen Luck straddled her small butt, clad only in a pair of her own underwear. She was glad, perhaps oddly, that she had worn one of the nicer pairs today, instead of the cotton stuff you could buy in three-packs at Bradlee's. She reached out and touched tented, tentative fingers on the fabric, which stretched to accommodate what was inside them. She closed her eyes and inhaled. Her own scent – not her mother's Dream Clouds, but the lighter, more summery Beach Breeze – was the room's scent, the scent of the two of them. It was a *girl* scent.

You want some brownies? She heard it so clearly in her ear, an echo, said with just a hint of a come-on. Surely she hadn't simply imagined that flirty look in Mrs. Dear's eyes, the way those eyes lingered on Karen's face. It had been real. It had all been real and ... and now, here it was, in the flesh. Sure it was. Just beneath her fingers was the first hidden part of Mrs. Dear. She was going to let Karen do anything she want to. Her best friend's mother had wanted this for awhile, hadn't she?

Karen laid her hand flat against Mrs. Dear's ass ... then snaked up under the waistband and dipped below the skin. She tensed beneath the future bestselling writer's hand, but said nothing, and didn't move away. Now it was Karen's turn to tense. She was building a world in the darkness inside her mind, a world that was becoming clearer to her by the second, and now she was going to have to shatter it. Hopefully briefly, hopefully only momentarily. But necessary. Her heart slammed in her chest. Her brain whirred.

"I want to do something," she said, not opening her eyes. There was breathing in the dark. "I would like you to let me do it. If it's too much, I'll stop. But I don't want to. Don't say anything unless you want me to stop."

Hesitantly, she put her finger in her mouth, made it wet. Then she tucked it back under the waistband, trailing down until she found the center of Mrs. Dear's warmth. Then, with no preamble, she poked in. Again, the woman tensed against her; she hadn't expected this intrusion. Somewhere up ahead, the woman made a low gasping grunt sound. Masculine, maybe. Or maybe just stunned. Yeah, that was it. Stunned.

Without realizing it, she'd dipped her other hand under the waistband of the boy's boxers she wore, and slipped her own finger inside herself. A lot less resistance. A lot wetter.

She pushed both fingers in deeper; she knew just where to hit with one and was groping blindly in the dark with the other. The dichotomy made her mind tilt. Raw lightning bolts screamed up from deep inside her, cascading into fireballs inside her hollow parts. A thin, shuddering gasp exploded out of her. Pulses of sensation caromed through her thighs and belly and heart. Karen was unprepared for the swiftness or intensity of her orgasm. She wanted to scream. She couldn't scream.

The finger inside Mrs. Dear prodded in further, fast now, and now there was a sound beneath her, low and rumbling and unexpected. A cry? A moan? She didn't know. All she wanted was to feel that again, feel that cannonball of pleasure inside her. The future novelist took a risk and opened her eyes.

That hair wasn't right, and the setting wasn't right. In her mind, the room had been nondescript, the bed in the middle of an abstract concept of a room rather than something concrete, something that tied her to this reality. Karen's eye kept going to the hair, which was 100% wrong; everything else was 100% right. That bra, open and on either side of the person below her. The heel of her hand against the silk of underwear, her middle finger deep inside ... *her*, it can still be *her*, even with her eyes open.

She pressed in deeper, deepest, and something inside Mrs. Dear brushed up against her fingertip. Something round, warm, and now that voice below her changed. Not a groan. Not that odd rumble. It was pleasure. Karen was almost sure of it. Unable to push her finger in any deeper, she instead attempted to twirl it, like someone putting a finger to their ear to indicate *cuckoo*. Again that sound, low and surprised, as though the person creating it had discovered something new and borderline shocking. It was a good sound. A righteous sound.

Karen moved her own finger inside herself, bracing for another orgasm. It didn't come, not right away. Maybe the first one scared all the rest away through the sheer force of its impact and power. Then she tried twirling it, as she was doing inside Mrs. Dear. Within seconds, both fingers matched rhythm, moving in tandem. This wasn't how she did things back home. She found her spot and flicked it or pressed on it, the pressure gentle then forceful, gentle then forceful; she never moved like this inside herself, her finger providing that somehow awful, somehow glorious feeling that consumed everything, then moving away a moment, ratcheting up the anticipation, until she brushed by again. New. This was new and this was ... this was...

Her second orgasm fluttered through her. Not as powerful as the first, but when it gripped her, it refused to let go. Seasons changed. Epochs rose and fell. That feeling in her roared and dropped off, roared and dropped off, like the engine of a muscle car. And then, just like that, it drifted away.

In the midst of all that, Karen's eyes had closed again. The future novelist now opened them and took her surroundings in. There was universe inside herself in which she could envision Mrs. Dear in her son's bedroom with her; Henry would be away at CAP, and Karen would come by for some homework or something. While she was in his room, Mrs. Dear would come and lean in the doorway, her hair down and her glasses on, and she would ask Karen if she'd found what she was looking for. Things would progress from there. Karen would eventually write a scene very similar to that in her novel *Caught Over Nebraska*.

But here, it was too artificial, too much invention. It was adding layers to something that needed to be simple to work. Mrs. Dear wasn't *in* the doorway. Henry was actually below her. And ... and besides, why would she think about Mrs. Dear at all, right? That would be dumb, when her sort-of boyfriend was right here, *right here*, and had at least contributed to the two orgasms that had rocked her body.

She slid out of him slowly, not wanting to hurt him. The ridiculous confidence with which she'd come in here had tumbled away, like a clumsy Jenga tower. Karen missed that confidence ... and was glad it had gone away for awhile. It scared her, a little.

Henry rolled over and stared at her. Karen looked away, a little shocked, a little dismayed that the face looking back wasn't his mother's. *No. Stop thinking that way, Karen. He might hear you. Or sense you. Henry might figure you out.* She turned back to him, met his eyes. Held them.

"Near the end," he said quietly. "I liked what you were doing near the end."

"We don't have to talk about this."

"I think we should, though."

Her eyes hadn't left his. Beyond anything else, Henry Dear had been her best friend for almost a decade. She'd saved him that day of the tornado. Maybe she owed him something now. Maybe she owed herself something.

"I didn't know I was going to…" But she trailed off. Of course she had known. The second Mrs. Dear had set the brownies down, then descended that spiral staircase, Karen had known. Fooling herself wasn't going to do her any favors.

It's worked for me so far, she thought.

Has it? some alien voice shot back from inside her, betraying her shaky ground.

"Karen," Henry said, and sat up at the edge of his bed. The bra had been discarded somewhere, but her panties were still on him, stretching too far in every direction. But his erection had disappeared, and his penis had pulled inside the underwear. It bulged out in front; Karen wanted to reach out and rub her fingers over that bulge. It didn't make sense, a bulge like that in girls' underwear; in its way, it was like putting your finger in a boy's ass. None of this made sense. All of it thrilled her. "Would you sit here with me a second?"

Too exhausted for other recourse, she did what he asked of her, and when he put his arm around her, she allowed it. The hair on his arm felt course and the bones jutted out and into her shoulders and back, but it was still a comfort. He was still her friend.

"You don't have to say a thing," Henry Dear said. "I don't know what this is. I don't know if I like it. But if *you* like it, this is something we can keep doing."

Tears didn't fall down her cheeks, but they were close. She said, "I don't know if I like it. I just wanted to do it."

He nodded. "Anything you want to do, Karen. Anything at all. I will do. You need to know that there aren't limits, and I won't ask all that much in return."

"Jesus, Henry," she said, closing her eyes and putting her face to his chest. "Don't give me that much power."

When he laughed, it chuffed out, like something was caught in his throat and he'd finally cleared it. "Karen Luck," he said, pressing his hand to her lower back, holding her so she didn't fall off the bed. "You've always had that much power. Don't you know that?"

Maybe she did and maybe she didn't. Maybe that was why Henry had proven such a fertile testing ground. Here it was, a little over two years later, the taste of Burger City fries in her mouth, heading back to her place so she could strap on a dildo and enter her best friend. She liked all the parts of the arrangement, especially the slow buildup. A little lube on the strap-on as he put her makeup on in her vanity. He was already starting to grow a mustache and the makeup looked a little silly on him – but not, she had to admit, as silly as it had when he'd first put it on. He'd attained some skill. Karen wasn't sure if that was good or bad.

The point wasn't to make him look like her ... or anyone else real, for that matter. She didn't want him to *be* a woman, because if he really was a she, that would indicate some things about herself that she wasn't in any way comfortable with. But he could embody the *idea* of the feminine. Not in the way that drag queens did it, as little as she knew about drag queens. It wasn't supposed to be an act, nothing camp or silly. The future novelist wanted Henry real, but heightened. That was the word. *Heightened*.

They stole into Karen's house like ghosts.

Automatically, she tilted her head to hear if her father was clacking away at typewriter keys in either his office or her mother's. But that had gotten tricker, hadn't it? Nowadays, the only typewriter in the house was her own. A little over a year ago, Dad had replaced his own typewriter with a word processor, the words flowing down and down, green against a black background. After his first day of writing with the new machine, he'd tumbled out of his office, exhausted, dehydrated, needing to use the bathroom.

"It's alchemy," her father had said later, tucking into a Shake & Bake pork chop that was three hours cold. His eyes were wide. His hands shaky. For the first time ever, Karen wondered if her father was doing drugs in his office, something to help him through his ten-hour writing days. "The pages don't *stop*. There's no putting another page in, no hesitation. It's *all* there, right there in one document. I wrote *twenty* pages today. Karen, during my last week with my typewriter, I don't think I wrote twenty pages in a *week*."

Karen, who was picking at a piece of cake, wanted only to go back to her bedroom and work on her new story. "The Transmigration" was her school story – she could keep it away from her father and Henry and everyone else, because it only existed on a single floppy disk hidden away from everyone, and she never intended to print it out. At home, she was working on something she liked almost as much, but which was a little more standard. Something other people could read. It was called "Nobody Under the Stars." She didn't trust the narrator, a girl who believes she's not in love with her favorite teacher. The teacher, a flustered young man in his early twenties, knows about the crush but is determined to do nothing about it. Both of them are fooling themselves, but it was trickier when your main character was doing it, and you were telling the story from her point of view. You kind of wanted to shake her and say, wake up, you idiot, and see what's in front of you. That tension was keeping "Nobody Under the Stars" afloat, even if there was something about it that felt strange. Inauthentic. She couldn't tell if it was because the teacher probably would *also* want the girl back. That would throw a whole new level of complication into the mix, and she wasn't sure she wanted to get there with this story, even if it might make the story better. She would figure out more once she got back to her room and was once more able to fall into the mashmallowy strands of the story.

But now: "Dad, are you okay?"

He grinned up at her. "More than okay, Karen. I want to write *more*. I want to write *now*. Is that strange? I have *never* felt like this writing as myself. It's like there's a key to my brain and the word processor unlocked it."

Karen watched him skeptically. Mom's office didn't have a word processor. It had a brand new IBM computer, complete with WordPerfect – the best word processing software on the market, according to Dad. The obvious question was why her father, who was pumping out high quality, extremely popular novels under two different names, couldn't afford to get himself a new PC while he was at it.

"I dunno," he'd told her, not really looking around. "Too many whistles and bells for me. I just need words on a screen. Your Mom deserves better." It would have been the perfect time to remind him that Mom, despite her publishing career, was dead, and had been most of Karen's life. But it was a point she never quite got along to pressing.

Now, Karen said, "I just haven't seen you like this in awhile."

Dad gulped water and grinned. "The book is a mystery. Most of them are mysteries but this one's different, okay? It's about this guy, Mike Bull, and he's this private detective and he's *almost* cynical, but not totally. I mean, cynical private eyes are a dime a dozen, you know? I wanted someone with a little optimism. Anyway, he's got a daughter and she's sort of a junior private eye, you know? He's solving cases and she's solving different cases. I don't know if they're going to converge or not, the cases. I think maybe they will sometimes, but maybe not in this first book."

Karen started. "Sometimes? You mean this is like a potential new series?"

"Could be." Dad's grin grew even bigger.

"What about Sprouse and Apa?"

"They'll come back. People love them. People love them a lot more now than they used to, I think. But I think I need to *need* them. I don't want those guys to get stale, you know? I've been writing them for over a decade. Now I think it's time to try something new."

"Mike Bull. Sounds mean."

Dad's eyes went wide with joy. "I *know*, but he's *not*. That's *part* of it!"

Before too much longer, he retreated back into his office to continue his work. The novel, *Too Little, Too Late*, would be ready for proofread in just three weeks. In the past, Dad had barely gotten to his fourth chapter in three weeks. He'd never finished a full novel that fast, under any name.

Two days later, during which he mostly slept, he was in Mom's office, wearing his favorite wig, light makeup, a pair of tan capri pants, and a white-on-blue polka-dotted top with mammoth lapels. Karen poked her head in on the way to school. She noticed he'd been at it long enough to have kicked off his white strappy shoes. That normally didn't happen until he was a few hours in. *Was* he a few hours in?

"I'm off to the Academy," she said, careful not to call him *Dad*. She could, but it might interrupt his flow. Writing was a creature that existed to consume. Karen didn't know if that kind of consumption was good or bad; she only knew that it was necessary. Dad hadn't put ten hour days into *Too Little, Too Late*; he'd put *fourteen* hours. And none of them had been that awful start-stop second guessing writing he was usually stuck with when Gary Luck sat at a typewriter. All the hours were productive. He woke up before her and went to bed – barely – after her and when he finally emerged, it was with a new book. Writing like that was the goal. Writing like that was the pinnacle. Karen only hoped that it wasn't some delusion of optimism; she hadn't yet looked at the book, not sure she could take it if all that excitement had resulted in something terrible. It would challenge the very notion of putting everything of yourself into a book. The manuscript was in her backpack now; she was going to spend half her lunch hour reading it, and half up in the writing lab, working on her own fiction.

But she wondered how he was going to tackle the next Elaine Luck novel. Dad and Mom had always had different ways of writing. She'd flowed while he labored. She'd take that day's work to bed with her and do some spot-editing sitting up with a cup of tea at hand and a red pen at the ready; that way, she'd be ready to simply dive in the next day, with no time wasted. There were days when Karen looked through the hole in the wall and had seen not the confusing physicality of her parents, but the quiet time they spent in between those moments. Dad would be sitting up, reading a paperback. Mom would have her pen tucked behind her ear, flipping through manuscript pages. If Dad had finished writing a book, Mom would look that over, too, and vice versa. Dad not only knew how Mom wrote, he knew how she edited. He knew how she kept consistency in her own novels, and in his. Dad knew how she *re*-wrote, what strands she pruned and which ones she followed. All this was part of the reason why Mom was able to stay alive long after that tornado had taken her to Texas. When you give enough of yourself in life, you live on long past death.

Now Karen shook her head, clearing out those old memories. She stood frozen in the middle of the living room, trying hard to hear the tiny, sludgy sound of fingers on keyboard keys. The ones from Dad's office – the word processor office – were always slightly louder. He'd taken a little break after finishing *There's Something Wrong With Betsy* – what may be the best Elaine Luck novel yet – but now he was back at work on a new Mike Bull novel, *Thanks That Was Fun*. The going was a little slower than with *Too Little, Too Late*, but part of that was because Cynthia lived with them now. *She* was reading his stuff nightly, offering suggestions, giving him some insights. She did it from the comfort of her own room, formerly one of the guest rooms, on the west side of the house. The whole setup was weird. If she and Dad were having a relationship, wouldn't it just make sense to come out and say so? It's not like Karen wanted her Dad single forever. Were they trying to protect her feelings? That was stupid. Karen had always liked Cynthia, who had worn shoulder pads in the mid-eighties like the women on *L.A. Law.* She looked tough, but Dad always said it was a huge act. "Cynthia was your mother's best friend, not just her agent," Dad confided one night. "Except for me and you, I think Cynthia was the most devastated person in the world when your Mom died." And now, after all this time, she was here.

But not audibly.

"Come on," Karen whispered. "Let's go to my room. I have something new I want you to try."

Henry followed her into her house, all deep mahogany and dark paint. There was a painting on the wall in the living room behind the couch of a forest scene, with a deer in the foreground, looking out as if trying to sense what was going on in the world of humans. Maybe it wondered what it was doing here, hanging up in this foreign place, so far away from where it was supposed to be. That painting had hung there since before Karen had been born, and no one ever commented on it. It just existed. In odd moments, Henry would sometimes wonder how that painting had survived so long in the House of Luck; just existing here seemed anathema to the whole tenor of the house. Sometimes, when his thoughts turned to Elaine Luck, he would think that of course a tornado had to take her away; nothing else could have captured one of the Lucks. They simply never stopped.

Karen's bedroom had changed little over the years; it was one of the few places in the house where the walls didn't seem heavy and oppressive, where the dark-on-dark color scheme lightened up a little. Her walls were all a light sky-blue, and paintings from her childhood still hung in pastel watercolors at intervals along one of her walls. Some were nursery-rhyme scenes: Jack and Jill with the pitcher of water, Humpty Dumpty on the wall. Most were simple, folksy paintings of things like fruit and vegetables. Still life in isolation. He wondered why Karen had never replaced these paintings. Had her Mom created these? Mrs. Luck had died a decade ago. Was it time to replace stuff like this?

While Karen went to her dresser, rummaging in the drawers for whatever it was she planned on using on him today, Henry paused at her writing-desk, and ran his fingers along the typewriter keyboard. Karen was the only person he knew that was still using a typewriter to write. At school, they were all on computers. His Mom found this ironic. "You know, kiddo, when I went to that school, they had typing classes. Some boys, mostly girls. So we could learn how to be secretaries, you know? Ha! And now they've gotten rid of the typing courses the second the computer courses start. Tell me, Henry, where's the logic in that?" At this, Mom would knock back some of whatever was in her glass at the time – usually gin, sometimes rum. Mom drinking was a newer thing, and Henry was unsure if he should be concerned yet. He was out of the house more than he used to be. Tuesdays and Thursdays were Civil Air Patrol, where he was learning about the history of aviation and space flight, or doing calisthenics and wind sprints or working out in the gym, which was a lot better than the one at school.

Sometimes, Henry thought that the gym was the only reason he stayed on at CAP. Some of the kids there seemed to be getting a lot more out of it than he was. Following orders wasn't his problem. He *liked* following orders. The problem, Henry thought, seemed to be the fact that the orders were everyone's orders. If you were doing twenty pushups in the rain, your whole squadron was doing twenty pushups in the rain. Even if someone was called out for insubordination or something, it was because he – or, occasionally, she – wasn't falling into formation with the rest of the squadron. You were supposed to conform to the *group*. More and more, Henry was growing disillusioned with the concept of the *group*. It went counter to everything CAP stood for, but being *part* of something was starting to feel more than a little uncomfortable. Here, with Karen, he didn't always like the stuff they did, but at least she saw him as *him*, as an individual, as someone who had presence and weight and meaning in her life. Not just as Cadet Airman First Class Dear, one of dozens of Cadet Airmen First Class. Here he was Henry, and then when she put makeup and stuff on him, he was someone else, someone she wanted him to be, but he was still some*one*. Plus, it wasn't as if he wasn't getting something out of this. He didn't know why Karen liked to dress him up – she never gave him a straight answer – and it wasn't his favorite part of all this, but he *loved* it when she got him up on all fours and entered him.

He'd loved it since that first time she'd come into his room and stuck a finger inside him. He'd hated it at first – it hurt, for one thing, and for another it made him feel weird and vulnerable and a little scared – but he was willing to do it until she wanted to stop. That was the whole deal with Karen, you did whatever she wanted to do until she wanted to stop.

But something had happened in him before too long. Karen hit something in him that made his entire lower half feel like it was melting – melting and exploding at the same time. The only time Henry felt anything like that was when Karen had bit his nipple that time. It seemed as if she was uniquely adept at finding the parts in him that made his body go crazy with sensation. In the years since, she had upped her technique ... and her arsenal. Somehow, she'd gotten her hands on a variety of toys – dildos and vibrators of all shapes and sizes. One of the more recent ones was so big he almost laughed about it; he wasn't laughing twenty minutes later as she was pouring lube all over it and trying to get the whole thing inside him. When she did something to him that made him feel really uncomfortable, she made sure to reward him.

Usually, she would play with his nipples while he jerked off. That day, when it actually hurt him no matter how much lube she'd slathered on it, she'd actually given him one of her rare blowjobs. She wasn't very good at them, but he would never in a million years tell Karen that. Besides, they always made him feel better; it was the *effort* of it that mattered, the fact that she knew he needed something to make him feel better. The oversized dildo had hurt enough to bring tears to his eyes, and he had borne it, knowing that it would be worth it in the end, knowing that Karen wouldn't let him suffer for nothing.

There was a stack of papers next to the typewriter. A title headed the top sheet: "Nobody Under the Stars." He reached for it, but Karen stopped him.

"What are you looking at?" she asked, coming up behind him.

"I thought you said you weren't writing much."

"I said I was writing, but it wasn't ready for consumption," she told him, putting a hand on his lower back.

"So I can't read this?" he asked, picking up the top sheet.

The new science teacher strode to the chalkboard and Devan watched him go. Her best friend Lara glanced her way and Devan offered raised eyebrows, the very picture of innocence. Then, deliberately, she turned back to Mr. Peterson. Before the end of the day, she would know his first name. Then it would be game on.

"Game on?" he asked her.

"Put it down, Henry."

He would, but not just yet. "Do you have a crush on one of your teachers?"

Karen rolled her eyebrows. "Why does everyone think that the stuff I write about is always about *me*? Maybe I can invent stories, because that's what writers do?"

He placed the page back on the stack and turned to her. She had what looked like a black rubber ball with a small belt coming out either side of it. "I'm sorry," he said. "I always hear, 'Write what you know.'"

"That's not even what Hemingway meant. Write what you know can mean writing stuff you've seen and done, *or* the stuff you read about in books or heard in stories, *or*..."

There was a noise coming from the other side of the wall. Karen's eyes went wide. How long had it been since she'd heard *anything* from over there but the sound of her Dad snoring? She took a step toward the wall, aiming for the painting of the folk-arty strawberries in the little frame. Then, another noise, something low and guttural. It was a weirdly *familiar* sound, even if Henry couldn't quite place it.

"Wait," Karen said. "No, wait."

She went to the painting of the strawberries and pulled it off the wall, revealing a small, irregularly-shaped hole about the size of a ping-pong ball. Karen put her eye to the hole, then immediately jumped back, as if the wall had burned her forehead.

"What... What's over there?"

"No," Karen said immediately, but Henry was already moving toward the hole. "Henry, seriously, *no!*" Her voice came out strangled, almost terrified. She got to him too late.

Before she could put a hand on his shoulder to wrench him away, he'd already put his eye against the wall.

Cynthia Auburn straddled Mr. Luck across a big bed with brass fixtures. He knew it was Mr. Luck, even though the man was in full makeup and wig and some costuming. One of the dresses he wore when writing was in a puddle on the floor, but he still had on a bra and panties. Well, his panties had been yanked down at some point. Cynthia, fully naked, wore a strap-on the size of a Coke bottle and the color of bubblegum. Her hands were on Mr. Luck's hips and she was simply *slamming* into him, harder than seemed necessary, harder than the man should be able to take. But he *was* taking it. Henry saw his best friend's father very clearly; it was not the face of a man in terrible agony or sadness or grief. He was *transported.* The grin on his face, and the way his jaw hung slightly ajar, said it all. However aggressive Cynthia was, he could probably stand a little more.

Maybe they wouldn't have noticed anything amiss if Henry hadn't shouted right then, but really, he couldn't help it.

"*No!*" That was all.

Everything stopped.

Cynthia was so startled by the sudden sound that she tumbled backward, falling inelegantly to the floor with a crash. Her strap-on stuck up in the air like a quivering pink exclamation point. Mr. Luck scrambled up to the head of the bed, seeming at first to cower from Henry's shout. Then Henry saw he was grabbing one of the pillowcases and trying his best to wipe the makeup from his face. From what Henry could see, he was only succeeding in smearing it around. Karen hadn't moved from her place against the wall, seemingly paralyzed there, her face a giant O of shock and horror.

Now, Mr. Luck got out of bed and went to a dresser, grabbing jeans and a T-shirt for a band called Thunder Bravo. Karen murmured, "He's going to come in here. He's going to." Her voice came out strained, shuddery. But accurate: a second later, there was a light knock at her door.

"Karen? Honey?"

Henry looked at her, but she just closed her eyes, grabbing at the wall, as if she could find some purchase there. Except for the pictures her Mom had put up, this wall was bare. Henry went to the door and turned the handle. Mr. Luck strode in like a bad effect from a science fiction movie: his makeup streaked across his nose and cheeks and forehead and ears. Thinking quickly, Henry went to Karen's vanity, where the cold cloths were. He handed one to Mr. Luck, who looked at it a moment before going to the vanity and wiping the streaks off his face. As he did, Cynthia Auburn came into the doorway and leaned in. Henry couldn't read her face. She looked in, her arms crossed, not giving an inch of herself.

Mr. Luck went to his daughter first, who was still pressed against the wall. The strawberry painting hung askew. He went to straighten it, and instead lifted it off the hook. "Ah," he said, crouching and looking through it. "Ah," he repeated, setting the strawberry painting gently down on the floor. Now he looked to his daughter and said, "Your Mom noticed that hole when we moved in. She put the painting up to cover it and I guess we just forgot about it."

Finally, Karen spoke. "It's been there for awhile."

Mr. Luck nodded. "I know, honey." He took his hand in hers and lifted it. "What's this?" She still clutched the rubber ball with the belt running through it. If it had held a modicum of menace before all this, now it looked vaguely ridiculous.

Cynthia strode in. "It's a ball gag," she said, taking it from Karen. "You put it in someone's mouth to keep them quiet during sex."

Henry turned to Karen. "That's what you wanted to show me?"

Sudden scarlet raced up Karen's face and she turned away, "Jesus, Henry."

But Mr. Luck held both her small hands in his big ones. For the first time, Henry noticed just how big Mr. Luck was, both in height and girth. It occurred to him that he had only rarely seen the man standing up; over the years, he was either hunched over his own desk, or sitting up in a dress and a wig in his wife's office. You don't really get an accurate sense of a person if all they're doing it writing all the time.

"Karen, look at me, and listen to me. We're not having any shame here. This is a shame-free zone. You're not in trouble." He paused. "I hope I'm not."

Karen looked at him, her mind whirring and buzzing and clack-clacking like the sound of typewriter keys hitting a page. "No," she said. "You're not."

He nodded, satisfied. To Henry, he said, "I'd like to talk with you, Henry. Privately, if I could."

Henry blinked. "Am *I* in trouble?"

"No. I just want to talk."

Cynthia said to Karen, "So do I. Okay?" Karen nodded.

Mr. Luck shuffled Henry out and Karen heard them head downstairs, where the living room and the two writing studios were. She was left alone with Cynthia, who was holding the ball gag Karen had bought through a mail catalog. It was the same catalog through which she'd bought the dildos and vibrators she'd used on herself and on Henry, even that giant one she was sure he'd balk at. And had she *wanted* him to balk at it? Finding it in the catalogue had been like having a wide-awake fever dream. Heart fluttering, fingers tingling, she'd written the item number on the tear-out sheet and copied her credit card number. There was no *way* Henry was going to let her put this in him. No *way*. Every time he came here, or she went to his place, it was something new, something usually humiliating or weird or potentially upsetting. He'd taken it all, he'd allowed her to do *anything*, and that... Well, he had to say no to *something*, right?

And then that giant dildo had come. *Giant*, that was the only word for it. Almost as big around as her own forearm, and she'd opened it in her bedroom – this room! – and for a moment simply stared at it. "This is the line," she'd murmured. Of course it was. He'd say no, and maybe they'd argue a little, and that would be the end of it. The sex part of their friendship would end, and it could go back to what it was before all this.

Only Henry hadn't said no. He'd only sighed and begun undressing, staring at it as if it was some old nemesis, come back to settle a score. Before it was halfway in, he'd begun crying. She'd heard it and wanted to stop. "Henry?" she'd prompted.

"Is that all of it?" His voice was strained and tired.

"No, just half."

"Fuck," he murmured. "Fuck, Karen."

"Look, I can pull this out and we could..."

"Keep going," he'd said. "Just go slow."

And so she had, and he'd borne it, and afterward, the shame of what she'd done fell on her like an avalanche. *You weren't supposed to want to do it*, she'd thought, staring at him after, his face puffy and red. *You were supposed to tell me to stop.* The thing she hated most in the world was giving blowjobs, but Henry had earned one after that. It didn't take long. Even aching from what she'd done to him, all it took was three minutes with her mouth on his dick and her hands on his nipples. It was a small price to pay.

Besides, it wasn't as if she'd hadn't gotten herself off as she tested his endurance. It hadn't been his crying – oh God, not that, Jesus – but it had been something about the *letting*, the *allowing*. It wasn't just that he gave her total control over him; it was that he would *keep* doing it, forever. He would never say no. Especially after this – he wouldn't ever say no to her. That was dangerous, and not just for him. She needed to make him say no. She hoped he never would. *That* was what got her off.

These were things she understood only vaguely. Cynthia sat on the edge of her bed, looking down at the ball gag and sighing. "When I was your age, I barely knew what sex was. You guys are just ... so much more involved."

Karen took a step forward. "I'm so sorry I saw that."

Cynthia laughed. "I think in this scenario, I should be the one apologizing to you. This isn't something that we do. I mean we have done. Not a lot. I guess it's something that we do sometimes. Am I red?"

"Extremely. Me?"

"Oh yes." Cynthia paused. "What you saw... that's not how I usually am."

"You don't have to explain to me."

"I feel like I do. I don't want to embarrass you or anything, but if you have a ball gag, you're already at least a little bit versed in this stuff."

Karen said, "I'm not, actually. We haven't used that yet."

"Oh?"

"We um." Karen closed her eyes and leaned against the wall, feeling her cheeks run scarlet and her heart crashing in and out of her chest like a fist. "What you were doing is normally what I'm doing."

The silence lasted so long, Karen opened her eyes, unable to bear that quiet darkness. Cynthia was staring off, toward Karen's Wilson Phillips poster hanging next to her window. "I know that probably makes me a bad person."

"No," Cynthia said.

"Or fucked up. Really pretty fucked up, right?"

Now Cynthia stood and went to her. Karen's brain was suddenly on overload. Thinking was impossible. She groped for the agent before she even got to her, grabbed her around the back and pulled her close. Cynthia grabbed back, holding tight, matching Karen's intensity. "You're not bad, and you're not fucked up. Don't say that, Karen. Don't ever say that, okay?"

Thick, hitching sobs stuttered out of her and she held Cynthia tighter. "I don't know what I am, Cynthia. And my Dad is sort of confusing. And I miss my Mom. I miss my Mom every day."

Cynthia, who had never comforted a child before and who was sure she was doing it wrong, now closed her eyes and said, "I do, too, Karen. I miss her every day, too."

"Why do I do this stuff to him?" Karen suddenly blurted. "He loves me so much and I love that he loves me, but I don't, Cynthia. I don't love him like that. And I think I'm just using him, and I don't think he minds, but *I* mind. Goddammit."

Holding the girl tighter for a moment, Cynthia then held her out at arm's length and said, "I want to tell you something, but only if you promise not to be angry with me."

Despite everything, curiosity twisted through her like a mutant vine. She wiped her tears away. Oh, and by the way: did Cynthia have hazel eyes? How come she'd never noticed that before? Mrs. Dear had hazel eyes. "Yes, I promise."

"I'm not in love with your Dad, either. To be honest, I don't think he's in love with me. It works out better that way, at least for us. We're using each other, and it's working, at least for now."

Karen only looked at her for a moment, silent, pondering. "You don't love him."

"Sometimes sex is okay without love," she said. "If you're careful. Always be careful, Karen."

"Okay. I will. But..."

Cynthia interrupted. "I'm in love with somebody else."

"Who?"

Turning away, Cynthia went to the window, and looked down at the yard below. The two pines seemed to stretch up toward her from the ground, their branches swaying as if beckoning her into their embrace. If she jumped, she wouldn't have to answer any more questions. A thin, rueful smile passed over her lips. Was she really going to tell this girl the truth, after everything she'd seen? After everything she'd been through? If there was one thing Karen Luck didn't need in this life was more complications ... and yet, what did Cynthia expect when she'd moved in? That first night, when Gary had come to her in her bedroom, dressed not in an expensive dress or pearls or anything, but in jeans and a button-down shirt he had tied in a knot in the front. He wore a kerchief in his hair and his makeup was light and understated. He looked like Eileen sometimes looked, on Sunday afternoons when Cynthia would be visiting for the weekend. Eileen would take a break from writing and the two of them would sit in the kitchen, sipping coffee and reading together. Somewhere else, Gary would be writing and little Karen would be running around or playing some game with her friend Henry, and Cynthia would have this moment with Eileen all alone. It seemed to her that the further she got away from Eileen's death, the more memories accumulated. She didn't know if she was getting more adept at pinpointing individual moments, or if she was simply making it up. Was it possible that she could be remembering those Sunday afternoons wrong? Was it possible that Gary's outfit only recalled the *idea* of Eileen, like his novels had, as opposed to the *fact* of her?

    Maybe it didn't matter. The way he stood in her door that night, dressed as he had been, smelling like her scent, she didn't care if she remembered the past wrong or not. She was pretending anyway, wasn't she? Pretending not to see Gary's little beer belly, hairy and protruding; pretending not to see how tall he was, or how the wig he wore wasn't quite the right shade. Pretending that he was not Gary Luck at all. That was easy. He knew what she wanted and she knew what he wanted, and in the dark it was the same thing. They could both have Eileen Luck; they could both *be* Eileen Luck. The ghost between them was a gift.

"Your Mom," Cynthia said, not looking around. "I'm in love with your Mom, Karen."

Finally, she turned, and Karen was sitting on her bed, staring at Cynthia. Tears streamed down her face and she made no move to wipe them away or cover her face. Her hands gripped the edge of the bed so tightly her knuckles were white. "Wait," she said, and her voice was woven with ache and tremor. "You mean I'm not alone?"

"So let's just assume," Gary Luck said to the shaking boy sitting in his favorite chair. He was holding a Diet Dr Pepper but he hadn't opened it yet. "That I'm furious at you for having sex with my daughter. That's what Dads do, right? Get furious at the kid having sex with his daughter?" He had taken a moment to change out of his dress and high heels and wig and was now in a T-shirt and khakis and a baseball hat with the Supersonics logo on the front.

"Um," Henry Dear said, "I don't honestly know, Mr. Luck. The only Dad I really know is my own Dad. Actually, I don't *really* know him all that well, either. Anyway, he only has a son. Me. And even that's... Well, you know."

"You're talking about the makeup?" Gary asked cautiously. The kid had seen something no kid should ever have to see, but wasn't it strange that except for that first "no!" that started this whole thing rolling, the kid didn't seem so much horrified as ... what? Resigned? Contemplative? He was nervous, but that wasn't all of it, or even most of it.

Henry nodded. "You wear it when you write sometimes. I see you here. You're in a wig and stuff."

It occurred to Gary that he was in a room with a boy who had just seen him getting fucked by a woman wearing a strap-on while he wore a dress and a wig, and the boy in question had been in that weird military thing for years and now had muscles that had only been hypothetical when he and Karen were kids. If Henry wanted to, he could stand up and come at Gary, fists blazing, screaming "tranny" at the top of his lungs while he rearranged Gary's face for him. *Then* who would he be? Would it be at all useful to tell this semi-hulking kid that he *wasn't* a tranny, not really, not in the classic sense? No. If people want to beat you up for being different, nuance wasn't going to win you any points.

"I wear that when I write as my wife."

"You used to when you wrote as yourself."

"You remember that?"

Henry nodded. "I think I was here more as a kid than I was at my own house. I remember the first time I saw you coming out of your office. You scared me, but Karen just said, 'It's okay, he's being Doreen right now. It doesn't last.'"

Gary smiled and nodded. "It's lasted awhile."

"Not Doreen," Henry said. "Mrs. Luck." Okay, so maybe this kid *did* understand nuance.

"Listen, Henry, what you saw…"

Suddenly, Henry stood up and started pacing. "I need to talk about what I saw. And I need you to like ... *not* be furious if you can help it, okay? Because I need to talk to someone and I can't talk to my Mom, and I *really* can't talk to my Dad, and I can't talk to my CO, or *anyone*. And I think I can talk to you but only if I can talk to you like you're not Karen's dad. Okay? Can you just be a person and not Karen's dad for a couple minutes?"

The boy was looking at him, frantic. Perspiration showed on his forehead. His eyes were wild. Gary said, "Okay, son. Go ahead."

"I don't *like* wearing makeup? Okay. I got good at it because *she* likes it. And I thought, like, she got the *idea* from what you wore and not ... like, anything else. I didn't we were doing the same thing. I didn't know."

Gary blinked. Oh. Oh, this was a *highly* inappropriate conversation to be having. But he nodded.

"And I don't want to wear the stuff she tells me to wear. It's the part I hate, but I think it's the part she likes the most. And guess what? I'm good at it. I'm so good at it now. She likes that I'm good at it. But I don't want to *do* it. And I like all the other stuff, like *really* like it, so how can I tell her I don't like one part but I like all the other parts? What if that's a dealbreaker? What if she breaks up with me?"

Still blinking, Gary said, "I think I'm going to have a little scotch. You want scotch?"

Henry raised his can. "I have a Dr Pepper."

"Right, good." Gary went to the little bar by the TV and poured some scotch in a glass and tossed it back, neat. It wasn't how scotch was meant to be drunk. Scotch was meant to be an ingredient in an Old Fashioned. You added bitters and ice and club soda and some sugar and a cherry and you had a real drink. Construction mattered. Creation mattered. But right now he just wanted to take the edge off. "Look, Henry, I've known you your whole life. Maybe you're not like a son to me, sure. Maybe we don't have that relationship. But I care about you. I care about what happens to you. And I don't think you have fathom how very much I don't want to talk about what you and Karen do when I'm not around, but I think ... I may be uniquely qualified to do so.

"I don't know if I like wearing women's clothes, either."

Henry blinked. "But I..."

"I like what *happens* when I'm in them. They're magic, in a way. I can write as her – as Eileen – when I'm in them. I can *be* her. And when it's the ... the other stuff, I got used to it. It was Eileen's idea. And like you, I liked some of it. Not all. But we did that for a long, long time, Henry. Now it's all I want."

Miserably, Henry said, "But what if *I* want something else?"

Gary put a hand on the boy's shoulder. He had only been to the Dears' house a dozen times over the years, almost exclusively when Welton Dear was out of town. Welton Dear was always out of town. Most of his visits came after finishing a novel under his own name, and he'd call up Skylark Dear and ask her if she was still making that righteous meatloaf he liked so much. Every time she said yes, and sometimes he'd go over to her house with Karen and the four of them would eat together, and sometimes he'd go over alone and there wouldn't be food. Skylark Dear would spread out before him and push his head down on her, suffocating him against her vagina as his tongue explored and probed and found her private world delicious and soft and wonderful. For his part, he never really got off this way, never really even got hard. It was enough to have companionship and a place to feel welcome when his latest act of self-exhumation was finished.

This boy didn't have a father, not really, and while his occasional dalliances with Skylark Dear didn't *make* him a father, he might be the closest thing to it. What an absurd life.

"You don't have to do anything you don't want to do, Henry," he told the boy. "You just have to be happy. Aren't you happy?"

Tears began to flow down Henry's cheeks. "I don't know. Mr. Luck, I just don't know."

The writer first tightened his hand on the boy's shoulder, then pulled him in, hugging him close while the boy cried against his chest. He held him like that for a long while.

"We're going to find out what makes you happy, Henry," he said, hating this boy's father. "We'll find out, and then we'll have you do that thing as long as you can, all right?"

Henry, crying too hard to speak, nodded against Gary's chest, now wrapping his own arms around the man.

"Okay," Gary soothed, looking around his living room. The deer in the painting Eileen had liked so much stared at him. He stared back, his mind racing, his heart matching the pace. For the first time in a very long time, he wasn't feeling guilty for being away from writing; he wasn't feeling as if he needed to get through this moment so that he could settle into one of his office chairs and get some pages down. He'd written some this morning and afternoon – his hands ached, but his hands always ached – and then he'd heard Cynthia making lunch and then went upstairs to become Eileen. He'd felt guilty *then*, of course – sex usually took an hour or so, and he was on a crucial moment in the latest Mike Bull story (but then, what wasn't a crucial moment in a Mike Bull story?) – and every second away from the word processor was a second he wasn't going to pour into the novel. Still, he couldn't deny what Cynthia offered, or what he offered her. It was different from what he could give to Skylark Dear. Different for Cynthia, different for him. He couldn't get hard with Skylark, but he was undeniably a man when he was in her bed. He got off every time with Cynthia, but his gender was far more fluid. Not to mention his identity. He would become Eileen, but somewhere in the middle, *Cynthia* was the one who became Eileen. Only Eileen had ever entered him in that way. Only Eileen had ever made him feel that kind of pleasure, the kind that sent ball lightning all through his body and caused his brain to short-circuit in the infinite explosion that was always too short. He would never, could never, replace his wife. But every once in a little while, he could pretend. Pretending was what he did, after all.

Pretending was who he was.

But he couldn't pretend with Karen.

He rapped on her bedroom door. Cynthia had long gone to bed in her room on the other side of the house. The day had exhausted her. Through Karen's bedroom door, Gary could hear the click-clack sound of typewriter keys moving furiously. Normally, he would never interrupt, but tonight was special. Important. He waited a moment before knocking again, wondering as always why she shut her door when she was writing. Neither he nor Eileen had ever done that. Writing was a private thing, a sacred thing, but both of them knew that to shut their girl out of the process would be to shut a part of themselves out. Maybe other writers needed more privacy or solace. The Lucks had needed Karen.

Gary knocked again, louder this time. The typing stopped.

"Hello?" The voice was timid, tentative.

"It's Dad, Karen. Can I come in, please?"

For a moment, a little more nothing. Then the door opened a crack and she peeked out. "Are you going to yell at me?"

"No," he said. "Are you going to yell at *me*?"

"I don't think so."

"So let's talk."

She moved back and opened the door, allowing him into her room. His eye immediately went to the place where the strawberry painting had been; the hole in the wall glared back at him, like an all-seeing eye. Which, he supposed, it kind of was. He sat on the bed and she sat on her writing chair.

"I know you like the typewriter, but I think it might be time to get you a word processor. Or a computer. We can afford a computer."

Karen looked around at her Underwood and nodded. "I'm writing faster. I have to keep replacing the ribbons. I really hate replacing the ribbons."

"What are you working on?"

"It was supposed to be a short story. Maybe it's a novella now. It's called 'Nobody Under the Stars.' It's about a girl who has a crush on a teacher and the teacher might have a crush back. Maybe. I haven't gotten there yet."

Gary smiled. "You know, you sound like her, especially when you talk about writing."

"I do?"

"You do." He paused. "Do you want to talk about today?"

"Kind of. What did Cynthia tell you?"

"Not much. She thought I should talk to you." He scootched almost imperceptibly closer. "*Do* we talk, Karen? You and me? Do we talk enough?"

Karen looked at her father. There was something in her eyes, something he couldn't puzzle out. She looked as if she were struggling with something. Maybe more than one something. "I want to make you feel okay about today. I'm not freaked out about today. I mean, a little, but not ... I saw you and Mom doing it, too. I know it's something you do. I didn't used to understand it but I do now."

Gary couldn't help but turn back to the hole in the wall. Damn. Dammit. "You never should have seen that stuff."

"I'm glad I did. Now I am. You loved each other. You just had a weird way of showing it."

Clearing his throat, Gary said, "What if we warped you? I know you ... I have some idea of what you and Henry do."

Now it was Karen's turn to look away. "Well, I never thought I'd be having this conversation with my father."

Despite everything, he grinned. "And sometimes you sound like me."

"What?"

"Nevermind. Are you happy with what you're doing?"

Karen continued avoiding his eyes. "Are you?"

Gary leaned over and tried to catch her eye. "You keep avoiding my questions."

"Maybe I don't want to answer them."

"Because it's hard?"

"Because it's invasive. I'm not asking you questions."

"Maybe you should," he said. Now she looked up. "Until today, I thought I had a pretty good handle on our relationship. I've always told myself that writing was the second-most important thing in my life after you. And today, I don't know. I'm not sure if you know that."

Her eyes found his. "I love you, Dad. More than anything. And I know you love me more than anything. But writing is the most important thing in your life. Don't lie to yourself, or to me."

Gary recoiled as if slapped. For a moment, he could only gape at his daughter. "Karen, I…" She gave him ample time to finish the sentence, but he didn't have a way to finish it. You could refute the truth as hard as you want, but it doesn't stop being the truth.

"That wasn't meant to hurt you," Karen said.

"Well."

She sighed. "It's not like I want you to change, Dad. Writing *is* the most important thing."

Gary blinked. "But it's not. At least, it's not supposed to be."

Reaching out to touch his shoulder, she said, "If not for writing, we would have lost Mom ten years ago."

He closed his eyes. They *had* lost Eileen ten years ago. Hadn't they? She'd been found in a tree in Texas. You don't get more lost than that. But ... there was the smell of her in her writing room, wasn't there? And her books had come out, one after the other, and she was more popular than ever. If Eileen Luck could keep writing and publishing novels, *was* she lost? The story they'd sold to the public – that these were a treasure-trove of novels that Eileen Luck had left behind – worked on a surface level, but Gary knew the truth. He was inside his wife's memory, so much so that she was no longer a memory. She still lived. Karen knew it. Hell, Cynthia knew it. You're not truly dead if you're still writing.

"Can I read your story?" Gary finally asked.

Karen went over to her typewriter and picked up the stack of neatly typed pages. "It's not done yet.

"I'll read as you go. You want me to edit?"

"Not until it's done. Just read it. I want your opinion." Now she blushed again. "I really hope you like it."

He took it to bed that night, staying up late to finish what she had written. This wasn't a short story; it was a novella. Maybe more. If we knew a little more about the girl's home life, and a little more about the teacher – he's kind of a cypher throughout; Karen hadn't yet mastered the art of writing characters outside her own experience; but she would get there. His edits would help.

Nobody Under the Stars, fully rewritten based on his and Cynthia's suggestions, would hit bookstores five years later, when Karen Luck was twenty-one. It wouldn't be her best book, nor would it be her bestselling book. But it would be her start.

Part Two

Los Angeles

Chapter 5: Maura Moves In

Maura McKinnon had rules about the shower. You had to know her pretty well to know all the rules; Karen Luck, the novelist, knew most of the rules. Actually, she knew most of the rules about everything, and that was part of the reason Maura loved her. The other part was the part that was keeping her out of Maura's shower this morning. Her back would go unwashed this morning, and she would have to do her own hair. Neither of these things were tragedies; but Karen *knew*. And it's not as if Maura hadn't alerted her. "Hopping in the shower now, babe," those were her exact words. Karen had barely looked away from her computer. Maura could sense her in there now, typing hard, squinting at the screen like she did when she was trying to make a concept come. Sometimes Maura would stand in the doorway and watch her work. She only rarely interrupted, and that was only when they were rushing to get somewhere and Karen had gotten pulled back to whatever she was working on. If they had dinner reservations or a movie started at a certain time, do *not* leave

Karen alone near her writing office. That was another one of the rules.

They didn't have a rule about writing in the morning. Maura had half-heartedly tried to implement one a few months after they'd moved into together. Karen hadn't laughed at the suggestion, but by then, Maura knew Karen well enough to know that she was just trying to spare Maura's feelings. When they'd signed the lease on the apartment in the Valley, Maura did so knowing that she was playing second fiddle to Karen's writing, that the writing was going to always come first. But knowing a thing when you were dating was different from knowing that thing when you lived together. When you lived together with the woman you loved, you started expecting things might shift a little. That your constant presence in her life would start to shift her priorities. It had been over a year now, and if anything, Karen's devotion to her writing had only increased.

It's because you're old, Maura's traitor brain whispered. *You have to know that. When you were dating, being the older woman was exciting and fun. Now that you live together, she's begun to realize that you're actually an old woman. Hell, you read her mother's books while she was still in diapers. So she's buried herself in her writing, shutting you out because she's too kind to break up with you and demand that you leave the apartment. Just look in the mirror, Maura. You're no one's idea of a prize, especially not someone like Karen Luck.*

Maura shook her head, hating the invasive voice, the one that always came when she was most vulnerable, most susceptible to its dark charms. It was silly, wasn't it? Karen *liked* older women. She'd said that on their first date, and all the women she'd pointed out when they were at the coffeehouse or the mall were all at least ten years older than Karen herself, if not more. One time, a woman with stark white hair in a complicated chignon had wandered into their coffeehouse, and Karen looked up from her book and only stared a moment. The woman had to be in her sixties. Maybe even late sixties. She'd worn a smart pantsuit and glasses on a chain around her neck and she certainly looked *elegant*, but *elegant* didn't preclude *elderly*. Karen had been absolutely smitten. At the time, Maura only rolled her eyes and poked fun about it. Now, alone in the shower, she wondered how much of that had been performance, designed to convince Maura that she was not an anomaly, that at forty-one, she actually skewed on the younger side of Karen's older-woman thing.

So stop worrying, a different voice in her head commanded. *You're not even a generation beyond her and you're worried that she's going to toss you out with the coffee grounds.* Which was good advice. But how long would it last? She could jog until the end of days and still parts of her would sag. She could get lipo and tummy tucks and botox and attempt to look younger and become a freak in the process. It's not that Maura thought Karen would suddenly be into younger women; it's that Karen would eventually get older, too, and what was once older was going to become her own age, and what once might have been appealing about forty-one was going to wither and twist and sag and wrinkle. Karen was going to age gracefully into a vivacious, striking older woman, while Maura McKinnon was only going to get old. And was it so much to want Karen to join her in the shower before that happened? Karen Luck would always have her writing; who knew how long Maura McKinnon would last?

She reached out to turn the water off and suddenly felt arms wrapping around her from behind. The hands that had created two fairly successful novels were now on her stomach, trailing up to cup her breasts gently. "Does someone want her back washed?" Karen asked.

"Someone does." Maura closed her eyes, hoping she wasn't suddenly crying. God, what has gotten *into* you today, Maura?

"Well, let's see what we can do about that."

As it turned out, they could do a lot.

Maura had three auditions today – two commercials, one pilot – and had to hurry after they'd finished up. Foreplay was fine in the shower, but actual making love had to be done in the bed. And after, you were supposed to shower again, especially if your whole day depended on your look. Karen understood some rules about the shower, but some seemed awfully obscure. Was Maura getting weirder lately? It seemed like she was getting weirder.

Karen rolled over and laid her head on Maura's pillow, inhaling her scent deeply and letting it resonate in her sinuses and lungs for a moment before letting her breath out. Taking breaks didn't come easy for her, but she did enjoy a good revel after good sex. Especially when Maura had to head out and she could have the bed to herself for a few moments. The apartment was all her own, and quiet, and the whole writing day stretched out before her.

The phone rang.

Karen's eyes, which had been about to drift shut, now sprung open. Had she been preparing to take a nap? She'd earned it; she'd been up since 5:30 AM, getting her rewrites for *Up in the Air* taken care of for the day so that she could focus entirely on the new novel during daylight. The 5:30 thing hadn't entirely been her fault, either. Those damn dreams were back, just when she thought she'd fully purged herself. She's wandering down a road. It's pitch-black. No stars. And that's when a door slices through the darkness and the giant man in white strides out, holding something huge and sharp and slathered with blood in his hand. Then he locks eyes on her and grins, a huge toothy grin, and starts to stride her way, purposefully, with intent. Just before Karen could wrench herself out of the dream, the man's eyes start glowing like that bit in "The Raven" – "his eyes have all the seeming of a demon's that is dreaming." Then he raises his weapon and begins to run, and it was a miracle she didn't wake Maura up with her screams when she comes fully awake in their dark bedroom before dawn.

5:30, a full half-hour before the alarm, but it turns out okay. Of course *Up in the Air* needed more triage than she'd anticipated – there was a whole melodramatic sequence involving the mother holding her dead son's arm, and it didn't need to be there at all, but cutting it out meant amending so much of the rest of the book – and then Maura needed attending to and it had been the sort of morning that warranted a pre-afternoon nap.

And yet, the phone.

She rolled over and picked it up, affecting her sleepiest sleep-tone. "H'lo?"

"I know you've been awake for hours, Karen."

Cynthia. Of course it was Cynthia. What else could spoil this morning idyll as thoroughly as a call from an ex you had to work with?

"Cynthia. So good to hear from you."

"I just bet. You know why I'm calling, don't you?"

"The edits are almost done. I worked on them for three hours today."

"You have something of a momentum right now, Karen. *Nobody Under the Stars* got good reviews and people bought it, but they didn't buy *enough* of it. Not for the daughter of Eileen and Gary Luck."

"So, right out of the gate, I'm competing with two of the most successful authors in the world. If I don't live up to those lunatic standards, I'm dead in the water?" Ooo, *Dead in the Water*. Was that a common phrase? Had it been used as a book title? Karen thought it might have been.

"Not dead in the water," she said, "but if you want to stop being known as their daughter and start making some waves as yourself, you need to generate excitement for your brand." Cynthia didn't used to speak in corporate drone-talk, but once she'd gone from literary agent to literary editor at Chanler & Cushing, the talk seemed to come easily. Karen couldn't tell if she just had a natural proclivity for it, or if being at the biggest publisher in the world had a way of changing you. Not that Karen had any right to complain; Chanler & Cushing had done good by her, and bitching that she had to compete with her parents in the crowded bestseller marketplace was the whinging of a spoiled brat. She knew that, as a first time novelist who'd only placed a few short stories in magazines, a publisher like Chanler & Cushing didn't owe her a thing – not even a contract. Cynthia had negotiated like a woman possessed, even though they'd been broken up for a year by that point, and Karen had already moved out to Los Angeles. But she'd come back for these negotiations, and because she knew that Cynthia would do right by her, despite the stuff that had happened between them.

Of course she'd had nothing to worry about. She walked out of the corporate offices of Chanler & Cushing in New York City (a little wobbly because she never wore high heels unless she was seeing Cynthia) with a three-book contract and a six-figure advance. She'd taken the advance back to LA, invested some, bought a new computer, and had begun work on *Up in the Air*.

And then came Maura.

She wasn't supposed to meet Maura, that was the thing. She'd been perfectly happy living the single life out in California, aside, of course, from a few discreet dalliances. Carolyn thought it best that she keep the whole truth out of the public eye, just for a little while. "Just for a little while" had now extended the three years of her publishing career. It hadn't been right to come out before the first book had been written. "You'll get typed."

"Typed? As what?"

"A lesbian writer. Or a feminist writer." Cynthia had been naked at the time, lying across her bed in Oklahoma City. Both of them had long moved out of her father's house, and OKC was large enough that you could still live in the same town and not be anywhere near walking distance. She loved her Dad, loved it when he was working on his own books ... but she couldn't live with her mother anymore. She'd never found it weird that he was wearing women's clothes to write, and even knowing what else he wore those clothes for hadn't really bothered her, at least not any more than her Dad having any sort of sexual kink she knew about it. It was his adherence to being *her*, to being *Mom*, to being Eileen Luck. That was what had begun to get to her. Before she left, he wasn't just wearing her clothes to write in; he was trying to inhabit her all the time. Watching TV. Making dinner. Even reading in bed. When he was writing her novels, he would sit on her side of the bed, reading a book from the collection she'd left behind. It creeped her out, and she couldn't get Dad to talk about it directly, let alone change. So she'd moved out, and Cynthia moved out, and now she only visited when he was working on a Gary Luck novel.

"Would it be so bad to be typed as either of those?" Karen asked. "I *am* a lesbian. *And* a feminist."

How long had they been broken up by that point? A year? Two? Why were they still having sex? God, that had been a mistake. But Cynthia, after all her years of hiding, had come so furiously into her own that making love with her was like riding a rabid bull. You held on for dear life. Things hadn't been like that with Henry; *nothing* about Cynthia was like Henry. The passivity she'd come to expect during sex was never part of it. She found that she missed that sometimes, but Cynthia's excited determination to throw her all into everything couldn't be denied. Not even after they'd split.

Now Cynthia sat up. "Karen, it would be one thing if you were writing a book about lesbians. We could use the gay thing as a marketing push. You'd be going after a smaller audience, of course. You'd be typed and thought of as a niche writer. But that's how we *could* go. But your book is about a heterosexual kind-of romance. There's a single gay character and it's a guy, and he's tertiary. At best. You're not writing *for* lesbians, so why trumpet the fact that you *are* one?"

"I'm writing for everyone," Karen said, starting to feel a little helpless. Cynthia once told her that coming out was an ongoing process. You had to keep doing it, every day, to everyone. Admitting it to herself and Cynthia when she was sixteen had only been the first step. Telling her Dad a year later had been easier than she thought it'd be; maybe the fact that he was wearing an outfit that very closely resembled one that Mom wore around the house all the time when she was working on *No One Knows Where Sarah Goes* had something to do with it. Henry had been the toughest. They'd broken up on good terms. At least she'd thought they were good terms. He'd thrown himself into school and CAP and on Henry's graduation day, he'd seemed content enough to just be friends. She'd sat in the stands applauding along with her father, and then after the ceremonies, they'd gotten drunk together, leaning up against the back of the IHOP downtown. When the whisky was gone, she'd taken his face in hers and kissed him on the lips, crying and telling him how she wished they could have been different. And it was bad, because as he'd gotten older, his body had filled out and gotten more masculine. But his face, with his high cheekbones and delicate eyelashes and soft chin, had never been more feminine. From the neck up, he looked like a picture she'd once seen of Skylark Dear that hung in the hallway at their house. Her hair was short in the picture, and she wore a jaunty white-and-red polka dotted scarf around her neck. She stood on a beach and there was a boy with her – probably Welton – and her face was lit by a setting sun. Henry's face looked exactly like that now, down to the style of hair, which was short but no longer cropped to the skull. Sometimes, after the breakup, she wondered if he wore his hair like that as a way of enticing her. She'd never mentioned her feelings for his mother, but some of it must have come through subconsciously.

Now she was kissing him and once more thinking about Mrs. Dear, Mrs. Dear, what soft lips you have, Mrs. Dear.

"I like girls," she whispered to him. "I'm so sorry, Henry. You deserve so much more than that, but I really am sorry."

He hesitate, his hand on her shoulder. Would he scream at her? Cry harder? Stalk away? He'd never done anything physically against her, but now, with his tightly muscled body, maybe he would. Maybe whatever power she'd once had over him had evaporated.

"You don't ... Karen, don't be sorry. If that's who you are, don't be sorry. I only wish I'd known sooner. I guess I should have."

"How, though? I never told anyone. I didn't even tell myself until I was ... old enough to know better." She didn't want to give the concrete age. He didn't need to know that they still had sex for another six months after she'd known.

"Karen, you made me put on women's clothes and makeup before we had sex. I thought it was weird but I went along with it. After that day at your house, I just kind of thought you learned it from seeing your Dad do it. I didn't ask questions. I didn't think too much about it. Being with you was the important thing. I would have done anything you wanted."

Her voice cracked. "You should have said no. At least once, Henry. You should have told me no."

He smiled at her, and wrapped her gently in his arms. "I'm not in the habit of doing impossible things, Karen."

That's what made it harder. Because coming out to her Dad had felt like telling the truth, and coming out to Henry had felt like confessing a lie. Where was Henry now? Back in OKC, last she heard. Sometimes he and her father hung out, a thought which gave Karen the shivers. She was destined to a life populated with exes.

And what would happen now if, God forbid, the whole lesbian thing emerged later?

"Once you get established, it will matter less," Cynthia told her, though she didn't seem all that convinced herself. "Get a few books under your belt. Grow your audience. *Then* live your truth. But not just yet."

"A few books?" Karen asked, incredulous. "How long do you expect me to hide out?"

"Well, if your output is anything like your parents', maybe a year or two."

"It's taken me eight years to get this one written, Cynthia."

"Well, then get cracking."

And she had. The opening lines for *Up in the Air* were ones she had been carrying in her head for nearly four years. She'd dreamed them, and after waking up, screaming, she scribbled them down in the notebook she kept by the side of the bed. Her nightmares often proved good fodder for her work.

I was six years old when I saw my mother carried away by a tornado. The last thing she said to me before pushing me out of the path was to find safety, to get to safety. But over the next ten years, that tornado would carry away almost everything else, too. Mom's last words were lies: there was no safety to get to.

It had been chugging along at a steady clip for the first six chapters, somewhere between 1,200 and 1,600 words a day – between three and four pages, if she was thinking in terms of physical typing. A good clip. A good output. But the problem with writing in a brand-new city with, suddenly, six figures in your bank account – six figures that *you'd* earned – was that everything else was pulling you away. Hollywood wasn't the bastion of fame and fortune that she'd been led to believe, but her apartment in West Hollywood was nice and if you got used to the grime and homelessness, downtown was actually not bad. At night, she'd get into her Jeep and play Alanis Morissette with the cover off and drive into the Hollywood Hills, which was a lot more in line with her image of the city than the rest of it had been. At night, you could look down and see all of L.A. spread out before you like glittering diamonds in the desert. Everything in Oklahoma City was flat and spread out and dense and claustrophobic. Not here. You got a sense that anything could happen here; there was *elevation*. Here, *up in the air* wasn't a scary phrase. She was learning that at roughly the same time as her main character, Charlotte, was learning that. And it was exhilarating to be living the same life as her main character, at least for a little while. Of course, she had plans for Charlotte that would push her beyond her own experience, but in the right now, things were steady. Good.

After these drives into the hills, before heading back home to work on the book, she would stop at a bar called Muffs; what the local Gay Guide called, "the best dyke bar in WeHo." Karen didn't find Muffs particularly dykey – the most in-your-face part of the whole bar was the name – but she could buy "best." She would usually get herself something weak, sit at the corner of the bar and watch the dance floor. Mondays were country nights and Patsy Cline was always pumping out of the loudspeakers. You didn't have to line dance to get out there, but some talent was necessary. It was always fascinating to watch some of the women on the floor move in complete synchronicity, tapping and swaying to choreographed commands only they could hear. One of those women was Maura McKinnon, and Karen Luck had fallen for her the moment they'd first locked eyes across that crowded dance floor.

What type of car do lesbians drive on a second date, the old joke goes. A U-Haul. It wasn't quite that quick for Karen and Maura, but they hadn't yet been dating half a year before Maura moved most of her stuff into Karen's house and began subletting her own apartment across town. Karen had torn open a box of Maura's books to shove onto the shelves – organization could come later – when she encountered a stack of her mother's novels ... including the ones that said Eileen Luck on the front but which was 100% Gary Luck inside.

"Background research?" she asked Maura, who smiled and reddened.

"I didn't want you to know I was a fan."

"You're an … Eileen Luck fan?"

"Since I was a kid. I had to hide them from my parents. Mom thought she was like V.C. Andrews, but worse. Eileen Luck was another thing, like rock music and video games, that were just inviting the devil in."

"I just had no idea."

"Well, I didn't want you thinking I was sleeping with you just because I read your Mom's books. That would be weird." She hesitated. "*Is* it weird?"

"Only a little," Karen said, placing the books on the shelf. How much weirder would it be if Maura knew the whole truth? "I mean, she's a pretty massive writer. It might be weird if you *didn't* read her."

"She's not why I'm here."

Karen held Maura's hands in hers and kissed her lightly on the lips. "I know." Then she paused. "You're here for my money." And they'd giggled together. Like Karen, Maura had come from a family of money. They'd invested something and that investment had turned into bigger investments and now they were living the American dream. Maura wouldn't get more specific than that.

"Sometimes I think they throw money at me in the hopes I'll go away," Maura had said on one of their early dates. They'd both been drinking and the sex had been good and Maura was lying with her head on Karen's lap. They were both naked, and for once, Karen wasn't thinking about *Up in the Air*.

"What about the other times?"

"The other times I know," Maura said. It came out sounding a little rehearsed, but Karen didn't mind that. As a writer, she liked lines that felt spontaneous but read easily. As a girlfriend, she just hoped that Maura didn't expect clever conversation at every turn. A lot of that stuff came to her when she faced the screen and poured it out through her fingers. Often, though, the *bon mots* and the witty repartee that came naturally to her characters tended to seize in her throat.

"Are you out to them?" Karen asked, because it was obligatory.

"Yeah. My father understands it better, I think. Mom is ... convinced it's a phase. You know that book *Stick a Geranium in Your Hat and Be Happy*?" Karen shook her head. "It's by this woman, this fucking *awful* woman. You want to feel bad for her, but she's fucking awful. She's lost three sons, right? One in a war – I think it's Vietnam – and one in a car crash or something. And the third one? She's *lost to the gay lifestyle*. In her mind, she has three dead kids. Isn't that goddamn horrifying?"

Karen breathed through her nose and out through her mouth. Sadness, profound and total, crept up on her for a moment, then dusted away. "And your Mom...?"

"Not *as* bad, but close. She told me once when I was fifteen that I could tell her anything in the world, literally anything ... except that I was gay. So of course, three years later, I did just that."

"How long did you know before you said something?"

"Oh, Karen, I've known my whole life. But I made myself aware of it when I was fourteen. There was a girl in my class. Sadie Marie Jensen. I couldn't avoid it after seeing her. How about you?"

"Best friend's mother."

Maura's face broke into a wide grin. "So you *are* into old women."

"Older than me, yeah."

"So, old."

"You're trying to bait me into something, Maura. It's not going to work."

"No, but I bet if I asked you to take a shower with me, *that* bait would work."

It would, especially because Karen didn't know about Maura's weird stuff about showers yet. And also because she didn't know what would happen with the book when Maura started spending more and more time there. Suddenly, it wasn't three pages a day; it was eight pages. Sometimes ten. Over the phone, Cynthia said, "So you found a girl and you feel comfortable and it's easier to write. It doesn't have to be more complicated than that."

Cynthia's bitterness was apparent over the phone and she'd wished, as usual, that she had literally anyone else to talk with. She hadn't made any real friends out here, and the only friend from the old days was Henry Dear, and calling him often felt like a mistake. She could talk to her Dad, probably – talking about sex and writing was their bread and butter – but he was in the middle of one of Mom's books right now. One of the last ones. It was harder going for him now than ever; it was like how writing books under his own name had gone before he'd started working on the Mike Bull mysteries. She wondered what would happen to his writing when he had to stop writing as Mom. Would he be able to keep going? Or would he put that part of himself in the past, as he had with Doreen Daley?

The writing faster – and better? – when Maura was here probably had something to do with nesting, being comfortable enough to throw herself even more into the book. But it was something more than that. Part of it was telling Maura the rules of her writing. She had to write until she was done. The door was open but that didn't automatically mean you could come in. Sometimes, if she couldn't sleep at night, she'd get up and go to her writing room and try to get out a couple pages before sleep finally came.

"I'm under a deadline, that's all," Karen told Maura. "My agent wants this book sooner rather than later." None of this was precisely a lie ... but it wasn't the whole truth, was it? Writing was the most important thing – not just now, but always. That's how it was always going to be, and telling Maura that without saying it out loud was a balancing act.

For her part, Maura was positive that she wanted someone as driven and as ambitious as Karen in her life. Her dad had been both. Her mom, who spent most of her time shopping for expensive clothes she would never wear and forming opinions about people she wasn't even going to try to understand, was the laziest person Maura had ever encountered. She'd laid around all day watching TV until it was time to go to the gym or get a massage or go to some gala or event. And she only went to the gym because her father made her go. "Appearances, Bedelia, appearances," he'd say. Dad worked out every day for two hours without having to be told. So did Maura.

Sometimes, in those crucial weeks before she moved in, Maura would stand outside Karen's office door and watch her type. She had never seen anyone approach anything with the intensity that Karen Luck approached writing. The woman would stare at the screen, *into* the screen, her face bunching up, releasing, bunching up, as if she were trying to remember something so important that her life would fly off course without it. Occasionally, she would feint toward the door, wanting to remind the woman she was falling in love with that writing should probably feel *good*, and that whatever she was doing looked like it hurt. But of course Maura would do no such thing. She interpreted words, she didn't create them. That act of creation scared her, a little.

So Maura had moved in and a month later, the first draft of *Up in the Air* was complete. Karen had emerged from her office looking worn and haggard and unsettled. "I finished," she said, looking on the verge of tears. Not happy tears, not quiet tears. Karen looked like she'd wrenched some curved, sharp object out of her flesh, and was now standing in the doorway, bleeding out.

Maura went to her, holding her, kissing her lips gently, kissing her forehead. For a moment, Karen only stood there, a lump of warm clay, then she grabbed Maura back, holding her so tightly that Maura couldn't get in full breaths.

"Don't leave," Karen whispered into her ear. "Don't leave, Maura, please don't leave."

Maura had smiled, but it had been a troubled smile. "I just got here."

"Everything hurts. I need you. I need it to not hurt now."

Sex with Karen had been thrilling and a little weird before Maura had moved in. Maura wasn't so used to taking the passive role in bed, but Karen loved wearing that strap-on and taking Maura from behind. She was good at it, too – Maura was consistently satisfied – but she would have liked a little variety. Now, following the completion of her second book, Maura laid Karen down in bed and got her undressed. She badly wanted to wash her makeup off, but Karen always liked her to wear makeup when they were having sex. To tell the truth, it made Maura feel a little like a whore, but maybe that was part of Karen's fetish. Her own sexual habits were malleable, so Karen having a very clear idea what she wanted was a bit of a relief.

But right now, Karen was lost. Maura trailed her fingers up Karen's thigh as she kissed her small belly, moving as gently as she could. How had the two of them been together this long and she was still unfamiliar with the geography of Karen's thighs? Had they *always* done it Karen's way? Unable to help herself, she stopped kissing Karen's belly and started kissing those thighs, mysteries she'd slept beside for months. Up above, Karen moaned, and Maura had to restrain a smile. She was on a mission.

In the end, Karen came at least three times, each time bucking up off the bed, her legs pressed so tightly against Maura's head that Maura was sure each time that her skull would pop open, spilling its contents all over Karen and their brand-new bedsheets. She hadn't gone to their bedside drawers for toys or lube or anything; Maura was determined that this time just be her body and Karen's body and nothing else. After the wreck of the end of the book, Maura thought it was crucial that Karen felt safe and grounded; it was less about sex and more about assurance. The book could end, but I'm still here, love. I'm still here.

With *Nobody Under the Stars*, she'd finished that first draft and had spent a year tinkering with it before letting Cynthia read it. She didn't want to give her the novel she'd written in high school before she'd had a chance to make it feel a little less like she'd written it in high school. She knew that with her three-book deal and six-figure advance, she didn't really have a whole year to putter around with *Up in the Air*. The next day, she'd overnighted the manuscript – warts and all – to Cynthia, and waited to hear back. She did, three days later.

"It's messy," Cynthia said at first, but her voice wasn't barbed as it often was. It was quiet. "But not a bad messy. The timeline thing, Karen. You're bouncing so fast between past and present and future that it's a little confusing. All it needs is a little streamlining. And the main character? She seems a little mean. Maybe she doesn't have to be *that* mean."

"Mean?" Karen asked. She knew Cynthia would have concerns about the timeline stuff. She had concerns about it. *Nobody Under the Stars* had been a straightforward narrative. She hadn't gone back and forth, exploring Charlotte's past for a few pages before bringing her back to the now, only to jump back to a whole different part of the past. It was bold and different – there were flashbacks inside flashbacks; learning to *not* do that was Fiction Writing 101 – but she wasn't sure if *different* meant *bad*.

Cynthia said, "You have opinions about Charlotte that I don't think your readers would have. You're judging her over and over in the text. But she's not bad. She's not as cruel as you try to assert she is. She's just a little lost."

"Oh."

"And Charlotte isn't the reason her mother dies," Cynthia said. It was almost a whisper.

Karen swallowed. "That's an important part of what the book is about, though. I can't take that out."

"I know. I just wanted you to know that Charlotte's just a little girl when her Mom dies. It's not her fault."

"That's something I'll consider."

That conversation had taken place over three months ago, before she'd gotten the edits back from Annie Telluride, her editor at Chandler & Cushing. They were good edits, but

Annie had agreed with Cynthia; Karen was way too hard on Charlotte. The timeline stuff as a whole wasn't bad, Annie had explained; she'd just needed to streamline a couple of passages to make sure the reader knew what era she was in. Karen had taken all the edits into consideration, and had brought the marked-up manuscript into her home office and gotten to work. Two days after that, she'd begun work on the new novel, tentatively titled *Where'd She Go?* That was when the getting up at 5:00 had started. If she was going to edit one book and write another, she needed to devote a *lot* more time to her writing.

Her whole plan was to finish the edits on *Up in the Air* just as *Where'd She Go?* was streaking toward its conclusion. That way, she could keep waking up at five, stealing out of bed to click on the small light in her office and fire up the IBM and slowly wend her way through Charlotte's life, from the death of her mother all the way to the death of her son. She hadn't entirely agreed with Cynthia or Annie about going a little easier on Charlotte. She tended to use people and she was a little selfish, and at some point, she couldn't keep blaming her messed-up childhood on the way she was. But she'd come down hard on blaming Charlotte for her son's horrible death, and none of it was Charlotte's fault at all. That was the part she'd been working on this morning before Cynthia called ... which meant she really was nearly done with the edits. She had, what, two chapters left to go through? How much longer would *Where'd She Go?* take? A month, maybe two. Mild panic had filled her that morning as she'd put *Up in the Air* away for the day. Maybe she could start editing some short stories or something in the morning. Would Chandler & Cushing be interested in a collection? She had something like ten, eleven short stories floating around. She could—

"Karen?" Cynthia prompted. Karen blinked.

"Yeah, sorry. Here."

"Speaking of your parents, we should probably discuss your Dad." *Had* they been speaking about her parents? She'd gotten to woolgathering and then everything else flew out the window. It was like when she was writing sometimes, with Maura in the other room going over her lines or whatever, and the path seemed clear to whatever came next. One sequence leading easily to another, and nothing else in the world seemed to matter.

"My Dad? What's with Dad?"

"You know the Eileen Luck books are almost done."

"Yeah," she said, and didn't add *years too late, probably.* She wanted to. Shuddering, she imagined her father in Mom's old office, almost completely untouched since 1981, with the obvious exception of the new computer. Would his makeup now reflect who Mom was in her late thirties? Would he be wearing Mom jeans and sensible shoes, or would he have gotten punked-out in preparation for forty, wearing torn band T-shirt and miniskirts that showed off his still-great legs? Every option made Karen uncomfortable.

"I think he's taking it hard," she said. "Harder than anything. I'm a little worried about him."

Karen sighed. "I don't know if you're allowed to worry about him."

"Oh, get off it, Karen. That was a long time ago, and we're all adults."

Sucking in air, wanting not to take up this old argument, but hating how it always felt unresolved, she finally said, "Okay. What should I do?"

"Maybe go to him?" Cynthia said. "I think he needs you right now."

Karen swallowed. "I'm not sure I want to go back to OKC, Cyn. Lots of memories for me there. Ghosts, too."

"Maybe you could bring him out to La La Land?" Cynthia suggested, breezing right past her old nickname. "Maybe it will help him to finish the last Eileen Luck novel, if he knew you were around." Karen bristled at *La La Land*, but Cynthia couldn't help it. The time she'd lived in OKC loomed large in Karen's own mind, but Cynthia was a New Yorker, and thus thought all of Hollywood was fake and airy-fairy and macrobiotic. New York was *gritty*. New York was *real*.

"Would he come?"

"He would once the Eileen book was finished."

Cynthia nodded, wanting suddenly to get back to her own writing. Then again, when didn't she?

"All right. I'll talk to him."

"Look, maybe you *should* go to him. Just to convince him, not to stay."

Karen closed her eyes and she could see her mother, flying in the air in her car, like a special effect in a movie. Then trying to climb out. Why would she do something like that? The car had been found just a little ways up the road. The tornado had dumped it on its head and the thing had accordioned inward, but there was a *chance* she would have survived that, right? Surely there'd been a *chance*.

"All right. Let me talk to Maura."

"How is Maura?"

"Green is a terrible color on you, Cynthia."

"I was asking an honest question."

"And I was stating an honest retort. Has everyone forgotten that *you* broke up with *me*? I'm supposed to be the scorned one here. I'm supposed to be the jealous one. Only I can't be, because I'm just a little bit too famous to be out of the closet, so I have to keep all of this bottled up, especially when you call, because I still fucking *like* you, even though I won't ever stop being *mad* at you."

"Yeah, well," Cynthia said. Karen waited, but there wasn't any more.

"I'll let you know about Dad," Karen said, and then hung up after a quiet and terse good-bye. For what seemed to be only seconds on her personal timeline, she and Cynthia had said "I love you" at the end of every call. Sometimes, Karen wished they still did.

She had to call Maura. She had to call her father. There were a lot of real-world things that needed tending to today, and even though she'd showered with Maura, she probably could use another solo shower to clean off the sex and the sweat. All these things needed doing.

So she went to her office and kept the door open, and fell immediately into *Where'd She Go?* Karen Luck wrote for five hours.

6: *The House Where You Lived*

Sylvia entered the room where she and he used to sleep. It was empty now. Maybe it had been empty for a long time.

There was a dark patch of wall above where the bed used to sit. That old picture of the two of them with their daughters. The room had grown paler in the time since Dan slept here last. Paler and older and sadder. But right there, that small square of wall – that was the same as it had been before Dan had fallen. It had remained unchanged in all this time.

"I don't know how to do this," Sylvia said, laying her hand on that patch, which felt warm. Maybe it was Dan's ghost. She'd come up here today hoping to sense him somehow, hoping to feel him one last time. But that was silly, wasn't it? The megrims of a silly old woman who doesn't want to believe she's alone.

The worst of it was that she wasn't old, and that she wasn't silly. The worst of it was that even after all this time mourning the love of her life, she thought she had the capacity to move on. To be a person without Dan. She hated *knowing that. She hated her damned resilience. It had gone dormant for so long. She felt it starting to emerge again, and it made her so sad. So fucking sad.*

Then she left the bedroom where they'd slept. She passed thorough the kitchen where they'd eaten. The living room where they'd read. The porch where they'd hung their coats and taken off their shoes.

Then, without a look back, Sylvia Gregory walked out of and away from the house where they'd lived.

Gary Luck had been crying for over an hour. He'd started when he'd begun writing that last page and hadn't stopped yet, wandering from room to room, looking for something he'd never find. A mighty voice inside told him that he should call Cynthia up and tell her, surprise, they'd found another manuscript. Or five! The publisher would be happy. Well, eventually. *The House Where You Lived* was being touted as "The Last Eileen Luck Novel!" and the marketing people at Chanler & Cushing were already having a field day with the promotional materials. "Finding" new manuscripts now would throw a monkey wrench in everything, but they'd eventually make it work. And they'd love it. Five, six, ten more years of Eileen Luck novels? How could they *not* love it?

He tamped that mighty voice down, even though it took an equally Herculean effort to do so. Gary had been working in endings for his entire life, and this was one of them.

The girls would be here at the end of the week. He'd never met Maura and wasn't quite sure what to think about Karen bringing her home. He'd never met one of Karen's girlfriends. Well, except for Cynthia, of course, but that was better not thought about. Karen's coming-out moment hadn't been all that hard for him; it wasn't as if he, Gary Luck, were particularly on the mainstream side of sexuality and identity. She'd told him tearfully in the living room, as if terrified that he would start ranting, or screaming. Maybe he'd kick her out of their nice house. Gary knew things like that happened, especially in conservative enclaves like Oklahoma City. The fact that she'd told him while he was still wearing his wife's eyeliner and perfume should have comforted her some, but it didn't. Only after she'd finished and he'd wrapped his arms around her and assured her that her being happy was all that mattered did she stop crying. If it had ended there, maybe the rift that *actually* drove her from the house wouldn't have happened.

But finding out that she and Cynthia had been sleeping together had been one bridge too far. That they were sleeping with Cynthia *concurrently* was simply abhorrent. What happened? Cynthia would fuck him in his marriage bedroom with the door closed and the hole in the wall finally plastered over, then, when he went back down to write, she'd steal into his daughter's room and fuck her, too? When it came to sex, Gary had been willing – eager – to bend norms and challenge the traditional ways of doing things, but this was too far away from the norm. It felt, he admitted to himself later, a little like incest. The very thought sent nauseated shudders through him.

Cynthia had found a new place on the edge of town, and soon enough, so did Karen. And while he was certain that the two of them were *still* sleeping with one another, when Cynthia came by to talk about books or contracts or other business, they'd still end up back in his room, wearing his wife's clothes and makeup, allowing her inside him, closing his eyes and trying to pretend it was Eileen back there. Maybe it was the fact that she'd been having sex with both of them *in the house* that felt so wrong. At least now, he could *feign* ignorance.

But that had been long ago, and Cynthia had long moved to New York and Karen had long moved to Los Angeles. This giant house was his alone, now. Where once there was only Eileen's ghost, now there were more. And he was afraid, really afraid, that he was becoming one of them.

He picked up the phone.

"Mr. Luck?" Henry answered on the first ring. The very first thing he wanted to ask was if his Mom was around. But that wouldn't be kosher. It wouldn't make sense, not according to the way things had always been done, at least. He hadn't finished *his* novel; he'd finished *Eileen's* novel. Now wasn't the time to see Skylark, even though he wanted to. Would she even be into it, knowing that he was attempting to change the rules?

"Henry, I wondered if you wouldn't mind coming over," he said, unaware he was going to ask and startled that he had. When was the last time Henry had been over? For a time, after high school but before college, the boy had been by often. He assumed at first it was to catch a glimpse of Karen, and it had almost felt inappropriate ... until he realized the kid was actually, legitimately there to see him. On weekends home during college, Henry would come over and bring food his Mom had made – casseroles, mostly, but still better than the stuff he tried to cook himself. And then after college, Henry had moved right back home and had begun working in a bookstore at the mall. And still came by, just a lot less frequently. Once or twice when Gary had finished another Eileen Luck novel. More often just to sit and talk and watch TV and drink a couple beers together. Gary wanted to ask where his real father had gone, where Welton was. But that was a subject he hadn't dared to bring up. Karen had first moved to the other side of town, then all the way out to the coast. She wasn't drinking beers and watching TV with him. She wasn't talking about what books she was reading with him over casseroles. That was all his fault. When she'd said that writing was the most important thing to him, she'd been right. A child doesn't deserve to play second fiddle to the fiction in your mind.

But all Henry Dear needed was a part-time father. Gary thought he could do that, at least. If the kid needed him, he could be that.

And now, it seemed, Gary needed Henry. "I just finished writing a book, and I thought ... that is, would you like to take a look at it?"

The briefest of pauses. "I'll be right over, Gary."

He was, holding a bottle of white wine in one hand. "I didn't know if we celebrated or something," Henry said as he walked into their home.

"Sounds good," Gary said, heading to the kitchen to get glasses. It didn't sound good; it sounded *great*. Right now, all he wanted to do was to get drunk and stay drunk for a little while.

When he returned, Henry had already found the manuscript on the coffee table and was leafing through it.

"It's big," he said.

"Her biggest yet."

"So it's hers?"

"Her last."

"Okay."

They clinked glasses over the pages. Henry sipped. Gary guzzled, liking the immediate lightness that swam into his head. Maybe it would keep further tears away. Maybe not, but maybe. You could sustain yourself on maybe.

"Is it too soon to ask what's next?" Henry asked. "Another Mike Bull novel? I really like what you've been doing with him over the last few books. He—"

"I don't think ... I'll be writing again," Gary said. "I think that's what's next. I stop writing."

Henry stared at him, placing the first few pages of *The House Where You Lived* back onto the stack. "Gary, you're not serious."

"I am, Henry," he said, sighing. "I'm tired. I spent so much of my life inside this thing, maybe hiding inside it. I was pretending the whole time."

"Well, that's what writing is, isn't it? Pretending?"

Gary shook his head. "Not like this. Not like me. I'm heading toward fifty, Henry, and I've done it without a whole lot of self-awareness. I think, over the course of this last book, I've been waking up, bit by bit. My wife is dead. I've known that intellectually for fifteen years. But it's hitting me now. It's all crashing in on me. The reality of it."

"But that's understandable, isn't it? You've been writing as her to keep her alive. It only makes sense that now..."

"I haven't been keeping her alive," Gary said bitterly. "I've been propping up her corpse and making it dance. I'm a ghoul, Henry."

Henry swallowed and looked back down at the pages. Then he stood and went over to where Gary sat, squatted, and put his arms around him. "You're a good person, Gary," he said. "You're a great writer."

Arms hanging limp at his sides, Gary said, "That's all I am, is a writer. I don't have anything else. I pushed my daughter away."

"But..." Henry seemed to struggle with his words. "But you were *here*. I don't think Karen ever got how important that was. And besides, Karen pushes people away on her own."

"Just being here wasn't enough. *Isn't* enough. Because writing *was* more important to me. More important than she was. Writing *novels*." He spat this last, meaning for it to come out sounding angry and defiant, but it turned into a sob instead. He grasped Henry hard around the sides and cried like that until he couldn't cry any more. Eventually, he said, "You know, a long time ago you asked me a question, and I didn't get it right."

Henry let him go and stood apart from him. "What question was that?"

"Do I like wearing women's clothes? I told you no. But I do. I did, at least. The sexual stuff was good but secondary." He didn't notice Henry's wince at that; for Henry, that day of the hole in the wall was etched permanently in the memory at the front of his brain. "But wearing it, becoming her – that meant the world to me. With Doreen Daley, it was a costume. *Writing* like her was a costume. With Eileen, it was more." The words he wanted were out of his grasp. How could he tell this young man who had once loved his daughter more than was safe about how profound his loss really was? It wasn't just that he had lost his wife, and that he was doing it today for a second time. It wasn't just that he'd alienated his daughter, long before they'd begun sleeping with the same woman. Those things were all true, and all deep shards of ache inside his heart. But what he was really mourning today was the loss of himself that was her. He'd been living two lives for a decade and a half, only one of them had begun to seem more and more like the real version of who he was. Eileen was taking over, and he was more than content to let her take over. What had he accomplished as Gary Luck, anyway? He'd written a handful of generic bestsellers and in the process, been a bad parent to a daughter that needed at least one good one. Eileen, on the other hand, had written wonderful novels that were designed to be remembered long after the last page was closed. She'd nobly sacrificed herself for her child and then had resurrected herself. She had been the object of adoration of the best agent in New York City, and had even managed to fall in love with her a little. Life as Eileen was better because *Eileen* was better. The best version of him. And now she was dead. And now she was really dead.

Henry said, "You're not the only one in this room who still wears women's clothes."

Startled, Gary shook his head, breaking the maudlin reverie he'd been lost inside. "What? I thought…"

"And it's still true. I don't like it. But I do it. I do it a lot."

For a long while, Gary Luck and Henry Dear looked at one another, saying nothing, doing nothing. After a while, Henry began to talk.

Chapter 6: Encampment

Civil Air Patrol had begun to lose its luster for Henry Dear years before the encampment at Fort Still. Every time he tried to quit, something would happen that would keep him in just a little longer. Normally, that something was his father.

Throughout Henry's high school career, Welton Dear became an increasingly rare presence in his son's life. The only time he was guaranteed to show up and make his presence known was when there was some big, public CAP demonstration – if his squadron was being promoted, or if there was some sort of demonstration before a football game. Afterward, Dad would find him and take his cap off and tousle his hair. "Looking real official in that uniform, kid," he'd told Henry more than once. Sometimes, he'd grab his arm and look down in disbelief. "Man, have you been working *out*?" Henry had been, almost daily, since sophomore year in high school. Dad had worked out in high school. When Henry would leaf through Dad's old yearbooks, it was impossible not to notice his father; he ran track, he was on the wrestling and football teams, and one picture, of Welton Dear warming up before a wrestling meet, showed him shirtless, drenched with sweat. He had muscles Henry never suspected existed. Biceps on biceps. Quads on quads. He was astounding.

Sure, maybe he didn't quite look like that anymore. He was still buff, but a lot of that quarterbacking weight had redistributed in Welton's adulthood. A few times, Henry had tried to get Dad to hit the CAP base gym with him, but Dad was always so busy. Just constantly busy. So he worked out alone, usually blasting his Walkman. Nirvana was his copilot, usually. You wouldn't think hard yet introspective grunge rock would be good workout music – Nirvana didn't seem like the kind of band that would appeal to most meatheads – but it absolutely did. He listened to his cassette of *Nevermind* every time he hit the gym, and when the tape snapped, he bought another. Routine was the best way to go. Routine was the only way to improve. And who knew? Maybe some time Dad *would* say yes to working out, and Henry could show him the routines he did, how he switched things up on a weekly basis, how you had to alternate between bodybuilding and cardio. Dad would probably get a kick out of that stuff, and then he could tell Henry how *he'd* gotten all those muscles in high school, and they could compare notes, and it wouldn't just be a quick mention after a CAP event. Yeah, that could all totally happen.

Sure.

The night he'd gotten his Cadet Staff Sergeant insignia pinned to his lapel – it was the last rank you could get before you started getting leadership roles, and just the thought of being a CAP leader made Henry's stomach churn – Dad had cheered louder than anyone in the bleachers set up in one of the Yeager Air Force Base hangars. Henry had worn his dress blues and had executed every position in stationary drill flawlessly, even *about face* which always sent some cadets stumbling dizzily to right themselves. Throughout the whole ceremony, Henry could hear his dad shouting, "That's my kid out there! That's my kid!" Everything about it embarrassed him ... but every time his dad hooted or hollered, a funny warm feeling exploded in his gut and worked its way up to his chest. He *knew* that was dumb. Intellectually, he understood that he was doing his absolute best for someone who didn't deserve it. But when had that ever stopped him before?

The encampment at Fort Still seemed like a nightmare. They announced it right after flight simulator class on a Friday – a class that his CAP friends couldn't get enough of and which Henry found boring. Had he *ever* wanted to be a pilot? *Top Gun* had been an awesome movie – it still was – but Henry never really saw himself up there, flying upside-down, doing complicated barrel rolls, all so he could get good enough to go fly over some other country and drop bombs in the name of America. Henry was smart enough to know that his worldly cynicism was only a part of the whole problem – namely, he just didn't want to fly, and he didn't want to be in the military, and he didn't want to look back on these moments of his high school life and have these as the dominant memories. Putting this much effort and perfectionism into something you didn't care about seemed insane.

One of Henry's biggest problems, though, was that he didn't *know* what he cared about. He cared about Karen Luck, but after that day they'd seen her Dad though the hole in the wall, they didn't spend as much time together as they used to. They still met up for sex occasionally, but it was always in his house, and it was always more of an effort than it had been in the past – even more of an effort than that afternoon of the giant dildo. Writing was something he thought he might be good at; composition had long been his best subject at school. But how do you even pretend to be a writer when you lived next door to the Lucks? Even before she died, Eileen Luck was already hugely successful; in the years since she'd died, she'd become something of a phenomenon. And Gary Luck was no slouch, either. Under his own name, he'd become a bestseller in his own right. Henry had read both their books and loved them ... but neither of them were as good as Karen was.

Henry was aware that this *could* be absurd bias. Maybe. He couldn't always be objective when it came to Karen. But in this case, he thought he was right: Karen Luck was a better writer than either of her famous parents. Eventually the world would figure that out. Eventually she would, too.

So it was silly to think that he could even pretend to be a writer, wasn't it? Henry had written a few short stories for classes and had consistently gotten As, even one A+, the only one Ms. Goulding had given in six years. That one was called "One Cup of Coffee, One Cup of Tea." It was a story about a marriage that was crumbling, but neither the husband nor the wife knew it was crumbling. Henry snuck up on the story's theme, deliberately not writing dialogue – something he was pretty good at. The words he chose to describe their past were light, airy nouns and verbs and adjectives: the sun-dappled pond, the way they sprinted toward each other at the airport, their first kiss in the gazebo; *gazebo* was such a fun and silly word to say that it felt perfect for this part of the story. Now, they shambled. The sky was *pockmarked* with stars. He tried not to do something as deliberate as them looking out of opposite windows, but the story's title indicates a massive change in who they are. In the "happy" part of the story, they would stop at coffeeshops and ask for two coffees, and drink them together. Near the end of the story, the wife orders one cup of coffee, one cup of tea, and the kicker is that the husband doesn't even notice anything is amiss.

Ms. Goulding had read the story aloud in class, embarrassing Henry to a degree that, after class, he bolted to the nearest bathroom and puked up his whole lunch. He found himself glad that Karen went to that fancy-rich academy instead of Uxbridge High. How would she have felt in a class where Ms. Goulding chose *his* amateur shit to read, when Karen was writing professional-level stuff and she was doing it in high school? The thought of that made him puke again. When he went home that night, he sat down at his own typewriter in his room and started a new short story, trying his damnedest not to pay attention to what he was doing.

The encampment, though; the encampment. You were going to be spending nine summer days at Fort Still, five hours away from OKC. It was going to be right after high school graduation, so while all the other kids were lazing around on their last summer before college, playing video games or reading or just hanging out with their friends, the members of Henry's squadron were going to be spending nine scorching days on an Army base, sleeping in real barracks, participating in a bivouac (which meant sleeping outside without a tent, basically), and living, breathing, eating CAP for nine days. It was to give the squadron an idea of what real basic training was. To Henry, it sounded like an endless journey through Hell. It was time to quit CAP, quit for good.

Then, somehow, his father found out about it.

Henry had been writing and hadn't even known his father was home when the man burst into his bedroom, scaring a scream out of him. He'd been inside a short story at the time, and the writing was going very well. The story was about a teenager who had never left his house and didn't know anything about the outside world. His father was the one who kept him there – not because he was cruel, necessarily, but because he was trying to protect his son from the larger world. Henry thought maybe the kid was going to walk out the front door at some point and immediately get run over by a car, but that seemed a little too bleak. Henry did his best writing while improvising; he had no idea what his endings were going to be until he was almost on top of them. Usually this worked out for him, especially when he was trying to pretend that he *wasn't* writing. If he could be surprised at his own endings, then it wasn't really *him* doing this, right?

Although ... although sometimes, he thought about telling Gary Luck that he was working on some short stories. The writer trusted him enough to read some of his books and offer insights. Might he be able to take a look at a couple of his stories and tell Henry if he was wasting his time or if he should keep going. Henry had no doubt that, if he caught Mr. Luck at the right time, between books or very late at night, the man would take him seriously about this stuff. But approaching Mr. Luck about his writing meant talking about his writing, meant presuming his writing deserved to be thought of in the same capacity as his own daughter's. Surely Gary Luck knew that his daughter was one of the best writers in the world, and who was he? Henry Luck, next door neighbor.

These things were playing at the back of his mind when Dad burst in and he screamed and tried to throw his body over the typewriter. Dad was wearing a loose, humungous grin, the sort grin some big dogs have when they're at their most satisfied. "Kid! Did you hear about this?"

And for a moment, Henry only wanted to turn on the man and shout: "Get the fuck out of here! Can't you see I'm doing something important? Whatever it is you have to talk about can wait! What if I'd been jerking off in here, Dad? What if I'd been doing other stuff? Get out. Get the *fuck out!*"

Instead he said, "Hear about what?"

"What are you doing there?" Dad said, looking suspiciously at the typewriter. Dad wasn't a reader.

"Book report," Henry said, forcing himself away from the typewriter so as not to draw more attention to it. "What's up?"

For a long, excruciating moment, his father just stood silent, looking from his son to the typewriter. Then his face shifted, and that sloppy, doggish grin was back. "This encampment! Did they not tell you about it yet? I heard about it from Freddy's dad!"

Freddy – who Henry knew as Cadet Technical Sergeant Moss – was a wheezy, pompous jerk in Henry's squadron. He'd been on the leadership track since day one. Even though he and Freddy were both technically sergeants,

Moss took his position way more seriously. Henry knew plenty of guys (and some girls) in CAP who were on the command track because they thought they could be good leaders and they believed in the ideals and mission of CAP. Not Freddy Moss. He wanted to be in command of the cadets around him because it was like sanctioned bullying. He wanted to scream at younger cadets until they cried. A girl named McAdams who went to school with Moss told Henry that he was a big fan of pushing kids into lockers and knocking lunch trays over. "Leadership will always attract guys like that," she'd said before aircraft history class, her eyes steely and focused on something Henry couldn't see. McAdams *did* want to fly planes. That's all she'd ever wanted. Henry wished he could be more like her; knowing exactly what you want out of life seemed an unattainable fantasy.

But Dad didn't know any of that. Why would he? What he knew is that there was going to be an encampment after graduation, and at the end of it, there'd be a huge presentation where he'd once again be in his dress blues, marching and presenting arms and saluting the flag and all that. Dad was jazzed beyond reason.

"You know what we should do? This weekend? We should go shopping. Just me and you. Freddy's dad said they had a whole list of stuff you'll need for the encampment. You have the list?"

Nodding and trying not to let his misery show, Henry said, "Yeah, it's in my backpack."

Dad had never been this excited about anything in Henry's recollection. "Like Sterno and stuff?"

"Yeah. For during the bivouac."

"Oh *man!*" Dad shouted, clapping Henry on the shoulder. "What I wouldn't give to be living your life right now."

Henry opened his mouth to say, "I wrote a story. I think it's a good one. Ms. Goulding read it in class. If I wanted to, I could submit it to a magazine and they'd publish it, I bet. Are you proud of *that*?" Of course, Henry said no such thing. Not only because he'd have to directly confront the fact that he was not only a writer but a pretty good writer, and not only because he'd have to deal with the uncertainty of his father's response, but also because he kind of brought this all on himself. Hadn't he? Dad and he had watched that dumb movie four years ago, and Dad had gone cuckoo banana cakes over it, and Henry's first reaction – his *first* reaction – had been to join Civil Air Patrol. At first that was okay, even if he wasn't particularly fond of CAP, because Dad could be happy that he did it and then he could maybe drift out of it after a while and Dad wouldn't care, because Dad had make a whole habit of not caring about him. Only Dad *did* care. Just enough to make everything suck.

Mom came in later that night as she always did. Henry's bedside light was on and he was reading the latest Roger Cobb mystery. The guy wasn't as good as Gary Luck at his best, but he'd do. Mom sat on the side of his bed and he put his book to the side while she smoothed out his hair.

"This encampment," she said to him, then stopped short.

"Sounds like fun, doesn't it?" Henry couldn't even try to keep the tremble out of his voice.

She sighed. "I think your father heard all that stuff about Dads missing the big events in their kids' lives. Birthdays and graduations, stuff like that. But I think he got the wrong message. You're not supposed to *only* be there for those moments."

"It's not just that," Henry said, and realized he'd never discussed this with his mother before. "I don't know if he even likes me. I think he just wants to be me. Not real me. Like a person he thinks I am."

"Or a person he used to be when he was young. That was a boy I fell in love with, and I... Well, he's not that boy anymore." She paused. "I don't know why you're trying so hard. Not with him. I mean, buddy, I'm here. I've always been here."

In the quiet, unthreatening light, Henry looked at his mother. Perfect? No. She worked, too, and there were some nights Henry went to bed in his too-big house, all alone. There were days when he didn't see her at all. When he and Karen had still been together, that had almost been okay. She could come over after school and play Nintendo and then they'd have the sort of sex Karen fully liked and he, Henry, half-liked, and then he could fix some supper and take his book to bed and that felt okay. Grown-up, kind of. But when you're alone, you're alone, and the house sometimes felt like a mammoth, creaking mausoleum of dark corridors and gaping maws that might be doors in the daytime but were mouths at night, hungry mouths that feed on loneliness and flesh, and on those nights his sleep was thin and fitful.

But mostly that didn't happen. Mostly Mom was there when he went to bed at night and there when he woke up in the morning. While Dad drifted in and out of his life like a driverless motorboat passing a buoy from time to time, Mom was mostly solid. Mostly steady. Mostly reliable.

Now he looked at her miserably, not knowing how to explain that in order to be truly good, truly remarkable, you had to try to be the best for someone who didn't care about you one way or the other. That he was so grateful for her in his life, and that having someone like Mr. Luck – Gary – available to him when he couldn't take the pain anymore and needed – fucking *needed* – a father to see him and know him and understand him – those were necessities. Those were the backbones of his stability and sanity. But, through some malevolent alchemy he didn't understand and didn't want to understand, *having* love and understanding was not nearly as important as *craving* love and understanding.

"I love you," was all he could say, and soon after, she kissed his forehead and told him to not stay up too late, reading.

Then she was gone and he silently went to his drawer and pulled out one of the candles he'd wrapped in Saran Wrap. There was a tub of Vaseline in there and he spread it liberally. He didn't have Karen's access to the stuff she used to bring over – was there a catalog somewhere? – but what he lacked in professional-grade stuff, he made up for in improvisation. When it was just him, he didn't need the makeup or the clothes or anything like that ... but he needed something inside him. He could get off without it, but it always took too long and wasn't all that satisfying. The candles had served his purposes nicely.

They served them now, too. He maneuvered it inside him slowly, wishing he had a third hand that could easily move it in and out, hitting *all* the spots. One of the things they don't tell you about having muscles is that you lose some of your flexibility, and getting the candle up in him was far more of an effort than it would have been a few years ago. But he managed it, and when he did, he turned off the light, and thought of Karen in bed with him, actually him and not a version of him with girls' clothes and makeup, and she was moving the candle up and down, in and out, and she went harder, and harder, and oh God there oh *God* oh *God*.

By the time Henry Luck actually got on the bus to the encampment at Fort Still, graduation had come and gone and Karen had dropped her massive revelation he should have seen coming. In a weird way, he could see it as comforting. She didn't even like boys, but she'd given him access to the world of her. Henry didn't know if it was right that he felt proud about that, but he was going to let himself be. Knowing that nothing at all was going to happen between he and Karen, nothing at all? That was too big to process, too big to fully comprehend. With high school behind him and college ahead, everything seemed uncertain and large and scary. He didn't know how he was going to survive in a world without even the possibility of Karen coming back. Dark, fleeting thoughts of suicide had drifted through his mind like smoke, never tangible but absolutely real. A future without Karen seemed like a hellish future.

And now he was going to this fucking encampment.

The bus ride was five hours. He was in his CAP fatigues, the uniform with the blue patch that said DEAR in white embroidery. Of all the bright spots to find in this awful mess, the uniform was actually one of them. When he was wearing it, it was easy to pretend he was someone else. Someone better, someone worthy of both Karen and his father, someone who was actually excited about being in CAP and going to this encampment five hours away from home. If he worked at it, really worked at it, he could almost make himself believe that he wanted to go. Sure he did. A guy wearing this uniform would *have* to be excited to be going, wouldn't he? And he'd be confident and sure of himself, and able to process the fact that the girl he loved more than he loved anything was never going to love him back, and that without Karen, there was a giant void in his life that he hadn't thought to fill with anything else. The absence of her underscored the absence of everything else. Wearing his cadet uniform was currently the best way to make believe he made sense of that.

They pulled in to Fort Still shortly before noon, joining the other buses already parked in the vast lot. The encampment wasn't just for the squadron from Yeager Air Force Base in OKC; kids from all over Oklahoma were encamping here this week. A massive flagpole, its flag flapping patriotically in the breeze, stood sentinel over the neat row of barracks – squat and white and rectangular, all exactly the same. Well, maybe not exactly: above the front door of each, a small, neat letter had been painted in black. A through E – or, in military parlance, Alpha through Echo. Echo was where they put the girls. Henry was in Delta, right next door.

Stepping into Delta Barracks was like stepping into a minimalist funhouse. A dozen sets of bunkbeds were set at intervals at either side of the room, mirroring one another; each bunk boasted a thin pillow and an olive-drab woolen blanket. At the foot of each bunkbed, two small trunks squatted like conspiring toads, green and hunched. Lockers ran the length of the side wall, interrupted by windows whose thin white curtains let in milky light. Pale linoleum tiles stretched to the far back wall, where one door – open – led to the facilities and the other – closed – to the training sergeant's quarters.

Henry's skin crawled; this was a place where you went to have your individualism stamped out. The cadets were expected to be like these beds: tight, orderly, devoid of personality. Nothing in here breathed. Nothing lived. It was as if the word *antiseptic* had gained form.

He moved in and dropped his rucksack on the lower bunk closest to the front door. *So I can bolt if I have to*, he thought without knowing he thought it. His rucksack was overladen and he knew it; none of the other guys in Delta

Barracks had even half the stuff that Henry had hauled with him from OKC. He couldn't really leave any of it home. What if his Dad happened to find out that after haunting OKC's four Army-Navy stores all afternoon before having a late lunch at Friendly's, just the two of them, Henry had just discarded a bunch of the stuff they'd found together? The thought was unacceptable. Thinking of Dad, and that afternoon together, forced a wave of homesickness so powerful that he staggered under it. *I want to go home*, he thought. *I want to not be here*, he thought. *I want... I want...*

Henry swallowed and gripped the side of the bunk. *I want to write some stories. I want to sit at my desk at home and write stories, and spend the summer doing that, and reading. I want to figure out a way to make peace with who Karen is, and figure out who I am in the wake of that. I want to work out and listen to music and go to movies and deal with my fucking broken heart, and I'm here instead. I'm here instead.*

Just then, a tall man with a red face emerged the back room, striding into the barracks in shiny boots and a buzzcut. Immediately, he began shouting. "All right, cadets, for this week, you are under my command. You may address me as Sergeant Pellin. I will be your training officer for the duration of this encampment, and I am to ensure the wellbeing of each and every one of you. I will also make sure that you adhere to strict military guidelines, that you will exercise, that you will learn and grow and be fit to wear the uniforms you are currently in. You will not satisfy me but you will try. Is that understood?"

Finally, Henry thought, his nerve endings suddenly sizzling, and having no idea why he was thinking it. With the rest of Delta Barracks, he shouted, "Sir, yes *sir*!" Because things get ingrained after a while.

Sergeant Pellin broke down the rules for them: how their uniforms were supposed to look, how shiny their boots were supposed to be, how to make their beds with those military corners. Their days would start at 5:30. Lights out at ten. And in between, a lot of stuff that wasn't writing.

Delta Barracks marched to the big mess hall at noon for orientation. He was used to someone barking *left, right, left right left* when he marched; he'd been hearing it for nearly four years back at Yeager in OKC. What he wasn't used to was cadence songs, which you were supposed to, like, *chant* as you were marching, repeating Pellin's lines like it was a rock concert. The concept was fascinating. No one ever told him that singing was a part of military service.

I know a girl from OKC (*I know a girl from OKC*)

She's as pretty as can be (*she's as pretty as can be*)

I know a girl from OKC (*I know a girl from OKC*)

She shows everything to me (*she shows everything to me*)

Henry wondered who the other guys in the squad were thinking about.

Inside, the mess hall looked like what would happen if their barracks decided to dress up as a cafeteria for the day. Instead of bunks, long tables had been set in a double column that stretched the length of the hall. Off to the right was the kitchen and the buffet line. Henry didn't know what he was expecting from the mess – glop from a giant rusty pot, maybe, an image gleaned from countless movies about crappy high schools and prisons and old movies about life in the Army – but what he smelled was decidedly not gloppy. Hamburgers? Chicken? All in all, it smelled as good as what his Mom cooked, and way better than what Mr. Luck cooked. Henry felt his stomach rumble. He hadn't thought about food all morning, what with nerves twisting his stomach around.

"Are they giving us *burgers*?" said a voice behind him. Henry turned and there was McAdams. Her cap was pulled down a little low on her head and her fatigues were loose. He wondered if girls' uniforms were made like that to make them look more like boys – or, at the very least, sexless.

"I think so," Henry said, happy to see a familiar face. "Well, there's one good thing, at least."

A slight grin touched her mouth. "Aw, the barracks are cool. It's all about precision. I'm a big fan of precision."

"It's not precision, it's … whatever the opposite of individuality is. It's like the Borg."

"Is that from *Star Trek*?"

"Yeah."

"You're a nerd." But she smiled when she said it, then looked down at his arms. Even the uniform that was designed to make them all look like clones couldn't entirely mask Henry's muscles. He followed her gaze, stupidly wondering how his arms actually got like that. He'd taken to the working out so naturally, and his growth had happened so gradually, that only now did he start to realize what he actually looked like. For the first time, it occurred to him that there might be parts of him that were appealing to the opposite sex. Not just what he could do, but what he *was*. The thought scared him a little. It actually scared him a lot.

"You want to sit next to me?" McAdams asked him. "I don't mind the single-sex dorm, but this place is supposed to be co-ed."

"You call it a dorm?"

"Yeah, what do you call it?"

"A barracks." He swallowed. "Because it's a barracks."

She smiled crookedly at him. He found himself smiling back. Huh.

Orientation was okay. They got packets giving them a list of activities throughout the week, a set of guidelines for comportment, a listing of where to go if you have an emergency. Then came lunch, and it wasn't just burgers and fries but also a selection of chicken and tacos and fruit. Henry realized in line that he hadn't eaten any breakfast that morning as his misery roped his stomach in knots, his father's grinning, exuberant face the last thing he saw as the bus pulled away. The knots were a little looser now. He sat down next to McAdams and scoped her tray as she pored over the itinerary. A small bowl of fruit. Some yogurt. A carton of chocolate milk.

"Is that enough?" he asked, nodding to her tray.

"Absolutely," she said, not looking at her tray, or him. "You want to see pictures of a blister?"

Henry flicked his eyes from her tray to her face. "Um. No?"

She showed him anyway. Inside the handbook was a black and white close-up of a foot, a huge angry red blister pulsing on the heel. Henry dropped his fork. "Why would you show me that?"

"They do blister checks every night. Your training officer. To make sure you're not going to leak pus everywhere." At that, she put her itinerary down and took a big scoop of yogurt, popping it in her mouth.

"For someone who wants to sit next to someone, you're making any other possibility really attractive." Why can I talk to her? Why is this easy?

"Sorry," she said, grinning that crooked grin again, but she put the handbook away. Henry bit into his taco and was stunned at how richly flavorful it was.

"I didn't know the food was going to be this good."

"You know what I'm excited about?" she asked. "Two days from now, we get in the air. No more flight simulation. Actual flight."

Henry blinked. "Do we actually have to ... you know, fly the plane?"

"With zero in-flight training, I don't think so," she said, but her smile was wistful, and faraway. "But someday. That's the only reason I'm doing all this. It's not that I don't love my country or that I don't like things regimented. The military part is kind of secondary. I just really want to get up in the air."

For the first time in a long time, a memory of Mrs. Luck's car being sucked up into the tornado walloped him full-on, and he dropped his taco to the plate. Why did she climb out that window? Did she think she'd be safer? Did she think the car was the reason for her predicament? Or was it that she just didn't want to die in a coffin before she was buried in one?

"Whoa," McAdams said.

"Sorry, weird memory," Henry said, his heart hammering in his chest, bright spots dancing across his vision. "It's fine. Really, it's nothing."

"You sure?"

Henry wasn't sure, but he nodded. The last thing he wanted to talk about was Eileen Luck … or, for that matter, the entire Luck family. Here he was in a place almost fully removed from his real life. He knew McAdams from back in OKC, but mostly from sight. She'd said more to him here in the last twenty minutes than in the last four years they'd been in CAP together. This place was a chance for him to be someone completely different, wasn't it? Someone who he wasn't at home. Hating CAP had always been just part of being in CAP; hating CAP and still trying to do his very best had always just been a part of him. But maybe he could look at it differently here, at the encampment. He didn't have to be trapped in love with Karen Luck, who couldn't love him back. He didn't have to try to please his Dad, who wouldn't be here until the very end. All the stuff he hated about himself, all the stuff that held him back, could take a temporary break while he was here at Fort Still. He didn't even have to hide being a writer, because here, no one knew he was Karen Luck's neighbor and friend, and no one knew how much better she was than him.

"Yeah. Something you said reminded me of something I heard once. Did you know that supersonic jets used to fly over OKC like all the time?"

McAdams punched him on the arm. "Of course I did, dum-dum! That's part of the reason I wanted to be a pilot. Faster than the speed of sound, can you believe that? That *people* can do that?"

"Yeah, but they canceled them."

Shaking her head, McAdams said, "Just the ones over land. You can still take the Concord from New York to London and back again, and the Lockheed YF is still pretty new. I mean, they cost a *ton* to build and maintain, so they don't make a lot, and because they can't go over land, they're not really, you know, cost effective."

Are you pretty? I can't tell. Maybe it's okay that I can't tell.

"You really get into this flight stuff."

"And you don't?"

He paused. "To tell you the truth, I'm not totally sure why I joined CAP."

"Oh." She tilted her head and watched him a moment. "Haven't you been in awhile?"

"Yeah," he said, then added, "I like the gym."

"Well, that's obvious," she said, casting an appreciative glance down at his arm. The bicep bulged slightly under his olive drab sleeve and he thought, *Am I pretty? I can't tell.*

His cheeks blasting hot color, he said, "I just like to write. I do writing. I am a writer, I mean."

"And now is when I ask what you write."

Blinking, Henry said, "Is there a script I don't know about?"

"Is there?"

Her eyes were blue and there were freckles on her cheeks and her hair, what little he could see of it, was dark brown, almost black. She looked nothing like Karen Luck. After this encampment, he would leave Civil Air Patrol and they would go off to different schools and never see each other again. "I'm bad at this because I've only been in love once and I've only had one best friend, and they were both the same girl. If there are patterns and prerequisites, I don't know them. So there isn't a script."

McAdams watched him for a long moment. "We've been here for ten minutes and you haven't asked me my name."

Henry swallowed. "What's your name, McAdams?"

"Thomas. It's a boy's name but my mother liked it and she overruled my father."

"Do you go by Tom?"

"Never."

"Do you hate your name?"

"No."

"Thomas McAdams, do you want to know my name?"

"Henry Dear of OKC. Both your parents do something with money. You joined CAP in 1989, when you were a freshman in high school. Which is Uxbridge, and from which you just graduated."

His eyes were now giant moons in his face and his mouth hung open. "So you're a witch. Or a, what's that called? Clairvoyant."

"I just do research. I'm good at research."

His cheeks flushed red again, anticipating what he absolutely could not say but could not stop himself from saying. "What else are you good at?"

Thomas McAdams' grin widened. "Let's see if you find out. Until then, Henry Dear, what is it that you write?"

Until the trouble happened, Henry had decided that the encampment was the best way he could have started off his final summer before college. The whys and wherefores of how he got here had begun to mean significantly less the longer he stayed at Fort Still. Occasionally, it seemed as if the life back in OKC were his other life, some distant memory of a dream he once had. Fort Still was real life.

Thomas McAdams was only part of it. Every morning at 5:30, Pellin would barge into the sleeping room of Delta Barracks, banging the metal lid of a trash can. The guys would all jolt awake and shower and get their uniforms on, making sure every stitch of it was in place. You made your bunk according to strict protocol, and every morning, Pellin would rip a bunk apart for not adhering to regulation, and make whatever cadet got the treatment remake it. It was always a different kid, and Henry suspected that whatever bunk got demolished probably *was* regulation, but that Pellin had to make an example of someone every day. On the second day, that example was him. Henry watched as Pellin pointed out insignificant imperfections in his folding and his tucking, then tore the bedclothes off and made him do it all again while he watched. Henry didn't exactly *like* what was happening, didn't exactly *want* it to happen, but there was definitely a sense of familiarity here, a sense of feeling most like his real self. Much later, he would assign this feeling a name: my happiest misery. It summed a lot of his life up.

Then a march down to the mess hall in the dark, singing cadence songs and staying in step. Henry didn't love the cadence songs – so many of them seemed to be about girls being sluts or guys *wanting* girls to be sluts, couched in a double entendre so thin you could read newsprint through it – but he liked the rhythm of it, the camaraderie. It was too early for his own thoughts to really crowd in, and the whole morning was so regimented that he was actually freed from the burden of having to think ... but still, every morning, he cast his eyes up and saw with perfect clarity the constellation of Orion, his belt shimmering the brightest in the summer sky, the rest of his shape forming around those three brilliant stars. In these moments, he thought of Thomas McAdams – just her face, and a suggestion of her personality. Maybe someday she would fly fighter jets. Maybe someday, she would pilot spacecraft. Sometimes he cast his mind into the future and thought he could almost see her up there, in some futuristic rocket, clicking buttons and flicking levers on her way to the moon.

The days were long and grueling and every night, Henry fell into his bunk, exhausted. He didn't exactly hate that, either. It wasn't part of his happiest misery; it was the simple joy he got from putting his all into making use of his time, making use of himself. Back home, Gary Luck would pour ten hours of his day – *ten hours* – into writing novels under two people's names, and he did it until it wore him out. He was willing to bet that Karen did the same, and that Karen *would* do the same when she went off to college. Not that he was thinking of her, because he *wasn't*, but he could still admire who she was, what she did, without focusing on the fact that she had probably never loved him the way he loved her, never *could* do it because she was gay and he wasn't a woman, no matter how much makeup he'd worn for her. Besides, it was easier to think about Mr. Luck, who had been kind to him for years, and who had allowed him into his house while he wrote and read and talked about books.

What was most interesting about Henry's thinking was that he didn't associate it with either of *his* parents. Welton Dear worked so much that he was barely home, and his mother maybe worked even harder, putting in all her hours down at the office, bringing work home, often making him dinner and desserts and hanging out with him when he knew she couldn't really spare the time. But for Henry, a lot of his parents' work was vague, intangible. They both worked with money and they both made money and that was great ... but they did it elsewhere, and the parameters of it never quite gelled in his brain. Whereas Gary Luck sat down at a keyboard day after day and created something, something real that you could hold in your hand. Something that he, Henry, could read and remark upon before any one of his – or Elaine's – rabid fans could even see.

So pushing himself daily at Fort Still was actually a good thing, a righteous thing, the sort of thing he wanted to take home with him. Getting up this early before anyone else was stirring, when you could still hear the crickets and look up and see the nighttime constellations: that seemed the definition of joy, the right way to structure your day. Accomplishing that much before most anyone else has even woken up, and then spending the day accomplishing even more? That sounded all right to Henry.

Sometimes he would see McAdams at breakfast, but she usually ate with her barracks – her dorm. They'd nod at each other but that was it. Maybe that was okay, too; in the morning, his brain was still gearing up for the day, and not really up for the complicated conversations McAdams liked to dig into. But after morning calisthenics, classes in either the history of flight or the history of the Air Force or what it means to have honor and to really be part of something important *like* the Air Force, and afternoon drills, he'd usually have some unstructured time before lunch. That was when he would head out to the mess hall early, and Thomas McAdams would head out there too, and sometimes they'd talk a bit and sometimes they'd make out, and once he'd put his hand under her shirt and once, she'd done the same.

"Would you pinch it?" he'd asked her, terrified, his voice shaking. They'd only made out twice and he was beginning to suspect she was much better at it than him. His penis was already a hard slab of rock in his pants; back home, his thoughts had almost entirely been occupied with Karen Luck, and he hadn't honestly suspected that anyone else could make him feel this excited. But Karen, for all her outré thrill, had been safe. They'd been best friends since birth, had lived through the scariest experience in either of their lives together, and were already naked when he'd first asked her to bite his nipple. She wasn't going to run away screaming or telling people how weird he was. McAdams was a lot more of an unknown quantity, and asking her to get weird with him, especially in a place like an encampment, could be dangerous.

But her only hesitation was a fiery look in her eye, maybe a confirmation that he'd really asked her to do what he'd asked her to do. Tentatively, she'd squeezed his nipple between her fingers, and he'd let out the sort of gasp he could only let out when his Mom was home and he was taken with the need to masturbate. As quiet as possible, but with real force, trying not to let sensation overwhelm him.

"Really?" she'd asked, grinning a little, and she did it again, harder. For a bare moment, he squeezed his eyes closed so tightly he could only see kaleidoscopic light pulse across his field of vision. He grabbed her arm and pulled it away, almost unable to speak.

"I want it so bad," he said. "But things ... can get messy if you do."

A large grin appeared on her face. *She wants to*, he thought, feverishly. *What else does she want me to do? Is it something I won't like? Let it be something I won't like.*

These things were thought and dismissed in the same picosecond, never fully acknowledged. Before she could go back to what she was doing, a bugle sound called over Fort Still, signaling that lunch was upon them. Hastily, Henry and Thomas tucked in their T-shirts and checked to make sure the other looked presentable.

"I like you," she told him as they wound their way to the front of the mess hall, looking as conspicuously inconspicuous as possible.

"I like you, too."

"You've never made out before, have you?"

Stunned to near-paralysis, Henry sputtered, "Yes, of course I have. Absolutely." His mind, unbidden, cast back to that moment on graduation day, right before Karen told him what she was and who she was, and why she and he would never be together again. They'd kissed then, kissed deeply; last time pays for all, and all that. But objectively, even Henry had to admit that the kissing itself hadn't been great. They'd bashed teeth a few times, and he'd been hesitant and withholding the whole time ... perhaps sensing the same from her. How often *had* they made out in the past? Had they ever? It was all bodies and what could be done to them.

"Well, she failed to give you pointers," Thomas said. "We'll work on it. But first and foremost: don't fucking grab my face when you're going in. It's goddamn creepy."

"Oh."

"They do that in the movies, maybe for cinematic effect. It's not real life."

Henry, feeling less like a high school graduate and more like a recalcitrant twelve-year-old, asked, "Yeah, but ... but what do I do with my hands? Just hold them at my side?"

Thomas stared at him. "You know, I didn't think I was coming to this encampment to teach a boy how to kiss me, but here we are. Let's eat. Maybe during free time later, you can wander out near the latrines and I can show you what you can do with your hands."

And so he had, and again, his hands went up her shirt and hers went up his, and this time she *did* squeeze hard enough, and he had to go back to Delta Barracks and change his shorts before the stain had a chance to spread to his fatigues.

The following day, they went out onto the shooting range and practiced shooting rifles at faraway targets. Perhaps ironically, Thomas was a poor shot, only hitting the actual target a few times. He supposed that made sense. He'd always been far better at *Super Mario Bros.* than Karen, but she always crushed him at *Duck Hunt*, which utilized laser guns and featured a cartoon dog that laughed at you when you missed a shot. Henry kept expecting that dog to start appearing behind the blind, pointing at him with one accusatory paw.

That was the night that Thomas McAdams finally let Henry put his hand down her pants. If making out had been a mystery, this was a full-on secret. She gave him no guidance here, no roadmap. He simply felt around this foreign territory, desperately wanting to see what he was touching, desperately wanting her to tell him what to do instead of just leaving him to literally feel around in the dark. Eventually, he slipped one finger inside her, marveling at how wet the passage was, how yielding. It wasn't like the candles at home at all, which required nearly a handful of Vaseline to get to even consider gaining entrance. Thomas gasped, then gripped his arm, forcing him out of her. "A little further than I want you," she said. Then, as an afterthought, "And your nails aren't regulation, Dear. No girl liked jagged fingernails."

When he went back to the barracks, he slid into a stall and jerked off as fast and as quietly as he could. It didn't take long.

The plane was a four-seat Cessna Skyhawk. It sat happily on the runway at Agnew AFB, under a blue and blameless June sky; the whole thing had a Disney quality to it, as if at any moment, the Cessna might start singing. Henry approached it with some trepidation that did not show in his march. You could be scared if you needed to, but don't you dare break protocol. Two other cadets from his barracks marched behind him, Deaky and Curtis, both more junior members of Delta Barracks. Up ahead, the pilot – a bulky guy with a half-grin wearing sunglasses – stood by the door of the Cessna. Henry shot a salute up. The pilot met it with his own a moment later, and they both dropped at the same time. *I'm going to remember saluting like this my whole life. What's that statistic? If you do something sixty times, it becomes a habit. It gets in your bones. Well, this has been way more than sixty times. Will I ever stop wanting to do it?*

"You've trained for this" – the pilot, whose name patch said **Sasto** – intoned. "You've studied. But books and simulators can only take you so far. We are about to do the thing on which the essence of Civil Air Patrol is based. We are going to fly."

A thin rime of terror slid icy fingers around Henry's heart. He thought back to something he'd said to McAdams: *I don't entirely know why I joined CAP.* That was true enough, even now, even as his days were better than they normally were, with distance from OKC and his life there. The night before, he had lain awake longer than usual, thinking about what they were going to do today, thinking about how he'd been in Civil Air Patrol for four years, had been calling himself an Airman, had been prepping and learning and saluting and marching, and all of it had been on the ground. He'd known this day was coming. Even back when he first signed up, knowing little about the program and even less about his reasons for joining, he'd known this day was coming.

So why was he suddenly so scared?

He climbed into the co-pilot seat after Deaky and Curtis made it known that they would prefer to ride in back, sir yes sir. Henry glanced around and saw the same fear on their faces that he felt inside himself. He wondered why Sasto wasn't calling them cowards or sissies or pussies, something Pellin had a habit of doing if you broke formation in a march or you couldn't do the number of pushups he'd wanted. Even though he couldn't read Sasto's eyes through the sunglasses, Henry thought he understood; this *was* scary, especially on your first time. Being bullied about it would probably be counterproductive. Maybe other pilots and officers had their own ways of doing things, but Henry was willing to bet if he or Deaky or Curtis needed to simply cut and run or else risk having a meltdown in midair, Sasto would allow it. More than allow it. Maybe he'd say something like, *Don't be ashamed to be scared. But don't let your fear stop you. Maybe you can't do this today, and that's okay. But tomorrow's wide open. Don't shut the door on it.*

You're putting a lot on a guy who's said three sentences to you, Henry.

I'll take what I can get.

Strapping himself in, he went through the whole safety check with Sasto and the other guys. This was nothing. This was rote. Henry found it fascinating that he could look at the

Cessna's panel and understand everything on it, even though he'd never been in a non-commercial plane before. Then they were taxiing down the runway; two days before, Henry and the rest of Delta Barracks had been out on this runway, picking up rocks and pebbles as a service to Agnew. At the time it had seemed like tedious busywork. Now, Henry desperately hoped they'd gotten them all. Who knew what a single pebble could do to send the Cessna careening off course? Henry's heart thudded dully. He thought he heard one of the guys behind him – Deaky – groaning under his breath. Then Sasto pulled up on the yoke and suddenly they were airborne.

Later – after the trouble had long receded and he allowed himself to have good memories of the encampment – this was the moment he would keep coming back to. The second the Cessna's wheels left the ground, a sense of utter serenity stole over him. In front of him, the ground tilted and then receded. Ahead of him, the bright, almost ethereal blue of the sky filled the Cessna's windshield, and then the sky was all around him, enveloping him. Leaving OKC for the encampment had felt like leaving his real world behind, but this was like leaving *everything* behind. Karen couldn't be his everything up here when the sky was so much bigger than everything; pleasing his father didn't mean that much when the ground was so far beneath him, and his relationship with his dad was by definition so much smaller.

Over the course of Henry's CAP career, he'd heard so much about honor and duty, about history and tradition. He was sure all those things were important – of course they were important – but none of his textbooks or drill sergeants or superior officers had ever talked about magic. Flying was magic, plain and simple. You only had to look out across that endless sea of blue to understand that. He felt like a sailor of old, setting his sails to fill with the wind, drifting across a vast ocean, undisturbed by squalls or storms or pirates. The thought of storms carried with it an immediate and unwelcome question: *What if we hit a tornado?*

Henry waited for the inevitable panic, the rough flashback of seeing Mrs. Luck crawling out of her car and being taken away by the black and twisting sky. But none of that happened. Serenity suffused him; clarity steadied him. *I'm above tornados*, he thought. *They're low-altitude events. We're high up. We could look right down into a tornado and not be affected.* This was mostly true. Without even trying to, Henry Dear had picked up more knowledge about tornadoes and flying than most people he knew; tornadoes were usually 500 feet tall or less, and the Cessna was cleared for flight of up to 1,800 feet. They were safe up here. Safe above every storm.

Sasto turned to him. "Feel like taking the wheel, cadet?"

Henry looked at him, saw his own face reflected in the man's sunglasses. He was stunned to see a small smile had blossomed on his own face, and that his eyes seemed faraway and dreamy. A snatch of a Pink Floyd song he liked crept into his brain: "tongue-tied and twisted, just an earthbound misfit, I."

"Yes," he murmured, then caught himself. "Yes, sir. Thank you sir."

Henry turned to the controls and grabbed the yoke on his side. "Right now, all you want to do is stay steady with the horizon line. Do you see it?"

The yoke moved somnolently in his hands. There was power here, power beyond any he had ever experienced. *I've been in Civil Air Patrol for four years*, some very distant part of his mind marveled. *How come they never talked about the magic?* "I see it, sir," Henry said, so quietly that it was almost a whisper. What would the yoke feel like when you were taking off, defying gravity and challenging physics and leaping into the sky? Or when you were making a steep turn or diving a little. How much would your gut lurch? How much would it feel like riding the Sonic Boom at Sooner City? Henry guessed that a roller coaster ride was a mere approximation of what flying – taking the yoke and actually flying – really felt like.

"You're dipping a little," Sasto said. "Pull up."

Doing as he was told, Henry Dear felt the entire aircraft move up, just a little, steadying itself. *I did that*, he thought, marveling. *Me.* Henry had never given much thought to anything approaching spiritualism, but up here it was like touching God, like witnessing Heaven. For the first time in his whole life, Henry felt truly and wholly free.

Sasto headed the Cessna back toward base soon after, taking control of the yoke back from Henry. "You did good, cadet. You'll be a pilot yet."

A wordless shudder of warmth blossomed from Henry's gut and radiated outward, as if a small nuclear reaction was happening in the middle of him. "Thank you, sir," he said automatically, almost not even aware he was saying it. The sensation carried him through to the ground, where the Cessna landed a little hard on the tarmac, jostling Henry and shaking him out of his brief but total reverie.

Thomas McAdams, her brow stitched together in a knot of consternation, approached him later by the mess hall, not really looking at him. "McAdams?" he asked, swallowing.

"What." It wasn't a question. The bright white energy that had been pulsing through him ever since they returned to Fort Still dimmed somewhat. Henry tried to catch her eyes, to maybe see a little more of the emotional weather there, but she wouldn't stop staring at the ground.

"Is there something you want ... if you want to talk?"

Now she glanced up at his face. The possible future pilot was trying to suppress a grin but it wouldn't entirely leave his face. He'd practiced this moment in his head all afternoon. She would come running up to him, barely able to contain her excitement. Flying for the first time, *flying* for the first time, and it had been all she'd ever hoped. And how could it not be? Thomas McAdams had known a lot longer than him what a profound experience flight was, and he would apologize for not being on her page sooner. And he would ask her if the experience felt somehow spiritual for her, if she felt *moved* on the level that he had. They would talk about planes, and flying, and how if you lived long enough and practiced hard enough, you could get to a place above storms, above even tornadoes.

"I threw up," she said simply. "I threw up twice. I filled two barf bags. One in the air, and one on the way down. I suck at flying. I will never be a pilot. I'm quitting CAP."

Henry leaned forward, his grin finally subsiding, and attempted to put a hand on her shoulder. She shrugged away.

"I don't want fucking comfort. I want to hurt you. Let me hurt you."

Now inside himself was that same blossoming sensation in his gut, only now it was cold. Not exactly a bad cold, either; more like a sharp edge, a blade of ice, something darkly anticipatory instead of whatever that feeling was in the air. Only he knew what that feeling was, despite having only had a passing familiarity with his over the course of his life. Bliss. For a little while, he'd felt bliss.

Then how, he wondered vaguely, could he be as excited at what Thomas had suggested, on the same day that he'd felt something as pure and rapturous as what he'd felt up in the sky? Why was he like this? What *allowed* him to be like this?

He could have stopped her, maybe. He could have told her no, that talking about what had happened would probably be better. But instead he untucked his shirt and let her slide her cold hand up his belly and chest, the stubs of her fingernails running up the skin and sending sizzling cold electricity throughout his hollow spaces. Then, without warning or words, she clamped those fingernails over his nipple, and pinched as hard as she could.

The thing that should have happened didn't. He was only semi-hard, and nowhere close to ejaculating. Everything should have been working: Thomas' icy-blue eyes were almost rapturously beautiful, and her command of the situation both thrilled and chilled him. Wanting to please her and knowing he couldn't set off that cold fire in his gut. But it wasn't working, and Henry thought he knew why. Being used wasn't a bad thing, he knew, not *always* a bad thing at least, but being used in this way *was*. He wanted to talk to her. He wanted to assure her. He wanted to make sure Thomas McAdams knew that one setback wasn't the end of the world, and that she could work to overcome what had happened. Henry wanted to kiss her when he told her all that, in the hopes that his earnestness would convince her.

Instead: this. Tears sprung to his eyes. He thought he could feel her fingernails meeting in the middle, breaking through his delicate nipple skin. Wanting to howl, not daring to, Henry Dear felt a thin runnel of warmth spill down from her pinch point, down his chest, onto his belly, where it pooled in his navel.

Thomas jerked her hand away. "Henry." Her eyes met his, and they were miserable eyes, eyes that wanted to overspill into raw, jagged emotion, but that didn't quite dare. Maybe she knew that letting herself feel anything meant that she would have to let herself feel everything. That was too high a price to pay.

Swallowing, Henry said, "It's only blood, Thomas. I'll recover."

She stared at him. "You're an asshole, you know that?"

He blinked. "Wait, what?"

"You're a fucking *asshole*," she grunted under her breath. "What, do you want me to make the other one bleed, too? I can do it. Do you want me to do it?"

"Not especially, no." He was trying not to gape. What the hell was happening now?

"I came to you for ... why are you letting me even *do* this?" Now she sounded tired. Not regular tired, either, but full-on exhausted. How worn out must you be on the day you saw your lifelong dream crash and burn in front of your eyes? How tired must something like that make you?

"Thomas, I..."

"No, seriously." She had yanked her hand back and Henry saw a small streak of blood on her index finger. *I've been doing marching and calisthenics and all manner of grueling physical activity all week, and only now do I start bleeding. What a dumb world.* "This is stupid. And *you're* stupid. I feel bad for whoever marries you."

The dark thing which had kindled in his belly when he first glimpsed her anger evaporated. Worse, the warm thing that had suffused him all day ever since seeing the sky from above now dried up and dusted away. That had been his. Something just for him. It was gone now, and Henry didn't know if he was going to get it back anytime soon.

"Well, you got your wish," Henry said, tucking his T-shirt in, then his fatigues shirt. "You wanted to hurt me. Congratulations, Thomas."

For a moment, he thought she would demur, or apologize, or maybe even try to play it off with a laugh or a joke or something. Instead she stared into his eyes and nodded once and said, "Good." Then she headed into the mess and he ran-marched back to Delta.

The barracks was empty. Back home, when Henry would step into a completely empty room, sometimes he thought he could feel the presence of the person who lived there. Especially in a place like Eileen Luck's office; when Gary Luck wasn't in there, pretending to be her, Henry thought he could absolutely feel the echoes of his best friend's mother in the walls and the floor and the chair and the desk. It wasn't like sensing a ghost, necessarily; it was more like being open to an echo of the person whose personality created then infused the room in which they spent so much time. Being in the barracks during lunch was the opposite of that; there were no personalities here, no echoes. This place was a triumph of anonymity; the fact that he'd bled in here would never make an impact. No one who came after him would have any idea that he'd ever been here.

Henry stripped off his fatigues shirt and T-shirt and tossed them unceremoniously on his bunk. A furious red streak slashed down the front of his T-shirt, topped with a darker, rounder pool of blood at top. It was like an inverted exclamation point, the kind that goes at the start of a Spanish sentence when something extreme is about to happen.

The lights in the bathroom were bright and harsh and artificial. Henry stood at the bank of sinks, looking at himself in the mirror. The blood had stopped flowing and had already begun to dry to his skin. Wincing, he touched his nipple; bright pain flowed like mercury, traveling down through his gut. The thing that should have happened outside the mess happened now: as he watched himself in the mirror, his penis suddenly galvanized. It pushed out the front of his uniform pants almost comically, like a gopher trying to burrow out from under a blanket. Funny, but Henry wasn't laughing. His brain was conjuring an idea deep inside itself, so that Henry could follow his brain's commands while still ignoring what they meant. All that he allowed himself to focus on were the broad, direct sensations of time moving quickly, of a need for release, of a sudden sexual imperative. If he was going to do what he wanted to do before lunch was over, he was going to have to move fast. Lust doesn't wait.

He raced toward his locker, triple-time, misfiring the combination twice before shaking the hasp free on the third try. His heart galloped: it was like being in the air, it was like being with Thomas, it was like being with Karen, it was like none of these things, all of these things. One of the imperatives his father had made absolutely sure they bought and packed was a short, thin flashlight, about five inches long and one and a half wide. Its black stainless-steel body was smooth, gleaming mutely in the sunlight filtering through the barracks window. He slammed his locker shut and clicked the lock home without thinking about it, and was in front of the mirror again in seconds.

The air was still, unsullied by the tumult of people or the weight of history. For a bare moment, Henry only stared at the flashlight, his conscious mind repeating only one thing: *don't, Henry; don't, Henry; don't, Henry.* The voice was soft and easy to ignore. Dropping his pants and underwear to the floor, he tweaked his hurt nipple again. Again, his penis responded at once, convulsing once, twice, as if celebrating its freedom. A thin, clear runnel of precum dangled from the tip and spattered to the cold tile floor. *Clean that up after*, that soft, receding voice in his head murmured as he reached out and pumped three handfuls of liquid soap into his palm from the dispenser on the wall. He watched himself, sure he would start imagining Karen's accoutrements – the makeup, the jewelry, the wig. None of that happened. Instead, he had a vision of Thomas banging through the door of Delta Barracks, calling his name out once, twice, and then finding him in here. She wouldn't shout or scream. She would only take the flashlight from his hand and look in the mirror with him, one hand snaking around to his hurt nipple, pinching it a little more tenderly this time, a little more in fun and urgency and lust, and then she would start to slide that flashlight inside him. Slowly at first – soap isn't Vaseline, and it isn't the lube that Karen used to bring over. Karen, Karen, what if *she* was here? She would know exactly what to do, what his rhythm was. She'd perfected that rhythm, practically *invented* that rhythm. So she didn't like boys, she didn't like *him*, but maybe she'd make an exception for old time's sake, maybe she'd ... because she was so smart and so good, and maybe she hadn't shown him her writing for a little while but she still *was* writing, her Dad had told him that, she *was* writing, and she didn't hide that from people. God, Karen here, working this flashlight inside, easier for her than him because she didn't have to contend with arm muscles that didn't bend backward that easily. Karen in *this* place, and this place would *never* get its anonymity back, would never feel as bland or as blank again. She would corrupt it with her presence, ruin it with her perfection. Karen *here*. Karen *now*.

And then, with his left hand by his bloody nipple and his right hand working hard, Henry Dear began to ejaculate harder than he ever had in his life, coating the sinks and mirrors, and a quiet, sublime panic had begun to seep in when he heard Sergeant Pellin's voice behind him saying, "What in the holy hell is happening here, cadet?"

Chapter 7: The Luck You Make

"I called you an hour later. Pellin was so furious with me I thought he was going to start punching me."

Gary Luck nodded, but not necessarily in agreement. He had spoken with Pellin when he'd arrived at the encampments, and there he'd found a man who was not angry so much as deeply bewildered. "He's been such a model cadet until now," Pellin had grunted. "Not just here, but at his home squadron, as well. There was just no indication that something so ... aberrant as this was in him."

Taking in Pellin's squared-off crewcut, square jaw, and rigid posture, Gary had a feeling that the man's concept of what was aberrant was wide and encompassed vast swaths of things he didn't understand. That didn't make him a bad man, just a narrow one. Fifteen minutes later, bundling Henry into his car, he knew that trying to get someone like Pellin to understand the nuance and complexities of sexuality would be impossible. He couldn't help but wonder what, if anything, Pellin was hiding deep inside himself, keeping from his harsh and rational mind. What would this military man say if he, Gary, told him that his wife used to fuck him with a strap-on while he wore the wig she'd bought him. The man would likely have a conniption. Gary giggled a little as they drove out of Fort Still and pointed toward home.

The moon had ridden low in the sky as night started to gain a toehold. Henry's silence baked off him in waves. Finally, Gary asked, "Did you call me because your parents wouldn't be available or because they wouldn't understand?"

Without turning away from the window, Henry said, "Yes."

Gary nodded, turning toward the boy and touching his shoulder. Henry didn't shrug it off. That was a good sign. He asked, "What are you going to tell them?"

"That I got homesick. I'm eighteen. I don't have to tell them what really happened."

He took his hand away and heard Henry's breath pull in, shuddery. "What did really happen?"

"I put a flashlight up my ass and got caught," Henry spat bitterly, staring out at the moon. Gary sat silent for a moment, maybe digesting what the boy had said. Then Henry heard a strained, almost tight sound escaping his best friend's father. He turned to see Gary biting his lip, his eyes bulging.

"Are ... are you *laughing*?"

Gary looked at him, his mouth twisting in a huge, irrepressible grin. "So you got caught with a flashlight *up* your ass?"

Henry's eyes went wide. This had been a long, mostly terrible, rollercoaster day ... and this man he *trusted* enough to call was *laughing* at him? Henry said, "Yeah, and I was cumming at the time, too."

The novelist could no longer hold it in; he let out a long, braying laugh that filled the car and seemed to fill the night. "Holy shit, you were *cumming*?"

"Like in the *middle* of it. This girl I met at the encampment had squeezed my nipple so hard that I was bleeding, and..."

Gary pierced the inside of the car with another shrieking peal of laughter. "What the hell *happens* at these things? Are there orgies in the barracks?"

Now it got into Henry, who threw back his own head and howled laughter. "This is an *important* thing, Gary! I might be *damaged*."

"Oh yeah," Gary laughed, "you're really fucking damaged. Call me when your lesbian literary agent fucks you because you remind her of your late wife."

"Oh my God! *You're* damaged!"

"Guilty!" Gary raised a hand and glanced at Henry, who looked a little husked-out and exhausted, but a lot better than he had when he'd gotten in the car. Sighing happily, Gary said, "You really aren't weird, you know."

Henry was nodding too quickly, as if trying to believe it but not quite daring. "I feel weird. I feel like I was finally starting to get something out of CAP and then I went and ruined it."

"I thought you hated CAP."

"I flew today," Henry told him. "Before all this, I flew."

Now Henry told him everything, from getting used to the encampment to Thomas McAdams to holding the Cessna's yoke steady on the horizon. "And one other thing," Henry said. "I've been writing. Short stories mostly, but I've been writing."

Gary's eyes went wide. "For how long? How come this is the first time I'm hearing about it?"

"A couple years," Henry said. "I'm not very good. Not as good as Karen."

Slowly, Gary sucked in air, and let it out slowly. "You can be the best writer in the world and still feel like you're not as good as someone else, Henry."

"I'm nowhere near the best writer in the world. I don't just feel, I know."

The highway in front of them was deserted. Gary pulled over to the shoulder and put the car into park. Henry stared at him. Gary stared back. "So *what?*"

A long silence. Then: "Huh?"

"I mean it. So what? Karen had two novelist parents. Still does, sort of. Her entire life has been books and writing from the day she was born. She's edited my books and her mother's books, and she's been proofing since she was *eight*. She's been a voracious and omnivorous reader since she was three years old. If Karen *hadn't* turned out to be a writer – and a very good writer – I would be surprised. She's excellent. She's going to be big, I think. But listen to me, Henry. Just because someone is better than you doesn't mean you're not great. Do you understand me?"

Henry, wanting only to placate this man and move the conversation along, attempted to nod. "No. Not really."

Unlatching his seatbelt, Gary said, "Come on. We're getting out of the car."

"What?"

"Get out." To the left, great swaths of empty. To the right, similar empty, marred only by a dilapidated farmhouse that hadn't held people in years. Ahead of them, the two-lane highway stretched for what seemed like a hundred miles. Henry was a suburban kid for the most part (even though he technically lived in the OKC limits), and it had never really occurred to him just how empty so much of his state was. For a bare moment as he climbed out of the car, the sight of all that empty land under the vast endless tapestry of stars made him feel suffocatingly small. Then, just before Gary Luck came around to his side, he thought, *Could I fly at night? Man, I'd like to fly at night.*

"Do you know who's a better writer than me, Henry?" The man came around the front of the car and began pacing. He looked nearly manic.

"Um," Henry said. "Tolstoy?"

Gary pointed at him. "I'm serious." Then: "Although, yes, Tolstoy is a far better writer than me, thank you for bringing that up.

"My wife is, Henry. Eileen is one of the best writers I have ever had the privilege of reading, and then she ... she went away, and not only was I losing *her*, I was losing her *stories*. Okay, her *books*. And sometimes you get to a place where you have to step up or stay down forever, no matter what the consequences. I knew I would never be as good as Eileen when I sat down to write as her. I *knew* that. And I did it anyway because it's what needed to be done. You know what happened? I got *better*. Trying to be as good as Eileen made me *better*. Why would you give up on yourself for not being the best before you even tried to be *your* best?"

Hot tears had begun to fall from Henry's eyes. This had been the longest day in his entire life and there was still a long way to go. "I don't know, Gary. I don't know."

For a second, Gary Luck stood before him, and the wide, endless plains stretched out beyond. Then Gary leapt forward and grabbed Henry, as he'd done on that day when Henry first glimpsed the hole in the wall. Startled, Henry grabbed Gary back, and held him, crying into his shoulder. *This is what he'd needed. This was something his Dad couldn't give him, even if Dad understood about the sex stuff. Gary got the sex stuff, and he at least tried to understand the flying stuff, and most of all he knew that sometimes what you needed was human contact from someone who likes you, and cares about what happens to you.*

"I love you, Henry. Okay?"

"I love you too, Gary. Thank you. Jesus, thank you." Then words fell apart and they just held each other like that for a very long time. Anyone passing by who happened to glance at them might very well think that they were father and son, but no one drove by. The Oklahoma night was empty around them.

"I took your advice," Henry said now, seven years later. Gary looked up from his place on the couch, a soda can by his side, open but forgotten.

"I hope it was good advice."

"I started writing. Not as me but as the person I wanted to be."

Absently, Gary grabbed the soda and popped it open. It was warm but he drank it anyway. "Dressed up?"

"Yes."

"Makeup?"

"Yep. Even shoes. I couldn't get her shoes exactly because my feet are so damn huge, but..."

"You're writing as my daughter," Gary said flatly. "You're writing Karen Luck novels." He wanted to stand and pace. He wanted to ask more questions. He wanted to laugh. Instead, all he did was glance down at the last Eileen Luck manuscript and sigh. *You started this, Gary*, he thought. *Where does it end?*

"Not exactly." Henry explained his process. Gary was stunned that he was deep enough into this to even have a process. What he'd do is sit down and get the first chapter out without any help. He'd wear what he thought of as his Henry Dear Writing Clothes: baseball hat, blue jeans, a T-shirt for a band he liked, Chuck Taylor sneakers. The first chapter was always the hardest, and Henry had a sneaking suspicion that it would be a lot easier if he were to start off as Karen, too. But that was one of the ironclad rules.

"Are there other rules?"

"We'll get there," Henry said, smiling.

Henry built the first chapter slowly, laying down his main characters' motivations and backgrounds and likes and dislikes – as much of a narrative dump as he thought he could reasonably work in without the chapter feeling labored or laden with exposition. Then, starting with chapter two, he'd let his version of Karen take over. Wig. Makeup. Sometimes a dress. And it was almost always a shocker to see where Karen would maneuver the story. Almost always, she drove it into a place he never could have imagined.

"It's a true collaboration," Henry told Gary, not meeting his gaze. "She's constantly surprising me. I definitely wouldn't do half the stuff she does. Like, I started this one book, *Valerie*. And my whole intention was for it to sort of be this funny novel, right? I spent all this time figuring out Valerie's life. She has a boyfriend and she's got this ex-husband who's silly but not really bad, and this sister who she doesn't get along with, and a mother she's half-estranged from. Right? Lots of conflict, lots of different ways to go with the story, and so I put all that into chapter one. I went into *Valerie* with the hope that I'd explore some themes I'm trying to work on – loneliness and singularity, kind of, but in a funny way. And what does Karen do the second I turn the novel over to her?"

Gary, who had read enough of his daughter's work to make an educated guess, said, "She killed the main character."

Henry's eyes went wide, but he grinned. "That's *right*. Karen hasn't done that in a book yet and she only kind of did it in that short story of hers—"

"'Their Tiny Knuckles.'" Gary's voice was flat, affectless.

Eyes blazing, Henry said, "*Yeah!* I love that story. But she *always* likes to shift expectation. And she did that with my book."

Gary, who had been listening with growing discomfort, knew that he was the first person to which Henry Dear had confessed any of this. And of course it was with good reason; Gary Luck's entire literary career could have been an encyclopedia entry under the word *precedent*. Not only that, but this boy – who was no longer a boy not really – trusted Gary implicitly. In so many ways, he'd acted as Henry's father when his real father wouldn't do. Hadn't he been the one Henry called from the encampment? Hadn't he bought Henry his first computer? And yet this … this wasn't anything he would have wanted for the boy. Not in a million years.

"*You* did that, Henry," he whispered, and something in his brain tilted, like a universe of stars going off its axis. "*You* shifted expectation."

For a bare second, Henry could only gawp at this man, who had taught him most of what he needed to know about writing. The rest he'd learned from this man's daughter, and maybe that was the thing that had given Gary pause. He only had one daughter, and here dumb old Henry Dear was, trying to co-opt her.

"Well," he said, trying to assure him. "It really is her. The writer version of her, at least. But it's not *just* her. Okay? Because I write the last chapter."

"You...?"

Henry grinned. "That's right. As we're getting to the end of the book, I take off the wig and the dress and the makeup and even the perfume, and I take the book back. She hands it to me neatly and sweetly. She's done. So here I have to wrap up all the messy stuff that she's put those characters through, even the ones I hadn't created at the start of the book. I have to make sure it all comes to a logical conclusion. She has these wild narrative flights of fancy that make literally *no* sense, and I have to make sense of them. But that's exciting. That's why writing is so vital, right?"

Gary Luck, who knew exactly what he was talking about, could only nod numbly.

"Anyway, that's the only reason I feel like I'm justified in putting my name on the book. Because I start and finish it, you know? Oh and then, get this, this is the best part. I put the book away for a few weeks and think on it some, and then when it comes time for the rewrite, *Karen* actually starts it."

Swallowing hard, Gary said, "My Karen or your Karen?"

Henry blinked. Weren't they one and the same? But he said, "Mine. I put all the stuff back on – sometimes I call it my uniform and sometimes my gear, does that make sense? – and then she takes up the first chapter, adjusting it to make sure it's in line with the rest of the book. Then I look at what she did for the rest of the book and move stuff around and maybe try to make it fit my original vision for the book. But not much. Books are sort of delicate and they have their own momentum. You don't want to tinker too much with the bones of a book when it's finished. If I try to shoehorn motifs onto a book after

Karen kind of obliterated them, it would destroy the book. So it's gentle. Subtle. I can do subtle."

"Does Karen come back in and rewrite the last chapter?" Gary hated how flat his voice was. He wanted to support this kid. *His* kid? Sure. Maybe. You could say that Welton and Skylark Dear had written the first chapter of their son, but then Gary Luck had come in and took the story in a completely different direction. Jesus.

"*Yeah!* She puts her final stamp of approval on it and then lets me call it my book. The whole thing. Isn't that remarkable?"

Gary crossed to the other side of the room. His knees popped and lower back wept. He felt like the world's biggest hypocrite. What gave him the right to feel uneasy about any of this? Was it because Karen was his daughter and this boy was almost – but not quite – his son? Was it because, in the immediate wake of Eileen's last novel, he was beginning to realize how bizarre his own writing life had been, and that he hadn't meant for it to serve as a template? Or was it because Karen, unlike Eileen, was still alive?

All these things, all at once. But mostly that last one, and not just as it related to writing. Gary Luck wanted to mourn, and he'd wanted Henry to mourn with him before his daughter came home. But he'd forgotten that Henry, like Karen, had probably mourned his wife years ago. They'd seen her carried away, hadn't they? Both of them. Despite living with the literary presence of Eileen Luck all these years, she was only an echo for both of them. A pale ghost. Gary had *inhabited* her, and she had inhabited him, in a far more intimate way than what he'd allowed Cynthia to do when they'd both decided that Eileen could not only be alive when writing, but could also be *sexually* alive for both of them.

Gary had *needed* to resurrect his wife, because he hadn't been ready to let her go. But Karen wasn't gone. Karen wasn't dead. So what Henry was doing wasn't out of a desire to keep anyone alive. It was out of infatuation.

Slowly, cautiously, he said, "I'm not sure what you're doing is necessarily a good idea, son."

Henry, who had been looking dreamily off in the distance, perhaps considering the specifics of his writing process or the stories themselves, suddenly shook himself out of it. "What? What do you mean?"

Hesitatingly, he asked, "You know Karen is ... you know she likes girls, right? She's actually coming here with a girlfriend. I haven't met her yet. I guess her name is Maura."

"I know she's a lesbian," Henry said, rolling his eyes dramatically. "She told me the day I graduated high school. It's fine. I totally get it."

"Henry..."

"Oh. I see what this is. You think I'm still so in love with my high school girlfriend that I dress up like her just to be near her. Christ, Gary, I thought you of all people would understand."

Without any idea what he was going to say, Gary shook his head. "I don't. Eileen..."

Rapidly, Henry crossed the room toward the manuscript for *The House Where You Lived*, rapping on the title page with his knuckles. "Is here. Mrs. Luck exists here. That's it. I know that. Just as sure as I know that my version of Karen – and that's all she is, Gary, a *version* – is just the book. I know she's a good writer and I want to be a good writer, too. That's it. That's all."

But was it? Was it really?

"Besides, I'm just taking your advice. Trying to be as good as Karen is making *me* better. You should see some of my earlier short stories. Man, they sucked. Only when I started writing novels did things start to get better. Because she was my motivation." He paused, looked over at the deer. "I'm not still in love with her, if that's what you're thinking."

But Henry wasn't looking his way. He was looking at that damn deer. Why did they even have that painting? It was a terrible painting. It had always been terrible. Gary wanted to tell the boy to look around, to say what he said when he could look in Henry's eyes. Then, all at once, it seemed too much, too complicated. Did it really matter if Henry was still in love with his daughter? What harm could come of a crush, or a torch? Nothing was ever going to happen, so it didn't matter.

Tired, Gary slumped into a chair by the coffee table. Henry knocking on Eileen's last book was what had done it. The sound was a final sound, an ending sound. It still resonated in Gary's mind, like the Telltale Heart: thump-*thump.*

God, what was he going to do now?

Karen parked the car in the gravel driveway, the sound of those rocks crunching together under tires shocking an immediate sense-memory in her. Gravel was gravel was gravel, but to Karen Luck, this sounded like such *specific* gravel. Coming home from the video store with another Disney live-action film from the 60s on the seat next to her – *The Happiest Millionaire* or *Gnome-mobile* or *Darby O'Gill and the Little People.* Or returning from the supermarket or the Dairy Queen, or those occasions when Mom or Dad would pick her up from school instead of having her take the bus. The days when public school was an option and before Haveline Academy had come into her life and changed it. That sound of gravel meant they were home.

She got out on one side and Maura got out on the other. For a moment, Karen could only stop and stare at her old home. It was a Tudor revival, huge angled roofs chiseling the sky. Natural wood laced throughout the house's pale stone, geometric storybook patterns facing the gravel driveway as the front gable pushed forward to greet you. Twin columnar chimneys poked out from the top of the house, odd amidst all those sharp angles. The front door dwarfed all that stood near it: heavy wood with massive black iron hinges, arched at the top; decorative stonework limned the door frame with faux-rustic brickwork.

"Holy shit," Maura said, coming around to the front, "you live in a *castle*."

"*Lived*," Karen corrected, and reached out for Maura's hand, who took it. Anxiety pinged through Karen's brain. Why did it feel like correcting Maura was a lie?

"Where's your old room?" Maura asked. Grinning, Karen pointed up at a huge window with a wooden overhang; it looked like the kind of overhang you'd see above a well in a Grimm's Brothers illustration.

"The place I had my first sexual fantasy, my first period, and wrote my first short story."

"That's a lot of firsts to put on one room."

"I only shared two with my Dad."

"Which two?"

"Scared yet?"

Maura said, after a moment, "Is your relationship with your dad weird?"

Karen nodded at once. "Oh yeah. Super weird. But not gross weird. I don't think."

"Well, my parents sort-of-but-not-totally hate me, so anything will probably be better."

"We'll see." Maura noticed that Karen had left all the luggage in the car to pick up later ... except for the leather satchel containing *Where'd She Go?*, her latest novel. For a bare moment back in Los Angeles, Maura had allowed herself to believe that this weird trip to Middle America was going to be something of a vacation. Of *course* Karen was going to work here.

The door loomed in front of her. It was bigger than she remembered, which was strange; normally when you confront places from your past, they seem smaller, diminished. Not this door. Not this house. She thought of knocking and instead walked in. You didn't have to knock if there was still a bed you could call yours inside.

Dad was in the kitchen, standing in the middle island and chopping vegetables and doing a ramshackle job of it. Pepper juice and tomato pulp oozed everywhere, coating the cutting board and most of the tile beneath. He was dressed as Gary Luck, a revelation that filled her with an almost palpable relief. But the thing that hadn't happened at the door happened now: Dad looked smaller. There were wrinkles around his eyes that hadn't been there before. His arms were thinner than they had been, bones wrapped in bandages wrapped in skin. His hair had gone more salt than pepper, although she was heartened to see that most of it was still there, combed in that almost-messy writer's hairdo he'd been favoring since the 80s.

"Well if it isn't my first and only born, Karen," he said, putting the cutting knife down and throwing his arms open wide.

Reluctantly, Karen put the satchel down, not wanting to get it anywhere near water or vegetable ooze. Eventually she settled on one of the barstools and went to hug her father. She hadn't exactly been dreading this moment, but she and Dad weren't really all that close these days, and that fact had made her feel both sad and guilty ... only not so guilty that she was willing to change it. But the hug made her feel the opposite of those things. It was *his* scent he smelled, that boring but familiar Old Spice aroma that hung around his office, even when he wasn't there. There was warmth in his embrace, and fierce love, and a desperate longing that she understood all too well. Dad laced his hands behind her back and squeezed her tight, the way he'd hugged her in the days after Mom died, and after they'd found her body. He'd lost someone he loved, and it was his sacred duty to make you know *you* were loved, here on this earth. Karen understood immediately, and was glad she had come home.

"You've finished."

"It's called *The House Where You Lived*."

Karen smiled. "You went with my title."

He nodded. "*Leave* seemed like the wrong kind of final." Then tears, all at once, came to his eyes and he hugged her even tighter. Karen hugged back. One of the reasons she'd moved out of this house was to escape the persistent ghost of her mother. Now her mother was gone. For real gone. And she found herself crying, too.

Maura McKinnon stood in the corner of the kitchen, looking alternately at Karen's satchel, and the Lucks holding each other as if they wanted to never let go. She thought that she had never felt this lonely in her entire life. She wanted a shower, and bad.

But first: dinner.

"Okay, so my big attempt was lamb," Dad said. "I *bought* lamb. Like a *lot* of lamb. But then two things occurred to me. One, what if Karen and Maura are vegetarian or vegan, because that happens in California. And two, I don't know how to make lamb. So that's why we're eating spaghetti."

"It's really good, Mr. Luck," Maura said. It was true, Karen thought. Which meant Dad hadn't made it.

"So, Dad, what's my ex up to lately?" Very casual, Karen.

Maura blinked. "Your ex?"

"The last boy I dated before I started seeing girls. Before I could *admit* that I wanted to start seeing girls."

"Oh," Maura laughed. "*That* ex."

Gary looked up. "Do you know Henry?" he asked, "or does Karen just talk about him a lot?"

"Actually, this is the first time I've heard of him," she said, and shot Karen a quietly dark look. It didn't remain. "But when you're ... you know, like us, you always have that one last opposite-sex experience that sort of puts paid to it."

Karen grinned and took Maura's hand. "You can say 'gay.'"

"Or lesbian!" Dad nearly shouted, and they all laughed. "I'm not uncomfortable," he explained, "just new. I don't know any of this stuff."

Maura shrugged. "For me, it was this guy named Bob. Nice guy. A little younger. Kind of ... very masculine. Like, *hyper* masculine. Not really in a bad way, but he went to the gym a lot and he was, you know, kind of hairy. *Very* hairy. And he drank beer and watched football. A cliché of suburban masculinity, right? I think he was there so that I could test myself. I like men, and to prove it, I'll be with an *uber*man. One man to stand for all men.

"What kind of shattered it all for me was the way he kept trying to ... I don't know, let me know if this is too much information, but he kept trying to shower with me. You don't know how invasive that is. He did it at least once a week. One time, I even made sure he had showered and dressed and everything before I got in, and he still stripped down and climbed in. I turned around with soap in my eyes and my elbow brushed his hairy gut. I screamed and almost fell over. If I had, I guess my head would have connected with the faucet and I'd probably be dead now. But Bob grabbed me and held me a minute. I think he thought it was romantic, but for me..."

Karen watched her for a long moment. Maura didn't have many slippery spots, but the showering thing was one of them. There were myriad rules about Maura in the shower, and Karen had no idea what most of them were. The main one seemed to be to read Maura's mind whenever she headed to the shower, and anticipate her every whim and need. Karen thought she had a pretty good average when it came to making sure Maura's shower needs were met – maybe even exceeded – but the fact that she was constantly standing on slippery ground made her nervous.

"So of course that didn't work," Maura continued. "And there's irony it it I didn't see until after. It wasn't just the shower thing. I picked Bob because he was supposed to both prove *and* disprove that I liked men. My two warring sides battling for supremacy. The disprove side won."

"And Bob?" Karen asked.

"He waited a respectable time before he asked me if I had any friends I could set him up with."

Dad gaped. "What a pig."

"Yeah, but I knew that going in. He didn't know I was gay going in. So I had the upper hand."

"But you didn't know, either," Dad said, and both Maura and Karen looked his way. "So no one had the upper hand."

Everyone was silent a moment. Karen felt her stomach cramp. Being here was a bad idea. Taking Maura here was a bad idea. How come this was the first time she was hearing about Bob, by the way?

"Cynthia tells me you're working on a new book," Dad said. That cramp in Karen's stomach punched deeper.

Karen glanced at Maura. For support? As a warning? She didn't know. She liked the way Maura held her silverware, her long fingers elegant as they moved. The nails flashed deep maroon, the perfect shade for a woman like Maura. Bright red was for college girls. Maroon was for someone a little older, a little wiser. Someone with a few years on her, a few years of experience and knowledge. And yet ... some of that polish had chipped. Maura's additional decade didn't mean she wasn't vulnerable, maybe even a little fragile. Karen wondered what those fingers would look like typing. All at once, she wanted to be back in the place in Los Angeles, just her and her girlfriend, and she wanted to feel those fingers on her body, inside her body, surprising her by doing the things she couldn't anticipate. More than the physical, she wanted to step out of her home office after a day of writing and find Maura in the living room, going over sides. And Karen would take some pages from her and run lines until Maura had them down cold. They'd eat and watch *Jeopardy!* and Karen would go back and do a little more writing before bed, and then in bed they'd maybe read or maybe sleep or maybe have a little fun with each other, and all of that was to the good, all of that was to the great. She wanted all those things forever. The knot in her stomach loosened.

"Yeah. It's called *Where'd She Go?* I have no idea if it's good or not yet, but it's nearly done."

"What about that second one, the one I can't read?"

"*Up in the Air.* And it's not that you *can't* read it. I just think you *shouldn't.*"

Gary swallowed. "Is it about what I think it's about?"

Karen nodded. "Probably the same thing your book is about."

Slowly, Gary's eyes closed. "It's your mother's book."

Karen glanced again at Maura, who was watching this interplay, enrapt. There was too much here to put on her girlfriend, who had never anticipated visiting Karen's weird childhood home and getting into the whole deal about her mother and her father and the way that sometimes they were the same person. She should have outlined all this on the plane, or before. It was unfair to bring Maura here, not knowing if Dad was going to be wandering around the house in a dress and makeup. The fact of that might be hard enough to explain, but what about telling her that Dad actually believed he *was* his dead wife, at least sometimes. She'd pack it up and run screaming from the stately little mock Tudor and from Karen's life forever.

Maura, sensing tension she didn't understand, said, "I just think it's remarkable that Mrs. Luck had all those finished manuscripts hidden away." Both Karen and Gary slowly turned to look at her. "I've actually been reading her books for a long time before I knew Karen. Jeez, I read *No One Knows Where Sarah Goes* when I was fourteen and my Mom almost had a fit."

Gary nodded. "It's a ... it's a very good book."

"It really is. That's why it's such a shame that ... well, what I mean to say is that the manuscripts she left behind got even better than that. I can't even imagine how tragic losing her must have been to you two, but for someone who's been reading Eileen Luck since she was a teenager? It's like each of the books improved on what went before. Those first books were so special, but the later ones just went beyond that. I guess it's just a shame that she never lived to see how her efforts paid off." Maura paused. "And suddenly I remember she's not just a writer but a real person."

"It's okay," Karen said. "She died a long time ago."

Dropping his fork to his plate, Gary said, "No she didn't." Then he got up and headed out of the kitchen. Karen stood and Maura followed.

"Oh God, I'm so sorry," Maura said. "I'm so stupid."

"You're not stupid. Things are just ... complicated right now. I was actually waiting for this. This is why I'm here."

"Is he going to be okay? God, maybe I should have read his books, too. I could have talked about that instead, maybe. I just don't really like those macho crime novels, you know?"

Karen suddenly felt the weight of a thousand unspoken truths attempt to land on her shoulders and crush her into the ground. She took Maura's hand and said, "Why don't you head back to the room? Leave all this. I'm going to go check on him. I'll be up in a bit."

Maura nodded and stood. She kissed Karen on the lips and told her she loved her.

"I love you, too." Karen said, and as always, hoped she meant it.

Entering her father's office was like entering the lair of a feral animal. Karen knew that a maid came in every week to do some light cleaning and tidying up. She could only guess her father had barred the woman from this room. Dishes were stacked up unceremoniously on every available surface. Clothes littered the hardwood floor. An inset bookcase dominated the back wall of his office; research books and foreign editions of his own novels and some of his favorite fiction had long been stuffed lovingly, if haphazardly, onto the shelves. That gentle chaos was now fervent chaos, as if her father had pulled every book out, glanced at it, then shoved it back on the shelf upside down in an entirely different place. There was a slight rotting smell emanating from the trash bin by the far window. Dad had cracked the window a little as a concession to the smell; otherwise, he was willing to live with it.

Worst of all, though, was her father himself. He'd managed to throw a ratty robe over his clothes and now sat at his word processor, staring vacantly at the screen.

"You're here to tell me it's time to stop mourning," he said, tapping the spacebar a few times with his thumb, then the backspace key with his pinkie. Three steps forward, three steps back.

"Should I?" she asked. There was a small wooden chair in the corner; more dirty clothes had been piled on top of it. As delicately as she could, she picked the piled up and set it on the floor, wondering why she was being delicate.

"What else? That writing as her for so long was damaging, that doing it in the way I did was absurd, that I should have gotten all this all out of my system years ago."

Karen sat. "Do you want me to tell you that stuff? Or is it stuff you want to tell yourself?"

He glanced at her. "I can't write, Karen."

Of all things she was expecting him to say – more about her mother, or about mourning, or about how Karen shut the door on Elaine Luck years ago and only he had tried to keep her alive – this was not one of them. Reflexively, she glanced at the black-and-green glowing screen of his word processor. Two words, *I went*, appeared at the top of the screen. That was it. That was all.

"That's as far as I've gotten," he said. "I've been at this almost a week."

"Jesus," she said, leaning closer to the screen, as if she could will more words to come. "You've had writer's block before, right?"

"I've had writer's *pause* before. When I was writing my last book on the typewriter, there were days when I would just stare at the page for an hour, and then type out a sentence, then realize it was crap. The words were coming, but they were sluggish. I had all the ideas in my head and *wanted* to write them, but it was slow. I was in a *pause*." Dad sucked in a deep breath through his nostrils and Karen wondered how he could stand the smell. "This isn't that. I don't have ideas. I don't have words. I don't have *writing*.

"And Karen," he said, looking up at her with wet eyes, "if I don't have your mom and I don't have writing, what do I have?"

"Me, Dad," she almost whispered, hating that she felt hurt that he hadn't said it first. "You have me."

He blinked savagely, then asked, "But do I? You're so far away and you have your own life. I don't fit into that. I don't know where I fit in, actually."

Karen's heart was speeding in her chest, speeding so fast that she worried it might explode. "I was thinking you might come visit me for a while."

"In Los Angeles?" he asked dubiously, staring at those two short words glowing on his screen. *I went.*

"A change would do you some good. Actually, it might do me some good, too. I wouldn't mind having you there to look at the new book when I finish it."

"Before Annie?"

"You've always read my stuff before Annie."

"Before Cynthia?"

Karen paused, looking out at the window and the deepening night beyond. Beyond the canopy of those old, massive twin pines, the night sky stretched on forever. The stars were brighter here in OKC. "Yes," she said. "Before Cynthia."

Dad stood and went to her, hugging her from behind and looking out the window. "Before we leave," he said, "could you take a look at her last book? I'd like you to read it in the old house. Maybe ... I don't know, maybe you could finish your book here, too."

"I don't know, Dad."

"Just maybe."

"We'll see."

Later, she would wonder if the millisecond between his "just maybe" and her "we'll see" is when she decided the course of the rest of her life. Everything that came later was willed, subconsciously, into existence in an instant shorter than it takes to exhale.

Why don't you try writing on Mom's computer? she thought she asked out loud. But she didn't.

She didn't.

Four days later, Maura emerged from the bathroom, a towel wrapped around her. Karen looked up from her desk, knowing she should feel guilty and feeling guilty for not feeling guilty.

"I know I'm shirking my responsibilities," she said quietly, not looking Maura in the eye. "I'm sorry, Maur."

Maura raised a hand and smiled, a little tightly. "I know this is a special circumstance. The shower isn't as important as your Mom's last novel."

Reluctantly, Karen put the red pen down. How many more pages in *The House Where You Lived*? A dozen? Two? "It's not exactly my Mom's novel," she said, "and I know how important the shower is to you."

"Well," Maura said, and went to the dresser. It was beyond weird to see Maura pulling out her pajama bottoms from the drawer where she, Karen, used to keep her sex toys.

Even more weird: Karen had kept sex toys in that drawer when she was *fourteen*. Did Dad know that? Or Cynthia? What about Henry? All she'd needed was the credit card her Dad had given her "for emergencies" and an address. That dildo she'd bought mail order, the one she thought would finally cause Henry to run screaming from her bedroom, had arrived at the house in a huge white box, with her name right on it so that the entire world could have witnessed her filth. Dad never saw it. Cynthia never saw it. It was so big, she'd had to keep that one in her closet. When had she thrown it out? Right before college?

"Well what? I know that well." A vague panic alarm started to bleat at the back of her brain. She should have been less weirded out that Maura was taking pajama bottoms from her drawer and more weirded out that Maura was wearing pajama bottoms at all. Maura slept in the nude; it was one of the coolest things about her. Occasionally, if Karen was restless and needed to get up in the night, she'd glance back and see Maura deep asleep in a cozy shaft of hallway light. The way her shoulders rose out from under the covers, cream-white and so vulnerable. Maura would breathe in so deeply and hold it for just a second, as if every breath was an anticipation. In these moments, Karen would think, *you blew it with Cynthia. Don't blow it now. She's trusting you to keep her safe and well. So don't fucking blow it.*

Then she would turn from her sleeping girlfriend and pad down the hall to her computer room to write. She could flip on the TV or crack a book or find some other way to fall asleep, but there was nothing like accomplishment to really relax you. Getting real pages in when Maura was asleep was always a bonus, because she could jam out on whatever she was writing for as long as she wanted, but didn't neglect her girlfriend. It was a win/win.

But she'd been neglecting her on this trip.

Karen got into bed, still fully dressed, and gently kissed Maura's neck. Her smile loosening a little – *just* a little – Maura said, "Well it's okay. Mostly okay."

"Only mostly?" Karen kissed the back of her ear, one of Maura's tingle spots. There were more and she knew all of them, she thought. Maybe she could hit them all and get Maura to forget all about that *mostly*.

"You're trying to woo me."

"Will wooing work?"

Maura gasped, and for a moment her legs shot out, straight and straining, galvanized. Then she said, "Wooing won't work."

"We'll see," Karen said, and whatever calculation had crunched in her mind evaporated. Mom's book had been stuffed away elsewhere. Her own books – both of which were very nearly done – were similarly hidden at the back of her brain. When they did this the way Karen liked best, it involved at least one toy and a bit of costuming and staging. She loved wearing the strap-on and seeing Maura look back at her, her makeup not garish so much as a little obvious. The kind of makeup a suburban woman in her late forties would wear if she was trying to impress the women at a PTA meeting or at Kohl's. Not to impress a husband; that probably *would* be garish. Karen liked makeup that women wore for other women.

But when they did this the way Maura liked best, all they needed was each other. Exploring Maura's body was thrilling, finding those spots on her that Maura didn't like and highlighting them with lust and love. Because she was a working actress in her forties and she wasn't a megastar, the roles Maura tended to get were moms in TV movies, long-suffering wives in failed pilots, or occasionally the cruel guest star prosecutor who is destined to lose against good-guy defendants. And she got commercials. Mom in a pizza rolls commercial. Mom in a fruit drink commercial. Mom in a dog food commercial, who gets to wear an expression of serene relief that her pooch is *finally* eating the right food, and not the bullshit they *used* to cram down its gullet. There was an undeniable erotic charge catching her girlfriend on TV in one of those commercials, or catching her still in her costume when she came home at night after one of those shoots.

Maura didn't see it like that. All she could do is point out her perceived flaws. A patch of cellulite here, a cluster of stretch marks there. Wrinkles she didn't used to have. Grays she worked hard to cover up. Just lately, she'd been talking about going in for some plastic surgery, or at least Botox, but so far she'd listened to Karen and had kept it natural. It was hard keeping it natural when the world is looking at you. It was in these moments when Maura was feeling especially self-conscious that Karen would do her level best to make her see what she, Karen, saw in her. She wouldn't ignore that cellulite; she'd kiss it, moaning a little at how sexy it was. If she found a stretch mark, she'd run her tongue over it, tracing the lines as gently and as delicately as possible. Lust *for*, not lust *in spite of*. Only after she'd done a full survey of Maura's outer body did she move to the inner, and oh the things she could do there.

She did those things now, and Maura closed her eyes and went, and went.

After.

"I'm going to shower again," Maura said quietly.

"Do you want me to come with you?" Karen was drifting, lost in the haze of their sex, dizzied by the cognitive dissonance of being in this room again, the taste of a woman on her tongue and the smell of a woman on her bed. It had been a long time. She wanted to keep drifting, but this had been intense, seismic, and she was still tethered to the woman now standing by her childhood bed. If Maura wanted her to come shower, Karen wouldn't hesitate.

A long pause, then Maura shook her head. "No. You rest up. Try to be awake when I come back."

Karen smiled, nuzzling into the bedsheets and making satisfaction noises. Maura went.

Her eyes were already brimming with tears before she closed the door of the en suite, and she forced herself to hold them in until she got the shower going and Karen wouldn't hear her. This ... this was of course ridiculous. Wasn't it? It was. She was standing here, naked, sodden, expecting Karen Luck to literally read her mind. Dumb. Ridiculous. Wasn't it? Maybe.

Something had happened between them in Karen's old bedroom tonight; she knew she wasn't the only one who felt it. Sex with Karen had always been fun, despite her overreliance on toys and dressing up. But tonight, a frisson of unexpected passion had clutched both of them, rocked them, disarrayed them. She could still feel Karen's tongue, gentle at first, then almost sadistically aggressive, seeming to anticipate Maura's most receptive spots. It wasn't just that making love with Karen had never been that easy or natural or explosive; it was that making love had never been like that, period. Had it been like that for Karen? She thought it had.

Maura supposed some of it had to do with the tension of the last few days – days during which they were supposed to be headed back to Los Angeles, with or without Karen's father. She hadn't accepted any gigs while out here in the middle of Nowheresville, USA, and because Karen couldn't give her a definite return time, she was hesitant to accept anything. The problem with not accepting things is that after awhile, your agent stops sending things. That had *also* been part of the tension.

But now, in the heat of what they'd done, the tension seemed to have evaporated, like lake mist when the day comes on hot. She'd lain back against her pillow – a pillow that Karen might have slept on when she was still dating boys and writing her first stories – and let her long exhale stutter out and looked over at the woman she loved. Karen seemed dazed and spent, her eyes unfocused, hazy. It *had* been the same for her.

So why hadn't she followed Maura into the bathroom? Why *ask*? It was almost a violation to ask. When Maura had first swung her legs – still tingling with sensation – out and dropped her feet to the floor, she'd simply wanted to begin walking, then extend a hand backward, expecting Karen to simply take it. Maybe she'd wiggle her fingers in an insouciant come-on gesture. And Karen would come, too, taking her hand and standing under the spray and letting Maura soap up her back and her front and wash her hair. Then Karen could return the favor. Maura saw this all very clearly in her head. And yet Karen had asked. Dammit. Goddammit.

The water was warm and clean and when she stepped out, she grabbed a new towel from under the sink because her old one was still wet. She'd cried herself out under the spray. It was fine now. Absolutely fine. Years from now, the two of them would only recall that absolutely mind-rending sex, not whatever bullshit surrounded it. Maybe they'd come up with a cute nickname for it, like, "your father's house," and they could say in front of people, "hey, want to go to your father's house tonight?" It would be one of those inside jokes couples have, and it would be good, because she wanted to feel what she felt tonight – not the tears, but the passion. She craved that passion.

Fully wrapping herself in a towel, completely forgetting that she'd intended to wear pajama bottoms tonight, Maura stepped from the bathroom to the bedroom. She'd hoped to find Karen lying there, bedroom eyes, looking back, suggesting but not demanding a round two. She'd expected to find Karen fully asleep, a small but contented smile on her pretty face.

What Maura found was Karen up at her desk, her red pen in hand, flipping a page of her mother's last novel.

Her only thought – *I don't want this* – passed through her head without leaving an impression.

Maura McKinnon stayed in the doorway for a very long time. Karen didn't look up once.

Chapter 8: Burger City Again

"I didn't want to push," Henry said across the booth. "But it's really great to see you, Karen."

"You too, Henry," she said cautiously, looking around. "You know, I never thought I'd be back here."

The décor in Burger City hadn't changed much in the five years she'd been away, done up as it was in American Imitation. The style of the 1950s as remembered in the 1970s, constructed in the mid-1980s; the vinyl seat cushions were pale and, in some cases, cracked. The Formica tabletops all seemed more faded than fun. The jukebox in the corner no longer accepted quarters and was merely there for decoration. Back when this was their place, the pitstop between their respective schools and their respective homes, that Wurlitzer glowed and played actual 45s. You could actually watch the mechanism inside swap old records for new ones through a window in the front: a little robot hand would select the disc from a slot on the left, then sweep up in this beautiful arc before dropping it on the spindle in the center. It was pure science fiction to Karen, which had gone with the mid-century aesthetic somehow. Until her last year in high school, the only records they featured were doo-wop and pop and rockabilly, all from the wayback years before The Beatles came to America. They'd started spinning 70s records around the time she'd started coming here alone in her senior year. It didn't fit the look, but they played a lot of David Bowie and Elton John and Heart, so Karen hadn't much felt like complaining.

"Welcome back," he said, picking up a French fry and then, reluctantly, putting it down again. "I'm sorry. I feel stilted. I really wanted to see you and now I have no idea what to say."

"To tell you the truth, I don't know either. It's been awhile."

"You know I left CAP."

She nodded. "Dad told me. Oh, and you're writing?"

"Dad told you that too?"

"Yeah. Jeez, our neighborhood and writers, right? Maybe we should have started an OKC version of Bloomsbury."

She laughed. He laughed. She wanted to fucking scream. Had she spent most of her childhood and young adulthood being friends with this man? It had only been five years; how the hell did she have nothing to say to him? Instead of answering that, she looked around again.

"You looking for someone?"

"There used to be a waitress here. Enid?"

Henry grinned. "You remember Enid?"

"How could I forget? All that hair. Those cat glasses. She was memorable."

All at once, Henry's grin grew wider. "Wait a minute."

Blood rushed to Karen's cheeks. Was she honestly that transparent? "What? You should tell me about your writing. Is it novels? Or just short stories. Fill me in."

"You had a thing for Enid, didn't you?"

"Would you keep it the fuck down? I'm not exactly out of the closet, especially in OKC."

Henry blinked, trying to force his round mind into a square concept. "Why aren't you out of the closet? Don't you live in LA? Isn't everyone gay out there?"

"That's San Francisco. And there's a lot of reasons, okay? Cynthia, for one. If I'm out and proud I'm not going to sell novels."

"That's dumb," Henry said. "Wait, *is* that dumb?"

"I don't know. I don't write gay lead characters so I guess it's fine." The taste on her tongue was salty and dry, like sea sand. "I really do want to hear about your writing."

"And I really do want to hear about Enid."

"There's nothing to tell," Karen said.

"That's how I know there's definitely something to tell."

For a long while, Karen simply watched this guy, this man, her ex, and thought of how she wanted to tell it. She'd wanted to write about it in the past and had never quite dared. Not directly, anyway. She closed her eyes, took a breath, and traveled back in time. Not distance, though. Finding those days was easier now. She was already here.

Haveline Academy was a sprawling Streamline Moderne campus on the outskirts of Oklahoma City. Built in the mid-1930s, the main building resembled nothing so much as a classic ocean liner, with long solid walls ending in curves, not edges. All of the windows were round, the accents chrome and almost entirely decorative. For Karen Luck, going to classes felt like time-traveling to Paris during the Art Deco movement; at any moment, she could hope to see a can-can dancer lifting her petticoats and riffles and skirts and showing her ankles and breasts in one of the airy open spaces in the main building. Maybe an artist with bizarre facial hair would be painting a surrealistic elephant in one of the halls. All of it felt too fancy and foreign and too non-Oklahoma City to be a place where she had to learn science and math and social studies. And yet.

The Academy was a hybrid school, meaning that while most of the students were borders, a few of them came from local families and went home at the end of the day. Karen believed it was the ultimate tragedy of her life that she hadn't been sent to a school in another city – or maybe even another country. So many of the books she'd read as a child involved girls or boys being sent away to school somewhere and then stumbling on mysteries either tragic or magic. Finding grand adventure in Oklahoma City didn't seem to be on the agenda. If she wanted actual excitement, she was going to have to head to New York or Los Angeles, like the singers in a lot of her favorite songs. You either found yourself or lost yourself on the coasts, and by the time she was a junior at Haveline, she was ready for either option.

Then she met Hartford.

The girl was in her Advanced Comp class, but you'd barely know it from the way she never spoke. Karen didn't really have a plethora of friends at Haveline – she suspected it was because the borders bonded together and the locals didn't really have to – but even she was more social than Hartford, who sat at the back of the class with her frizzy hair and old flannel shirts and didn't raise her hand. There was something weirdly familiar about her that Karen couldn't place; something in the set of her nose or the color of her eyes that triggered some vague association back deep in her brain. Whatever it was, Karen didn't think it could be that important, or memorable; the girl's name was *Hartford* for chrissake. If Karen had any connection – even remote – to her, that name should have cemented it.

It was two weeks after Halloween that Hartford first approached, and things inside Karen were officially weird. She'd "come out" to herself only a month before, and all the scary repercussions she was terrified of facing hadn't yet happened. In every class, she waited for everything to go suddenly silent, and then all heads would turn to her and the teacher would point a shaming, accusatory finger and start shouting, "*Sinner! There's a sinner among us!*" And then the other girls would fall on her like an estrogenic *Lord of the Flies* and gleefully rend her apart.

So much of this was absurd. Haveline wasn't in any respects a religious school, a feature Dad had particularly appreciated. Plus, just admitting to yourself – and your dad's agent – that you liked girls didn't mean that all at once, a red pulsing sign appeared on your forehead, blinking LESBIAN on and off to the beat of your racing heart. No one else knew. No one else even suspected. Well, maybe Dad. And, okay, *maybe* Henry. But no one at school.

Which she'd nearly convinced herself of when Hartford stopped her in the hall with a hand on her shoulder and a wide-eyed look of terror plastered on her face. *This is it,* Karen thought, *I waited for this. I knew it was coming. They're going to kick me out of school. They're going to cast me out. I'll go to public school and then all the kids will get weird around me because my Dad's famous and my Mom died in a tornado and I like girls and I'll drop out and start doing heroin and die before I'm eighteen.*

"Karen?" Hartford asked in small, meek voice. "Luck?"

"In the flesh," Karen said, wishing she felt as confident as she sounded. She attempted a small smile. "You're Hartford, right?"

The girl's eyes widened. "You know my name?"

"It's a name you don't forget."

Hartford sniffed. "Well, that's my mother's doing." Karen couldn't read the look that came over her her classmate's face – somewhere in the valley between a moue of disgust and an indulgent love. It was disorienting to see all at once in the same face. "Listen, I just ... this is weird, maybe. I feel weird."

Oh my God. She's a lesbian. This is my first lesbian thing. Well, not really my first. *Henry doesn't count. Wait,* does *Henry count?* "Don't feel weird." Karen felt *supremely* weird. It took every ounce of fortitude in her body to not turn tail and bolt down the hall.

"Do you remember the Halloween Storytelling Round? In Ms. Dorian's class?" Of course she did. The assignment was to write a story inspired by Halloween in some way, and then they would spend the week in class reading three or four stories aloud each day and offering critiques – constructive, not destructive. Karen loved assignments like this, loved being told she had to write on a specific topic but otherwise, write free. After school that day, she'd rushed home and plunked herself in front of her typewriter and let the words flow through her.

And it sucked.

The story – called "Gust," a title she'd come up with on the bus ride home; a *good* title, she thought – concerned a woman running from a tornado. It was going to have all the elements: suspense, inner monologue, literary allusions to *The Wizard of Oz*, maybe even a shifting point of view. She had a thought to include another character watching this woman from afar, a little girl in a barn who can see everything but do nothing. The idea of writing a story like this scared her a little; nothing she'd written so far in any class or on her own had hewn so closely to her own life. Would reliving the memory of her mother's death screw her up in some real, defining way? Would she have to write through tears? Would she have to vow never to show "Gust" to her father, for fear that it would hurt him in a way she couldn't repair? Karen Luck was willing to suffer these literary trespasses. If it was for the writing, the *work*, then personal comfort be damned.

Only none of that happened. What happened was this:

Evangeline looked over her shoulder and she ran. She was wearing high-heeled shoes, impractical, and the heel came off for her left shoe in a pothole the city never got around to repairing. Still she ran, limping now, and the tornado was closer. Wildly, Evangeline thought of The Wizard of Oz, *but not the movie version. The book version. The main difference between the two plots was*

"Oh my fucking God," Karen said, hating Evangeline for refusing to exist correctly and attempting to offer a compare and contrast essay in the midst of running for her life. She hated herself for watching thin, lifeless prose spill out of her as easily as some of her good stuff had done. What did it benefit a girl to write fast and and nearly effortlessly if the resulting work was so damned godawful.

The excitement she'd been riding high on all day deflated. She tore the paper out of her typewriter and tossed it, half-crunched, toward the garbage can. Nothing but net. The crowd goes wild. Yippee.

She peeked into Cynthia's room, knowing she wouldn't find her. Cynthia had been called back to New York City for a few days to deal with a difficult writer who was demanding a percentage of the profits from any toys made from a movie of the book he'd written. The book he'd written was a sci-fi slog from beginning to end, the kind of hard SF packed with scientifically accurate machinations and a good handle on theoretical physics and little else. Cynthia had brought a galley of it home and Karen gave up by page twenty. It kind of sucked when Cyn wasn't around; if she wanted to talk to someone about being gay, she had to go to her dumb journal. In a few weeks, she'd come out to her father and things would be easier, but that hadn't happened yet. And if she wanted to talk to someone about the literary business beyond just things like plot and character, Cynthia wasn't too shabby either.

Soon, Karen Luck thought, and stepped away – for now – from Cynthia's door.

Downstairs, Dad was working on the newest Elaine Luck novel, a long and involved novel about a female architect in the 1940s, and the estate she builds in Los Angeles for a lunatic billionaire. Loosely – extremely loosely – based on the actual story of William Randolph Hearst and his architect Julia Morgan – *Nothing So Fine as Huckleberry Wine* was a classic gothic book, at turns lurid and literary. When he tore himself (herself? How were you supposed to refer to him when he was being her mother?) away from the computer, he'd rhapsodize about the work.

"It's like Daphne duMaurier," he said. "She was the queen of that stuff. Old creepy houses, someone who *knows* something, forces that are against your main character. Supernatural? Maybe. Your mom has such a great understanding of how to work in that genre. I never really got the knack."

It was one of those times when it was all almost too much, and Karen had wanted to throw the fork down and start screaming, and screaming, and saying, *My mother died! She doesn't have a great understanding of anything anymore! Who are you trying to fool – me or yourself?*

But when she glanced at him, there were tears in his eyes, brimming but not over spilling. Dad wasn't fooling anyone.

Now, she leaned in the doorway of Mom's office. There were some fresh-cut wildflowers in a vase on the side of the desk. Mom liked to have fresh flowers when she wrote. Dad was hunched in his chair, peering at the computer screen with intense, almost fervid concentration. He wasn't wearing his normal wig today; this one was a deeper color, and was cut short in an almost-bob. Mom had never worn her hair like that, but Karen could absolutely see her doing it. That was one of the trickiest things about Dad's drag act: he anticipated what Mom *would* do, not just what she *did* do.

"Dad?" Karen asked quietly. For a moment, the person in the chair did nothing but stare into the glow from that computer screen. Was what was in there so much better than what was out here? "Dad?"

Now he looked up, and his cheeks were smeared with Mom's mascara. It rolled down his cheeks in ugly brown tracks. Usually, Dad's daily transformation was quite good: elegant enough to get to the essence of Mom, workmanlike enough so that it could withstand all the hours of sweat and tension and full-bore creativity that writing a novel took. Karen wondered how he could stand it every day. She didn't wear makeup when she wrote. She wanted to feel as unencumbered as possible. Everything that made up who she was had to flow out of her and into the story, onto the page. How Dad could go from writing without any of that stuff on his face when he worked on his own books to coating his cheeks and eyelids and lips to write as Mom utterly baffled Karen. And today, it all looked haphazard, hastily slapped on by an indifferent man without an interest in being a woman. And now, with those mascara tracks, it was even worse. He looked like a clown right now. A sad, tragic clown, but a clown nonetheless. Pagliacci in mom jeans.

"What's going on, Karen?"

"Are you okay?"

He let loose a humungous sigh. "Not really, Karen. Do I *look* okay?"

She leaned in the door. This wasn't Dad. This wasn't the way he was, especially when he was writing Elaine Luck books. When he was on his own stuff, sometimes she would peek inside and he'd be crying there in his chair, his hands hovering over the word processor's keyboard. Never when he was her. What did Mom have to be sad about? She'd been resurrected to do the thing she loved the most.

No, her mind immediately amended. *That's what* he *loves the most. Mom loved you the most. You know that.*

"Dad, I..."

"I'm writing this novel because it's one I think she would want to write. She would tell me all her inspirations for her stories and books. Random stuff. The way she'd see a news story on missing women and then someone rams into her cart at the supermarket, and she combines those things and gets *No One Knows Where Sarah Goes*. I loved talking with her about that. I loved knowing that stuff about her.

"And I think that there'd be something like that for this book. You know, before you were born, your mom and I went out to Los Angeles, in California. I wasn't all that impressed, but she thought it was the best place in the whole world. She said something like, 'I love everyone dedicating their whole realities to artifice. That's what we do, Gary, isn't it?'" He put a big hand to his face and a choked sob escaped him. "And I miss her, Karen. I'm trying to forget that I miss her and just ... just fucking *be* ... I'm sorry I swore. I didn't mean to swear."

"It's okay, Dad." Karen wanted to go to him and wrap her arms around him, but it seemed like there was something more in him, something he needed to get out before he could continue. She waited.

"Out in California, we went to this museum on the architecture of Los Angeles. Your Mom was in awe. She loved art and buildings and city planning; I think that's part of why she liked writing so much. A lot of that goes into books, but usually it's invisible. You have to learn a little about everything to make a seamless book. And she wanted to learn all about the architects who built LA. And on the second floor there was a whole exhibit on Julia Morgan, one of the only women architects back then. Your mom was enrapt. She ... she just went insane over it. And she said, 'Gary, when I come back, I want to be a badass woman architect. I don't just want to break glass ceilings, I want to build new ones.' And we laughed a little bit about that because it was so silly, and..." Dad smiled softly, and now he didn't look like a clown. He looked like a man in too much makeup, trying his hardest to keep it all together. Now Karen went to him and put her hand on his shoulder. The tears spilled over and he cried quietly, his chin on his chest. She crouched down and tried to hold him. Maybe she cried a little, too.

Eventually he sniffed and blinked and said, as if he hadn't interrupted himself, "After you started sleeping through the night – this is years later – after she would put her office to rights at night, she would come out into the living room with me and we'd read and drink wine together. And every once in a little while, she'd raise her glass to me and say, 'Nothing so fine as huckleberry wine.' Even if it wasn't huckleberry wine. I don't even know if they make that.

"But your mom liked the way it rhymed. It tickled her, you know? So I'm just bringing those two things together, Karen. The way she always did it. She really *is* writing it. I know that. I feel that."

"Okay, Dad," Karen said, standing.

"It's just that in those moments, I forget that she isn't here anymore. Because I can feel her when I'm writing, I think I'm going to poke my head out of the door and see her there, and she's going to ask me why I'm in her office, get out Gary.

It's not the remembering that hurts so much. It's the forgetting."

Slowly, Dad turned around in his chair, dabbing at his eyes with some tissues he kept by the side of the computer. He took a deep breath in and placed his hands on the keyboard. Karen asked, "Is it going to bother you if I bring my typewriter into your office and write awhile?"

"*My* office? You... Oh. Yes, sure."

How quickly he became her, how shatteringly quickly. She nodded and grabbed her typewriter and paper and the one draft of "Gust" that wasn't completely terrible. In Dad's office – which smelled, as always, of years of soaked-in Old Spice – and set up at the table by the window. For a time, she looked at the cover over Dad's word processor, beige and draped and ordinary. His books weren't ordinary. He thought they paled in comparison to Mom's, but they were so much better than he gave them credit for. He was better now that he wasn't Doreen Daley, but all his books had been at least good; some of them had been astounding. Some of them had been *better* than Mom's books, both when she was alive and now that she wasn't. He would never understand that, Karen didn't think. Dad saw himself as a hard worker, as a dedicated novelist. Not a great novelist.

Karen dragged her eyes from the covered word processor and turned back to "Gust." The first paragraph of this draft wasn't bad. The onus wasn't on Evangeline anymore, but her daughter, watching from the front porch of an old woman's house.

The cyclone, which would haunt Annie Evanston for the rest of her life, thundered down the dusty road toward the porch on which she stood. The old woman inside was trying to call 9-1-1, but the lines were dead. Communication with the world beyond that horrid, trainline bellow had been severed. Even from this distance, Annie could see her mother going up, going in. That connection had been severed, too.

Good. It was a good paragraph. But for what? A short story? A novel? The next few paragraphs followed Annie Evanston inside and the old woman brought her some cookies on a China plate, all while the sound of the tornado outside kept getting closer and closer. There was *something* there, a kernel of something inside those words, but not *of* those words. The prose limped, the dialogue fell flat. Was she writing a coming of age story? Was Annie Evanston going to be forced to grow up fast and live the way her mother couldn't because the tornado was a metaphor for the chaos of life? That sounded a little silly ... but also a little too expansive for the confines of a short story, and she wasn't really ready to write a novel yet.

"What if it's not about the mother *or* the daughter?" Karen asked out loud, startling herself. "What if that's not the story I want?"

She reread what she'd written, and two words jumped out at her from the center of the second page. *Bone China.* The old woman brings the girl cookies on a bone china plate, and...

"That's the title," she murmured, shoving a new piece of paper into the spindle and twisting. At the top of the page, she typed those two words. "Bone China." Karen glanced out the window and the skies were perfectly clear. She wrote:

The sound of the cyclone shrieked and galloped up the road to Jessica Walther's house. Some people said that the sound of a tornado was the sound of a train, but after living all her seventy-two years in this little house in Oklahoma City, it wasn't the sound of a train she heard. It was death.

Her husband had been taken from her two decades earlier, found in whatever rubble was left of the supermarket after a tornado had plowed through it. Her daughter had been carried off in her car five years earlier; Jessica had watched from the window of her own house and had seen the whole thing. The girl had been bringing her a new stock of huckleberry preserves. One minute she was there, and the next she was up in the sky. And the next she was dead.

Now, it seemed, the tornado was finally coming for her.

Karen didn't outline, moving from hunch to intuition to words streaming across the page. She was on page three before she realized that there were creatures living in Jessica Walther's house. Tiny creatures, birthing themselves out of the wood grain and cracks in the tiles on the bathroom floor, in the worn-down warp and woof of the carpets in the upstairs library. They were warped, misshapen things that came out of the warped, misshapen parts of Jessica Walther's refuge, coming to life while the tornado swirled and screamed around the house. The counterpoint thrilled Karen – the small sounds inside, the trainlike howl outside, both packed with endless menace.

"It's not fair," Karen murmured to herself as she got closer to the climax, but she was smiling. "She's just an old woman, this isn't fair."

It wasn't fair, the story wasn't fair. There was appeal in that, excitement in that. The fact that this woman could have suffered so much and that she was just going to keep suffering – well, that was a juggernaut of truth, wasn't it? The last lines of the story spilled from her like liquid fire:

Her face, drawn, twisted, stared up at the thing on her table. The angle was bad and her vision was fading, but she could make out what was happening up there on top of her good tablecloth. God help her, she could. The thing with the small mouth and the huge fangs lifted her mother's bone china cup to its hideous lips, tilted, and sipped Jessica's blood as delicately as a woman would sip a cup of warm tea. Sated, it placed the cup onto the matching saucer and leapt about the table, capering, gibbering in its unknowable language. Outside, the cyclone continued its unearthly shriek, and Jessica only wanted to shriek along with it. But she was so weak. So very weak.

Then, a new sound. Small. Almost imperceptible underneath that mammoth sound of the tornado. Clink-clink. Clink-clink. The sound doubled, trebled, magnified in her ears until it was all around her. Using up what had to be the last of her strength, Jessica got herself up on her elbow and looked around her room, horror steadily building inside her.

There were creatures on every surface of her kitchen: on the little island, on the sideboard, on the stacked cabinets, in the sink. These misshapen things that had somehow come to twisted life out of the cracks and warps and imperfections of her home were now everywhere, and all of them held a cup of her mother's good bone china. Lightheaded, Jessica knew what was in each of those cups. Oh, she knew.

Then, in grotesque unison, the things began rapping on those cups with their tiny knuckles. The sound surrounded her – nuk, nuk, nuk – as the sound of the tornado did. Horrors within horrors, swirling around and within each other like some demented Möbius strip. The sound their tiny knuckles made was the sound of nightmares, a rallying cry for insanity and instability. It—

Then pain, searing and immediate, screamed from her leg. Jessica turned that way, knowing that one of those creatures had leapt down to the floor and was now sinking claws or fangs into her loose flesh; when she saw that, she would go mad. But that wasn't it. It was worse.

Out of the wrinkles and folds of her leg, a new creature was rending itself into the world, literally tearing its way out of her skin and onto the hardwood floor. Its single eye was a dark liver spot that opened and looked around. Its dozen sharp teeth protruded out of a line of mouth that had once been a varicose vein. As Jessica watched, it turned that rheumy, malevolent eye her way, smiled, then dropped its tiny knuckles to the floor and began rapping on the wood. Nuk-nuk. Nuk-Nuk.

Jessica screamed.

Outside, the tornado fell silent. In here, things were just getting started.

Karen pushed herself away from the typewriter and stared at it. Then she stared out the window for a long time, not wanting to look at the page anymore. When her eyes finally fell on the last words – *in here, things were just getting started* – she wanted to scream. Had she managed to scare *herself* with a story?

Then she pushed that thought away. It wasn't useful, not yet. The first few pages of the story needed to be reworked, and hard. You wanted to feel bad for this woman, but the story couldn't be needlessly cruel. These creatures had to be a reaction to something the woman had done, a reaction to bad behavior of some kind. Not even *bad*, but ... but what if the woman had shut out everything after her husband and daughter were killed? She cut everyone out of her life, her terror or tornadoes forcing her into a life of solitude and wariness. Yeah, that was it. She didn't need to be *nice* to Jessica, but she needed to be *fair*. This house was the thing she used to shut out the horrors of the outside world, but as it turned out, the house was the horror all along. Yeah. Yes.

Karen stood up, looking around the office, all dark wood and Old Spice. A masculine smell. A masculine place. Did Dad try to be masculine when he was in here, to counterbalance the stuff that went on in the other office? If so, was it conscious? Whatever gloss you want to put on it, Elaine Luck was a costume. The question was: was Gary Luck *also* a costume? Karen wasn't sure she wanted answers, because those answers might apply more than to just her dad.

She was about to straighten the pages and lug the typewriter back up to her room when the steady sound of fingers on keys wafted to her from the other office: *tappa-tappa-tappa*, nonstop, ceaseless. When did she suppose she was going to go back and edit those first three pages and bring them into line with the rest of the story? Tomorrow? The next day? Or never? What if the story got into her and she found it simply too fearsome to face? It was scary as hell. She could barely believe it had come from her. All at once, she could almost hear the sound of those tiny knuckles on the keyboard in the other office, her Mom's office.

Tappa-tappa-tappa, those tiny knuckles birthed out of her story and into the real world, and she shuddered, revulsion slouching up her spine. Sudden, blank fear swept across her consciousness. What if she went in there now, and her father was on the ground, the wig on his head askew, barely able to move, pale as paper. And on the keyboard, a half-dozen half-melted things with razor teeth and glowing idiot eyes tapped their tiny knuckles against keys, perverting her dead mother's newest novel? It was so horribly *plausible*, so sickeningly *possible*.

And if she put those pages off, attempted to recreate the churlish horrors within her on a later day, what might happen? The story she was working on at school, the forbidden one no one could ever see, "The Transmigration," was scary, but it was low-level scary. The dread crept. She could sustain that. Could she sustain this?

Karen Luck sat and spooled a page into her typewriter. She was going to be here as long as it took to make it right. To make it perfect.

She was in her father's office deep into the night. When she finished her story, she meant to leave it for her father on the coffee table, but he was still writing.

Always writing.

Hartford was looking at her. "Yeah, of course," she said. "I liked writing it. Well, sort of. I mean, it was scary to write."

"I bet!" Hartford said, maybe a little too enthusiastically. "I just ... that was the first time I think Ms. Dorian actually read a student's story aloud in class. If it's not the first time, it's rare as heck. Mostly, kids just read their own stuff. It's such an impressive story."

Oh my God, Karen thought. *She's a fan. I have my first fan. Well goddamn.*

"Thank you very much, Hartford. I…"

"I wanted to know if I could publish it." All this came out of the frizzy-headed girl in one breath: *Iwanknowficupublshit.* For a second, Karen had no idea what the girl was trying to say. Then it all dawned on her.

"*Publish* it? Did you say...?"

"It's not because of your parents!" Hartford nearly shrieked. She clamped her hands over her mouth and stared, wide-eyed at Karen, looking miserable, looking fraught. "I'm sorry. I'm never like this."

The exaltation had drawn some looks from the girls in the hallway, all of whom almost immediately glanced away, rolling their eyes. "Oh," those eyerolls said. "It's just *Hartford*. We might have *known*."

A little nervously, Karen turned back to the girl, who she discovered she liked, in spite of herself. "That's fine, Hartford. It's..."

"All I wanted to say is that it's not because of your parents. Some people have rich parents here. Well, most people, I guess. Not my mother. My mother's a waitress. Anyway, you're kind of the only person here whose parents are rich *and* famous. So you're probably sensitive to that."

In truth, Karen wasn't all that sensitive to it. Maybe it was because they lived in OKC or maybe it was because the richest thing her family ever did was fly to Disney World every other year or so and ride Space Mountain and Horizons. Fans tended to write letters instead of showing up to the house. In that way, it was lucky that most of Elaine Luck's novels were being published posthumously; of her two parents, Elaine had the most strident fans, the ones who thought they were owed something because they read a book. Her being dead tended to keep those fans away. As for her father, he got his share of weird letters. For a time, he was getting letters every week from a woman named Ms. Nessa Balanchine who claimed she was engaged to Mike Bull, and wanted Dad's blessing to marry him.

"How do you marry a fictional character?" Dad had asked, handing one of the letters to Karen. "It just seems so improbable."

"I saw a thing on TV once where a guy married the Golden Gate Bridge, so maybe it's not so weird," Karen had responded.

Ms. Nessa Balanchine had grown furious when Dad didn't respond, and downright livid when, in a later book, Mike Bull meets Betty Alameda and the series' first extended romance starts heating up. "I'm burning all your books," the lunatic wrote. "And I'm never going to read another word you write." The threat was either idle or short-lived, because every time Dad published a new Mike Bull novel, Ms. Nessa Balanchine would shoot off a spate of hateful invectives about how Dad was "destroying the story you've been sharing with us all these years."

"I think I might have killed Alameda off three books ago if not for her," Dad confessed to his daughter one night after the writing had gone particularly well. Fifteen pages in one day was unusual, and Dad had done eighteen that day. "For a while, I was just keeping her in there out of spite. As it turned out, she's what the series needed. Thank God for crazy fans."

Now, Karen said, "I mean, a little. I don't really think of them as famous, really."

"Well, they *are*. And *you* are. But you're also *talented*, and I didn't know that. Now I do. I'm the senior editor of Haveline's literary magazine. It's called *Merry Lives* and it's good but I think it would really benefit from your story. Can I publish it, please?"

It hadn't taken much convincing. Hartford had walked away grinning, and Karen watched her, feeling at once elated and lonesome. When she spotted the girl with the frizzy hair the next day at lunch, her nose deep in a Lauren Kincaid novel, she approached tentatively. "Hi, Hartford. If I'm interrupting, let me know. I can just..."

"You're not!" Hartford said, jamming a Juicy Fruit wrapper into the book to mark her place. "Not at all, not one bit! Have a seat!"

So began the unremarkable and short-lived friendship of Hartford Geary and Karen Luck. They were close enough long enough so that "Their Tiny Knuckles" appeared in the next issue of *Merry Lives*, along with a commissioned cover illustration that Hartford must have paid out of pocket for. By the time the following issue arrived, Hartford would no longer even look at Karen Luck in the halls, a miasma of deep and unforgivable betrayal hanging about her like a cloud of dust.

Now, Henry's eyes widened. "Enid's her mother. You slept with her mother."

"I was *getting* there."

"Karen, you have always had a way with backstory, but sometimes..."

"I know, I know, get to the point."

The point was that a few months into their friendship, Hartford tearfully confessed that her mother, divorced and single and living on waitress's wages, had revealed that she no longer liked men. "I don't even know what that *means*," Hartford had wailed to Karen. They were in the academy's vast library, both on beanbag chairs chocked up against the back wall. "How do you stop liking *men*? I like men. They just don't like *me*. It feels like she's mocking me, you know?"

Sitting stock-still, Karen's finger paused halfway through the book she'd pulled from the shelf – a volume of the TimeLife series *Man, Myth, & Magic*. There was an entry on the transmigration of souls, and though she'd studied it fervently for the past few weeks, she wanted to make absolutely sure she got every detail right. You couldn't take the *Man, Myth, & Magic* series out of the library; even though they discussed the supernatural, they were considered reference. The librarian, Ms. Doherty, always gave a little sniff of disapproval when she saw Karen with that one; Karen had an idea that Ms. Doherty hadn't been the one to requisition the series. She wondered what the elderly librarian would have to say if Hartford confessed to her that her mother liked girls. How distraught would it make her?

Terror pulsed through Karen. Later, she would occasionally chastise Cynthia for not being out at work, for letting the publishing house keep her in the closet just so she didn't make waves. That older version of Karen forgot how abjectly numb with fear she had been only a few years before, facing her kind-of-friend and hoping she couldn't see into her soul.

"I don't know if it's *mocking*, really," Karen ventured. "She probably can't help it."

Hartford rolled her eyes. "I mean I *guess*." A slow sigh. "I mean, I *know* she can't help it. But like, why be a lesbian *now*? Okay? Why not when I was little, so I could get used to it a little while? And it's like ... she could date *any* guy, right? She *has* dated any guy. And she sends me away like her fucked-up little secret. And *that's* when she decides that it's okay to ... look, I don't know."

"It's okay."

"I don't know. I don't *hate* her. I keep thinking I'm going to and I don't. I *wanted* to come here. The literary magazine and the whole creative curriculum is awesome. Of course we couldn't afford it – she's a *waitress,* right? – but she filled out all the grant stuff and the scholarship stuff and like went to town. Which is *great,* okay? I get how much she did for me. But it still feels like she was *waiting* for me to go away, you know? Like I was holding her back."

Karen still couldn't move. There was too much here to fully process. For a few moments, she'd thought Hartford had hated her mother. Maybe she could have understood that. Hated it but understood it. It would have been easy to know just not to ever, ever come out to Hartford. But Karen didn't think this was about the lesbian thing at all. Or at least not most of it; it's just the easiest thing for Hartford to hang her misery on. When Cynthia had convinced Karen that *Nobody Under the Stars* could work as a novel, Karen went to work deconstructing her main character, giving her frizzy red hair and glasses and a mother she didn't understand. In the library, Karen didn't know then that Hartford – who would become Houston in her novel – was going to be the main character of the first book she wrote. She also didn't know that every moment spent for the rest of her life would be a moment spent gathering material. Every confession she heard or gave, every kiss, every terrible conversation: it would all echo in her fiction eventually. Some nights, when she was desperate for a reason to hate herself, this made for a good fallback. Everyone who encountered her thought they were talking to Karen Luck, the person, but not even Karen knew who that was. They were always *really* talking to Karen Luck, the writer. And writers are great at disguises.

Waitress, Hartford had said. She'd said it before, too, but now it was sticking in her brain like a harpoon. Something about that word. That word and Hartford's nose.

"I don't know your mom, but I'd say she's just figuring out who she is. I don't think she got rid of you to do it or anything, though. She probably thinks you're doing good on your own. Like you got this, you know? She can work on her because you're doing a great job of working on you."

Hartford barked a laugh. At the front desk, Ms. Doherty looked around, irritated. "Do I *look* like I'm doing a great job of me?"

This one was easy. "I think so. More important, though, what do you let your mom think?"

Hartford was quiet for a few long moments. Karen felt her body unclench, but only a little. "Yeah, okay, I get your point. Kind of."

She couldn't hold it in any longer. "Hartford, you said she was a waitress."

Another one of those barking laughs. Ms. Doherty stood from her desk and shouted, "*Quiet, please!*" which to Karen seemed antithetical. "Yeah," Hartford said. "Actually, you probably know her. She works at that burger place downtown."

Karen's eyes went wide. Oh shit. Oh *shit.* "Burger City?"

Burger City.

Karen Luck ordered a cheeseburger deluxe meal with tater tots and a vanilla Coke. Enid Geary brought it all to her with a smile, then asked if she wanted a slice of pie to go with it.

Jesus.

"Yeah," Karen said. "Do you have lemon meringue?"

Enid cast a glance at the glass dome on the front counter; various pie wedges whispered temptingly. "I'll see what I can't rustle up for you," Enid said, and had she said it with a wink? Karen couldn't tell. Her heart was thumping harder than the one under the floorboards in the Poe story. Surely Enid could hear that. From her place at the counter, Enid glanced over at Karen, lifted the glass dome, and presented the slice of lemon meringue with a flourish of her hand. *She's a mom*, Karen thought, and a not-unpleasant shiver shot through her, like electricity.

She flashed a thumbs-up sign and casually glanced around the diner. The place was empty. Karen tried to tell herself she hadn't planned that, but she did leave school three hours early today, claiming terrible cramps. During the school year, Burger City didn't really get going until 3:30, even at lunchtime. The Wurlitzer in the corner was playing some old country tune, Patsy Cline or Tammy Wynette or Dolly Parton in a mournful mood. Enid reappeared at her table with the pie and a huge grin. She was wearing cat glasses today, giving her the aura of a woman displaced in time, bouncing around alternate eras before she could return to where she came from.

"Enid, right?" Karen asked, her face on fire.

"Are you okay, girl? Something not agreeing with you? Jeez, I hope it's not food poisoning." She paused. "I did *not* say food poisoning. Ignore me."

"Enid, can I tell you something?"

The question knocked Enid a little off-kilter. She set the plate of pie down on the table with a loud clink and her brow furrowed. It was a look of a small-town woman with a secret, though technically OKC was one of the largest towns in the country. "Maybe you'd better not."

"I have to," Karen said.

Glancing around, probably ascertaining that Burger City was, in fact, empty, Enid slid into the booth across from Karen. Behind her cat glasses, her eyes were bright and wide and intelligent. And there was that thing with her nose: sharp and angular, unexpected in the middle of a face with round cheeks and a soft chin and those wide eyes. The nose matched her glasses, not the rest of her face, and Karen couldn't stop staring at it. Hartford had that nose, but not the face to carry it off.

Karen swallowed hard. There was a click in her throat. She murmured, "Enid, I'm gay."

Very slowly, Enid offered an almost imperceptible nod. Removing her glasses, she rubbed the bridge of her nose between her thumb and forefinger, looking exhausted. *At night, she goes home and takes off her stockings and dress and bra and leaves them wherever, and she probably doesn't have the energy to cook dinner, so she heats something in the microwave and flips on the TV and watches whatever's on. Her daughter is off at school because that's what's best for her, but she goes home and has this quiet, unremarkable life that she thinks is so small, but it's not, it's not.* Another of those shocks of electricity bolted through Karen and the tremor through her was absolutely noticeable, but both she and Enid were pretending it wasn't.

Enid dropped her hand. "What's your name again, girl?"

"Karen," she said. "Karen Luck."

Nodding, the waitress said, "That writer guy comes in here sometimes. He always looks sad. Does he know about you?"

"Not yet," she said. "But his agent does. She's gay too."

"Oh." Without her glasses, her nose looked even more angular. Her face had the air of royalty about it. In another life, she could be a queen. Maybe she even was, if she was as unstuck in time as Karen had supposed. She could actually picture the woman wearing a purple velvet cape and a gold crown, holding a scepter and looking down upon her subjects from on high. It was an appealing image, but not quite as appealing as the one of this woman at home alone with her single TV dinner. Thoreau talked about men leading lives of quiet desperation, dying with a song still in them ... but Karen thought Thoreau never considered the lives of women. They *raged* lives of quiet desperation, and the song in them was a scream.

"Karen, why are you telling me this?" Enid kept glancing away, then flicking her eyes back to Karen's face.

Here it was. Oh God, this was the moment of absolute truth. Karen started to shake. "I think you're real pretty, is all. I think you're so pretty and you make me so happy every time I come in here."

For a long silent moment, Enid said nothing. Karen said nothing. On the jukebox, classic country gave way to something contemporary. Distantly, Karen thought it was one of the new Aerosmith songs, "Cryin'" or "Crazy" or "Amazing." She couldn't tell the difference. Enid simply looked at her, not speaking, not breathing. Finally, she put her glasses back on and said, "You're not the only one at this booth who's gay, Karen."

What a bizarre, rococo way to say that! What a relief to hear that! What the hell was going on inside her right now? Was she going to puke? She thought she might puke.

"You'd better not be putting me on, girl. You don't do that to someone."

Karen said, "I'm not putting you on, Enid."

Enid bit her lip. "Jesus God."

"I guess the question is, what next?"

"I don't know, Karen. I don't have a clue." She paused. "You know you're beautiful, right?"

"I don't know any such thing," Karen replied, self-consciously tucking a lock of hair behind her ear. "But it's awfully kind of you to say."

Enid suddenly, jerkily, reached across the table and touched Karen's hand. More jolts of electricity, jumping from Enid to Karen and flowing up her arm. Sometimes Carolyn had touched her hand but it was never like this. Carolyn wouldn't even attempt anything behind touching hands for another couple years. "It's the God's honest," Enid said. "I don't ... I'm very new at this and I don't always know what I'm doing."

"You think you're new at this?" Karen laughed, then stopped suddenly, realizing that the laugh hadn't been forced. Everything in her body was either on fire or on pins and needles; how could she possibly be in any way at *ease*? "I just came out this year. My Dad doesn't even know."

"Your Dad," Enid said, looking around, troubled. "Do you still live with him?" she asked, taking her hand away.

There was a pitfall here, one that Karen could only guess the shape of. "Yes, but..."

"But it must be tough to not find work after college and have to stay in your old house."

Karen opened her mouth to say the dumbest thing – maybe that college was still years away, Enid, I go to school with your *daughter* – and then closed it again. "It is tough," was all she said.

"I see you come in here sometimes. You remind me a little of me back when. Burger City's been here forever, you know. I guess it'll always be here. I guess maybe I will be, too."

She paused, then slowly reached her hand out again. "I don't want to make a mistake by you, girl."

Squeezing Enid's hand and wondering where the confidence was coming from, she said, "I know how to make my own decisions, Enid."

"Sure, but are they the right ones?"

Enid looked to the door, as if expecting a tinkle of chimes at just that minute. Stuff like that didn't happen in real life, only in movies and books. You are rarely, if ever, saved by the bell. But she stood up anyway, and grabbed a napkin from the dispenser, scribbling something on it with her waitress' pen. "I live here. I'm off at seven. Home by seven thirty. Can we talk more then?"

Karen looked down at the napkin. Enid Geary lived in Lawton, one of the poorer neighborhoods. Sometimes the kids she knew called it Laterville, maybe because it was one of those areas of OKC that got tacked on during the city's growth sprawl in the 60s. Opposite of the Sooners, who got here early. Or maybe because it just sounded like a doomy word. Laterville, land of potholes and low-income housing and schools you wouldn't want your daughter going to. That's where Karen would be going tonight at seven thirty.

Three miles separated her house and the first sizzling, popping arc-sodium streetlight marking the outer edge of Laterville, but to Karen Luck it might have been another world. She would doubt her memory later; what her mind conjured up when she thought of Laterville was damp, Dickensian streets where smog hung low in the air and rats the size of small cats ran the streets. But her memory was far from faulty. If anything, she was attempting to put a writer's romantic sheen on everything. But there was little romantic about Laterville.

The bus dropped her off three blocks from Enid Geary's apartment. She passed that first streetlight just as it turned on, the daylight giving up its last gasp with a sigh of relief. The light's stuttering glow cast capering epileptic shadows against the aging brick edifices of the buildings towering around her. Sounds permeated the air like threats: cats hissing in some alley, a man screaming at a woman named Doris – *I swear to God, Doris! I swear to fuckin God, Doris!* – and

Karen was sure he was also crying when he screamed it, someone with their stereo up too loud, playing a song from twenty years ago, something bombastic and comforting and Karen guessed they probably needed it.

Karen wanted to move her purse inside her jacket, but didn't want to stop on the street long enough to take her jacket off and put it back on. Worse, she was feeling a little klutzy, and it wasn't just the uneven sidewalks with the canyon cracks running through them. Right before she left the house that night, she swapped her pink Chuck Taylor sneakers for one of her three pairs of high heels. She hated high heels, but could admit to herself they had a way of showing off her calf muscles. Plus, she was already wearing a fairly showy skirt – not quite a miniskirt – and a peasant top that showed the top of what little cleavage she had. Karen knew she wasn't ugly ... well, okay, *usually* she knew. But she also knew she wasn't the beautiful Enid Geary had said she was earlier that day. Plus, maybe Enid had to say stuff like that to customers. Oh, you're so handsome, you're so beautiful. When you live on tips, you do what you can, especially for a girl whose parents were rich. Whose *parent* was rich.

Still, making herself a little more girly, a little more exciting wasn't going to hurt anything, so the clothes went on and the shoes went on and she'd spent a little more time at the makeup mirror than usual. She could have called a cab but she'd heard stories that some cabs wouldn't go to Laterville and she didn't want the whole thing to get weird. It was easy enough to take a bus to the mall and then take another bus out to where Enid lived. Besides, she could listen to her Discman and take some deep breaths and think about what might happen, until that got too anxious and then she would just focus on the music. Concrete Blonde mostly but she had Ani DiFranco and Kenny Rogers and Billy Joel CDs in her purse. If she got mugged out here – holy shit, she could actually get mugged out here – the guys would make away with a small CD collection they would never be able to make sense of. Was this girl crazy or just eclectic?

She heard a murmur of voices to her left. A group of kids her age were sitting on the crumbling steps of an old brownstone. They stopped talking when she looked at them. Slowly, they watched her walk past, her heels click-clacking on the sidewalk, uneven and skittering. Why the hell did she wear these? She hated these. Why did she even own these? Cynthia bought them for her for "special occasions." She—

"Hey baby!" a voice called out. Not from on the stoop with the kids. Further away. She couldn't see who said it. "How much, honey?"

Then she did see him: a tall, lanky guy with slicked-back hair leaning against a rotting phone pole. He was chewing gum loudly, deliberately. A foot above him, two sneakers tied together dangled from the wire in the breeze. The position of the nearby streetlight – not quite as flickering as the one nearer the bus stop – threw muddy shadows over him, bisecting the guy's face diagonally. Karen could only see one brown eye peeking out from a thick eyebrow; it crawled over her like a rat over a fatty piece of discarded meat.

"I'm not for sale," she somehow managed, her knees feeling weak as her feet tried to pick up speed. *Keep moving, Karen, keep the fuck moving.*

"Could've fooled me," he chuckled, and blew a bubble. It popped almost at once, startling her so much she almost fell over. Her mind insisted that none of this was really bad, people actually *lived* here, this wasn't a movie where everything was menacing and bad. People *lived* here, and if people lived here and came home after work every day, or school, there were certain ways that people lived, that people behaved. They weren't all animals. You don't just go into a neighborhood *in your city* and suddenly people are rapists and murderers or whatever.

He thought I was a prostitute, Karen thought. *And I think it wouldn't really matter to him if I was willing or not. Jesus Christ, Karen, what are you doing here?*

She tried to conjure up Enid's face, the heart-pounding excitement of sitting across the booth from her and pretending she was older, pretending she wasn't in the same grade as Enid's daughter. All that seemed so long ago, in the daylight.

"Hey girl," another voice said from the recesses of an alley. "What you looking for?"

"I'm not for sale," she repeated, and the voice – disembodied and chuckling wetly – said, "I wasn't askin if you wanted to sell. I was askin if you wanted to *buy*."

"My Mom's calling me." Karen felt on the verge of tears, every extremity shaking, her stomach churning and burning.

"Better get home then," the voice said, and even though she couldn't see him, she got the sense that the man stepped back deeper into the shadows. *Does he live there? Is that alley his home? Where am I? Where the hell*

And then her thoughts cut off neatly as a set of double doors flew open across the street and a man wearing white pants and a white shirt stepped out. He was large, his gut rounding out in front of him, hefty and solid. His clothes were covered in blood. He wore a white hat cocked back against his fleshy head. His brown eyes

(murderer's eyes, Karen, murderer's eyes)

found her and seemed to mark her. A cleaver, its blade winking in the streetlight, depended from his fist. More blood dripped from the blade, making a small maroon puddle on the ground below. The meaty man opened his mouth and Karen saw that several of his small teeth were missing. "Hey, what you lookin at?"

Too terrified to scream, Karen simply gasped in air and broke into a run. Streetlights, seemingly triggered by her movement, came to nictitating life as she passed, casting cataract glows against the crumbling landscape. Her high heels click-clacked, click-clacked, as if she were trying to signal the nightmares upon her. She struggled to stay upright, terrified of losing her balance and falling, knowing that the man with the cleaver was back there, knowing he was chasing her through these dark streets, knowing that she was an interloper and that no one would ever think to look for her here. Horror stole into her like a secret, then darted solidly inside her, pinballing and caroming through her hollow places. By the time she reached Enid Geary's apartment building, she heard – actually heard – the giant mere steps behind her, nightmare incarnate, scraping his warped and bloody cleaver against the side of the building, sharpening the blade, making it hungry for the flesh of a girl.

She barely had time to perceive the name GEARY at the side of the doorbell before she jammed her thumb down, an atonal, blasting buzz roaring from the door into the night. A sheen of arctic sweat broke out all over Karen's body; she'd been expecting a voice through the speaker just above the door buzzers. In the extremity of her terror, she hadn't noticed that the speaker had been pretty well wrecked, the wire mesh bashed in and a few wires, like lost worms, poking out and scenting the fetid air. She'd been fully ready to start screaming at the speaker; this deviation paralyzed her. She could still hear the giant in the bloody whites scraping up the street, slowly, deliberately, knowing that she would never make it inside before he could take her. For the first time since high school, she wished Henry Dear was with her, a big strong man who could physically fight off the thing coming toward her, who could stand in her stead while she made her escape. Even in her paroxysm, she hated herself for thinking these things, not only for wanting to rely on a man like that, like she was some weak and helpless thing, but also for wanting to use

Henry like that, for wanting to make him sacrifice himself for her. Maybe she'd done enough of that already.

Only as the sound faded away did she realize that she'd missed her escape.

Karen, you're standing here in your short skirt and high heels and bloodred lipstick and thinking about how bad you feel and are and maybe those are valid things to explore but right now a maniac with a cleaver is coming after you and YOU DIDN'T DO ANYTHING TO SAVE YOURSELF.

With that, her paralysis broke and she jammed a thumb down on the Geary doorbell again and held it. Before she let go, that deep, almost insectile buzz resounded back and now she did yank the door open and pulled it closed behind her. As she did, she swung back and looked into the street. It was empty. No maniac with a cleaver. No nothing. From somewhere, two dogs got into a brief barking argument, then fell silent. Then it was just the streetlights.

On numb legs, Karen climbed the stairs, last carpeted and cleaned in the 1970s. The smell in here was like boiled dinner and Beef-a-Roni had been thrown against the dark wallpaper and had been left to rot. Her only thought was, *this is where Hartford lived? And she's* mad *that her mother found a way for her not to be?* The door on the second floor swung inward and there was Enid Geary, wearing a pink gingham dress and an unreadable expression on her face. Karen bolted up the rest of the stairs and hurled herself against Ms. Geary, wrapping her arms around her so tightly that she could feel the muscles in her back straining. Only then did she feel the terror of the neighborhood flow out of her, and involuntary shakes wracked her whole body. Hated tears sprung to her eyes and soaked into the fabric of Ms. Geary's dress. This is not how it was supposed to go. This wasn't how it was supposed to go at all.

But she let herself cry anyway, and soon enough, Ms. Geary shut the door behind them with her foot, closing out the rest of the world, and soon enough, Ms. Geary wrapped her arms around her, and Karen felt lost and found at the same time.

"That's Bob," she said eventually, as they sat across from one another in the Gearys' living room. "Bob the Butcher. He's a real butcher. Actually, he supplies a lot of meat to Burger City. Isn't that something?"

Karen wouldn't be deterred by prosaic reality. "I thought he was going to kill me. He *looked* like he was going to kill me."

"Who'd want to kill someone pretty as you?" Ms. Geary asked. Karen blushed and felt part of her start to float. The adrenaline had sputtered out of her as she sat here drinking pops and having cookies at Ms. Geary's splintered little coffee table. Karen noticed that both the sodas and the cookies were the Sureway store brand. Yesterday, Haveline Academy had served smothered pork chops with blanched green beans and a wedge of cheesecake for dessert, and that was *lunch*. Ms. Geary leaned closer and put her hand on Karen's leg. "But it's going to be late when you leave. I'll make sure to drive you home."

Karen looked up sharply, "Well, I don't want to leave *yet.*"

"Oh. No, I didn't mean now. I just…" Ms. Geary broke off. Without her waitress uniform, she looked strikingly different. Usually at Burger City, her hair was up; now it was relaxed and down and cascading over her shoulders. She wore no makeup, a stark contrast to the way she usually looked at work, with her ruby-red lips and blue eye shadow. Unadorned, her face maybe looked a little older … but that actually served to enhance her features, somehow. Her cat glasses didn't look as much of an affect now, part of a studied look. They just looked like glasses someone's mom would wear to read a book. Maybe that was why she'd begun thinking about her as Ms. Geary instead of Enid. Maybe that was why she was calling her that in her head. That dress, washed-out pink gingham, sat more comfortably against her pale skin than the fluorescent-yellow uniform they made employees wear at Burger City – red shirts for men, yellow dresses for women. To reflect ketchup and mustard, maybe, Karen mused silently, while her eyes kept drifting to the woman's knees protruding from just under the hem of that dress.

"I'm so new at this, Karen," Ms. Geary said, looking nakedly at her. "And I'm scared, a little."

"I'm scared a lot," Karen said.

"I can drive you home right now. Right now. I should drive you home right now."

Karen swallowed but her throat was dry. "Please don't."

"Okay." A pause. "I didn't want to."

Karen moved over to the couch, but found herself pressed to the arm at the extreme opposite side, where a tired afghan had been draped. "I've had sex," Karen blurted, grabbing her can of pop and guzzling. "With men. With *a* man. With ... he was dressed like a girl, though. I kept thinking he was a girl."

"Oh."

Hiccupping once, twice, Karen put the can of pop down and looked back down at Ms. Geary's knees again. They were perfect. Unblemished. No cuts, no bruises, no scars. The dresses at the diner were short-sleeved but long-hemmed: you could see almost all the waitress' arms but only the calves of their legs. These knees were private. Hidden. Karen very badly wanted to reach out and touch one. "But I didn't want him to be a girl, not really."

"No?"

"I wanted him to be a woman, I think. A woman ... like you."

Ms. Geary reached out tentatively and touched Karen's fingers. A dull charge of electricity jumped from the waitress into Karen's hand and Karen dragged her eyes up to look into Ms. Geary's face. Blue, watery eyes looked back through those cat glasses, slightly magnified, seeing everything clearly. "Are you sure you haven't done this before?" A small, wistful smile touched the corners of Ms. Geary's lips.

"You've had sex," Karen said.

"Yes."

"With men ... *and* women?"

"Yes. The latter only recently. I don't think my daughter approves."

There was a bare second in which Karen almost blurted something out, something about how Hartford *wanted* to approve but she didn't know how to. But that would have been a mistake, and Karen didn't want to make any mistakes, not now. Her heart thundered in her chest. Was it like this with Henry? The first time, maybe? Or the first time she got him to wear makeup?

No. Only the time with the giant dildo. And she'd done it because she wanted him to say no. When he didn't, it was even more exciting. Shameful, but more exciting. Now she wanted Ms. Geary to say yes. To what? She didn't entirely know.

"What's it like?" Karen asked instead. "What's the difference, I mean?"

"Not much, at first," Ms. Geary said, and she slid over to the other end of the couch. All internal thought ceased. She was as tense and edgy as she'd been outside Ms. Geary's apartment house door, but this time she didn't mind. This time, she wanted to be caught. "A lot of the sensations are the same. Hands are similar. Mouths are similar. Men have rougher tongues, though."

"Women's aren't rough?"

"Not that I've noticed." Then Ms. Geary's hand was on her leg and her lips were on Karen's. When Karen's lips parted, she discovered Ms. Geary was telling the absolute truth. Women's tongues were softer.

This was not a harbinger of the women Karen Luck would meet over her long experience. Before Maura, even the one-night stands were long negotiations; food or drinks or coffee were a must first, getting to know one another, getting to the core of the real person before getting to the carnal. By the time she was twenty-seven, Karen had heard pretty much every coming-out story in the greater Los Angeles area. Doubtless there were women out there – gay and straight and otherwise – able to change sexual partners as often as they brushed their teeth, but Karen had never had much luck with what Maura called cunnilingus roulette. That first time with Ms. Geary had been a false precursor. But what a false precursor!

When Ms. Geary stood and reached her hand out, Karen felt everything inside her tremble. It wasn't fear and it wasn't excitement; it was somewhere between those two, pushing and pulling inside her in an emotional game of tug-of-war. Karen took that hand and followed Ms. Geary to her bedroom, which was small and shabby, the carpet a dirty-champagne color and the ceiling marred with thin hairline cracks; a rust-colored water stain spread out from one of these like a tumor. Ms. Geary's hand was on her face, gently turning away from the ceiling and toward her face. For the first time, Karen noticed that there was a stain on the front of Ms. Geary's gingham dress, just between her breasts. Smears of black and red smudged across the pink, and Karen realized that *she* had put that stain there, when she had cried against Ms. Geary's chest in fear and dislocation. Ms. Geary had held her until she'd felt safe, and she realized that she felt safe now. Ms. Geary would not hurt her.

"All I want is for you to feel good," Ms. Geary said quietly. There was a forlorn look in her eyes. Karen wondered what she was thinking about.

Then she was lying across Ms. Geary's small bed. It sagged in the middle and she wondered distantly if Ms. Geary had a bad back because of it. Her clothes were on the floor and so were Ms. Geary's, and that tremulous butterfly of thrill was again loose inside her. Then Ms. Geary was inside her, only slightly, only barely, her face gently brushing against Karen's downy thatch of pubic hair, her tongue taking long, slow dips. In bed alone or with Henry, Karen had always jabbed her fingers and toys deep within herself, like she saw girls do in the porn movies that Henry's dad never locked up. Sometimes she had orgasms that way, but not always, and almost never the way Henry seemed to, seeming to buck and explode with his whole body. Ms. Geary knew secrets about Karen's body that Karen had never even suspected. Just those tiny flicks of her tongue sent shivers down Karen's spine, chilling it, galvanizing it, turning it to jelly. Oh wow. Oh wow.

At some point later, Ms. Geary came up for air, kissing her again, and Karen could taste herself on Ms. Geary's tongue. The intimacy of that taste was almost overwhelming. Tears sprung to her eyes and she felt like crying, even though she had never felt less sad in her life. *It's too much*, she thought. *This is too much. I can't feel this good because if I do, I won't know how to live without it.*

"Do you want to try me?" Ms. Geary asked, placing one hand on Karen's breast. She hoped that the waitress wouldn't suddenly decide to pinch her nipples. That was Henry's thing, she wanted to explain, but this woman had no idea who Henry was. She needn't have worried, anyway; Ms. Geary just ran the tip of her finger lazily across Karen's aureole and nipple, tracing it, her finger as gentle and hesitant as her tongue had been. It was the exact opposite of what sex with Henry had been like: instead of those hard gestures, bigger and and more violent each time, everything with Ms. Geary was a study in economy. The smallest actions yielding the best results. Karen's head spun.

"Yes," she said, meaning I don't know, meaning what if I do it wrong, meaning I'm a little scared, and moved down to the end of the bed as Ms. Geary stretched out. She wanted to stop herself a moment and simply stare, simply watch, simply look. A few hours ago, this woman, waitress, mother, was wearing a uniform that she had to stuff herself into every day because that's how jobs work, and now here she was, naked, lying on a bed, and not worried that Karen could see her. Ms.

Geary's breasts, so much larger than her own, hung down at her sides at opposing diagonals. Karen wanted to trace the geometry of them with her finger. Maybe her tongue. Would she *let* Karen touch her breasts with her tongue? If she was going to let her put her face *down there*, it stood to reason … but the idea still made Karen flash red. When you're little, you call what's in your pants your *privates*, but now with Ms. Geary stretched out, Karen realized that *all* of it was private. You hide *everything* when you're a grownup. Except for now; except for right now.

Two things occurred to Karen Luck in rapid succession: one, that Ms. Geary was naked every single day at least once or twice. She took showers during the day, maybe in the morning, washing her body, her fingers trailing over the open stretch of skin between her breasts and navel, the curve of her belly sensitive to the soap and the warm water. Karen invented her shower: cracked porcelain, chipped tiles, a shower curtain with torn rings and with dried-on soap scum skirting the bottom. An objectively filthy place and yet she got clean there, naked and clean.

The second thing that occurred to her was that Henry's Mom, Skylark Dear, was probably just as naked, just as often. Of course, Karen had thought about Skylark Dear more often than almost any grown woman over the course of her entire life, beyond Cynthia Auburn and maybe even succeeding her own mother. But now, all at once, she had context. If she closed her eyes right now, this woman in this bed could actually *be* Mrs. Dear. Henry had been a fairly effective simulacrum, but all you had to do was open your eyes or touch his body or even hear the sounds he made to know he was a man. No matter how well you played pretend, you couldn't get around that fact.

Well, she had gotten around it now, and for a moment, she allowed herself a brief vision of Skylark Dear in her own shower. The contrast between grime and beauty with Ms. Geary was intoxicating, but the idea of Mrs. Dear in her giant shower at home, the one with the water jets that came from the top and the sides because that was something rich people could have. The pristine cream-colored shower, those expertly manicured fingernails – red, almost always – and the soap, gliding over her ivory skin. When she stepped out of the shower onto the mat, the way her bare foot would crush the deep-pile fabric. Had Karen ever seen Mrs. Dear barefoot? She must have. The Dears had a pool, didn't they? Also, what happened when the woman traveled? She traveled sometimes and stayed in hotels. What was it like when she went to business meetings in her smart suit and high heels and then back in the hotel, tired, worn out, slowly removing her clothes and putting them on the chair, maybe folding them, and then she would go into an unfamiliar shower and she would be *naked*, okay, that was the thing, Mrs. Skylark Dear, wife of Welton who didn't know the treasure he had, and *she* knew, *Karen Luck* knew, and all it would take was to show her, just *show* her, and thinking these things, Karen dipped her head and opened her mouth and discovered a new type of paradise.

Later, on the ride home, Ms. Geary said, "Are you hungry? Do you want to grab some food? Anything but burgers."

Karen smiled a little and nodded. "There's a Kentucky Fried Chicken up here. We can do drive-through."

"Why don't we go in? We didn't have much of a chance to talk afterward."

"Okay."

Guiltily, Karen shut the car door behind her, trailing a little. Somehow, Ms. Geary knew that she'd been thinking about someone else – someone else's mom – while she did what she did. And had she been good at what she'd done? Karen couldn't tell. Ms. Geary had assured her that her performance had been mind-blowing – that was the word she kept using, mind-blowing – but Karen wondered. And if she really *had* been mind-blowing, was that because her own mind had been all over Mrs. Dear?

They ordered their chicken – Karen desperate to pay for the two of them but holding her tongue – and sat across from one another at a small table in the corner. Ms. Geary looked at her box, then placed her hands palm-down on the table and said, "I wonder if I made a mistake."

Startled, Karen dropped her drumstick and stared at the woman. In this harsh light, she could see the bags under the woman's eyes, the slight wattle under her chin, the way the lines around her mouth indicated more frowns than laughs. All of these were exciting to Karen; she could single out any of these apparent flaws and make them assets, because all of them added up to Enid Geary, who was objectively beautiful. Karen said, "What did I do wrong?"

Before she could even finish her sentence, Ms. Geary shook her head. "You didn't. You're wonderful, Karen. You..." The waitress cut herself off and looked around, as if the words were somewhere in the scent of fried chicken and mashed potatoes with gravy. "I kept thinking that I was helping you, you know. To figure out what this was before you spent so long wondering. I was your age when I knew I liked girls, Karen. And then I got married to Holt Geary before I was even out of high school because you were supposed to do that. Everyone thinks we got married because I was pregnant, but it wasn't so. I was saving myself for marriage. Back then, I didn't have any idea what saving myself meant."

Not Ms. Geary, then. *Mrs.* Geary. Now why should that, something as innocuous as a syllable, send the excitement roaring back into Karen's stomach again? The things she liked, the visual things like eyes and neck and figure, were all well and good; but it was the other stuff, the intangibles, that sent Karen into her minor frenzies. God, she needed to be listening to what she said. What Mrs. Geary said. Oh God.

"Then he left," Mrs. Geary said simply. "Up and left. Me seven months pregnant and living in the same place I'm living in now. So it was easy enough to push all the stuff I was feeling deep down inside me. I had a baby to deal with, and bills, and everything that comes with being broke and alone in a place like this. You might have noticed that OKC might be a wonderful place to live, but it's not exactly a bastion of progressive thought."

Bastion, Karen thought, savoring the word. She'd read it but never heard it aloud. She bet if she'd heard it first from her father or even Cynthia, it would have seemed ordinary or even boring, but in Mrs. Geary's mouth, it seemed so exotic.

Because she's poor, Karen? her mind grunted. *Maybe don't be an asshole, huh?*

If Mrs. Geary noticed her whole face turning bright scarlet, she didn't say anything. "I had noticed, kind of," Karen said, although this was a bit of a lie. She'd lived in a big house and so had her best friend; Henry had Nintendo and she had an electric typewriter. She went to a private school and until recently had made her best friend dress up like a girl while she put things in his butt. All of these things, she realized on a vague level, had shielded her from the OKC that Mrs. Geary was talking about. When you were a lesbian as a rich person's daughter, it could be shrugged off. When you were a poor lesbian with a daughter of your own, she could be taken away.

All at once, the *exotic* word seemed so rapturously cruel that she reddened even more.

"I'm thirty-four, Karen. I'm too old to be finally doing something I've wanted my whole life. Something I didn't let myself do. Because I was ashamed. And I don't want you to be ashamed. I don't want you feeling like you're a bad person for wanting what you want. I thought I could save you from that."

"I don't feel ashamed about what we did," Karen said.

"But I kind of do. Not because of you." Mrs. Geary hesitated. "Well, yes, because of you. You're not in college, are you?"

"No," Karen admitted.

"See, I knew that. Of course I did. I knew everything. Do you think my daughter could go to school with Gary Luck's daughter and not tell me about it?" Karen opened her mouth to speak and Mrs. Geary raised a hand. "I took advantage of you, I think."

Karen took a deep breath. "You didn't, though. I wanted it just as much as you did. And I'm so happy."

"Are you?"

"Yeah! I mean you're so pretty and it was really fun." *Aren't you a writer, Karen?* Oh shut up. "What I mean is, if that was you taking advantage of me, I want you to do it again."

Mrs. Geary offered a tight smile. Were those the wrong words? Karen had meant them funny and maybe a little sexy, but maybe saying "taking advantage" again had been dumb. Things had been easier when they weren't talking, when they were just in Mrs. Geary's bed and naked and not having to say much of anything.

"I might forgive myself for once," Mrs. Geary said. "A second time would be pushing it."

Later, Karen would hate herself just a little for thinking about Skylark Dear in this moment, the way Henry's mom might wash herself and then step barefoot and naked into her bedroom. The king-sized bed was probably lonely a lot, what with Welton always away, and what a thought to lie down with her in that bed, to run her fingers along Mrs. Dear's exposed body, to taste her as she had tasted Mrs. Geary, winter warmth and spring honeysuckle. Then Karen forced the thought away and instead pictured Mrs. Geary in *her* shower, the one in her bathroom at home. How insane would it be to have Mrs. Geary in her own house, in *her* shower ... in *her* bed? The thought was too bizarre to contemplate, but she did contemplate it. Some day when she could be sure neither her father nor Cynthia would be home. She could sneak Mrs. Geary in through the back, out of view of the Dears next door. And then this women – *this* woman – would be in her house, her presence a beautiful intrusion, and then on her bed and in her room and maybe Mrs. Geary would even like to read a short story of hers and tell her if she liked it. Wouldn't that be nice? Maybe she could even read Karen's stories while the two of them were having sex. It was the word more than the thought that disrupted Karen's train of thought. She'd been thinking in the abstract, and they were talking around it, but the truth of it boiled down to seven little words she hadn't yet fully processed:

I just had sex with a woman.

"But there's nothing to forgive," Karen said. "Remember how scared I was when I got to your apartment? Well that stopped the second I was inside. You made me feel safe, and sure in myself and what we were doing." Was that a speech? Had it come off like a speech?

"Safe," Mrs. Geary said, and her eyes met Karen's. "Sure. Honey, there ain't no sure things in this whole world. Take it from someone who knows it firsthand."

"It doesn't have to be sure forever," Karen told her. "Maybe just for a little while."

"Karen," Mrs. Geary said, then stopped. She didn't speak for a long time. Then she said, "I've never gotten fully out of thinking I was probably a bad person for liking girls. And now you. Karen, you're half my age."

More than, Karen thought. "I think you're a good person. I think the way you got Hartford into our school was good. And I think what we did was good. Don't you?"

Mrs. Geary offered her a small smile. "I wondered if you would say her name. Come on, Karen, let me drive you home."

She got back into Mrs. Geary's beat-up old Buick, and tried to think about nothing at all as the lights of OKC sped past her. She waved as the car sped away, and when she went inside, all she could hear was the tappa-tappa-tappa of fingers on keys. Karen couldn't remember if her Dad was her Mom right now or not. Either way, she couldn't talk to him. Not when he was writing.

Karen Luck paused outside Cynthia's room for a very long time, wanting to knock, wanting to tell her everything. She would understand. She would try to help. More than any other person on this planet, Cynthia Auburn had the unique skills to talk Karen through right now.

But it occurred to Karen that she didn't want someone from this planet. She wanted her mother. She wanted to hold her mom and be held, and to cry a little, not for what she'd done but for what she'd likely lost. She wanted to be held and rocked to sleep and to not have the memory of her mother being blown away, blown away.

Thinking these things, she took her tears into her own bedroom, where Mrs. Geary would never lie, and cried into her pillow until she fell asleep.

Chapter 9: I Went

"So what happened to Enid?" Karen asked after a long silence. Obviously she'd left out everything about Henry's Mom, but she wondered, staring into her coffee cup, if he hadn't gleaned some of it anyway. Could that have happened only six years ago? Her first time, only six *years* ago? In the meantime, she'd graduated high school and college, dated and broke up with Cynthia Auburn, published a novel, wrote two more, moved to Los Angeles, met Maura, and fell in love. It seemed like an awful lot to pack into six years.

"I honestly don't know," Henry said. "I didn't notice her like you did. Also, I haven't really come to Burger City a lot since you've been gone."

Karen tried to take her eyes off him and couldn't. He was older, this Henry. Dumb thing to think, sure, they were both older ... but Henry *felt* older. There were no wrinkles on his face, his hairline wasn't receding, he didn't even have gray up on top. But something had gotten inside him and aged him beyond the twenty-three he was. Was it Oklahoma City, staying here while she went off to other worlds and other climates? Was it the fact that he still lived in the house where he grew up? Was it her? Was Henry Dear, after all this time, still in love with her? But that was absurd, wasn't it? You don't stay in love with the person from high school who couldn't love you back. Eventually you moved on.

"So," she said abruptly, "are you seeing anyone?"

Henry gave her a small smile. "Yeah. On and off. Right now off."

"What's her name?"

"Thomas." Karen leaned in and Henry grinned. "I'm not dating a guy. That's a girl's name."

"Oh."

Henry sipped his pop and said, "You know, I've been writing, too."

She surprised herself by breaking into an enormous grin. Excitement surged in her. Her story had drained her, and the question of where Enid went after Karen left town dangled over the booth above them like a scythe on a pendulum. Did she *want* to know where Enid was? What would she possibly say to her? Now all those questions vanished, as did all other Henry questions. "Have you? That's awesome! What have you been writing?"

Henry said, "A few short stories. I don't know, a couple of novels."

Karen's eyes went wide. "A *couple* of *novels*?" Fireworks exploded in her mind. She thought, *my God, if he'd been writing when we were having sex, maybe I wouldn't be gay now*. Unable to help a titter of laughter, she reached across the table and grabbed one of his hands. "Henry, have you shown them to anyone?"

"Your Dad," Henry told her. His face had gone brick red. "He liked them, I guess. He's probably just being nice, though. Nothing's going to be like his writing. You know, except your writing."

"Oh, my writing won't ever be as good as his."

She was distracted enough by this that she didn't notice Henry's eyes lock on Karen's hand lying over his; then his eyes closed and he thought, *it could be like this; I know it can't, but it could*.

"You're wrong about that, Karen. It's better. Already it's better. When you used to give me your short stories? I mean, 'Their Tiny Knuckles' kept me awake for two nights. You don't just pretend to have that kind of talent."

"That's very kind of you," she said; it was safe not to believe Henry because even if he wasn't in love with her now, he'd been very much in love with her when he read her juvenilia. She could have written a subliterate story with wooden characters and the scenes in an arbitrary order and he would have declared her the new Melville. What a fucked-up world when you couldn't trust the word of the people who liked you the most. She smiled, "A word of advice: don't write horror stories if you want to go into strange neighborhoods after dark. That butcher guy is the thing that kept me awake for two nights." Or, you know, off and on for the rest of my life.

Long silence followed this and Karen tried to force the image of Bob the Butcher out of her mind. It went, but reluctantly. The best thing you could say about the man in white was that he had eclipsed the nightmares of the tornado that had plagued her when she was very small. An enemy with a face was better than one without; if you could look it in the eye, you could defeat it. In theory. Probably.

She shook this off as thoroughly as possible. "What's your stuff about?" she asked.

Henry shrugged and looked down into his milkshake. "I don't know. Boys and girls and the stuff they do. They're sort of love stories but they're not really romances."

"Well, can I read them?"

Now he was very obviously refusing to look at her. "Not at this stage, I don't think they're really ready for … um, for your eye just yet."

Oh my God, Karen Luck thought, *they're about me.* But about that, she was wrong. They weren't *about* her. They were *by* her. Everything but the first and last chapter. And he knew that if Karen read his books, she would understand that immediately. Because she was brilliant, she would be able to intuit the method by which he'd written his novels, and she would get furious with him, and maybe she'd start screaming, and then she'd be out of his life forever. He could stand her not loving him the way he loved her – still, always – but he couldn't stand the idea that she could be out of his life forever ... especially if he was the one who had caused her to do it.

But Karen, who knew none of this, would not take no for an answer. "Do you remember all those times you sat across from me in this place and told me I *needed* to give you my new stories, even when *I* wasn't ready?"

"Yeah, and I remember you telling me no."

"And *I* remember you taking no for an answer. Almost always, that impulse is 100% right. About the stories, it was 100% wrong."

How much of their fairly recent past was Karen willfully forgetting, Henry wondered as he smiled sadly. 100% wrong didn't account for him sitting here, in maybe this very booth, begging her to read her latest stories, knowing he would be denied. Long before graduation night, he knew that they were never going to be together again, not sexually at least. But to be shut out of her mind, too, her creativity – the reality of that was almost too much to bear. And of course he'd had to bear it. When they were six, Karen had saved his life. When they were fourteen, she had changed it irrevocably. And two years later, she was almost entirely gone from his life. Karen might remember things a little differently, might remember her reluctance to share stories a playful sort of gambit, one he could have overcome with just a little bit more persistence. But she was 100% wrong.

None of which he would have ever told her, or accused her of. He knew she was going to force him to give her copies of his manuscripts, and he would drown in anxiety waiting for her proclamations. If she liked them, he would know he had a little talent. If she hated them, he would know he didn't. He wouldn't stop writing – nothing, not even Karen Luck, could make him give up writing at this point, and he ignored the small, distant, internal roar of triumph that came along with that knowledge – but he would never show it to another person. Not even Mr. Luck. His writing would be just for him, and for the version of Karen Luck he became when he wrote.

So it was with some trepidation that led her down the hallway toward his home writing studio an hour later. Karen had wandered his home for some time first, lost in let's remember. His old Nintendo had been swapped out for an N64 and he'd repainted his bedroom, but nothing much else had changed. This hallway remained all mahogany paneling and deep-pile wine-dark carpet. No windows looked to the outside. The darkness, so unlike the rest of the Dear house, was forbidding then and it was forbidding now. Karen ran a hand through her hair and tried not to think of the man in butcher whites, covered in blood.

"Where are your parents?" Karen asked, running her hand lightly on the wallpaper in the hallway, which was the same mid-century Googie print it had been when she used to come over every day. "I mean, I know your dad probably isn't..."

"Dad moved out," Henry said abruptly. He hadn't meant for it to come out so harshly, but thinking about Welton Luck had become something of a harsh endeavor. The last time he'd seen his father, he'd been screaming, and Thomas had been on the couch, sobbing convulsively, and on the TV, footage of the Alfred P. Murrah Federal Building crumbling into rubble played on and on, incessantly. "I don't *need you!*" he had screamed, his face inches from his father's. "I haven't needed you since I was ten!" And had he threatened to kill his father? The whole afternoon was such a haze, but he thought he had. He thought he had meant it.

"Oh. And your Mom?" A cocktail-party question, a wow-weather-is-weird question. But she felt her heart speed up just the same.

"Somewhere on business," he said. "And look, I know it's weird that I still live with my Mom. I like to say that *she* lives with *me*, actually. But she's got the whole downstairs and I have the whole upstairs and we share the kitchen, so I actually don't see her a whole lot."

"I don't think it's weird," Karen said. "I think when I head back to LA, I'm gonna take Dad to live with me."

Henry stopped dead in the hallway. All the breath had gone out of him. It felt like Karen had sucker-punched him in the gut. Everything in him went rigid. When he turned to her, he could almost hear the creak and moan of the tendons in his neck. "What are you going to do?"

"Well, he's having a rough time right now, and I think…"

"You can't take him," Henry told her, point blank. A deep and terrible part of him quailed at this; you didn't speak out against Karen Luck. Such things were just not done, not ever. But the rest of him didn't listen. "He belongs here. You can't take him away."

Karen stared at her old friend. There was a time, not so long ago, when Karen could say she felt a little hungry, and Henry would show up with a smorgasbord, curated specifically to her tastes. Hell, didn't he indicate less than an hour ago that he would never show her his writing? Now here they were, about to get his manuscripts. This tone was new. This stance was new. Karen didn't know what to say.

"Well," she blustered. "It would only be for a little while. Just until he feels okay again. And honestly, only if he says he wants to go."

"It's his house," Henry said, wanting badly to articulate what he really meant, knowing he couldn't.

Karen grinned, knowing it looked as false as it felt. "I'm not going to, like, drag him out of there, kicking and screaming.

I think, now that the last of the Eileen Luck books is done, he might want to spend some time with his family."

An inarticulate panic had begun to worm its way into Henry's heart. After that day in April two years ago, he didn't give a shit if he ever saw Welton Dear again in his life. But Mr. Luck, that was different. In this world, Henry knew, there were very few things you could count on. Your mom is often away and your dad is an atrocity; the love of your life realizes she's not compatible with you and your on-again, off-again girlfriend has been way more off again lately; you can't even count on yourself to write novels without the aid and assistance of the best writer in the world. Nothing's sure. Nothing stays. Except Gary Luck.

He's not yours to take, Henry thought. Then, immediately: *I won't forgive you, Karen. For everything else, but not this.*

"Speaking of family, where's your Mom? I haven't seen her in so long." Tension had built in this hallway so feverishly that it felt like the air before a major storm. She wanted to close her eyes and force the metaphors away, but they wouldn't go. There were good things here, but her nightmares were always closer in OKC: Bob the Butcher, screaming out of a doorway in the dark; the devouring cyclone that swallowed her mother whole. The look in Henry's eyes was like that cyclone, and she didn't know if it was going to swallow him ... or her.

"She's out," he said shortly, turning back to his studio door and swinging it open. After the oppressive darkness of the hallway, this was like stepping into the bright sunshine of Narnia through the dense wardrobe of coats. More, it was a room Karen didn't recognize at all; after planting herself deep in the situ of her past, this was comfortably brand-new. The walls were a light, honeysuckle blue; movie posters for *Back to the Future*, *Big Jet Planes*, and *Citizen Kane* adorned three of the walls. Midafternoon light poured in through a huge window with gauzy yellow curtains on the fourth wall; underneath the window, a squat bookshelf ran the length of the wall. She saw with no surprise that her whole family had been represented: those early Doreen Daley books kicked things off, then Dad's impressive run under his own name.

Then *The Absence of Sure Things, An Unexpected Island, No One Knows Where Sarah Goes*. The first and only hybrid work, *Chaos Logic* cozily nestled between *Sarah* and the first Eileen Luck novel wholly written by her dad, *Hannah's Window*. At the very end of the line, her own first novel, in pristine hardcover: *Nobody Under the Stars*. She thought, *I have a lot of catching up to do.*

"Good library," she said to Henry.

"Good teachers," he told her, settling into his writing chair and waking his computer up. "Sometimes if I'm stuck on a word or a phrase or something, I'll go to that shelf and pick something up off the shelf and read a few pages, just to get my head right again. That's not to say that I *copy* anything. There's just a lot of inspiration there. The three of you have this handle on style that I'm not sure I can ever really duplicate." Whatever tension had roiled the air in the hallway had suddenly dissipated – at least as far as Karen could tell. All she'd had to do was get him to talk about books and writing, specifically her *family's* books and writing. *And all along, I thought he was just* my *biggest fan*. She meant it to be funny and she forced herself to smile at it.

From a drawer in his desk, he pulled two large sheaves of paper, each wound around with a blue rubber band. "Which one do you want?" he asked, and Karen felt that odd hunger come back into her, that tripped-out excitement when she thought about Henry writing. Seeing these two manuscripts shot the point home to her: Henry Dear was a novelist. Not published. Not represented. But a novelist nonetheless. She wanted to grab those two manuscripts and sit on the floor right now and devour them both.

Karen plucked the manuscript from Henry's left hand and glanced down at the title: *Dance the Night Away*. "What's it about?" she asked him, running her finger over the title.

"Four hundred pages," he said, and when she looked up, he smiled. "I don't know what it's about. Men and women and stuff that happens to them."

She looked up from the title and locked eyes with Henry Dear. "I never wanted to hurt you, Henry."

"I know that, Karen." He chuckled, but there was no humor in it. "I never meant to hurt myself, but here we both are."

Only when she let out a long, slow breath did she realize she'd been holding it. "Can I take this?"

"If you promise to tell me what you think."

"I will. I'm not leaving right away. There's some stuff I have to get done here that I don't know if I can do in Los Angeles."

"I'm here," Henry said. "I'm always here. Always will be, I guess."

Her smile felt tight on her face, like plastic stretched too thin. She left his bright office and found herself back in that dark hallway. Claustrophobia threatened; it was too much like the night in here, too much like the sort of night a man in white could leap out at you, brandishing a cleaver and a will to do harm. She hurried along the hallway and even though she was wearing flats, she could feel the points of the high heels jabbing at her heels through the fabric of her shoes. By the time she got to the end of the hallway, she chanced a breath –

God, she was really finding ways to not breathe in this place – and that was when the door to the driveway opened, and Skylark Dear stepped inside.

"Oh!" she said, seeming caught off guard. "Well if it isn't Karen Luck, as I live and breathe. I knew you were in town and I was just about kicking myself for not having come round to say hello. How've you been?" The woman seemed out of breath and her eyes were not meeting Karen's, but Karen barely noticed.

It took every ounce of self-awareness not to drop Henry's manuscript to the floor, forgotten. A minute ago, it was somehow the most important thing in her life. Now it was such a distant second, she could barely see it in the rearview. Skylark Dear's hair had once been a golden yellow, the color of summer wheat. Now, lodes of white coursed through it, giving it more texture, more depth. Those eyes, always so deep blue and brilliant, seemed now to blaze with a new span of years, that sharp intelligence honed and shaped by whatever trials she had fought through. She wore a smart dark blue suit that complimented her eyes, and a short dress that complimented her legs. Once or twice or dozens of times in Los Angeles, she'd cast her mind back to Mrs. Dear and wondered if she could honestly be as beautiful in real life as she was in her memory. In all her private meanderings, she had never considered that Skylark Dear would *improve* on memory, that this woman getting older would be the best thing to happen to her.

"Oh," Karen said, forcing a grin she hoped seemed natural. "Oh, I'm good. I'm quite good. *So* good."

"You seem flustered. Let me get you a drink of water."

Karen thought: *just* be *my drink of water, Mrs. Dear* and dug her nails into the palms of her hand to keep from saying it out loud. "Oh no," she told this woman instead. "I really want to hang out and catch up and stuff, but my dad wanted me home for dinner."

Mrs. Dear hesitated a moment, then said, "Really? Now?"

"I think now. I mean, we didn't really nail down a time but I should get home. Besides" – she held up the pile of papers in her hand – "Henry gave me this to read."

"Oh!" Mrs. Dear shouted, maybe too loudly. "Which one of the two? I like them both but then again, I'm his mom. I think everything he does is brilliant. I wish he'd try harder to get published, though. He's up there in his office every *day* and spending hours just typing away, and I want to say, 'Kid, if you're spending *this* much time at it and you're not even *trying* to get published, what's the point.' Of course, he goes on about how it's its own reward, but I just don't know. What do you think?"

Karen, who could barely remember her own name at this point, glanced down and showed Mrs. Dear the manuscript. "Oh yeah, *Dance the Night Away*. He put some … you know, *racy* scenes in that one. They're well-written, but they're just – they're not what a mother wants to know what her son thinks about. But so well-written!"

Please kiss me, Karen thought. *All my life has led to this second with me in front of you and you in front of me, and all I've ever wanted was for you to kiss me and take me into bed and let me let you feel good. Doesn't that sound easy? Why does it have to be this hard?*

The thought passed through her mind in under a second. It resurfaced four years later, when she was in the middle of her fifth novel, the one that was going to be her most controversial ever. The one Cynthia would threaten to quit over. The one Maura couldn't abide. It would be called *Charlie's Mother* and when she wrote that scene, it would end differently. It would end the way it was supposed to.

Now, though, Karen only offered a polite giggle and said, "Well, I should get to reading! So nice to see you again, Mrs. Dear."

"Oh, for Pete's!" Mrs. Dear said, and touched her on the forearm. Chills shot through her, followed by a tense coil of heat, surging up from the base of her spine and detonating near her belly, sending shrapnel of excitement throughout the rest of her. "Call me Skylark. Or Sky. My closest friends call me Sky."

"Are we close friends, S-Sky?" The name stuttered out of her and she wanted to scream.

"Well." Suddenly, Skylark Dear seemed as flustered as she had when she'd first walked in. "I mean, of course. I've known you since you were itty-bitty, haven't I? And besides, any best friend of Henry's is a best friend of mine."

"Best friends," Karen said. "I'll take it."

Then she was outside the house and hurrying down the driveway and her house loomed next door, her dark bedroom window looking down on her like a sentinel's eye. Acknowledging her? Judging her? By the way, Karen, where was Maura today? By the way, Karen, have you even thought about Maura in the last few days?

She pushed these thoughts away and when she stepped through the front door, she heard someone set the phone in the kitchen back down on its cradle. "Dad?" she called.

He emerged from the kitchen into the living room as she put the manuscript down on the coffee table. It was re-emerging as the most important thing right now, a designation that she didn't quite understand. Her response to Henry's writing had been nearly Pavlovian. Would it have been the same if she found out Maura was writing novels? Or Cynthia? Or Skylark Dear? Karen didn't think so. It was something about Henry writing, specifically Henry. Suddenly, unbidden, an image of him running across that field when they were both six floated into her brain. Her mother had said to take care of one another. Had they done that? Maybe? For a little while, maybe? They'd escaped the cyclone together. That was part of it.

"Who was on the phone?" she asked.

"Nothing," he told her, smiling. "No one, I mean."

"Was it Cynthia?" Karen asked, then her heart sank. "Oh crap, was it Maura? Should I call her back?"

Dad's eyes suddenly brightened, as if a light had gone on at the back of his skull. "You know what, you *should* call Maura. Have you talked to her today?"

Was that an answer? "I haven't ... really called her in a few days. I'm letting her chill out a little."

"If that's what you think is right," he said.

She didn't think it was right. She also didn't want to call. Loving Maura was wonderful so much of the time. The sex was good, better than it had been with Cynthia. Maybe that had something to do with it not being with her father's ex-girlfriend; of course, that was just a guess. The way Maura laughed, the way she looked when she was reading. And she was a good actress. Not *great*, maybe, not like Laura Dern or Jodi Foster or Geena Davis, but *good*, and every time Karen saw her in a commercial, she sat, enrapt, marveling that someone she saw naked could be on the television.

But *wow*, did she have some problems. Not bad ones. Not insurmountable ones. And that wasn't to discount the fact that Karen also had problems. She knew that. She knew that Maura had to put up with her never sleeping in and coming to bed late and being sometimes emotionally unavailable when she was inside her fiction. But ... but the *shower* thing. Jesus, what the hell was the shower thing about? The last full night Maura had been here, she'd showered alone and then come out and they'd had *sex*, sex in the bed she'd slept in in high school, which was weird and a little unnerving but also cool. She'd slept with Henry in that bed, and then Cynthia, and neither of those had ever felt entirely right, entirely *good*. With Maura, it had been *great*, because with Maura, it usually was. But then was the whole shower thing. She'd *offered* to take one with her. Had been willing to stop writing for a few hours so that she could actually get in the shower with her girlfriend and make her happy in whatever weird way showering together made her happy.

That, however, wasn't good enough. If she *asked* to shower, it was basically like saying, *I don't want to shower with you unless you make me. Are you seriously going to make me?* Which wasn't what Karen had meant *at all*. She'd been willing. Into it, even. But then the shower had started running and she went to her manuscript and started doing edits and at some point, Maura came to bed and Karen didn't. And then next morning, Maura had been packed up and ready to head out.

"This isn't you," Maura said, in that tone that indicated how completely and totally it *was* her. "I should get back to Hollywood. I'm losing work and it's been fun to be here, but ... you know, this isn't my scene, really."

Karen had put her pen down and looked at her girlfriend. Her eyes were puffy and almost purple. Had she been crying or just not sleeping? "Is this about the shower,

Maura?" Not that she had a clue as to *what* it could be about the shower; it was just that with Maura, it usually was.

"I don't really ... that's not what's on my mind right now. You are here and you're working and you're helping your dad, and this is your past. Okay, and I'm having trouble feeling like I fit in with your past."

"Well, that's not the point, honey. You're my *future*. The fact that you're here refutes my past. At least the bad parts."

"And you don't see that that's the point." Maura smiled. "You don't really know what the bad parts are. You think you do, but being around you and your father this whole time, it's clear that what you say and what you believe are very different things."

Karen blinked. "Maura, I honestly don't—"

"You're working on your book while you're here, right? Your new book?"

Very slowly, Karen nodded. "Yeah. You knew that."

Maura's nod was quicker. "And what if I said let's take a day off of all that. Head downtown for awhile. Have you show me the sights of OKC. Maybe take me to a basketball game. Or that amusement park you keep telling me about."

Karen barked a laugh. "It's not like there's much to see here but urban sprawl and, you know, the site of the bombing. And you hate basketball."

Maura closed her eyes. "Okay, then. I'll be home when you get there."

Standing, shrugging, Karen said, "So ... what? You're leaving because I'm not giving you a tour of my hometown? Do you want to see the place where my mother died? Or the diner I used to go to with my last boyfriend?"

"You don't get it," Maura said, and sounded close to tears. "You *think* you do. It's actually kind of noble that you think you do. But you don't. So I'll see you at home."

So Maura took off, which sucked ... but was also kind of a relief, something she admitted to herself only after all the lights in the house were out, except for the one above her father's word processor. She'd spent the day reading *Dance the Night Away*, her first Henry Dear novel, and her brain was still trying to sort it out. Had the book been good? Hell, the book had been *great*. But it stuck inside her like warm taffy sticks to the fillings in your teeth. It felt somehow *familiar*. Not the *same*, not like he'd plagiarized something. But familiar. And the nagging question in her mind was: *why didn't I write this?* Karen had an idea that she *could* have written something like this. That if she'd sat down and really concentrated and honed her best instincts, *Dance the Night Away* could be a Karen Luck novel.

She put the last page down with tingling fingers and had immediately gone to her typewriter, which she'd lugged all the way from Los Angeles, along with the incomplete printout of *Where'd She Go?* How long until she was finished with this one? Three chapters? Four? She'd been dragging her feet in Los Angeles, hadn't she? She'd spent *years* on *Nobody Under the Stars*, and only a little shorter on *Up in the Air*. The *publication* of a novel should take years, maybe. Editing, rewrites, production, printing, all that – that could take years, maybe. But that first draft? That should be measured in terms of months. Mom – actual Mom – had spent no more than five months on each of her books before she died. Dad's books, the

Doreen Daley ones, his own, and the ones he'd written as Mom – none had taken longer than ten months, and that ten-monther had been an anomaly. The book, *The Girl in the Grove*, had topped out at over 250,000 words, his longest yet, and after finishing that one, he'd had that writer's pause for a couple months. By contrast, all Karen's books had been short – too short to spend the length of time she'd spent on them. What was holding her back? What was she afraid of?

Dance the Night Away had clarified all this; she knew that if Maura had been here, she wouldn't have been able to see what she so clearly could see now. She had to write faster. She had to write better. And she had to write *more*.

Karen stared at the green letters against that black background on her father's antique word processor. *I went.* Nothing less, but that didn't mean nothing *more*. Was it Michalangelo who said when he looked at a block of marble, he just carved out the stuff that didn't conform to the sculpture he had in mind? The other day, Karen had stared at her father's writer's block and seen nothing more than one small chip away. *I went.* Now, at 4:30 AM Central Time, she saw a lot more. She saw the sculpture inside the block.

I went downstairs for my first cup of coffee of the day. The elevator was still broken so I took the stairs. Before I could get out the front door, the woman in the mink coat came out of nowhere and grabbed me by the front of the T-shirt. "Mr. Bull?" *she asked, and the desperation in her face was easy to read.*

"Yeah," I said, and before I could ask any more questions, a bullet slammed through the front door glass, shattering the pane to pieces. The woman screamed and I threw her to the ground, covering her with my bulk. That was how I first met Ralinda Love. I never did get that cup of coffee.

Two paragraphs. That was all she had in her right now. It was enough. It was a foundation. Today, in order, she would finish her last edits on *Up in the Air*, get a few more pages written in *Where'd She Go?*, finish the edits on Dad/Mom's final novel, and return *Dance the Night Away* to Henry. He had a second finished novel and she wanted to take a look at that, too. It was going to be a big day ahead. A big week. A big month. And somewhere in there, she had to call Cynthia. There was a lot to talk about. Her brain exploded with the possibilities. She wasn't getting to sleep tonight. Right now, she didn't care if she ever got to sleep again.

Chapter 10: Bull in a China Shop

The elevator doors swept open and Karen stepped out, only to be faced with a sad-eyed woman holding a box. "Wrong floor," the woman said flatly. "Me too, I guess. Did I hit the up? Goddammit." Then she laughed ruefully, the expression on her face never changing. Uncertain, Karen stepped back into the elevator, almost tumbling ass over teakettle. She groaned inwardly. These heels were absurd. The fact that she was wearing them to a contract negotiation was even more absurd, but this meeting had to go perfectly, and things had a way of working out more perfectly with the Cynthia Auburn, Editor, if your heels were high and your calves were long. Did Henry know about Cynthia's thing for long legs? Is that why he said what he'd said? Karen shook her head. She had a couple of fairly precarious ultimatums in her attaché case, and she knew she was walking into Chanler & Cushing without a whole lot of leverage.

The door to the top floor opened and Florence at the front desk looked up and offered her warmest smile. "Well, if it isn't Karen Luck," she said.

"But it is." At this, Florence giggled. Karen had been making this joke with Florence ever since she was a child, and it never failed to crack Florence up. "Hey, what's going on downstairs? I passed a sad woman."

Florence's face grew suddenly stern and serious. "Oh, it's awful. That's that Devlin Associates company."

"What happened?"

"From what I hear" – Florence's voice dropped to a *sotto voce* whisper, as if any of the Devlin Associates could be lurking around any corner – "the president got caught in some fraud scandal. I don't know everything, but I have coffee with one of the secretaries, a Miz Lawrence? She's seen the writing on the wall for awhile. That Mr. Devlin is going to jail, to hear her tell it. *Everyone* is jobless. No money for severance packages. No 401(k) matching. Can you imagine that? Everything gone in thin air, just like that."

Karen's mouth was dry. "I can imagine that, I think. Hey, Florence, is Cynthia around?"

"She is indeed." Cynthia strode into the little lobby with its blondewood paneling and replica of an antique printing press under glass. Gutenberg wept. Cynthia was in a pale gray wool suit with a matching skirt; her dark hair was pulled back into a severe ponytail and she wore glasses she didn't need. Unlike herself, Cynthia was in flats. She was the only editor at Chanler & Cushing with a vagina, and Karen wondered how much of her outfit was meant to remind the higher-ups that she was a woman, and how much was meant to cover up the fact that she was a woman. Somewhat ironically, Karen was glad she wasn't in Cynthia's shoes. "What do you have in that satchel, Karen? You look like you're smuggling an elephant in there."

"You guessed it in one," Karen laughed, still unnerved by what Florence had said, and now sweat broke out on her brow. "A tiny baby elephant. I thought the office could use a mascot."

Cynthia chuckled. Florence wailed laughter. *Oh my God, this is hell, it's literal hell.* Then Cynthia put an arm around Karen's waist and led her into her office. The small one. The one with the view of the parking lot.

Only with the door closed behind her and Cynthia on the other side of her desk did Karen manage to relax a little. But only a little; this was where it all started. It had been a month and a half since she'd read Henry Dear's *Dance the Night Away* in the course of an afternoon. She'd been very busy since then. So busy that at one point, she'd collapsed in her father's office from sheer exhaustion. An ambulance had to come to revive her and she'd spent two days in the hospital getting fluids. She'd asked Henry to bring her a pen and a notebook in while she convalesced. He'd said no. Dad had come through, though. He got it. She hadn't bothered to tell Maura. Why worry her?

"All right," Cynthia said. "You told Florence this was urgent. Color me intrigued." Literary agent Cynthia would never have said "color me intrigued."

Without speaking, Karen unzipped the attaché case and pulled out four bulky manuscripts. *Up in the Air*, fully edited and rewritten, was the first one. Karen laid it on the corner of Cynthia's desk, facing her. She pulled out the next, *Where'd She Go?*, and slid it in next to *Air*; it was about twice the size. The third manuscript was *Valerie*, written by Henry Dear. It went next to *Where'd She Go?*. The fourth and final was the longest manuscript yet. It was called *Bull in a China Shop*, the latest Mike Bull mystery by Gary Luck. It dwarfed the others. That was the one Karen had been working on when she collapsed. It just barely fit on the other edge of Cynthia's desk.

"What am I looking at?" Cynthia asked, unable to rip her eyes off the titles. That was good.

"Millions of dollars," Karen said, and saluted herself for not letting her voice quaver. Cynthia looked up. Karen, who'd been about to sit, instead tented her fingers on *Up in the Air*. "If you crash production, you could get this one out in time for Christmas. Why do you want it out for Christmas? Because for the last three years, you've had two Luck titles out during the holidays, and you don't want to miss out on your Double Luck promotion."

"'Two Times the Luck,'" Cynthia corrected, finally looking up.

"Isn't that a little clunky?"

"It's worked so far."

"Point taken. Two Times the Luck, and it's going to be an easy sell for you. Elaine Luck's final novel, *plus* her daughter's novel, which is *about* her mother."

"I thought you said *Up in the Air* wasn't about you and Elaine."

"It's not," she said. "But it's about a girl whose mother dies in a tornado. You don't think marketing can capitalize on that?" Was this what selling out was? If so, it didn't feel as bad as she'd always thought it would. She thought about Florence saying, "everything gone into thin air," and she held steady

Cynthia offered nothing but the briefest nod. "This is your third novel?" she asked, tapping *Where'd She Go?*

"It's my best novel. And if *Up in the Air* does the numbers I think it will, I think this could be a summer novel, all by itself, next year."

"Big if."

"Big confidence. You know that I'm the hardest on myself, Cynthia. And I *know* these books are good. I think *Where'd She Go?* might actually be great."

"I guess I'll be the judge of that. I have a question."

"Why not crash production to get to my father's latest book?"

"You read my mind."

"It's not that hard to do."

Cynthia raised her eyebrows. "What am I thinking about right now?"

Karen smiled. "How to remain professional even though I want to lay my writer down on this desk and ravage her?"

Taking off her fake glasses and laying them on the desk, Cynthia grinned. "You're good. *Ravage* was a great touch."

"That's why I'm a writer. And we'll get to my father in a second. Let's talk Henry Dear."

"Your ex-boyfriend."

"I'd like to think I can have a good working relationship with all of my exes," Karen said.

"You'd like to think that, would you?" Cynthia slid her glasses back on. "What does Henry Dear bring to the table?"

"A knockout first novel. A book I think you'll like and I think readers will like. It's accessible but a little off-kilter."

"Mystery?"

Karen shook her head. "Mainstream."

"Non-genre is a harder sell."

"But better longevity."

Cynthia sighed. "Sometimes. Why are you going to bat for your ex-boyfriend. And why isn't he here?"

"Because the book is good," she said. It was mostly the whole truth. "And the second book is better. And because I insisted I do it like this." She hadn't had to insist very hard. Henry had stood in his living room, dazed that she'd liked his book well enough to go to bat for him. She liked dazing him.

She liked how easy things were with him, especially if you ignored why things were easy with him. And then he'd said that thing, something so incongruous that it momentarily shook her off balance. "Good thing you wore heels," he said, his eyes a little glazed over. And some flash, some memory, barrelled into her so hard and so abruptly that she only caught a glimpse of it before it sped past her. Hadn't Henry said something about sneakers once? A long, long time ago, hadn't he said something about her sneakers?

Cynthia roused her from her reverie. "There's a second book?"

"He's close to finishing a third book. If this first one hits – and I have to believe it will – you'll have a steady earner on your hands."

Nodding, Cynthia said, "I'll read it and let you know. Now tell me about your dad's book."

Now Karen sat, grateful to be off her feet. She crossed her legs. Cynthia sat at the other side of the desk and did the same. "First, you tell me something. How many more books does my Dad have on his contract?"

"Two," Cynthia said at once. "But you knew that."

"Of course I did. And if he were to sign another contract, how many books do you think he could negotiate for?"

"That's not up to me," Cynthia said, but it was a rote response. She was making calculations in her head. Karen could see it in her eyes.

"I'll ask the question in another way. Who is Chanler and Cushing's most popular writer?"

"Elaine Luck." No hesitation. Karen had known that, too.

"Right. And this is her last book. I'd be hooking to her star and hopefully end up shining on my own." She hesitated. "I've begun the fourth novel, Cynthia."

Cynthia's lips parted and she licked them. "Your contract's up in three."

"I think we can negotiate that, too. Who's your second most popular writer?"

"It's not your father," Cynthia said, her voice clipped.

"Maybe, maybe not. But he's up there. His last book was at #1 on the *Times* chart for eight weeks, and I know it's gone to a fifth printing already."

"Your point?"

"Gary Luck is one of your most popular, reliable writers. Each of his novels sells over a million copies. He's a cash cow." Karen stood, towering over the desk in her stiletto heels, and laid her hand on *Bull in a China Shop*. "And he has writer's block."

Cynthia looked from the stack of pages on her desk to Karen's face and back again. "Wait, you mean…"

"I wrote this. I'm Gary Luck now. *And* Karen Luck. Right now, you need one of us. By next year, you'll need both of us. Both of *me*. So let's talk contracts."

Cynthia blinked. "You Lucks are fucking crazy."

Karen smiled. "Runs in the family."

By the time she headed back out into the lobby, her throat was raw from talking and her legs were screaming. After some initial hesitation – well, what seemed like hesitation; for all the talk that Karen could read Cynthia's mind, the woman could be awfully cagey – Cyn had warmed up to almost all of her ideas. *Almost* all. Cyn wasn't going to give her everything she wanted, because that's not how the two of them operated. No one was going to get the lofty multiple-book contracts Karen had lain out. Karen had shot for the moon and had ended close to the stratosphere. Not the worst place to be.

Dad got another book tacked onto his contract; instead of the second book in an existing three-book contract, *Bull in a China Shop* would be the first book in a *new* three-book contract. Cynthia had only been willing to put in an offer for *Valerie* when it came to Henry's books. No contract, no advance for a second book. Being friends with the Luck family didn't make someone a Luck. The offer Cynthia had written into the paperwork was almost insultingly low, but to even do that without having read a single page of the book showed remarkable confidence in Karen's acuity. She had no doubt that Henry would accept the offer, either, and she thought the lowball would be good when it came to paperback and foreign rights. *If* he got them. She thought he would. She thought *Valerie* would do well. Maybe not gangbusters, but well.

The real surprise had had to do with her own work. Late in the meeting, Cynthia had slid open a drawer and pulled out a stapled pile of papers that had been folded and re-folded several times. "What's that?"

"Millions of dollars," Cynthia had said with a smirk. "I've been holding onto this for quite awhile, Karen. I was planning on showing it to you when the edits for *Up in the Air* were done. Why do you think I've been on you so hard about that one?"

"If I recall correctly, you were always hard on me."

"If *I* recall correctly, *you* were the one hard on me."

"Touché. So what is this?"

Cynthia met her eye, suddenly serious. "You know I have immense faith in you, right?"

The question, so soon after their pseudo-sexual banter, threw her. "I ... what do you mean?"

"Look, we work together because you're a good writer and I'm a good editor and it makes sense. We have a past and that almost doesn't matter. I was in love with your mother and that kind of matters. And maybe I'm still in love with you a little, and I *want* that not to matter. What actually *does* matter, for real matters, is that you are a very good writer. That's the only part of our whole history I've never questioned. So I'll stand for you ... for Karen Luck, writer."

So much of this meeting had been planned – or, at least, planned for. Karen had known Cynthia Auburn her whole life and had known her intimately for a good chunk of that. Either knowing how Cynthia was going to react or at least anticipating her general mood had long ceased being a trick and was now just instinct. But Cynthia threw curveballs sometimes, and this was one of the sometimes. Those four manuscripts stood against the edge of the woman's desk like sentinels between the two of them, and that millions-of-dollars contract sitting right on top, like a conquering hero. All at once, a massive and somehow majestic weight seemed to settle on her brain and shoulders and heart and gut, dragging her toward the floor. If she hadn't been sitting, she might have simply fallen over. All of that, all those pages, had largely been the work of a month. A *month.*

Even *Valerie*, the one book before her that she hadn't written, had her fingerprints all over it. She'd taken it to Burger City and gone through it, almost line by line, first alone and then with Henry, teasing a better story out of his rough first draft. Keeping Valerie alive longer, lulling the reader into thinking she was the main character throughout the whole novel, that was the trick of the book. The gimmick. You didn't want to blow the gimmick in the first chapter. But what Henry hadn't realized was that the rest of the book couldn't exist simply in service to that gimmick. It had to transcend it. You wanted readers to come back to *Valerie* and find an even richer story, one not dependent on the authorial trick. They found that story together, found a deeper thread between all the characters who *weren't* Valerie, and how they existed in relation to the dead girl, and to each other. The weirdest part of working with Henry on the book? At times, it felt like she was actually editing her *own* book. She'd never written anything remotely like *Valerie*, and the book wasn't exactly in her style (Karen actually wasn't sure she *had* a style, not yet, not three books in), but sometimes ... sometimes it was like déjà vu. A turn of phrase would leap out at her, and she would read it and re-read it, convinced that the words had sprung from some locked chasm inside her and onto this page. She hadn't written them, she hadn't consciously *thought* them, but she was convinced they had still somehow come from her. Wasn't that strange?

Strange.

And now *Valerie* was a little longer and a lot stronger and it was going to be published. *All* those books were going to be published, and more books were working as hard as they could to bust through her skull, even as they spoke. She had a room at the Hilton nearby, and there was a business center just off the lobby. Karen was going to dash to her room, take off these godawful heels, throw on jeans and a T-shirt and head straight down to the computers. She was about a quarter into Dad's new Mike Bull story – *Running Out of Ink* – and things were starting to get crazy. Mike Bull was on the case of a manuscript stolen from a literary convention. A J.D. Salinger type named Farris Holden had come out of hiding to read from his first novel in twelve years; and the brand-new novel was stolen out of his green room. Bull, at the convention at the behest of his protegee, comes to the rescue right away. What Bull – and the audience – didn't know yet is that the J.D. Salinger type hadn't written a word, and the stolen manuscript was a whole ruse so that the guy could feel relevant again. So far, the Mike Bull novels hadn't really experimented with downbeat endings, but Karen thought readers would enjoy this one. She had plans for Holden in upcoming books. God, she had ideas for the next *twelve* books: Dad's, hers ... and she even, just maybe, had one Elaine Luck novel in her. How that would work would be up to Cynthia to determine.

The elevator door slid open.

The giant man in white, down the hall and covered in blood, turned around and grinned at her. Something sharp and metal gleamed in his hand.

Karen Luck saw everything: the body slumped against one of the cubicle walls, a woman with lank hair and dull eyes staring off into nothing. It couldn't be the woman Karen had seen earlier; that woman had been leaving, she'd just been leaving over an hour ago. That couldn't be her on the floor, she'd just been leaving. Directly before her, mere inches from the lip of the elevator doors, a thick runnel of blood flowed into view. A picture sprang, fully formed, into her mind: there was a person to the right of these doors, just out of her sightline. A man, maybe. An intern with a young wife and baby at home. He had been slaughtered by this man in white, this giant, this butcher from the shadows and her nightmares remade into living flesh in the fluorescent mundanity of this New York office. How many times had the man in white cut him until he'd died? Karen saw him raising a cleaver and sinking into the man's thin shoulder. Blood in a geyser splattering the walls and the young intern's face. Then into his side, where the organs were. Maybe the butcher had cut him so deeply, the wound so large and gaping, that right now the man's intestines were birthing out onto the carpet, dead worms slathered in crimson afterbirth.

Karen's legs and arms were marble, heavy and immovable. What if the intern was still clutching to life, just out of her sightline? What if he was desperate to scream, desperate to live, and Karen simply stood here, stock still, imagining the butchery done to him? What if a hand clawed into sight, trying to drag the body it was attached to across the whispering carpet, to cast an accusatory eye toward her?

The man in white began to run toward the elevator, still grinning.

Karen's paralysis broke at once and she slammed her hand down on the DOOR CLOSE button. The butcher would be here in seconds. He would cut her. He would rend her. He would rip her flesh and meat from her bones. All with that grin on his face. Karen batted at the DOOR CLOSE button but nothing happened. Only when she flicked her eyes away from the madman for a bare second to look at her stuttering, shuddering hand did she realize she was pressing the DOOR OPEN button instead.

I'm going to die in an elevator, she thought wildly, just as the butcher reached her and raised his cleaver, the nightmare made bloody flesh. Panic instinct took over. Thought ceased. And without thinking, Karen raised her leg and shot her foot out the second the butcher breached the doorway. Maybe she only intended to kick him back into the office so she could escape. But that's not what happened.

She had kicked with enormous force. The man in white had gotten a running start. Karen's stiletto heel tore into the fabric of the butcher's shirt, then broke through his flesh, sinking partway into his gut. Blood gushed from the wound, slathering Karen's ankle and calf, warm and somehow oily against her skin. For a moment, she thought she might surely topple backward; her equilibrium sloshed in her head like loose water. She flailed her hands wildly at the doorway, wanting to steady herself, compartmentalizing that desire with the gruesome reality attached to her.

The butcher was screaming. Blood erupted from his belly in a geyser. He dropped his glittering weapon and it clattered harmlessly to the floor, half in and half out of the elevator. The man's eyes rolled. His hands were trying to go to his belly but there was some sort of short circuit in him; they only flailed at his sides.

Karen's fingers batted against nothing. Raw panic seized her and fell off, seized and fell off, like the motor of a muscle car. Then the elevator door, designed to start closing and only reopen if it met an obstruction, began to whoosh closed. Karen's hand at last found purchase and she yanked herself forward. The butcher tumbled to the ground and she went with him, her heel slamming even deeper into this man's soft parts. The man's screams escalated to shrieks.

Now that she was actually in the office, the carnage spread out before her in hideous tableau. The intern she'd imagined was actually an old man in a tan business suit, a rictus of pain and horror on what was left of his face. Later, she would discover that man was Stan Devlin, who had tried to declare bankruptcy, despite his personal net worth exceeding ten million dollars. If the butcher hadn't murdered him, he would have gone to jail for the rest of his life. One look at Stan Devlin convinced Karen that jail would have been better. The man's face was little but ground meat. One of his eyes had collapsed. The other stared out of a pulpy, blood-soaked pile of hamburger that used to belong to a human. Stab wounds, including the one near the man's heart that had caused the river of blood to surge across the carpet, pocked the man's body all over. Karen could see the butcher doing it, stabbing this man over and over and over until he died, grinning the whole time.

But he started with his face, Karen knew suddenly. *That's not what killed him. The butcher started carving his face up but he was still alive. The heart puncture is what killed him and that came after. His face ... his* face...

Then she threw up; the remnants of her meager, nervous breakfast torrented from her, splashing against the floor and onto her assailant's face. More bodies slumped and sprawled, covered in blood. Karen Luck thought: *he stabbed them all. Didn't bring a gun. He just stabbed them. How come nobody stopped him? Somebody had to have stopped him.*

But that was the thing: there *was* nobody. Karen realized she was looking at the last of the Devlin Associates employees. Five or six humans, probably devastated that their lives were now in shambles, slowly cleaning out their cubicles, aiming to be the last to leave.

That was when the giant started screaming. His screams were high, reedy, the screams of a young child who has been frightened badly. Then Karen heard screaming from somewhere else, a cacophonous harmony, and realized that the sound was coming from her. She was tethered to her nightmare, only now it was real and alive and spouting blood from a gut wound, and she was heel-deep inside it.

And *he* had regained his blade.

Still screaming, he raised it high and whickered it blindly into the air, managing only to scrape a new wound deep in his own belly. Still, Karen had felt the wind of its arc against her ankle and scrambled into a position with leverage. Leverage was important. She felt her heel dig into the man's insides and her own stomach slowly somersaulted, but she would *not* throw up again, she would *not*.

The man, calling on reserves of strength she didn't think she could have, lifted his weapon again. She saw now that it was a letter opener. Hefty. Stainless steel. But still: this lunatic had done all this with a *letter opener*. Jesus Freeze-Dried Christ. While she was musing on this, the man managed to swing his blade into the arc of her foot. It wasn't that hard and he didn't go deep, but blood still trickled out, and new, sharp pain sizzled into her foot. Instinctually, she yanked back, the sound like a hungry mouth sucking ice cream from the bottom of a cone. The geyser of blood now became a burbling hot spring, extruding blood and pooling it all over the man's shirt and the floor around him.

Karen Luck scrambled to her feet, wobbly but upright, making an *ooo-uuu* sound she couldn't hear herself make. The elevator behind her had finally slid closed. She reached behind herself, chancing a quick glance to make sure she was hitting the correct button, and jammed the heel of her hand down. The butcher – the killer – now emitted a sound like hiccuping, staccato and harsh. Blood bubbled out of his mouth, frothing. The door behind her slipped open like a secret. She stepped back, still wobbly, and jammed her thumb down. For the first time in a million years, a door closed between her and the horror show at Devlin Associates.

When it opened again, she was back on Cynthia's floor. Florence rushed forward. Karen stumbled out, utilizing the last of her strength to stay upright. The shag carpet she stepped onto was white and she discovered she was turning it red. "Hi, Florence," she said, and it came out almost casually, almost *want to get some drinks sometime*. Florence picked up the phone and pressed some numbers and spoke and none of it mattered. And Karen thought, almost randomly: *it's a good thing I wore heels.*

Cynthia burst into the lobby and said words. They didn't matter, either. Karen spoke. She wanted to say, *You have to rescue me*. She wanted to say, *I need you*. She wanted to say, *I love you, Cynthia, I'm sorry I couldn't be my Mom, but she's dead.*

But she only managed to get out the word, "butcher," before her eyes fluttered closed and she fainted dead away on the shag carpet. She wasn't aware of it and didn't believe it when Cynthia told her later, but she'd done it with a smile on her face.

Part Three

Goodbye,

Burger City

Chapter 11: Various Atrocities

Karen was on her third read of Henry Dear's latest manuscript, fuming, when Maura walked into the small attached living room and announced she was leaving Honolulu.

For a moment, Karen could barely credit what she was saying. Her fury was so overwhelming, so consuming, that nothing else in the world seemed to matter. One thing she knew for sure was that Henry Dear was on her permanent shit list. She and he were through, forever. This thing had blindsided her so thoroughly that the concept of thinking beyond her rage seemed absurd. And now here was Maura, demanding attention she didn't have the capacity to give, as she did so often when Karen was fully engaged. It was almost like she had a sixth sense about it. The second Karen had gone from poking along at her keyboard to completely locking into the world she was making, Maura would show up and start complaining.

Hawaii was supposed to change some of that. She had vowed to take a two-week break from writing and had completely managed it for a day and a half. To her way of thinking, if she got up after Maura fell asleep and set her laptop up on the living room table (or, better, on the lanai, overlooking dead volcanoes) and did her writing during the time when her beloved was asleep, no one had to get upset. Of course, Karen had to take some responsibility – sure, a lot of responsibility – for the fact that the new book had begun to require more and more of her time. A little over a week into their vacation, she and Maura would tuck into bed and she would attempt their normal pillow talk, but all she could think about was *Not Much Left*. It was *finally* the book she'd been wanting to write since 1997, since seeing that *Ellen* episode while she recovered from The Incident. In the episode, Ellen Morgan came out as gay to herself and to her friends and everyone was actually pretty okay with it. Paralleling her fictional counterpart, comedian and actress Ellen DeGeneres *also* came out. She appeared on the cover of *Time* magazine with the giant headline, "Yep, I'm Gay."

It was a *seismic* moment. Something had to be to rouse her. In the days immediately following The Incident, she holed up in Mom's old office and shut the door and wrote and wrote and wrote until she literally fell over, exhausted. Later, when she would read over what she'd done, she found clean copy, engaging prose ... and no memory of having written any of it. Her brain had ceased being the thing that thought for her. It had become a blank, black spiral. Her fingers did the thinking for her. When she slept, she didn't dream. When she wasn't writing, she was staring at the television in the living room with her Dad, who knew better than to question her therapy. She'd managed to get halfway through a chunky new Gary Luck novel – *Stunt* – in the three weeks following The Incident when that episode of *Ellen* shook her out of her stupor. On her television set, a woman leaned into an airport microphone and said she was gay. Everyone heard it. The woman she was attracted to heard it. And the laugh track boomed because it was a funny moment, but it was also a starkly *real* moment, a *raw* moment.

After the episode, Karen stood on shaky legs. She was barefoot, as she had been for weeks. The idea of putting on shoes filled her with such revulsion that she'd avoided it completely. The kitchen floor tile was cold beneath her heels and she relished the cold. It had seemed, when she'd been able to process any sensation beyond eyestrain and the aching in her wrists, that there was some muted fire inside of her, something that was trying to burn her from the inside out, but couldn't get enough oxygen to do it.

She called Cynthia's number from memory.

"Karen. It's sort of late. I have ... there's someone here."

"Did you watch it?" Karen asked abruptly.

A long pause. "The *Ellen* show? Yeah. It just ended."

"I want to write a book about myself, Cyn. My *real* self. No more excuses. You can be gay now. I want to write about my life. Who I am. Who *we* are."

A longer pause. "Can we talk about this tomorrow, Karen?"

"No. We're talking about this now."

Cynthia let escape a long, rueful sigh. "Look, Karen. This was big. Okay, I know it was big. But we have *no* idea how this is going to shake out. Ellen could get ostracized over this. Or worse. And I don't want that for you. You were in my office not three months ago with a whole plan for world domination. Do you really want to screw that up because you decide to write a lesbian novel?"

Anger spiked into Karen's brain so fast and so intrusively, she had no time to register it as the first emotion she'd experienced since fainting in the lobby of Chanler & Cushing. "No. Fuck that. People write novels with lesbians all the time and it doesn't *brand* them. Alice Walker wrote *The Color Purple* and she won a *Pulitzer*."

"All the time? Name one more lesbian novel."

Righteousness sizzled into Karen's heart. "I can name two! *Carmilla. Rubyfruit Jungle*, that one by Rita Mae Brown."

More of Cynthia's pausing. "All right, you got me with *Rubyfruit Jungle*. Very popular, too."

"See?"

"And I bet you can't tell me one other book by her. And I bet you never read it."

Now it was Karen's turn to hesitate. She turned around in the kitchen and looked out the window over the sink. After all this time not feeling anything, it was suddenly like every part of her insides had come to screaming, broken life. It felt, honestly, like there was a tornado loose inside her.

"*Carmilla* is a book about a lesbian vampire who feeds on living women. It's not really a positive light for lezzies."

The tornado was in her throat, and then her mouth. "*Why are you keeping me away from this? Why don't you want me to write about me, Cynthia?*" This had all come out in a shriek. Dad appeared in the kitchen door and leaned into it, looking at her. She turned away, not wanting him to see the sudden tears that had sprung to her eyes. What if they started to fall?

"Listen to me, Karen, and listen good. Being a pioneer is great. We need pioneers. But when you become one, you're always one. You remember three lesbian novels, only one of which was written by an actual gay woman, because they stick out. They're not the norm. Ellen isn't the norm. And I don't want your whole career saddled with the badge of being a *lesbian* writer. I want you to be known as a writer first."

"What if *I* want to be known as a lesbian writer? Don't I get a say?"

"Just think about it for a little while. Think about what you want to commit to."

"Oh, fuck *you!*" Karen slammed the phone down on the receiver, then slammed it down again, and again, and again. Shards of plastic flew. Wires unspooled. Karen kept screaming. "Fuck *you!* Fuck *you!*"

She glanced at her father, who looked so small and frail in the doorway. Was that what people looked like when they ran out of words? "I'll buy you a new phone," she told him.

"I don't care about the phone," he said. "You've been catatonic for months and now you're going ballistic. I care about *you.*"

Gary went to her, lifting his hands a little – maybe to hug her, maybe to grab her arms and hold her away from him

– then dropped them to his sides. His indecision baked off him like heat from a wood stove.

"This is supposed to be a happy night," she said. "That show – I mean a famous person who *is* a lesbian just said she was a lesbian in a popular comedy show. And Cynthia is treating it like it's no big deal."

"Is she?" Gary asked, his voice stringently neutral.

Karen looked away. "Whose side are you on?"

"Your side," he said without hesitation. "Always."

She still didn't look at him. The tornado inside her seemed to be sighing apart in tatters of ineffectual gales and gusts. "It's not about the show. I mean it is and it isn't. Maybe she's right. Mom always said Cynthia is always right. But even if she *is* right, it isn't *fair*."

Now Gary did approach her. If she'd been looking at him, he wouldn't have been able to. He had been living with a silent daughter for nearly three months. If it wasn't for the writing, he thought she might still be in that hospital room, nearly catatonic. But she'd snapped out of it enough in three days to want to come home to OKC. Maura had flown from Los

Angeles and begged to bring Karen back with her, but Karen had been firm on this point. She still had to recover, and she thought she'd do it better in her old home, surrounded by her childhood comforts. Of course Gary knew that she'd begun a book in his name before she'd left for New York, and she wanted to get back to it. Despite whatever conflicted ideas he might have about what she was doing, and about his own stupid goddamn writer's block, he wasn't conflicted about Karen going back to writing.

"No," he said quietly. "It's not."

She looked at him. "You mean, Cynthia is wrong?"

"I can't answer that," he said, then closed his eyes. "Okay, I don't *want* to answer that. Because I think she might be right. But that's not the end of it. I think you might be right, too."

Karen stood in the midst of the phone detritus, and again her mind turned to tornadoes. It hadn't drifted apart, after all. It had gotten out. "So ... what are you thinking?"

"I don't know what I'm thinking," he told her, but he did. "Except that ... does it *have* to be a Karen Luck novel?"

For a moment, she looked at him blankly. Then she got it. "Another pen name? A lesbian pseudonym?"

"Maybe it's not the worst idea."

She stared at the mess around her for a long silent moment. "It's not. But that's not how I want it. If I'm going to write that kind of truth, I want it to be *my* truth."

Gary nodded as if he'd expected no less. "Well, then. Does it have to be *published*?"

Now Karen lifted her eyes to his face. "You mean just write it and do nothing with it?"

Shrugging, he said, "Then when Cynthia thinks the world's come around, you'll have it ready to go. Your Mom had novels in reserve."

Karen blinked. "No she didn't, Dad."

Dad's forehead crinkled, his eyes incredulous. "Yes she did. She had thirteen…" He paused, then slowly shook his head. "No, you're right. She didn't."

"Dad, are you okay?"

"I'm just tired, honey. Just write what you feel. Write everything you feel. Publish the stuff she wants, hold the stuff she doesn't. It'll all get out eventually." He took a step toward her. "You *can* write it all, right?"

The idea floated in front of her like a spectral thing. *Three* strains of books. Mysteries from Gary Luck. The commercially viable stuff that Cynthia wanted, stuff in the vein of what she'd turned in already. And then stuff for herself, stuff about love and sex and danger and lust, and the women would be front and center, and the women would be reflections of her, what she was, *who* she was. She *could* do that. She had all those types of books in her somewhere. All she had to do was pull a thread or two and stuff would spin out. It never occurred to her to question her ability to do it, only her willingness. That spectral thing stared back at her, and she saw that it was enormous, and hungry, and that it would devour her whole life.

And she also realized that she wanted to be consumed.

"Writing is the most important thing," she murmured, and slowly, Dad nodded.

"Yeah. That's the only lesson that matters."

The fact that they might both be disastrously wrong never even crossed their minds.

And now: Hawaii, four years later. Early September. An idyllic morning except it wasn't.

"What do you mean, you're leaving Honolulu? Are you going to Waikiki? Or one of the other islands? I'm confused." Her mind was half-consumed with Henry Dear's newest novel, and half-consumed with *Not Much Left*. The book she'd been trying and failing to write ever since that phone call with Cynthia way back in the waning years of the 1990s. She'd been right about writing as a concept. It *was* the most important thing, and the fact that Maura refused to see that and support that was always going to be a wedge between them. About *her* writing, she was wrong. Dad had offered the perfect idea and something in her – she thought of it as the Voice of Cynthia – kept holding her back.

She could write Mike Bull novels. Those were almost easy, but you never wanted to get into the trap of being formulaic with them. Also, she was set on aging Mike a little bit with each book, in real time. She didn't want a Spenser on her hands. Karen thought Mike Bull should age. He had certain limitations as a character baked in – his anti-social nature, his endless trauma of letting a young boy get shot while he was still on the cops – that would eventually stagnate unless he could grow and learn and change. The changes were incremental but interesting, and Karen loved discovering where she might push him to next.

She could write short stories. She *had* been writing short stories all along, small Midwestern gothic stories about family tension drenched in a heaping helping of smiling kindnesses. One story, "The Sister I Knew," garnered a small amount of controversy after appearing in an issue of *Playboy*; its bare-bones portrayal of incest that isn't punished by man *or* God raised a few hackles. Everyone thought the girl in the story deserved to be put to death for seducing her older brother. The whole thing is told from the father's point of view, and it's implied that he and *his* sister had an affair back in the day, although the story never comes right out and says it. Their father killed the sister in a fit of pique one afternoon, and you get the sense through the whole story that *this* father is going to also kill his daughter, because sexual deviancy is always the fault of the woman. Instead, the Dad decides to break the cycle and instead builds them a small apartment above the garage where they can live if they want to. The last scene is the Dad hugging his daughter and whispering in her ear, "Don't have babies. You ain't wrong, but they would be." And the daughter looks at him seriously and nods and that's the end of the story.

There were uproars. Karen bore them easily enough. Her short stories didn't really pay the bills, but they were good for keeping the writing pump primed if there was ever a fallow period between novels. And one of them, that weird little horror story she'd written in school, "Their Tiny Knuckles," kept showing up in Halloween and horror anthologies, and while it might not be considered a modern classic, it was the one short story she'd written that had the same sort of recognition as her books. If she ever put out her own collection of stories, "Their Tiny Knuckles" could be the finale story. Maybe bookend the collection with incest and monsters.

Maybe that would be a good title for the whole shebang. Karen Luck's *Incest and Monsters*, coming soon to a Barnes & Noble near you.

But if the Mike Bull novels were ostensibly her father's, and the short stories were mostly under the radar, the books she thought of as "the Cynthia novels" were, simply put, wildfire. As it had turned out, they hadn't had to wait for *Where'd She Go?* to set the bestseller lists blazing. *Up In the Air* had done that all on its own. Karen was sure – *positive* – that the initial interest had a lot to do with the marketing, and her association with her father. And, as morbid as it might be, the *non*-association with her mother. Mom wasn't going to publish any more books, but here, right on time, was the closest thing they had to Elaine Luck in time for Christmas. Marketing and timing explained how the first printing sold out. Not how the second one did, and not how it had gone back for a third and fourth printing.

Paperback rights and foreign rights and movie rights followed. Those allowed her to move out of the little apartment in the Valley and situate herself in a house in the

Hollywood Hills. Maura hadn't wanted to move, but how could you really argue with the high ceilings, the glass walls that looked out onto a heated pool, and beyond that, over the glittering jewel box of Los Angeles, spread out like it was all theirs in the night. Dad got his own room just off the kitchen, an arrangement he liked. After years of shoveling whatever food was around into his mouth – anything to fuel the writing – he had begun to take an interest in cooking fine cuisine. On Mondays and Thursdays, he drove into the city and took cooking classes. On Tuesdays and Fridays, he went to the gym, where he'd made some friends among the middle-aged set there. After an entire life in Oklahoma City, Dad had fully acclimated to life in California. Karen, who'd known Maura would love the new house and who'd feared Dad would hate it, was thrown.

At some point in every novel, characters start behaving in ways you didn't anticipate. That was always the most exciting part of writing; it meant you created something so real, so vibrant, that the people you invented were taking on lives of their own. In *Where'd She Go?*, Karen had conjured a quiet, meek young girl who had been meant as nothing but a secondary – almost tertiary – character. Her name was Anna-Lucy, and she was best friends with the book's two main characters, twin sisters who sometimes hated each other. Then, in chapter three, Anna-Lucy killed the sisters' cat, just to watch it die. Karen had sat back from what she'd written that afternoon, knowing that this would derail the whole novel, that it would fundamentally change what she'd set out to write. She could rewrite it, omit it, save it for another book even. Instead, she'd spent the remainder of the novel trying to justify what Anna-Lucy had done, and the Elaine Luckian family drama she'd intended to delve into became her secondary concern. More, the hidden lunacy of Anna-Lucy *informed* the family drama, shading the edges and darkening the core of the sisters' fraught relationship. That had been an *immensely* satisfying novel to write. Every character lived and breathed; Karen felt like she was writing history, not fiction.

Which was all well and good when it was characters. People, on the other hand. People behaving in new and unexpected ways scared her. She knew she couldn't control everyone – she wouldn't *want* to – but she'd known Dad her whole life and she'd been with Maura for years when they'd moved. She should have been able to figure out who they were and how they'd react by now.

Then again, the world was crazy and made no sense. Her perfectly planned trajectory for her own career had gone wildly out of proportion, wildly fast. It was enough for you to wonder – idly, of course, just a little idly – whether you really deserved the success you'd gotten. Whether that marketing and cross-promotion you'd made such a case for had way more to do with the house in the Hills than your talent. And, by the way, who said you actually *had* talent? Maybe you didn't. There were a lot of bestselling writers out there that sold fast and were read hungrily who could barely write. Karen knew. She'd read plenty of them. So who was to say she wasn't *one* of them?

She kept a lot of those fears to herself, because the last thing she wanted to do was to destroy Dad's new feeling of idyll or burden Maura any more than she was already burdened. Instead, she'd made sure the house was equipped with two giant showers, both with rainfall heads above, and one with an actual waterfall feature, so that it felt like you were standing naked in the Amazon, bathing in the middle of nature. Like the old place in OKC, there were two writing rooms in the new house; one was ostensibly for Dad, but of course she used it when she was writing his mysteries. Keeping it warm for him until he could write again.

Both writing rooms communicated with the shower rooms, so that when Maura was in there, Karen could know she needed to pause her writing and get naked and spend time with her girlfriend. And how could she not? Maura standing under that waterfall feature, water sluicing around her breasts and down her tight belly and long legs – could anything else compare to how sexy that was? Or how connected she felt to Maura when she was in there, more than anywhere else, because it was Maura's best place. Maura couldn't come with her to her own best place, because writing was, by nature, a solitary activity.

For the first year in the new house, the status quo reigned. Maura calmed down about the new place. She even got more work. Then, two months after *Up in the Air* came out in paperback, Chanler & Cushing released *Where'd She Go?*

That's when everything changed. *Up in the Air* had been a bright, glittering flashpoint of publishing. But *Where'd She Go* was a *phenomenon*. Book signings at B. Dalton and Borders and Barnes & Noble. TV appearances. Interviews. Exposes in *People* magazine. A cultural re-evaluation of *Nobody Under the Stars* burbled up as a new paperback edition was published, with a cover flaunting Karen's name in huge type and "The Author of *Where'd She Go?*" only slightly smaller. For the first time, *Nobody* hit the paperback bestseller list, kept out of the #1 spot by John Grisham's newest. In other John news, novelist John Irving, whose novel *A Widow for One Year* Karen had liked very much, called her on the phone to congratulate her on her success. Perhaps most surreal of all, a reader's poll in the magazine *Fangoria* ranked Anna-Lucy at the top of the scariest literary villains, above Dracula and Hannibal Lecter and Pennywise the Dancing Clown. The character became such a pop culture touchstone of "evil children" that, for a time at least, being an "Anna-Lucy" was the same as being a "Bad Seed."

All of it was wonderful. All of it was thrilling. And all of it, Karen was convinced at some deep level, was fake. You don't just get *handed* adulation. You don't just *become* a household name. Karen knew she was a dedicated writer, a fierce writer, but she didn't know that she was a *great* writer. She lived in a bourgeois house in the Hollywood Hills, and her and her girlfriend and her Dad all drove expensive cars. Her dad and, by extension, her mom, had always had success, had always been popular writers who frequently appeared on the bestseller lists. But whether it was because Dad had remained mostly reclusive and gave few interviews, or because her mother had died before she really blew up, Gary and Elaine had never had even a fraction of this level of the success their daughter had.

"What you're saying," Maura said to her in bed one night, rubbing Karen's wrists so that they didn't ache so much after ten hours of writing, "is that you're afraid all this happened because of luck."

Karen looked at her, a slight grin on her face. "I get your point."

"See, I was doing one of those few double-entendres that aren't sexual."

"I'd roll my eyes at you if you weren't doing such a good job on my hands."

"I'd stop doing such a good job on your hands if you hadn't already done such a good job everywhere else."

"My fingers, their talent does not merely lie in writing."

"Nor your tongue."

She'd paused then. "You're good to me, Maura. Am I good to you?"

Maura grabbed the bottle of lotion and spread a little more on her fingertips. "Mostly," she finally said.

"Can you live with mostly?" Karen asked.

"Mostly," Maura said again, and Karen had closed her eyes.

And what of the Maura situation? Well, that was becoming harder and harder to keep secret, and the more acclaim her books received, the more she started seeing Cynthia's point. *Where'd She Go?* came out in 1999, two years after Ellen Degeneres did, one year after Ellen's show had gotten canceled and she'd faced a massive backlash for her actions. If the fame was fake, if the acclaim was for a person she was only pretending to be, then it could all fall apart at any moment. Her entire life was a Jenga tower. Expose the lesbian brick and everything tumbles to the ground.

    For her part, Maura got it. You didn't get far ahead in Hollywood by being a dyke. The *Ellen* backlash had proven some of that out. And in the world of publishing, it was *brave* to write a book about women who loved women, and often it was *tragic*, and no matter what it was about or who it was by, it was always a *statement*. Always a *big fucking deal*. And that, for lack of a more literary word, sucked. She believed in a world – or at least a country – bending toward justice, however many setbacks that journey might entail. She believed in a future where being gay was no big deal. All she wanted was to jump ahead in time and *get* there.

    So she'd been preparing.

By the time she and Maura had arrived in Honolulu in 2001, Karen had written four unpublished novels. Every one of them featured a lesbian main character. None of them were in the process of coming out, or having tragic – or, ye gods, suicidal – crushes on straight women. And none of them "just happened to be gay," a phrase that had long rankled Karen. It made her think of candy with a fun surprise in the center: normal straight exterior, surprise lesbian on the inside!

But it also kind of lessened what being gay actually *meant*. Karen Luck didn't just happen to be gay. Karen Luck *was* gay. It wasn't the only part of her, but it wasn't an unimportant part of her, either. It infused so much of what she did – from the way she dressed, to the way she did her hair, to the way she'd set up her writing rooms in proximity to her bathrooms. So her characters in these four unpublished novels were similarly homosexual: gay without a cause. *What Happened in Alina's Room?*, the first of the books, felt a little like an early Mike Bull novel. She had just finished her Dad's *Stunt* and had a little more juice in her for another short, punchy thriller. What had happened in Alina's room was that her parents and brother had been murdered by a serial killer. Having been off at sleepaway camp that night, Alina, seventeen and falling out of love with the first girl she'd ever slept with, had to track the killer down herself. Karen had been sorely tempted to make the girlfriend the killer, but that sort of thing was a cliché and she didn't want to make things obvious. The twist – that it was her *grandmother* – packed more of a punch, anyway.

Huff came next, written in the aftershocks of the fourth novel under her name she'd turned in to Cynthia, *Take with Meals*. The published book was about a boy addicted to his mother's prescription drugs, and what happens when she dies suddenly and he has to live without his pills or his mother's support. It was a dark book. Karen wrote obsessively, finishing five hundred pages in under four months and never once considering her words about the horrors of addiction ironic. The day after she'd finished the final sentence, she started *Huff*, about a woman whose girlfriend doesn't know she's addicted to sniffing glue and gas and Glade. The girlfriend is a recovering alcoholic and would leave this woman if she ever found out. *Huff* plays out messy and complicated, but it ends with a sense of hope and even optimism that *Take with Meals* could never accomplish.

Both *What Happened in Alina's Room?* and *Huff* had been short books – only slightly longer than novellas – and Karen wasn't so lost in the act of writing to see how both had riffed on their bigger sisters' themes. After *Huff* she took a two-day break from writing *anything* (Maura, who had never been to Disneyland, was ecstatic to have a whole day in the park with Karen by her side), and resumed with a very long book titled *Beverly Hatch*. Not an aftershock, and not a novella. She worked on *Beverly Hatch* for nearly a year, fending off discussions from her father and Maura and Cynthia about what she was creating. It was the story of a whole life, a sort of novel Karen had never written before. She followed Beverly from gestation to cremation, unearthing parts of herself she wasn't aware were inside, and festering. Mother stuff. Father stuff. Lesbian stuff. Even the stuff with Henry, stuff that she thought she'd atoned for by getting him a book deal. All of it went into the novel, and by the time she got to the home stretch, she *knew* it was one of her best novels, under any name. More, she knew for a fact that she could publish this as a full-fledged Karen Luck novel, and that it would be popular. In an alternate universe where her editor wanted merely her best work, not just her straightest, *Beverly Hatch* would be the logical follow-up to *Take with Meals*. Instead, she used *Beverly Hatch*'s aftershock – a slender book about a smaller portion of a life called *Really Restless*. Her audience wasn't really prepared for a novel that short – just under 200 pages – *or* a novel so comic. Since *Up in the Air*, people had been coming to Karen Luck for her dark and sticky tales of people and families and toxic generations. *Really Restless* had been a lightly funny book about a man named Conor Really who decides to become a rock climber at thirty-five with little to no experience. It's absurd because he's not good at it and he keeps doing it because it's fulfilling. What he *is* good at is pleasuring women, but he can't commit to them because he's afraid of dying during his climbs and leaving them alone, so the sex isn't fulfilling for him. He has a best friend named Sasha, and without even thinking about it, Karen had made Sasha gay. She doesn't have much of a personality, but aside from Conor, no one in *Really Restless* has much of a personality. She'd waited for Cynthia to say something, but apparently secondary characters being lesbians were fine, so long as they help out the straight protagonists. By the end of the book, Conor Really merges both sides of his personality, and, with Sasha's help, meets a woman who runs a rock climbing gym.

Really Restless was a tidy, funny, almost silly book that audiences bought but didn't seem to love. Cynthia *also* steadfastly didn't mention that her worst-selling book so far had featured a lesbian in a somewhat substantial role. She *had* sent an email in which she'd said, "Well, I guess we can't win everything. But onward and upward. I'm sure your fans will love your next book." *We can't win everything* was classic Cynthia. Karen had read that email over and over, alternating between rage and tears. She'd put as much effort and talent into *Really Restless* as with all her other books. But no one wanted light comedy from Karen Luck, and, who the fuck knew. Maybe no one wanted lesbians from Karen Luck, either.

So she dutifully wrote another novel. Longer. Better. Called *I Want You to Hurt Me*, the book allowed Karen to dig into the same parts of her soul that had made *Beverly Hatch* feel alive, and that had made Karen feel scared and a little lost. The scene that almost made her delete the entire manuscript, the one that she'd hated having created, ended this way:

Constance raised her head. Dennis sat across from her on the puke-green chair, watching her with an expression Constance couldn't interpret. There was blood on Dennis' fingernails, and dripping from the length of the belt he held loosely in her hand.

"I don't want to hurt you anymore," Dennis said, but his voice was flat, expressionless. Constance shifted and the pain sizzled up her back. Her shoulders shrieked against the restraints that secured her to the headboard. She tried to kick herself into a better position, but her feet were similarly tied. Everything hurt, but that hurt only went to just below the surface. She still couldn't feel anything. She still couldn't muster the real, honest ache she wanted to feel. The man with the belt had broken up with her only four hours ago, and the nothing

that was inside her blocked anything she wanted to feel. That nothing had been blocking every and any emotions since she was four and found a dying bird by the side of the road, and had stood to watch it die slowly, agonizingly. Did that make her a psychopath? Or was she something worse?

"Turn me over, Dennis," she said. "Make sure I can't move. And then keep hurting me."

"Why are you doing this to me?" Dennis asked, and twin tears slipped from his eyes. He still didn't blink. He'd been wanting to make Constance feel something, anything, for four years. Now was his chance. He might not want to do it, but he'd do it. And Constance thought he might like it, too.

"Because I can't do it to myself," Constance said, feeling her own tears patter to the coverlet. If she could be sure – sure! – that those tears indicated heartbreak instead of a biological pain response, they could stop right now. They could stop.

But they didn't stop for the next three hours. In the end, Dennis untied her and ran out of the apartment. Before she slipped into unconsciousness, Constance called 9-1-1 and explained nothing.

As the readership who had tepidly bought *Really Restless* surged back to Karen Luck with *I Want You To Hurt Me* (and the New York *Times* wondered whether the book indicated a bold, exciting direction or a distinct lack of taste), those three lesbian novels – *What Happened in Alina's Room?*, *Huff,* and *Beverly Hatch* – languished in two places: a folder in a folder in a folder on her laptop, the password to which no one knew, not even Maura or Dad; and printed out in a trunk under a bed in one of their two guest rooms. The maid, Rita, didn't clean there; only Karen did. And sometimes, when cleaning, she would open that trunk and look inside and lie on the bed and read over these stories of interesting people doing interesting things and hating Cynthia for being probably right.

It was a week after she'd finished *Hurt Me*, three days into Dad's new Mike Bull novel (she'd been toying with the title *A Load of Bull*, but Dad signed off on the titles and Cynthia wouldn't go for it anyway) that Karen had broached the Hawaii idea to Maura. "Time off. I love writing, but I need a break. It feels like I haven't stopped in years."

Maura had looked over from the book she was reading and rolled her eyes. "Hon, you haven't. Stopped. Ever. You do know that it's a little weird."

"It's not weird. Writers write. Stephen King writes like this."

"No he doesn't," Maura laughed, but the laughter was a little high, a little nervous. "He writes for like three hours a day and knocks off. I read that *Time* article on him, way back when. You write like *eight* hours a day. That's weird."

Karen had wanted to argue, but not much. She would be fully delusional if she didn't see Maura's point, at least a little. "Sometimes it's not because I *want* to."

"You have a calling." Was that a jab or an acknowledgment?

"I have *ideas*. Wouldn't it be irresponsible of me to *not* write when I have all these ideas?"

"I'm not sure irresponsible is the word," Maura had said, kissing her forearm. "But your Dad did what you're doing, and he burned out."

"After over a decade."

Maura sighed, then laughed a little. "You don't hear yourself, do you?"

"Look, aren't I lying here, acknowledging that I could use a break?"

"Okay, fair."

"And aren't I suggesting that we go to Hawaii?"

"Even fairer."

"Paid for by Chanler & Cushing?"

Now Maura sat up. "Oh?"

"I'm going to call it a research trip and see if they'll foot the bill."

"Doesn't that usually only work for nonfiction writers?"

"It usually works for Lucks, too."

Maura smiled, but the smile seemed guarded. "For someone who occasionally still worries about not deserving her level of fame and fortune, you sure don't balk at stuff like this."

"I don't deserve fame and fortune," Karen said simply. "Or you. But if I can get them, why not lament my good fortune in paradise?

"You make excellent points."

"After Dad's book. And no writing on vacation."

She'd been able to keep one of those promises. *A Load of Bull* had become *Bear and Bull*, a title which didn't quite make sense, given that there were no bears in the book, no one *named* Bear in the book, and it wasn't about the stock market at all. Dad had never used Mike Bull's name in the title before she'd taken over the books, and she'd vowed to go back to that with the next one. People didn't need reminding that Gary Luck meant Mike Bull anymore. She was already toying with a title, *Echoes on the Inside*, which had come to her in a dream after a short night of fitful sleep. Normally when Karen started a novel, she had at least the main characters locked in her head; stuff like plot and situation emerged out of what those characters did and wanted. Once in a great while, the plot would come first. *Really Restless* had mostly come about that way, and maybe that was why readers didn't take to it so readily.

Titles emerged during the writing of most of these books, and usually they changed. *Up in the Air* was simply going to be called *Tornadoes* until she was into the rewrite. *Beverly Hatch* was *Twisting in the Wind*, but Karen decided that it was too close to *Up in the Air*, especially if she wanted to actually eventually publish it. Sometimes, though – *Bull in a China Shop, I Want You to Hurt Me* – she'd come up with the titles first, spinning the story out around it like a spider weaving a web around a live fly. She had no idea what a book called *Echoes on the Inside* would be about, but it evoked the past reverberating up toward the now. Would Mike Bull have to reckon with something he'd done in one of his other novels? The series had been linear and moving slowly forward since Karen had taken over. Maybe something that happened to him when the books were exclusively Dad's could come back? She loved it when series acknowledged their canon, especially if the canon is long and deep and complicated. Every year, she dug back into her parents' old novels and found new stuff; this time, it would just be for research more than pleasure.

The important thing was to keep all these thoughts in her head when they were in Hawaii. Dad might have writer's block, but she, Karen Luck, was still *bursting* with ideas. More ideas than she could possibly write in a lifetime ... but she could sure as hell try.

Still: two weeks. Not too long to be away from all that, and a good way to recharge her batteries. Maura had booked them both a spa day, and Karen was actually looking forward to the massage portion. When you're a woman who finds the very concept of slowing down anathema to her core, sometimes you have to force it.

Then they'd gotten to the hotel and the showers were spacious and she'd indulged Maura in an afternoon of what Maura kept insisting they call "tropical indulgence." Karen washed her back. Her front. Made bold by her girlfriend's body – which, Karen had to admit, was a treasure she sometimes took for granted – Karen took her back to one of the big queen-sized beds (you had to get two; no need to arouse suspicions) and sat her down on the edge of the bed and kneeled in front of her. Maura smiled. Karen smile. And got to business.

She didn't even start the new book for three days.

And it wasn't like she'd planned it or anything. It wasn't even as if she'd wanted to do it. Sure, she'd brought her laptop here, but that was only to check her email and keep in touch with Dad. Calling long-distance from Hawaii would be murder. To be honest, she'd begun *Not Much Left* as a little bit of a lark to help her get back to sleep one night when she was feeling jittery. She could tell herself it was a lark because she knew immediately that it wasn't going to be a Chanler & Cushing book by Karen Luck. It wasn't, technically, going to be a book at all. It was only going to be a manuscript, something that Karen would hide in a folder in a folder in a folder, then print out and bury in a trunk under the bed in her spare room. She knew all that within the first couple paragraphs, she discovered that her main character, Mary Day, was a gay woman going through a divorce, who had just found an abandoned baby in a Walgreen's soda aisle.

But who was Mary Day? And who was the mother of the abandoned baby? And who was her ex-husband? Was he a bad guy? Or maybe he was a pretty okay guy who figured out his wife was gay before she did. And maybe Mary still loved him, but she was in love with another woman, a woman she barely knew, an *older* woman. And maybe that older woman had a secret.

That was how her best novels began: a series of questions, of *what-ifs*, of minor revelations that turned into major character beats. She started *Not Much Left* – the title rising up out of the first conversation between Mary Day and her husband Eddie – three days before the trip to Hawaii, forcing herself to wake up in the middle of the night and write in three hour intervals while Maura was asleep. When Maura had jobs, she *should* have been able to write in one of her rooms at the house, but what if Dad found her and told Maura? Maybe she could explain she was writing a novel in secret, but Dad wouldn't understand that. He'd always written with the door open.

The library was out. The Starbucks down the street was out. Paparazzi weren't exactly beating down her door, but the last thing she needed was for Maura to open *People* or the *Enquirer* in a week to discover that her beloved, trusted live-in girlfriend was having a tryst with a novel that shouldn't be happening. All it took was one candid and then the fights would start.

Oh but it *should* be happening. It should. *Not Much Left* was going to be the best thing she ever wrote, and stopping now would be like cutting one of her limbs off. So she got into her car and drove up and up and up into the Hollywood Hills, past the Spanish revival houses that hugged the road, past the grand mansions with the glass-front walls, past the point where the Hills started being anonymous. There, she would park her car and get into the backseat, turn on a little Fleetwood Mac, and write until her fingers hurt.

And did it feel like cheating? Yes. Cheating. Lying. Betraying. Karen understood that, regretted it. What she was doing was not fair to Maura. On the other hand, she wasn't entirely sure *why* it was such a bad thing. Maura was off acting, making *her* living. Why wasn't she allowed to do the thing that made hers? Not to mention that it was the thing that made her *happy*. Why was it so important to Maura that she have the ultimate forefront in Karen's mind at all time? Why was writing the other woman?

She told herself to leave the laptop at home when she was packing for the flight to Honolulu. Actually stood in the bedroom, looking at the thing plugged in and resting on top of her dresser, her heart beating hard and her breath coming in through a throat that felt like a thin reed. She cast her eyes toward the suitcase, then dragged them back to the laptop. Then back. Then back again. Maura was in the shower and was thus expecting her, but for the time being she felt paralyzed by indecision. The book was going along so well. *So* well, and it looked as if this was going to be the one she insisted on. Her other trunk novels, her other folder-in-folder novels, her other *lesbian* novels: those had all been good. *Not Much Left* was verging on great, and she knew it. She knew it might be her best novel yet; all the storylines and character development and author musings seemed to be coming from a place outside herself, and she was plucking it all from the ether and injecting it directly into her manuscript. There was no way she was going to write *The End* and print it out at Kinko's and slide it into a trunk to molder. She was going to storm into Cynthia's office and... well, okay, she wouldn't go to Cynthia's *office*, nothing would make her go back *there*, but she would bring Cyn out to lunch and show her the manuscript and tell her she was never going to publish another book with Chanler & Cushing until this got into the pipeline.

"I'm coming out," she would say to Cynthia, "and I'm going to do it with this novel. It's time, Cyn. I'm ready. Aren't you?"

She slid the laptop underneath the pile of Hawaiian shirts she'd bought for the trip, the ones Maura wouldn't even touch. There was going to be so much to distract her in Honolulu, she wouldn't even notice Karen sneaking off for a couple hours to write. Right?

As they headed out the door to await the taxi, their maid – a woman named Rita Burana who was short and stout and reminded Maura of her grandmother – sidled up to them holding a square white box. Without looking inside, Karen knew what it was: a manuscript box.

"Your agent sent this," Rita said. "She sent it overnight so I guess it's important."

Rita had never understood the difference between *agent* and *editor*, and Karen had long given up trying to explain it. Sometimes Cynthia sent her manuscripts so she could write blurbs to print on the back cover, but they'd never been sent with the urgency of an overnight delivery.

"Did it come with a note or anything?" Karen asked.

Sighing – Rita was fond of being world-weary – the maid said, "If it had, I would have told you. Do you really not have that sort of confidence in me?"

Maura jumped in now, because she was better with Rita. Karen often wondered if it was because they were closer in age, then wondered if the thought might not be uncharitable. "Thank you, Rita. You're always so good to us."

"And you're always so good to me," Rita said, gracing Maura with a beatific smile. Karen blinked. When Rita was gone, she wheeled on Maura. "What was that about?"

Unruffled, Maura said, "Rita responds to positive reinforcement, my love."

"She's not a child."

"And that's why I don't treat her like one."

Karen wrinkled her nose. "That's harsh. I'm going to cry all the way to Hawaii now."

"Giving me more reasons to start my tropical drinking schedule early." Maura nodded to the box. "You going to open that?"

Karen shrugged. "I guess I'll bring it. If Cyn wants a blurb that badly from me, it's probably a book she knows I'll like. We've got five hours in the air, and reading will calm me."

But of course it didn't calm her. Inside the box, Karen found Henry Dear's fourth novel. It was called *Goodbye, Burger City*, and it came with a short, handwritten note by Cynthia:

Karen,

All I ask is that you keep an open mind. – C

With some trepidation, Karen grabbed a sheaf of pages from the top of the stack inside and slid the rest of the box into the compartment above the seat. One of the best perks of first class was all the extra space you got. If she'd been in coach, maybe she wouldn't have bothered with the awkward box until they'd landed and gotten settled into the room, and maybe she wouldn't have ruined their vacation so thoroughly.

The dedication did nothing to alleviate her trepidation.

For my best friend Karen: this story from the outside in.

"Henry," she murmured. Maura, who was deep inside a John Grisham novel beside her, looked up. "Nothing," she assured, and Maura went back to whatever new tale of lawyers in peril Grisham had managed to cram between two covers. Karen turned the first page and almost immediately her insides felt watery. Her stomach turned lazily. A headache began to form behind her right eye, and by the time they'd landed in Hawaii, it would be screaming. Worst was her skin, which felt sick all over; not crawling, exactly, just *sick*, as if the inner lining of her gut had turned inside out and was stretched over her skeleton. She imagined the bile and bacteria crawling over the surface of her raw, striated pink flesh and shuddered. Before they were halfway to Oahu, she had finished Henry

Dear's latest novel, and knowing that she couldn't get up and start screaming made her feel lost and hopeless and hamstrung.

This was how Chapter One began:

Laurel Hunt was only six years old when she discovered the hole in her bedroom wall, and what she saw through it should have terrified her. Because she was only six, though, and a smart six, it only intrigued her. Mommy was on top of Daddy. They were both naked, mostly. Mommy was wearing something around her waist that Laurel couldn't quite make out. It was like a belt, cinched tight just above her bottom. And she was moving her hips back and forth, back and forth, in a rhythm like dancing. From where Laurel stood, it didn't seem exactly *like dancing. For one thing, Daddy wasn't moving at all. He was making nosies, though, some deep, guttural noises that Laurel had never heard before coming from him. And he was saying The Bad Word over and over again in that same deep voice: "Oh fuck, Ruth, fuck yeah, fuck yeah, goddamn!"*

Karen almost stopped reading right then. Raw, wire-thin fury wound its way through her, frayed and sparking. Her sudden capacity for hate was bottomless. Henry Dear was at the top of the list, but also Cynthia Auburn, Chanler & Cushing, even her father. Even her *mother*. Why had her parents, her fucking *parents*, been so disastrously fucked up? So much so that they'd fucked *her* up. She'd worn a fake dick and fucked the author of this book when they were both sixteen. Sixteen-year-olds shouldn't know what fucking *pegging* was. Goddammit. God-fucking-*dammit*.

She read on. And on. And when she finished, she found it impossible not to start again. Now here she was on her third read-through, and Maura was standing before her, wearing a flowered sundress, looking stately and radiant, her giant floppy hat tilted back so that it looked like a halo around her head.

"No," Maura said quietly. "Not going to Waikiki. Not going to another island. Going home. Getting my stuff. And then ... somewhere else."

The manuscript nearly dragged her eyes back down to itself; she was on the part where Laurel Hunt had begun fucking her father's agent, a woman named Tara, but it was framed more as something a lot more traumatic than her first trysts with Cynthia had been. For one thing, the agent was the one who initiated things; she never forced herself on Laurel, but it becomes obvious that she's not really going to take no for an answer. And in bed, she promises Laurel a recording contract, something even better than her father's. "His career is reaching the end," Tara whispers right before she sinks her fingers into Laurel for the first time. "Yours is just about to get started. And I want to be there. I want to help." It's abusive. It's a powerful person preying on the innocent. It was sick. And Henry Dear was sick for having thought of her relationship with Cynthia in such a disgusting way. What right did he – a straight man who couldn't understand *anything* about what two women can mean to one another – have to put this into a book? And what right did Cynthia have in publishing it?

All the same, she wanted to read those passages again.

Instead, she tried to focus on her girlfriend. "Somewhere else? Maura, what are you even talking about?"

"I know you're in some sort of writer's brain right now. I know this manuscript is doing something to you, even though you won't talk with me about it. But I've reached the point where I'm beyond my capacity to handle your idiosyncrasies. You can't give enough of yourself to me, Karen."

"Maura, what—"

"I'm leaving you, Karen. I love you and I will always love you. But you love writing. I know you've been working on a book in secret for weeks now. It's fucked up that you can't be healthy about what you do. You don't know it's fucked up. You think it's a virtue. It's not. I love you but I can't be the other woman in this relationship you have with your work. Goodbye, Karen." It had the cadence of a speech, long-considered and often rehearsed. But it wasn't like it didn't sting. The words were like tiny papercuts, slicing into the sensitive exposed gut she'd been wearing on the outside for days.

Karen opened her mouth to say something, anything. Beg her to stay. Coldly explain that Maura knew what she was getting into when she hooked up with a novelist. Mention how the shower thing was fucked up, and that was *her* fault. Plead. Reason. Try to get her to understand that this wasn't about

Maura, it was about Henry and her parents and Cynthia. But Karen knew it wasn't just *Goodbye, Burger City* Maura was talking about. Hell, that didn't even scratch the surface. This wasn't about now. It was about always.

What came out was this: "I'm sorry I'm the way I am. I know it's not fair. I'm not fair."

"I don't know what's fair, Karen," Maura told her. "I just know that this isn't where I can be happy. I just want to be happy."

"Are you flying out today?" As soon as the question escaped her, Karen knew it was the wrong one. Downshifting into the prosaic was the surest way to hammer home that you didn't really care. That if you could shrug your way through a good-bye, the years prior didn't mean all that much.

"Goodbye, Karen," Maura said, then made her way across the room and out the door. Karen watched her go, wondering when the tears would start. After awhile, she tried to force the tears to start. Then she turned toward the lanai; a light breeze was playing with the gauze curtains, making them dance like playful ghosts. Beyond: dead volcanoes, covered in green.

She looked back down at *Goodbye, Burger City*, shook her head briefly once, and sat down at the room's writing desk. Numbness pulsed through her, the same shock she'd felt in the aftermath of what had happened with the butcher in Cynthia's building. Maybe not the *exact* same, but close enough. Her breath whistled shallowly in her lungs. Her hands flexed and released, flexed and released.

"Oh," she whispered, and no one was there to hear her as she slipped out of stasis and into panic. She could see him as the elevator door opened, a man in white covered in blood, and she realized that she had been able to *smell* the blood even before she could see it. She could smell the blood now; it reeked, redolent in her nostrils as if the air were thick with it instead of hibiscus and honey. The pills she'd eventually had to take for her panic attacks were back in California. Why would she need them in Hawaii? Nothing was going to trigger an attack in the middle of paradise.

She felt her foot sink into the man's belly. Felt the heel tear the shirt; she could hear it, too, under the thump-thump-thump of her brain. Then the way the heel sunk into his flesh, his innards. She'd torn a hole in his gut and he was bleeding out under her. He *would* bleed out. He'd die down there while she lay unconscious in the lobby of Chanler & Cushing. Even as she slipped back into the world, that eerie catatonia wouldn't shake itself off. She wore it like a robe. A cape. It deflected reality, that cape. She'd murdered a man. It was accidental and he would have killed her if she hadn't done something, but she had murdered a man. She would know that for the rest of her life. She would have to live with his actual blood on her actual hands, and when she'd tried to go to the funeral, his pale, pinch-faced daughter had run up to her screaming, "*Murderer! I'll see you in Hell, murderer!*" And Karen had screamed back, "*He* was the murderer! He killed four people!" And she shrieked, "You killed my *father!*" and then collapsed to the ground, wailing, and later she found out that her name was Anita, and that she was in her twenties and that her Dad had long been unstable and losing his job had just pushed him over the edge. Karen learned this over two slices of pie at Anita's apartment. The catatonia still hadn't worn off or even down much, but knowing that her butcher alive was maybe as bad as he was dead had nudged her toward true awakening.

Anita had forgiven her, but she would never forgive herself. Of course it mattered that he'd killed people. Of course it mattered that he probably deserved to die for what he'd done. But what mattered most was that Karen had done it, and that at some point, she *would* make peace with what she'd done, and that was the worst of it all. In your life, you have to live with working the terrible stuff into the fabric, because if you don't, you'll go insane.

Karen fumbled her laptop open and looked into the screen. At the top of every page, a header in light gray reading **K. Luck / Not much left**. Without a moment to get a cup of water or trying to regulate her breathing, Karen sat down and began to type.

She was two pages in and things were getting interesting when the door to the room burst open. Karen dragged her eyes away from the screen and there, in the doorway, stood Maura, her bag with the pineapples on it slung over one shoulder, her sunglasses tucked provocatively in the fabric between her cleavage. Her eyes were red. She had been crying. Of course she'd been crying. And in here, she had been suffering her first panic attack in months. It occurred to Karen they'd been doing those things alone. It further occurred to Karen that she was going to *keep* doing things alone. The little nighttime banter she and Maura had before falling asleep. The way they'd read in bed together and sometimes tell each other what was happening. The mundane stuff: grocery shopping and going to concerts and arguing about what to watch on TV. All of that was about to be gone.

She knows I love her, right? Karen thought frantically. *Sure she does. Of course she does. She wouldn't be back if she didn't know that. Oh God, she came back. Oh God, I have another chance.* Adrenaline spiked in her veins. Excitement coursed through her. She could fix this. She could absolutely fix this. The excitement was immediately followed with the contradictory: did she *want* to fix this?

Maura, just tell me what to do and I'll do it. Or I'll try. Not the writing stuff, I need that, but literally anything else. You—

"Have you turned on the TV?" Maura asked.

Blinking, unprepared for the question, Karen said, "No, I was keeping it off. I thought ... well, you weren't here so I was going to write."

Maura closed her eyes and inhaled deeply. "The fact that you... You know what, nevermind. Turn on the television."

Karen did and settled on the edge of the bed. Maura also sat on the edge of the bed, as far away from her as she could go without falling off. The set warmed up. Karen was about to ask what this was all about when she saw it. Someone leaped from a high floor of a skyscraper. The camera didn't follow the person all the way down. They were too far away to see clearly, but Karen knew that person was now dead. That was the first certainty of that morning.

"Is it a movie?" Karen asked, knowing of course it was not.

"Two planes hit the World Trade Centers," Maura said quietly, inching a little closer. "I don't know why. Some people are saying it's terrorists. I don't know."

For an hour, they watched television in silence as the World Trade Centers collapsed, as people died or survived, as police and firefighters and EMTs raced to the scene and tried to save as many people as they could. It wasn't many.

Then Maua was beside her, and her hand was entwined with Karen's. In her periphery, she saw the Towers fall and fall and fall. She knew what she needed. Wanted, but also needed. She thought of prefacing it with saying, "I'm still mad at you," or, "I'm still leaving," but you didn't have to say stuff if everyone was on the same page. On the other side of the world, people from her country were dying horribly. Helplessness and horror intertwined inside her as she reached for the remote and flipped the TV off. Karen didn't protest.

"Make love with me," she said simply, and at once Karen touched her lips to Maura's. She broke apart and looked Maura in the eyes. She thought of prefacing this by asking whether Maura was still mad, or whether she would still be leaving. But none of that seemed important right now. In the wake of her panic attack and the writing that cured it, the shock of seeing Maura again so soon and the goddamned terror of what was on TV, the only important thing was giving into Maura's request.

She kissed Maura's neck, her breasts, the small concave curve of her belly. Fumbled her belt off and kept kissing. It was only as she drifted down to Maura's vagina, a place she'd found an inordinate amount of joy in over the last few years, did she realize she was once again in shock. Or ... or no. No. She was *still* in shock. She was *still* numb. What was happening in New York, Maura leaving, Henry Dear's book: all levels of bad, but they were all affecting her the same way. She was furious with Henry ... but did she *feel* furious? She wanted to scream and cry at the idea of a future without Maura, a woman she probably needed. But those screams and cries weren't hitting her, weren't erupting. And then there was the real tragedy. The real atrocity. And it sickened her and frightened her, but it did those things at such a far remove from the core of Karen's self that it was hard to even acknowledge them.

How long have I been like this? she wondered as she did the thing that made Maura groan deep, deep back in her throat. The sound was encouraging, but it was also far away, smaller than usual. Maura was also numb. God, had *she* done this to her girlfriend? Had *she* been so traumatized that it had flowed out of her pores and infected this good woman who'd only wanted love and showers?

People just either jumped to their death or burned alive in New York, Karen, her brain shot back. *Jesus, not everything is about you.*

Then she moved her tongue in the opposite direction and tried to shut out all the voices in her head.

It didn't work.

Chapter 12: Being Karen Luck

"He betrayed me," was the first thing she said to Cynthia Auburn when she finally got her on the phone. "And you let him. You *helped* him."

A pause on the line. "Yes, I'm alive. Thank you for asking."

"I've known you were alive for two weeks. Florence told me."

"Then how about some compassion? The Towers were literally within walking distance. I can't—"

"What, believe that you're using a national tragedy as a way to make me forget about what you did? I got him his contract. I paired you two up. And *this* is what happens?"

"It's a good book, Karen," she said. "What, did you *not* want me to publish a good book?"

Karen closed her eyes. "I wasn't allowed to write a novel with a lesbian main character for years, and Henry Dear just swoops in and gets to do it on his third time out?"

"He's not a lesbian," Cynthia said.

"Even more reason!" Karen shouted, and something in her brain twinged.

"Look, you keep making me out to be the bad guy on this, but I'm not. You coming out in fiction disrupts your real life. For a straight guy like Henry, it's just a *brave choice*. It's a different perception.

"Well *fuck* perception. I want to make a brave choice. Why is it *his* brave choice? Why not *mine*?"

A pause on the line. Karen didn't know what it meant. When Cynthia spoke, it was in a voice just above a murmur.

"I have been trying to protect you your whole life, Karen. Your mother…"

"You wanted to fuck my mother. And you couldn't, because she died. So you fucked her husband and you fucked her daughter and all these years after we broke up, you're still fucking me."

"How dare you." But the words were flat, emotionless.

"I dare easily. I'm glad you're not dead but that's as far as this goes. I want out. I'm done with you and with Chanler & Cushing."

Cynthia uttered a short, petulant bark. "You can't be done with us. You have two books left in your three-book contract and your father – should I put that in quotes? – has one left. That's three books you owe me, little miss Luck. And don't think I won't collect."

Karen hung up.

She went to the massive window that served as the south wall. The hills dropped off precipitously just outside, and she had the most gorgeous view of Los Angeles. Placing a hand on the glass, she looked out at the city below and tears welled in her eyes. She didn't know if they were for Maura, or for Cynthia, or even for Henry Dear. Maybe they were for 9/11, a concept that was already becoming abstract in her mind, only two weeks out. Maybe they were for herself. She had never meant to make loneliness an idea to strive for; now that she had it, she didn't know what to do with it. She thought she might hate it. What she knew for certain is that it would be good to have a woman standing next to her right now, helping her figure out what the next step was, squeezing her hand and telling her everything was going to be all right, even though it would be a lie.

Karen Luck stood at the window for a long while, then climbed upstairs to her father's room. Soft music was pouring out. Sheryl Crow, maybe. Dad had liked the first album, but the second one was, in his words, transformative. She lightly rapped on the door and turned the handle. Dad was at his desk, squinting at the desktop Mac she'd given him for Christmas. She leaned in the doorway and looked at him a minute.

"How'd it go?" he asked, still not turning from the screen.

"I have three books left spread over two contracts."

Dad exhaled slowly. "So she's alive."

Karen closed her eyes and nodded. "Yeah, Cynthia's alive."

"What are you going to do?"

Taking a step into his room and lowering the music most of the way – not all the way, Sheryl Crow had a voice she wanted to swim inside – she tented her fingers at the edge of his desk and looked at his screen. Word was open, and two paragraphs had been constructed.

"That depends on you, at least a little," she muttered, reading.

If someone needed to die, really needed to die, Jessica Cunningham was a good person to know. By the age of twenty-seven, she had murdered forty-seven people. Not a bad streak for a woman who hadn't even started killing until she was out of the Army. They'd trained her to do it for a weekly wage. Jessica had always wanted a little more out of life.

"That's not bad, Dad."

"It's good, isn't it? Not great, but pretty good."

"Hitwoman?" Dad nodded slowly. "What are you doing with it?"

He sighed. "Not deleting it like all the others. It's too good to just trash. But it's ... it's goddamn slow going. I've been working on these two paragraphs all day."

"There's no rule that says you have to write books quickly. John Irving doesn't. Donna Tartt doesn't."

"It's my rule. It was your mother's too, I think." He finally tore his eyes from the screen and glanced at her. "It's your rule, too."

Gravely, she moved over to his bed and sat on the edge. "Well, that's sort of what I need to talk with you about."

"Three books left in the contract."

"Two in mine. One in yours."

"Okay."

She tilted her chin toward the computer. "Do you want to finish this? Do you want this to be your final book with Chanler & Cushing?"

Dad let out a long, solemn breath. "We're moving?"

"I'm going to shop us around. We're two hugely popular writers. Other publishers will want us. Maybe they'll even pay us more."

"The pay's not important anymore."

"Maybe not. But it would be nice to be wanted."

He put a hand on hers. "Missing Maura?"

"Yes," she said at once. "But that's not what this is. This is about not being taken for granted. It's about having my own voice. I'm not going anywhere that won't let me have that."

"It would offer a certain ... I don't know, circularity to finish off my run with Chanler & Cushing with a book I actually wrote. But honey, I don't know when I'm going to finish. This could take years."

"Okay. Then it will take years. And it will be your first elsewhere." She looked at him and he looked at her for a long while.

"Why do I get the impression that you're asking me for something?"

"I need to go back to the house in OKC. I need to write these last two ... these last three books for Cynthia."

"Are you going to talk with Henry?"

"I don't know."

Dad stood and went to her. "How long are we going to be back in the old house?" She knew what his real question was: how long would it take her to write three novels worthy of publication, worthy of Karen and Gary Luck's names?

Because no matter how badly she wanted to get out of these draconian contracts and shut from Cynthia, she wasn't going to turn in shoddy work. Especially not if she needed her audience to follow her where she was going next.

"You're coming?"

"Maybe ... maybe Jessica Cunningham kills faster in Oklahoma City."

"Weirder things have happened."

"How long, Karen?"

She took a deep breath. "A month."

His eyes went wide. "Karen. No. You know that's lunacy."

"It's not. I can do it."

"Maybe. But you're going to kill yourself."

"I won't. Maybe I'll come close. But I have four brand new novels for whatever new publisher takes us. Four already written. I can breathe then."

He sighed. "You won't. Jesus, three books in a month."

"Unless you finish that one."

"Karen..."

"Now comes the important part, Dad. I have a lot of ideas in my head for Karen Luck novels. I'll chase a couple down and see if they stick. What I don't have is an idea for a new *Gary* Luck novel. Any thoughts?"

He went back to his computer and clicked open a few folders. Inside the folders, dozens of documents with a single sentence, maybe two, written. She looked at one of them.

Mike Bull drank coffee and looked out at the streets below, which were cold because it was winter. And because there was a lady he wanted to know who fuck fuck fuck

"I was going to call it *Bullseye*. He was going to meet Jessica Cunningham, actually. Then I thought, well, maybe this isn't a Mike Bull novel. Maybe this is a Cunningham novel. And if I can write one, maybe it's a series. But two paragraphs in a day don't make a series."

"How do they cross paths?"

"I don't know," he told her. "That was the hell of it. I think she had a hit out on him or something. But he stopped her and they went after someone else. Something like that. It never went anywhere."

"Okay."

He raised his eyebrows. "Okay?"

"Okay."

Against her strenuous objections, Dad called Skylark Dear to let her know that they would be coming home. "Would you mind calling a maid service and having them come in to air the place out some? I'd like it to feel like home when we get there."

"It'll be good to see you, Gary," she said. "Karen will be joining you?"

"Yes."

A pause. "And how is she?"

Gary looked around and didn't see his daughter around. "I think Henry hurt her. I think he hurt her a lot."

"He gave the book to me when he was done. I told him to stick in a drawer and never send it out to the publisher."

"Tell me something, Sky. Is it a bad book?"

She answered immediately. "No. It's a very good book. His best book. I can see why he wouldn't want to hide it away."

He had so many more questions. He wanted to know if he was still dressing up like his daughter when he was writing. He wanted to know if writing it was hurting him as much as it was hurting Karen. He wanted to know if he was still in love with her. Gary suspected the answer to all these questions was yes, but he didn't think Skylark would know.

When he hung up, Karen appeared from around the corner. She'd heard everything, after all. Of course she had. "How did she sound?"

"Skylark? Fine."

"Just fine?"

"Karen, I don't know if she knows all that much about Henry's writing."

Karen looked at him clear-eyed. "I wasn't asking about Henry's writing."

He sighed. "We didn't talk that much about Henry himself, either. Karen, are you sure going back home is a good idea?"

"It's the only idea," she said, deciding to drop any and all questions regarding Skylark. He'd asked about maids and he'd asked about *Goodbye, Burger City*. They didn't talk about whether she'd changed her hair since they'd last seen the Dears, or whether she'd been seeing someone, or how she was holding up since her husband finally, really left. Karen could picture her in her office downstairs, maybe the kerchief around her neck loose after a long day, her lipstick wiped free. She's done in. She leans back in her chair and all she needs is something calm, some release. She needs. She *needs*.

And then Karen Luck, who has been away for so long, slips into the house quietly, unexpectedly. With tented fingers, she pushes Skylark Dear's door open and the woman's eyes draw up toward her face. There's no lust there, not yet, but the immediate indulgent smile, the joyful way she welcomes Karen in – maybe that's enough. Small talk, sure, but Karen can already smell her perfume. Light and lilac, sprayed on her nude body so many hours ago. It's almost gone now, but just enough lingers on her skin and in the air around her to be intoxicating.

Coming around to the other side of the desk, she whispers, "It's been so long, Skylark," and even using the woman's first name makes her flush. She's a little girl talking to her friend's Mom. Surely she wasn't allowed to use her first name. But does the name feel right in her mouth? Of course it does. Because *this* is right. And Skylark Dear *wants* Karen to talk to her like this. You can tell by the way she tilts her head back and closes her eyes, the way her lips part just a little. Skylark is a woman who needs kissing, and Karen doesn't waste another moment in holding back.

The woman's neck, so long and

"Karen?" Dad, still in front of her, tilted his head. "Still there?"

"Yeah, sorry. Plotting stuff out," she said, reddening and not wanting him to see. "A week. Better get ready."

Then Karen retreated upstairs to her bedroom where she absolutely did not get ready. Then a shower. Then more work in *Not Much Left*. She was going to have to put this on hiatus for a little while, and she wanted it in good shape for when she returned to Los Angeles. She thought she *could* finish it before they flew out, but this wasn't something she felt like rushing. Writing this novel was like archeology; she was chipping decades of stone and rock and age to uncover new and unexamined parts of herself. A lot of the book was about Mary Day's long affair with an older woman named Steff Michaels, and Karen knew that she was going let the book pause on the moment the older woman revealed her biggest secret. Her father, Steff would explain, used to abuse her. Beat her, sure, but once in awhile he would come into her room at night and close the door and wake her up by climbing into bed with her and putting his hands on her. He didn't stop with his hands. At this point in the story, Mary Day, holding her baby, would clutch it tighter in her arms, as if Steff's father might barrel his way out of her story and attack the child. But he wasn't going to do much of anything these days. When Steff was sixteen, she had murdered her father while he slept. She'd done it with his nail gun; it had hung in the garage most of her life, and she had long been in awe of its raw power. Killing him had sent a surge of that power through her; it wasn't new, it was reclamation. She was taking that power back from him. She nailed him again and again, driving them through all his soft parts. Then she left her mother a note explaining everything he'd done to her, even though she suspected her mother knew. And then she'd skedaddled, changing her name and hiding out in state after state, never quite sure she was safe. "And that's his greatest legacy," Steff would tell Mary Day. "He's been dead for almost as long as you've been alive, and he's still after me."

That would be the line to end on until they were back in Los Angeles. Always pause in the middle of a scene; you can find the energy of that scene later a lot more easily than if you reach a natural stopping point and have to start a new scene. She'd done it, written until exhaustion and stopped at the end of a chapter, only to discover the next day that she couldn't rev the engine back up. That wasn't going to happen here. Not with this book. It was too important.

By the time she and her father were in the back of the Lincoln Towncar on the way to LAX, she had written fifty more pages and that scene she'd been striving toward was long in the past. Such was her nature.

Thomas McAdams didn't know if this was the best possible way to christen a new home, but she was more than willing to find out.

"Does it hurt?" she asked Henry, whose wrists were still lashed to the bed in this unfamiliar room in this brand-new cabin on the outskirts of the city, and whose ass was still in the air before her. His largest toy, the one he said he didn't much like, was lodged inside him. She kept trying to push it in further and he kept making the worst little yelping noise every time she did.

"Yeah," he said.

"Okay," she told him, and inched just a little more in. Henry yelped again. She dropped her hand down and found her clit and tapped it lightly, so lightly. This couldn't go on, but for now, it was exactly what she needed. She'd never talked to her therapist about S&M being a proper cure for PTSD, but then her therapist, a woman named Betty who wore her classes with a fine gold chain connecting the two stems around her neck, was kind of a prude who didn't like talking about sex at all. She was okay with survivor's guilt. An expert at discussing self-harm. Aces at clinical depression. But when she started talking about Welton Dear and what he'd tried to do to her as she watched the Alfred P. Murrah Federal Building – a building her own father was inside – crumble into dust and ash on TV, Betty would interrupt and say, "What a bad man. A terrible circumstance. But let's talk about your father, Thomas. My, how that must have affected you."

Of course it had. How many people can say they saw their parents die on television? It wasn't like she and Dad were super close, but she'd go over to his apartment once a month or so and make a big deal about his model planes. Sometimes he had a girlfriend. Sometimes he drank too much. But mostly he was a good dad who'd raised her himself and had never been prouder of her than when she'd joined Civil Air Patrol. There had been a time when he was her whole world. When she'd thrown up in the air, all she could think about was how much it would disappoint him. It occurred to her that she didn't have to tell him. If she quit CAP, it would be easier in the long run. He'd be disappointed in her decision, maybe, but he wouldn't know how flawed her *constitution* was. Her *character*. His daughter Thomas did not have what it took to be a pilot in the Air Force, and he would know that and judge her for that for the rest of her life.

It was always better to quit while you were ahead than to bumble through and eventually fall apart. That went for Civil Air Patrol, and for awhile it also went for Henry Dear. She'd quit CAP soon after the encampment, explaining to her father that it didn't hold the same excitement for her anymore. He'd been hurt by that; his father had been in the Air Force, and he worshipped his father. Thomas, at least for a little while, worshipped *her* father, and would do almost anything to please him. He hadn't been able to join the Air Force – something to do with his eyes that he would never talk about – but man, did he love planes. He loved planes more than anything else, save for his dad and his wife and maybe his daughter. It was easier to love dead people, Thomas reckoned when she was old enough to sign up for CAP despite a tepid-at-best interest. Dead people couldn't disappoint you.

Thomas's love for her father had been a complex, sometimes frustrating thing, but it had been a living thing:

mutable, different every day. It was something she was working on, by herself, with her shrink, and with Henry Dear, who had proven to be a remarkably keen listener. After sex, she would lie in bed next to him and orate on her day or on what she was feeling or what book she was reading, and he'd prop himself up on one elbow and simply listen to her, enrapt. Sometimes he'd ask questions, then fall silent as he digested her answers. She had rarely been the subject of such laser focus before. Dad mainly wanted to talk about his father and planes and how his father flew planes; her friends in school and in CAP weren't exactly shallow, but Thomas always felt that if any one of them were to go missing, it would take her a few minutes to place which one. Real personality was hard to come by, and hard to share. Henry wanted to share his, and wanted her to share hers. Falling in love with him after CAP hadn't been what she'd wanted, and she'd had a feeling it hadn't been what *he* wanted, either. But in love they were, and living together until that night her father died, and Henry's father had offered her comfort while she sat there, shocked. And when she wouldn't take comfort, he'd tried to force comfort. Thomas could still feel his hands, weirdly strong, grossly oily, running up the front of her shirt, his damp breath at her neck, his other arm holding her in place, explaining that she was hysterical and not herself, but that he would make her feel better, he would make her feel.

Instinct had kicked in and Thomas, not without training, had wrenched away from him, landing a punch into his soft gut and another to the side of his neck. He'd fallen back on the couch, his eyes wide, his body writhing, and she punched him again, this time in the balls. A horrible *urrrraaagh* sound vomited from him and she thought, her stomach lurching, that this was the man for whom Henry had joined CAP. *This* was the man he'd wanted to impress.

Then there were steps in the long hallway leading toward the living room, and when Thomas looked up, she was sure Skylark Dear was coming toward them. She hadn't anticipated this, but then she hadn't anticipated any of this. How would she explain herself to this terrible man's wife? What if *she* attacked Thomas? But then Thomas saw it wasn't Skylark after all. It was Henry. Henry in makeup and a dress, rushing toward them like Norman Bates in *Psycho*, his eyes wide and his fists raised.

"What happened?" he asked, and Thomas' head swam.

"Henry?" It was all she could manage.

He hesitated. "I was writing," he said, as if those three words explained everything. "Thomas, what happened?"

For the first time since Welton Dear had put his hand on her, she swung back to the television. As if in a bad dream that kept coming true, the Murrah Building just kept collapsing over and over. "My Dad," she said simply, and then let loose a long, righteous, ululating scream.

That's where the sequence of things got jumbled. What Thomas remembered was snapshots. The funeral. Moving out of Henry's house and into her father's apartment. Her friend Marie coming by with cake, then leaving almost immediately when Thomas refused to talk. Lying awake that first night, alone in a bed that wasn't hers, staring up at the plane models dangling from the ceiling via thin snips of wire. Maybe she cried. Maybe she slept. Her job at the bank had given her time for grief and she took it. Days flickered in and out of consciousness like shadows on the wall of an old-time projection booth. Then one day, Henry Dear was sitting across from her in a coffee shop and she had no idea how she'd gotten there. Only that that was when the narrative of her life seemed to regain its linear progression.

She picked up her coffee cup and saw her hands doing it; not as if someone else was doing it this time, not as if her hands were miles and miles away. She placed the cup to her lip and felt the porcelain rum against her lips. Inhaled and felt her brain popping awake from the smell. The bitter black coffee sloshed onto her tongue and she relished it, swallowing and finding pleasure in it. Then Henry was saying her name and she looked up, and there he was, no makeup, no dress, just the man she hadn't wanted to fall in love with sitting here, looking at her with eyes that seemed to communicate love.

"Thomas?"

"Your makeup," she said simply, and she knew at once that this would be confusing. He hadn't been in makeup for … for what? Weeks? A month? How long had all this been.

Henry made a noise deep in the back of his throat and looked away from her. "I was going to tell you."

"Tell me? Tell me what?" She remembered his run down the hallway, how it had reminded her of Anthony Perkins in *Psycho*, wearing his mother's wig and dress before he slaughtered that woman Marian Crane in the shower. Inside, she cringed away from this man across from her, this man whose internal life she thought she knew, around whose family she assumed she was safe.

Henry had closed his eyes and swallowed. "It's how I write. I can't write without it. I was writing that day … when all that stuff happened."

"Your father tried to rape me as I watched my father die." The sentence felt so absurd in her mouth, a soap-opera declaration that she should have screamed, her eyes wild, her hair matted but her makeup still so perfect. Absurd or not, though, it was their reality. She murmured it, loud enough for him to hear.

"I'm not going to make an argument for forgiveness," Henry said. "I think he's always been a … a wretch. I didn't see it because I was trying to impress him. I can't apologize for him, but I can apologize for letting him near you. If I ever thought…"

Thomas set down the coffee cup. "The makeup."

"I like being someone else when I write," he said, and she sensed he wanted to leave it there. She thought later that maybe it would have been best if he'd left it there. Thomas hadn't wanted to fall in love with this man across from her, but somewhere down the line, it had just happened. And now she was stuck in it, like a squirrel in tar. Henry said, "I like being *her* when I write."

Still reeling from the fugue state she'd found herself in for the last week or so, Thomas nearly asked who the *she* was. But it was really so obvious, wasn't it?

"Jesus, Henry," she muttered. "I thought you wanted to be your mother."

He blinked. "Why would I want to be my mother?"

"Why would you want to be Karen Luck?"

A shaky smile touched the corners of his mouth, and as much as Thomas didn't want to interpret that as a Pavlovian response to the woman's name, she didn't see how she could do otherwise. "Well, she's a success, isn't she? A wild success. If you want to be a writer, the kind that people read, why not emulate someone like Karen Luck?"

"Emulate, maybe," Thomas grunted, touching her temples. "That's not what you're doing, Henry. You're … you're *inhabiting* her. That's worse than cheating."

His eyes went so wide so fast they bulged. "It is *not* worse than cheating. I would *never* sleep with another woman. *Ever.*"

"Not even Karen Luck?" Thomas asked, hating the keening, sneering tone of voice in her mouth.

"She's a lesbian," he said, and that gave her some pause.

"Wait, for real?"

"For real. And it's kind of a secret, so don't spread it around."

Thomas shook her head. "How long have you known?"

"High school graduation." He bit his lip. "*That* was why we broke up, really. I didn't tell you the whole thing. We'd already drifted apart for awhile, but then we got drunk and she told me."

Thomas was letting the whole thing sink in. Now that she was aware of herself, there was going to come a moment that she would have to face the fact that she'd seen her father die, that she'd buried him, that her boyfriend's father had tried to rape her, that she had to figure out a whole new path of life. So she was glad for the distraction.

"If she wasn't a lesbian, would you still have sex with her?"

His eyes pleaded with her. "I don't know, Thomas." She thought she knew him well enough to know that he was telling the truth about that. It wasn't the answer she wanted, but it would be good enough.

"Are you still in love with her?" *Jesus, Thomas, why are you asking questions you don't want answers to?*

The pleading in his eyes fell away, replaced only by a soft sort of wistfulness. "Of course I am. Most days I don't want to be, but of course I am. Doesn't mean I'm not in love with you."

Thomas sighed. "So my options are working my ass off to try to make you forget her or pretending your high school crush isn't haunting our relationship and willingly subjugate myself to her memory. All for something you'll never have again."

"Thomas..."

"Of course there's the third option, which is just leaving you. Let me tell you, Henry, none of these options seem all that appealing to me."

"Why aren't you asking me to change? For you?"

"Because it won't do any good. I know what crushes are like. Hell, if Billy John Roberts from fifth grade called me up today and wanted to get busy, I'd probably say yes. He was my first crush, and even if he turned out homely and weird as an adult, I'd still say yes. That stuff lingers. And you've got this all wrapped up in your writing."

"Thomas," he said, tentatively reaching for her, then drawing his hand back.

"The simple shit of it is, Henry, that I can't stand to be alone right now. I don't have parents and my friend Marie and

I are maybe not as close as I thought we were. You're my best option, Henry. You're my only option."

And Henry moved in with her. The house where his mother lived was a lot bigger, and if they wanted to, they could move somewhere else completely. He wasn't living in Karen Luck's stratosphere, but Henry Dear had turned out pretty successful in his own right. Cynthia Auburn had given *Valerie* a big promotional push, and it had caught. None of his books had exploded, but every book was attracting new readers, and his last novel – *Slip Away* – had finally cracked the *New York Times* Top 10 Bestselling Books. He was doing well enough to afford an actual house. But if Thomas wanted to live in her father's old apartment, they were going to live in her father's old apartment.

Once, in the six years between him moving in and the morning two weeks after 9/11, the morning when she was attempting to see just how much pain he was willing to take at her hands, he'd asked her if she ever planned on taking the planes down from the ceiling. It had been a casual remark, offhand as he doodled in the notebook he sometimes wrote novel ideas in. Thomas had wheeled on him, her eyes blazing.

"If you touch those planes, I will *murder* you. Do you understand me, Henry? I. Will. *Murder*. You. You get dolled up every fucking day to look like your ex-girlfriend and I don't say boo. The planes fucking *stay*." Until that moment, Henry had been content to believe Thomas was living with his own form of weirdness out of a sense of pure loneliness, or some warped sense of duty she'd picked up in CAP. Until that moment, he hadn't quite realized she had plenty of her own weirdness. So he'd relaxed a little. Just a little.

Then came the morning, in February of 2001, when a snowstorm thundered into OKC so hard they closed the bank. Thomas had decided to luxuriate on the couch in the living room with a couple of novels and some hot chocolate. When Henry was done with his writing for the day, they'd flip on the TV and watch the episode of *Andy Richter Saves the Universe* they'd taped the night before, and then maybe they'd have sex.

Sex had gotten a little weird of late; Henry's seeming inability to get off without some sort of pain seemed to be escalating. Just lately, he'd begun asking her to put things inside him. "If you don't want to, that's cool," he told her, his face scarlet. He'd opened a box he'd been keeping in the closet full of toys – dildoes and vibrators, all a little bigger than the ones she sometimes used. Did he use these on *himself?* There was one in there that looked thicker than a can of Coke; how could he *possibly* utilize something like that?

    As these questions occurred to her, however, a sudden and unexpected excitement stirred in her belly. Henry's favorite way to get off had always been to have Thomas bite down on one of his nipples so hard that she sometimes drew blood. She wasn't too keen on that one. It made her feel like a vampire. She did it because he always attended to her needs first, laying her down on their bed, her legs draped over the edge so that her toes could feel the sensation of the deep-pile carpet she'd installed a year before. Something about the way the knobbiness of those fibers against the soft skin of her toes drove her wild. And he would kneel in front of her, running his tongue up her legs from the tips of her toes all the way to her vagina, stopping for awhile at the back of her knees to really explore what he found there. If the rest of it sent shivers through her, his tongue – expert, soft when it needed to be, hard when it had to be – on the back of her knees sent bolts. Orgasms sometimes – not usually, but sometimes – blasted into her that way. But she liked to hold out, because eventually that tongue would find its way inside her, and that was when the real fireworks would begin. It wasn't just that he found her clitoris; it was that he understood instinctually what to do with it when he got there. In those late-night confessional talks couples sometimes had – especially when they'd been drinking – she'd asked him if he'd done this with Karen Luck.

"Nope," he'd said, slurring a little. "She was kinkier than you. I honestly don't know how she's a lesbian because she never seemed into that stuff."

"Maybe she's into it with girls."

"Maybe," he said. "But this is a Thomas McAdams special. You like it *so* much."

"You're good at it."

"I'm good at it because it makes you happy. I like making you happy."

And he did – make her happy. But then he showed her those toys and something inside her seemed to wake up. She tried to ignore *she was kinkier than you* and the almost certain knowledge that Karen Luck and he had played with toys like this in high school. All she knew is that she wanted to try this with him, far more than she ever wanted to bite his nipples off.

The thought of doing that today, in the middle of the day while the snowstorm raged, was almost enough to distract her from the new Stephen King novel – a long book that seemed to be about snowstorms and alien invasions – but not entirely. She was deep into the second chapter when Henry emerged from his writing room, the converted pantry inside in which they still kept canned goods along with his small writing desk and computer. Rarely did she see him in the rest of the apartment with the makeup and the dress on. It was jarring; she had mostly gotten used to him dressing like a woman, like *her*, in order to get his writing done, but the idea of him dressing like that beyond the fiction was a little like carrying Karen Luck into what Thomas thought of as Henry's real life. She didn't like it. She placed a bookmark in her novel and sat up straighter.

"What's up?" she asked, only now aware that he was holding a small sheaf of pages in his hand. He thrust them out at her. When he spoke, Thomas almost expected a girly voice, or at least one at a higher pitch. Instead it was just Henry's voice, a little guarded and a little afraid. He said, "I need you to tell me this is shit."

She took the pages but didn't look at them. "Is this writing?"

Henry nodded, and now she saw he looked miserable, as if the writing had hurt him in some way. He didn't look like this when she was putting toys inside him. *That* misery was mixed with a perverse look of pleasure. Sex for Henry was agony mixed with ecstasy. This was straight-up agony. "Just please tell me to stop writing this now and maybe we can burn it. Delete the files from my computer. Hell, burn my computer. I fully defer to you here."

She looked at him, and the makeup and the dress ... it wasn't *her*. For the first time since she became aware of the way Henry wrote, she discovered that it wasn't Karen Luck, not exactly. Maybe he thought it was, but Thomas had seen Luck on TV giving interviews, had seen her picture in *People*. Karen Luck never wore earrings, but Henry did. The sort of frumpy dresses he usually wore – those were outdated, outmoded fashions Karen Luck probably wouldn't be caught dead in. Had Thomas ever seen a picture or a video of Karen Luck in a dress at all? She didn't think so. This wasn't Karen Luck her man was inhabiting; it was a memory of Karen Luck, back when they were next-door neighbors and his life hadn't been rocked by the truth of her. Was that sad or understandable? Thomas didn't know.

"Okay," she said. "Go shower. Clean that stuff off your face. I'll read this and we'll talk."

"It's the worst thing I've ever written," he said, his eyes imploring, pleading.

"Shower. Put on your Henry clothes. And we'll talk."

Slowly, he nodded, then wandered down the short hallway toward the bathroom. When she heard the water turn on, she sat at the Formica table her father had sat at alone for years and years, spread the pages out, and began to read.

Of course it *wasn't* the worst thing he'd ever written. Thomas could say with some impunity that it was the best thing. His novels had gotten progressively better, to the point where his first book, *Valerie*, now seemed almost like juvenilia. But these pages, this first chapter, represented a quantum leap forward in both maturity and emotional depth. It was his first book from the point of view of a woman. It talked about sex in a way that didn't seem embarrassed by it (as in his early books), or indulged in vulgar details that took you out of the story (as in some of his more recent stuff). It was only five pages at the start of a novel that already felt like it was going to be long, and if these five pages were any indication, it would be Henry Dear's first masterwork.

But it was about her. *Her.*

Thomas put the pages aside and tried to muster some anger. At Henry for wanting to write Karen Luck's life story as a novel. At Karen Luck, for having the sort of hold on him that she could never match and never compete with. For herself, for having neither the will nor the fortitude to tell Henry to cut the shit and get over this girl if he ever wanted to have a future in her heart.

But the anger took too much effort. It made her feel tired. It was getting to the point – hell, it was probably well past the point – where she was going to have to make a real decision about her and Henry. Whether her reluctant love for him was enough to sustain whatever they were to one another. Whether she could keep living with Karen Luck's ghost and still retain her own dignity and self-respect. Whether she could live with a man who became his ex-girlfriend so definitively that he was about to embark on a whole book from her point of view.

When he appeared in the kitchen doorway, his hair still wet and his OKC shirt damp and clinging to him, she said, "You will regret it if you don't write this book. And you will resent me. Maybe yourself too, but also me. I love you, Henry, but I can't live with your resentment. So you write this book. You edit it. You finish it. You get it out of your system. And then we are going to have a very real talk about what you wear when you write. And who you are when you close that door."

"Okay, Thomas," he said, and she didn't know if he sounded more relieved or scared. "I love you, you know."

"I know you do. I also know yours is reluctant. We didn't mean to fall in love, and here we are."

"Here we are," he said, and he sat across from her.

"Will it ever stop being about pain, Henry?" she asked suddenly, and she didn't expect her mind to flash to all those model planes hanging from the ceiling. She didn't expect to be thinking about her father at all.

"I don't know," he said. "Do you want it to not be about pain?"

She sighed. "I think I like hurting you. Sexually I like it. But I don't want it to be who we are. I don't want it to be our default."

"I like it sexually, too," he said. "But I … I think we need to think about changes."

"What kind of changes?"

Henry closed his eyes. "Your Dad was the best thing in your life, and my Dad was the worst thing in mine. One of the worst things in yours, too. I don't know how to move past either of those things. But I want to."

Thomas was silent for a long while. "I do too," she said, quietly.

He took her hand. "Do you want to hurt me for awhile, then watch *Andy Richter*?"

She did. And through that bitter winter and sweltering summer, he worked on the book he'd begun calling *Goodbye, Burger City*. She'd voiced some concerns about naming the book after a real place and some more concerns about referencing burgers in a book about a lesbian. "That's not a sexual term, is it?" he asked, but she didn't entirely know. It kind of *sounded* like one, was her weak argument. She read his chapters as he finished them, and did the light copyediting she always did when she was visiting one of Henry's books for the first time. The work didn't demand much from her. It was his cleanest copy ever. More, the story itself was getting in the way of her red pen; it flowed easily, dragging her along in its current, making her desperate for the next chapter before he'd even finished. More than once, she'd found herself pacing the kitchen near the pantry, her own pages in hand, wanting to trade off for something more. He was writing fast, but not *that* fast. Sometimes days would go by before he had new work to show her; she'd curse herself for devouring it so quickly.

The day he turned in the final chapter, she brought it into the bedroom, leaving the red pen on the kitchen table. She heard him in the shower, washing Karen Luck off of him. Maybe she heard him crying, too. Thomas would comfort him – this wasn't the pain she wanted him to be in – but right now she had to read.

Henry was leaning in the doorway, watching her as she placed the last page on the bed next to her. He was dressed in blue jeans and a Bruce Springsteen T-shirt. He said, "Well? Is it any good?"

Thomas took him in for a moment. Something had changed about him, this man she accidentally loved. Only it wasn't accidental anymore, was it? He'd been a good writer who'd somehow become a great writer, and somewhere in there he'd gone from an accidental love into being one with purpose. It wasn't just the book. Something had changed in him. Maybe something had changed in her, too. The book was part of it, maybe the catalyst of it. Now that it was over, it was just her and it was just him.

"Almost everyone had a happy ending," she said.

He swallowed. "Well, not the dead people."

"You know what I mean."

"I've never been a nihilist, but my novels don't really prove that out. So many of them end sad. I knew when I started this one that I didn't want to end it sad. I couldn't make it hokey or contrived, but I wanted it to feel satisfying at the end. I wanted to give it a good ending."

"It's a good ending," she said.

"I love you," he said. "I love you very much. And not just because you like my book."

"I love you, too, Henry. And those changes we talked about making? We're going to make them. Me and you."

He took a stop closer to her and felt himself shuddering. He'd cried in the shower some, but that was just the aftereffects of finishing a novel. He usually cried after finishing a novel. This was different. The fictional Karen Luck had been put paid to ... and Henry was smart enough to know that he didn't just mean the woman on the pages of his book.

When he cried, it was for the fact that his past might finally be over, and that *he*, Henry Dear, had been its agent of change. Maybe he would always love Karen Luck, but she didn't have to be a part of him anymore, and he didn't have to be consumed by her. If he was going to give himself to this woman in front of him, this good woman who had given him more chances than he'd ever earned, then he had to give himself completely.

But it wasn't *just* Thomas, was it? No, and maybe it wasn't even primarily her. The last month he'd slapped on that makeup and put on that dress, it had felt more like postponing the writing rather than preparing for it. For the first time ever, he made himself up like her all the way through to the end, when normally he'd write as himself in the final chapter. He'd dressed up as Karen the entire way through this book – it had felt apt, given the subject matter – but as the winter became spring and spring became summer, it felt more and more like an artifice he was perpetuating for no reason. The day he'd begun his final chapter, he'd drawn on the lipstick and eyeliner and looked at himself in the mirror, not feeling like Karen, not feeling like a woman at all. He felt like a boy with some paint on. He felt like a boy playing dress-up. He'd needed this until he didn't need it anymore. To hammer the point home, he *kept* putting on the makeup and the old-fashioned dresses; he didn't want to forget who he was anymore.

He cried because he'd put himself in a cage, and now he was free. When he kissed Thomas, that feeling of freedom flowed through him like water, purifying and cleansing.

They made love then, with the pages of his final chapter bunching up next to them. No pain. No toys. Just them, naked and unafraid. It was the first time they'd done it like that and it had felt weird to both of them, but they kept at it until they were both satisfied.

After, Thomas said, "She's going to read it, you know."

"I know."

"Are you prepared for that?"

"I tried not to think about it until now."

"And now that you have to think about it?"

"I don't know if she'll be flattered or pissed."

"Well, from her point of view, you're a man who co-opted her story for your own novel and wrote it better than she probably could."

It was on the tip of his tongue to say, *Come on, now, Karen's a genius, she could have written it way better.* But he stopped himself. "Do you honestly think I wrote it better than she could?"

"There's something to be said for distance," Thomas said vaguely. "And she's a great writer, Henry. Honestly, she is. I've read most of her books. But she's not the best writer in the world. I honestly think this book is written better than her books."

"That's high praise."

"Just the truth. You tapped into something with this one." She paused. "So what's next?"

Henry closed his eyes. "Well, I've been thinking about a totally different kind of story. Maybe a young adult thing. It's about a kid on vacation near the sea, and there's this haunted lighthouse..."

"No, silly," she said, grinning at him. "What's next for *us*?"

The cabin was on the edge of town, still within OKC limits, but then, *everything* in the sprawl was within OKC limits. It had a proper kitchen, a huge living room, a massive bedroom ... and *two* offices. Real ones. Henry had called the smaller one without a window; windows, he told her, would distract him from the worlds he wanted to create. The bigger office, overlooking their backyard, was hers. It was the only place in the whole house she allowed herself to hang Dad's model planes, and then, only three. Part of the reason for the cabin was for both of them to try to shake themselves loose from their pasts. But that didn't have to happen all at once. She got a couple of planes. And he got tied to the bed with his ass in the air, while she forced something way too large into something way too small.

In the morning, he would head into his studio; the walls were bare aside from a shelf of rare-edition hardcovers he'd collected over the years. "My only vice," he called them, which always struck them as funny if he said it after sex. It wasn't a bad vice to have: classic Steinbeck, Hemingway, several Brontes; more modern stuff with Atwood and King and Smiley. These used to hold a place of prominence in the living room, but Henry told her he needed some inspiration if it wasn't going to come from lipstick and eyeliner. In other words, maybe he *didn't* need Karen Luck's presence to be the writer he was supposed to be ... but he did need *other* writers. Thomas wondered if that was normal; weren't other writers able to draw inspiration just from themselves?

For her part, Thomas decided to quit the bank soon after they moved into the cabin. Now that Henry was all about discovering who he really was in the wake of being Karen Luck, Thomas had decided to discover who she was in the wake of being Mark McAdams' daughter, and Henry Dear's girlfriend. Eventually, she thought, she would be able to put away her father's model planes. But she missed *real* planes.

Flying might not be in her future, but she very distinctly remembered walking into that hangar, her eyes dragged from the middle distance she always stared at while marching, and taking in those fighter planes for the first time. They were grand, majestic, like great birds of myth roosting in this giant rook, wanting only to be in the air, wanting only to climb off the ground and soar into the clouds. Thomas wanted to be part of that in some way, and if she couldn't *fly* planes, maybe she could *fix* planes. And wouldn't you know it? Yeager Air Force Base, the same place she used to go to after school three days a week to attend Civil Air Patrol classes and drills, taught adult classes in aircraft maintenance and repair. There was something comforting going back to Yeager, despite the fact that Civil Air Patrol lost its luster after the encampment. Occasionally, she wondered if she had compromised too much of herself in the bubble of Henry's obsession with her ex, and sometimes she wondered if she had lost any part of herself in allowing him to be who he thought he had to be. If she had, she thought she could find it again in the last place she truly felt like her own person, unadulterated and uncompromised.

Then came 9/11.

It was like reliving her worst nightmare all over again, watching her father die, knowing that she would never see his face again, hold his hand, hear him talking about planes and places he'd been, and places he'd probably never go. Watching the TV that morning, Henry on the other side of the couch, not knowing if comforting her would freak her out or fuck her up more than this was already fucked up, the internal scream locked inside her, and for most of that morning, all she could think about was him, and how he'd gone into work that day thinking everything was totally fine, and had ended up dead. She saw him – flashes of him, imagined but real enough – in the windows of the World Trade Centers, saw him looking out at her, his eyes drawn, his face a mask of eternal sadness.

Then something beyond her comprehension for terror happened; a woman, not wanting to burn in the fires, leapt from a floor near the top of one of the towers. Thomas saw her clearly. Until this moment, she had paid little attention to New York and the skyscrapers there – Henry had visited a few times to meet with his publisher, but she was never tempted to join him. But now, her sense of scale widened. She comprehended just how tall those buildings were. That woman fell for a long, long time. And Thomas McAdams' myopia exploded.

Two days later, she quit the mechanics program at the base and signed up for EMT classes at Oklahoma State. Her father was dead. That woman was dead. But there were millions of people out there who didn't have to die, and if she could stop even one of those deaths from happening, she was sure as hell going to try.

Of course, saving people was going to be her day job. She could leave the Hippocratic Oath at the door when she came home, and her boyfriend *wanted* to be harmed, just as soon as he'd given her her own happy ending for the day. It was a weird life, a good life, and full days went by when she didn't think about Karen Luck until the writer showed up on her doorstep in early November that year, demanding to see Henry.

Here's how you make a long-scale emotional breakdown productive:

Up at four AM, that's how it had to start. Karen had gone to Sears and asked for the most obnoxious alarm they had. The counter girl had smiled a little shyly and scurried to find the correct one. "I'm sorry," the girl asked. "Are you Karen Luck?"

Karen, her nerves not just frayed but flayed, nearly snapped at the girl. This was the last place she wanted to have a fan encounter. The girl would probably try to push the clock on her, telling her to take it, it was on her. That happened with bizarre regularity, often in bookstores and grocery stores; people making minimum wage offering to buy her things. She wanted to tell them that she didn't need things, that the perks of being a famous person included actual companies sending her things, plus the perks of being rich meant she didn't need people to buy her things. Why didn't they give free stuff to writers who were struggling, people whose sales were a fraction of her own? Or people who had been trying to get a book contract for years, collecting rejection letter after rejection letter? *Those* people needed free watches and computers and groceries.

To the salesgirl, she said, "Yeah, but don't tell anyone. I don't want to cause a scene." She smiled and the girl giggled.

"My lips are sealed. I just wanted to say ... you know, I don't think you got enough credit for *Really Restless.*"

Karen blinked. "Seriously?"

"I know it's probably not your favorite of your books, but it's my favorite. It's funny, you know? I loved *I Want You to Hurt Me*, but that's the one I had to hide from my Mom. Even she liked *Really Restless.*"

Until this moment, Karen's only thought was getting home and getting to work. At once. Immediately. She'd been in OKC for four hours by this point. The house had been ready to receive her and Dad. The fridge and cabinets were fully stocked. Everything was dusted and put in its place. There was even a fire in the fireplace, roaring and ready to keep everything downstairs toasty. What there hadn't been was an alarm clock. She and Dad had brought theirs from the house in OKC to the one in LA and hadn't thought to bring them back.

Karen *had* entertained the notion of simply calling up Skylark Dear and asking her if she had an extra one ... but she didn't know what the situation with Henry was right now, and she thought if he surprised her by showing up at the front door, she might actually run him through with a fireplace poker.

"Thank you so much," Karen said. "I guess I needed to hear that today."

"Thank *you*," the girl said. Then, very quietly, she murmured, "You should write characters like that more."

For a moment, she could only gape at the girl. "Like Conor Really?"

"No. Like his friend Sasha. She was really cool."

For a moment, Karen said nothing at all. The girl met her eyes. Karen met the girl's eyes. In a voice she struggled to make normal, Karen said, "Just you wait."

"Oh yeah?"

"Yeah. I have some plans."

A smile dimpled the girl's cheeks and she nodded, as if confirming something to herself. "I have plans, too. There's a lot of evil in the world, isn't there?"

"Yes," Karen said, and for some reason, her mind didn't go to the Twin Towers, as it had been doing nonstop for the last couple weeks. It went to her eighth birthday, and seeing her mother carried away by that tornado. Terrorists were bad. Terrorists were evil. But they were at least human. They had faces and goals and objectives. What did tornadoes have? Chaos. Random. And when they were done with their destructions, they simply disappeared. They didn't even die. They just ceased to be. "But there's good in the world, too."

"You believe that?"

"I'm trying."

The girl sucked in breath. "Okay. Then I'll try too."

A younger version of Karen Luck wouldn't have believed it possible to have a conversation like this, to smile and mean it, in the midst of an ongoing meltdown. Nor did she entirely believe it now. How could she be in the middle of a meltdown if she had so much to write?

Up at four, that was the first thing. The main thing. Any delays – hitting the snooze button or attempting to sleep through it – would cause a ripple effect throughout the entire day, and that was not an eventually she was emotionally prepared to reckon with. She would drag herself blearily downstairs and get a cup of water and click the computer in her mother's office on. Two deep breaths, then reading what she'd written the day before. Her brain empty, trying like a stalled engine to fire up. Every morning she felt a little dizzy, and that was a good feeling. A great feeling, really. Discombobulation made you do weird stuff, and weird stuff was exactly what she needed if she was going to write three novels – three *good* novels – in a month.

Plus: there was something to writing with absolutely nothing in the tank. It felt almost noble. When your brain revved and fell off, revved and fell off, not catching, not clicking. When your fingers started to move and the words marched dutifully across the screen, even though your brain is begging for sleep, for respite, and there's nothing between the impulse to write and the writing itself. Revved, and fell off. Sometime during the morning's writing, the thing that drove the conscious part of her work would finally catch. Sometimes that happened almost immediately. Sometimes not until almost breaktime, 6:30, when the sun would finally decide that it was time to come out of hiding and start making itself known. She forced herself to stop at 6:30, even if she was in the middle of a great scene or a juicy bit of dialogue. There was a fine line between pushing hard and burning out. Saving the file and emailing the file to herself was part of the ritual, and it all had to be ritual. It all had to be a routine. It was the only way something like this made sense, if it made sense at all.

At 6:30, she got out of her pajama bottoms and ratty sleep shirt, tossed on sweats, fired up her Walkman, and entered the cool Oklahoma morning at a run. It was the same principle as her writing; her legs didn't want to go, especially not that fast, and especially not after having lain in bed for a few hours, followed by sitting for another two and a half. They got worried. They quivered. They screamed at her. And after about a mile or so, they acquiesced, and carried her as far as she needed to go.

Karen's philosophy for writing – besides tackling it like a maniac in a horror novel – was trying to improve upon whatever work she had done the day before. That happened infrequently, because she was a good writer and her standard of quality was already so high. But occasionally, a scene would flow from her, something so unexpected and brilliant that she would almost regret it. Scenes like that felt as if they'd come from somewhere else, from some dark ether that had reached out and tapped her to translate. Karen rarely felt like she earned those scenes, because they were simply too brilliant to have come entirely from her talent and craft and ambition. She would also regret them because she would have to spend the rest of the day, and the next day, and the next day, trying to live up to whatever had spooled out of her so effortlessly. Essentially, it was as if some invisible muse had whispered the words of her best work to her, and then plain old Karen Luck had to come in and try to stitch together prose and dialogue to match it. She was always terrified that the novel would come across as patchwork, that readers would see the seams between those elevated moments and her own clumsy attempts to follow up. The fact that, on rewriting, she often couldn't remember where the muse took over and left off never seemed to convince her otherwise.

Running was different. It was cumulative and qualitative. If you ran faster or further than the day before, then you were objectively better. The only running she'd done in Los Angeles had been at the gym, and she'd rarely put much effort into it. She pushed herself now, pushed hard, because she knew she would be depriving her midmorning self any exercise. Putting it all out on the streets of OKC as the sun dappled the asphalt and trees and early cars on their way from one place to another: that was the only way to keep in the shape she needed to be in to get through this month.

A week and a half into her routine, she started running past Henry Dear's new house. It was, somewhat absurdly, a cabin, situated far back from the road; a winding rock path meandered from the mailbox by the street to the cabin's front door. The first time she reached the cabin, she'd been tempted to dash up that stupid, calm path and bang on the door and scream for Henry to come out and explain himself. Maybe it would end with her punching him in the face. Maybe a bloody nose would teach him not to steal someone else's life story. Maybe.

Instead, she just sucked in breath and kept running. The next morning, she barely even looked at his house, and only vaguely wondered what he might be writing in there.

When the running was over, she'd finally shower and put on her hangout clothes – jeans, T-shirt, light jacket – and drive out to Nichols Hills, where the town was still abuzz with the opening of OKC's first Starbucks. Venti blackeye, all the coffee and triple the caffeine, and while it cooled, she'd situate at a table and put her headphones on and unfold the laptop, bulky and cumbersome. But it was only unwieldy until she downloaded the morning's work. Then the laptop stopped being its own thing and started being a tool with which to find her way inside the story.

Despite the fact that she was at least semi-famous and a hometown girl returning to do the thing that made her semi-famous, most people didn't bother her in the coffee shop. It was a new, anonymous place full of blank, anonymous people. It was the whole Midwest Nice thing, even though Oklahoma might technically be The South. No one wanted to be a bother. And in this null environment, Karen found that writing as herself was a lot easier than when she wrote at home. Writing *as* her mother was off the table, but when she wrote where Mom wrote, and where Dad wrote *as* her, it was almost impossible not to feel her presence guiding the work. Turns of phrase that would never occur to Karen popped into the prose, turns of phrase she was certain she'd read in Mom's books or heard Mom say when she was alive. Here, in the midst of the non-stop desperation for coffee, Karen could rely only on herself, and she found herself writing faster and more naturally that way. It's easy to be productive if ghosts are helping you. It's better to be productive if you're doing it on your own.

How many venti blackeyes? Two? Three? Chasing each one with an gargantuan bottle of water so that she wouldn't get kidney stones or something. She'd pee forever in the Starbucks bathroom, then defy every fiber in her being and go to the mall for a massage. In LA, it was easy to look down on the people who got daily massages. What was so stressful in your life that you could just drop all that money on some structured relaxation time? For Karen, it wasn't indulgence. It was triage. All that typing. It didn't matter if Mom was helping with the prose or she was doing it all on her own: her hands were the ones moving across the keyboard, pounding keys as fast as her brain could go. At the massage place, she'd put on headphones and slide in an audiobook cassette and let whoever was working that afternoon put her wrists and forearms back together.

Back home, back home, jiggedy-jog. Lunch with Dad, who had woken up whenever he'd woken up and poked out work on his own new novel. He'd tell her that it was okay to slow down and she nodded and plotted and when lunch was over, she'd retreat to the desk in her room and write for five hours straight. She didn't allow herself to stop. Didn't take bathroom breaks. Occasionally stood to stretch her legs and arm and then went right back to it. The writing was the important thing. The writing was the most important thing.

Her first novel was called *Jeremy Stain*; the title hung over the book like a noxious pall, informing the text, subverting it, casting every word on every page in a weirder, darker light. Jeremy, the only child of a rich software genius and her husband, is kidnapped in a harrowing, brutal scene at the start of the novel. The tension ratchets up to a fever pitch, then ratchets up some more. You know, going in, that things aren't going to go the standard route, but Karen wanted to follow the standard route just the same, wanted to see how long she could play in the world of ransom notes and well-meaning cops with alcoholic backstories. Then that phone call, and Jeremy's mother taps the *accept* button with a trembling finger, terrified that something has happened to her boy, something awful. Then it's Jeremy's voice, sweet and angelic, the voice that sang with her in the car and asked questions about coding that were clearly far over his head, the voice that laughed at cartoons and cried when he had strep. That voice now said, "It's over, Mommy. They're not going to hurt me anymore."

All of it's still inference for a long, long time. What happened to the kidnappers is tossed off in a bit of murmured dialogue between medical examiners – "All those cuts," one of them says, his eyes wide; the other, her face slack in horror, recalls that line at the beginning of Poe's "The Cask of

Amontillado," about the thousand injuries of Fortunado. Where the kid got the X-Acto knife was anybody's guess.

We don't see the bodies, we don't see Jeremy doing anything. But we know. We can imagine.

Every day Karen sat down, it was a challenge to herself to not go the standard route. Initially she wanted to give teenage Jeremy a girlfriend that he eventually menaces, then kills. His first "onscreen" kill, and she knew she could have done it justice. But the girl, a sweet young thing named Jolene, arrived fully formed on the page, and Karen realized that it was a boring trope and she didn't want to just kill the girl just to give Jeremy some motivation. What ends up happening is that Jolene very nearly kills *him* on the floor of the boys' locker room in school. They both have sex for the first time as he's bleeding out into the drain in the middle of the floor. Karen found herself reveling in the sexiness of the scene, trying hard to make blood sexy and seminal, allowing herself to skip inside Jolene's mind for a little while to talk about orgasms and how much better they were than the ones she gave herself. Violence was sex. Pain was sex. Blood was sex.

And *that* could have been standard, too. Karen, bleary-eyed with exhaustion, writing past one in the morning because the after-dinner work was free time, was time she didn't have to structure, writing even though she knew she had to be awake in three hours, almost cackled aloud. She *wanted* people to think this was a book about spree killing. About serial killers in love. About how the violence at the center of their relationship would eventually tear them apart. But that's not what *Jeremy Stain* was. When they broke up, it was mutual and loving. Karen tried desperately hard to make their breakup scene as heartfelt as in any "normal" book. The fact that both of these kooky kids were deranged didn't make you want to like them less.

Then – *then* – Karen jumped forward twenty-five years. Just passed everything that made Jeremy Stain the violent, random murderer that he is. When you see him next, he's drinking a beer poolside, his wife grilling burgers, his two kids playing in the pool. He's reading a news report on his phone about another random murder in Oklahoma City, and he knows it's Jolene. He'd been keeping tabs on her all these years, despite being married, despite loving his wife and kids fiercely. You never really forgot your first crush. It was in that moment that Karen realized what she was writing. In her hands was a romance novel of sorts. Guy loves his wife but can't quite let go of the girl he left behind. And maybe he wants to find her, maybe he doesn't. He ruminates. There's a chance meeting at a party and there she is. Maybe they have sex and maybe both of them spend a good chunk of the book terrified that they'd wronged their spouses, and wondering whether or not to confess. It was good stuff, riveting stuff, stuff that the literati love and that the *New York Times* Review of Books gave high praise.

But those types of books don't include scenes like the one where Jeremy's at the mall buying batteries, and happens to notice a kid wearing a baseball hat slightly too big for him. Just a little detail. Nothing major. But it sets off alarm bells in his head, and he knows that this kid who he's never met and has no connection to, will be his next victim. And now when we get to the murder, Karen pulled no punches. A few times, even she wanted to look away, especially at the scene where

Jeremy rends the kid's ulna from his arm and uses the jagged end of the bone to stab him in the face. Every detail was examined. Every cut, every scream. This time, she worked very hard to make the scene as *un*-sexual as possible, even though the multiple penetrations made it easy to slide into metaphor.

No one ever catches either Jeremy or Jolene. Their story is a tale of two lovers who didn't make it work, then couldn't make it work. But in the scene where they break down and have sex in a gas station bathroom, all they talk about is the people they've killed, and how sometimes they want to kill their spouses, and how – shamefully – sometimes they even wanted to kill their children. They never would, of course, not even if it meant they could be together.

Near the end of the book, before Jeremy goes back to his wife, burdened with the guilt of his affair, he asks Jolene if they could have ever really been a couple.

Jolene sighs, "You kill randomly. I do it systematically. Patterns, you know? I think your approach would drive me insane if we were to stay together."

"Doesn't love matter more than killing?"

She'd given a little laugh. "I don't know. What do you think?"

And he'd paused. "I keep waiting for it to feel like I'm living a double life. Like I have my wife and kids and suburbia, and then I have this dark secret. But it *doesn't* feel like that. I got the wife and kids and nice little house with the stone walkway out front, *and* I murder people. It's like I got the whole thing. I wouldn't want to give any of it up."

Jeremy talking about killing in such a blasé, suburban-dad way sent chills through Karen, and she knew that it would send chills through her readers. Some would be put off by the gore. She even thought some would get angry with her for "ruining" a perfectly good novel with all this superfluous violence, despite the fact that there'd been violence in almost all of her books and despite the fact that the violence is woven into the fabric of *Jeremy Stain*. You couldn't have the book without it.

Karen finished the novel at three in the morning a week and a half after she'd begun it. Nearly four hundred double-spaced manuscript pages. She'd gone to the all-night Kinko's downtown and had the whole thing printed out, leaving it on her father's desk the second she returned home at 4:30. Behind schedule. Sleep would have to wait. She sat down in her father's chair, flipped her laptop open, and got to work on *Bullseye*.

That one only took a week.

"Karen?" Dad was in the kitchen, crowding a bowl of oatmeal. The taste of her blackeye coffees were still on her tongue and her forearms tingled with a lack of tension. It was time to get back to work. She had a week and a half to finish her new book, a far less vicious piece of work than either *Jeremy Stain* or *Bullseye*. She was going back to family secrets and gothic houses and scrapbooks of exposition for this one. If *The Second Tucker Strong* was going to be her final novel with Chanler & Cushing, with Cynthia Auburn, it might as well fall into her wheelhouse. But that could be the curious thing about writing novels; even if you were walking on well-tilled earth, you still usually found a few live things fighting their way toward the sun. Sitting down to write didn't feel like a chore, didn't feel like useless repetition. The trick was to make the stuff you'd proven you were good at seem fresh and new. She could do that. Of course she could.

"Hey Dad."

"I brought you dinner." He was standing outside Mom's office door, a plate of something whose good smells wafted from it like physical things. On closer inspection, she saw that it was a plate of hot chicken, the skin golden and blackened in the right places. Mashed potatoes with the lumps in was drizzled with some hearty brown gravy on the side, and a small mountain of bright green beans completed the picture. Immediately her stomach cramped in anticipation.

"Didn't we eat dinner?" she asked, standing up. *Tucker Strong* was going fast and easy and well, and moving away from it was like pulling some partially-melted plastic off a hot patch of asphalt. She could actually hear the tearing, stretching sound in her brain. She reached for the plate and then her hands also cramped, and not so pleasantly.

"We ate dinner yesterday, Karen," he said quietly.

"Oh, okay." She flexed her hands and pain shot up her forearms. Dad was looking right at her so she kept her face neutral.

"Karen."

"Just say it, Dad."

"This isn't healthy."

She sighed, and, flexing her hands more – was it helping, hurting? – skittered past him through the doorway and into the kitchen. "Did you look at the *Bullseye* manuscript at all?"

"I did. You incorporated the Jessica Cunningham stuff in well. I put some thoughts in the margins." He hesitated. "It's a fucking great book, Karen. How the hell did you write a book that good with my brand-new character in a week and I've been struggling for months with this one novel?"

"This isn't a competition," she said, sitting at the kitchen table as Dad put the food in front of her. She glanced up and saw her reflection in the window above the sink. The woman staring back at her wasn't her. She was too skinny, for one. Skinner than Karen Luck had ever been. Which was fine, right? Skinny was good. That's what everyone was trying to be back in Los Angeles.

He settled across from her. "It goddamn well is and you know it. Everything about this is a competition. You're competing with who you want to be. I'm competing with who I am. And that's just where it starts."

When she felt confident she could hold utensils, Karen picked up her knife and fork and tucked in. Saliva shot into her mouth so powerfully it was almost like an orgasm. "You didn't make this."

"No," he murmured. "Skylark did."

Involuntarily, her mouth stopped chewing. When she swallowed, it went down hard, as if it was thick and solid like a golf ball. "She was here?"

"I know you don't like her son," he said, "but she's not—"

"Skylark Dear was in our house?" Henry was the furthest thing from her mind.

"Well, to drop off the plate of food. Actually a couple of plates." And, he didn't mention, to sneak up into his bedroom for a little while, and put her fingers into his ass, and to let him go down on her, bringing her to nearly silent orgasm three times before he allowed himself to get off. He further didn't mention that he was sending her away with new manuscript pages every time she came by, and that she was editing them as she did when he was still Elaine Luck part-time and she was still Welton Dear's wife. Some things you don't have to tell your daughter. Like the fact that he probably wasn't going to come with her when she left, and that he was probably going to ask Skylark to come live with him once he finished the new book. He had spent most of his life in service to Elaine, and he was never going to be over her, and she was never going to be over *for* him; he had spent the remaining years allowing his daughter to be in service to him. All of that had to end. Elaine was gone and he was coming back into himself. He'd been away too long.

"Could you let me know when she's here next? It's not about Henry. I just miss her. It's been awhile."

"Karen," he said, because his daughter was stalling. Why else would Karen lie about missing Skylark Dear? She never even knew the woman that well.

"Dad, I have one more book to go. Then things will get back to normal."

Gary bit his lip. "That's sort of what I'm afraid of."

"Don't do that," she said. "Don't Maura me."

"If you mean I need to stop caring about you, that's not going to happen."

She was finally able to push the plate away. "This has a stopping point, Dad. One month. I have another week to finish *Tucker*. And I will finish it. And then editing and the books go off to that lying fraud Cynthia and then we find ourselves a new publisher. One that will treat us with the respect that the both of us deserve."

He swallowed. "I don't know why you're taking all your rage out on her. All she did was publish Henry's book."

"That's not all she did," Karen told her father, "and you know that."

"Is this the lesbian thing?"

Blue rage exploded in Karen's head, nuclear and devastating. "The lesbian *thing*? The *lesbian* thing? How can you be so dense, Dad?"

"Karen, I only meant…"

"It's *all* 'the lesbian thing'. All of it. Every day of my goddamn *life*, it's the lesbian thing. How do you not get that? How do you not understand what she did to me?"

For a second, Dad looked cowed, withered in the radiation of her fury. Then, quietly, he said, "I think sometimes you forget she's also a lesbian," he said. "And that she's an editor who wanted a young person to have success before she got typed as a specific type of writer."

Karen's insides still felt hot, apocalyptic, but now the fire didn't feel as righteous. "You honestly don't know what you're talking about."

Dad nodded slightly. "You're probably right. Do *you* know what you're talking about?"

Now the fire inside felt muted, as if she were feeling the heat from a burning building two blocks away. No. No. It wouldn't do to listen to him … at least not now, not when she was close to getting everything she wanted. Later, maybe, after she'd finished *Tucker* and turned in her books, she could revisit this particular topic. Not now. She needed the fire.

Karen walked past her father toward her mother's old studio. "I need to work, Dad. Don't you have work, too?"

He laid a hand on her shoulder. She didn't turn. "What if I was wrong, Karen?"

Closing her eyes, she asked, "About what, Dad?"

"What if writing isn't the most important thing?"

For a moment, they only stood there in frozen tableau; he with his hand on her shoulder, she rooted to the floor halfway between her dinner and her work. Then Dad let his hand drop away and she got moving. It was still early. Somewhere up ahead, exhaustion would claim her and do it hard; until then, she was determined to get at least two more chapters in. Two more long chapters. All she needed was some Surge to get her into the wee hours. Ambition and drive and caffeine, that's all she really needed.

But when she sat down at her laptop, paralysis gripped her at once. The meal she'd scarfed down felt leaden in her stomach, like a ball of something molten now cooling and hardening. When she blinked—

she was at the top of the building, the woman at the top of the building

images crowded her brain, stuffed them like cotton in a scarecrow's burlap skull. Only not like that, because the crows had pecked their way inside and now reveled, madly, in the empty cavity.

she has two choices, jumping or burning, two choices only, jumping burning and Maura is here Maura is comfort Maura is

Karen's fingers clutch the arms of the chair, and for a screaming, endless moment she thinks it is a wheelchair, that she is confined here, that this is where she will spend the remainder of her days, alone and dying and terrified.

Maura is leaving, okay, Maura is leaving but she can't go now, no flights, no flights, so they make love because they have to, they have to because what's the alternative? As soon as Maura can leave, she will leave, and it's good she's going, isn't it? It's good that she's going because Karen Luck is no one's idea of a stable life. But now, oh now, if only she could stop thinking of that woman, that woman from the top of the tower, please Maura don't go please Maura don't leave please Maura help me forget because I can't do it alone.

Her mouth dry, her temples pounding, Karen forces her fingers to the keyboard. There's a blinking cursor at the end of the line she last typed before Dad came in with his food and his judgments. The line ran, "Tucker wanted to love his father. Wanted that more than anything else in this world. He clutched his broken finger and refused to cry. His father stared at him contemptuously. This was the face of every schoolyard bully Tucker ever had faced and ever would. He wanted to love his father but he could not. It would be madness. Instead, he launched off the ground toward the man's face, his hands high, his broken finger bobbing uselessly, and when he started clawing, he went for his father's eyes first."

If she'd stayed inside she might have lived. If that woman had just stayed inside, maybe she would have lived. The chances were small, sure, but it could have happened. Miracles happen all the time, don't they? And when Maura left her room for the last time, for the very last time, all she wanted to do was to call Henry. Henry would understand this. Henry would understand her. *But she couldn't call Henry, ever again. Karen's girlfriend had left and her best friend had betrayed her and her editor had fucked her over. She had her father and otherwise she was alone in the world, hundreds of miles from home.*

"Why didn't she just stay inside?" Karen muttered to herself, unaware that she was crying. Unaware that her hands had unclenched from the chair arms and her fingers were once again moving across the keyboard, completely working of their own volition, bypassing her brain altogether. "If she'd stayed inside she might still be alive. She didn't have to die. Doesn't anyone know that? She didn't have to die."

Karen wrote through the night, once or twice nearly fainting with the effort. Later, she thought she might actually have slept for some of it, because when she re-read her pages, she didn't remember a long chunk in the middle, where Tucker Strong finally meets his twin after thirteen years of not knowing he had one. It only occurred to her to lament the fact that she had been looking forward to writing that and only regretted not being present when the time came. She never considered – not then, anyway – that writing in her sleep might not actually be an ideal state of mind. That she was already frazzled beyond belief and she was working hard to frazzle herself more. Thinking beyond the scope of *Tucker* was out of reach at the moment, and she didn't entirely regret it. Dad had been right and was now wrong: writing really *was* all that mattered. For now, it was all she had.

Now, thin steam escaped her nose and mouth as she sprinted up the long walk toward the cabin – the fucking *cabin* – where her former best friend lived with a woman Karen couldn't remember Henry ever mentioning. Twenty minutes earlier, she had typed the words THE END after the last line of *Tucker Strong*, the last book she would ever write for Chanler & Cushing, the last book she would ever write for Cynthia Auburn. Over the last three days she'd gotten a total of five and a half hours of sleep, and all of those hours were in her mother's writing chair. No Starbucks. No massage. No jogging.

She'd gotten up to walk around the office, flexing her hands and arms only when she could no longer feel her toes, and her forearms felt packed with broken glass, moving around just under her skin. It was important to write through. If you gave your brain an inch, it would start getting a toehold into your consciousness.

First it was the images from the TV on 9/11, that woman jumping to her death, that more than anything. Then it might be the elevator door opening and seeing the Butcher standing there, grinning at her, coming for her; the way her stiletto heel so easily sank into his gut, how easily she had gone from bystander to murderer and no one even tried to blame her.

Then, sometimes, it might be tornadoes, sounding like trains come to steal precious things from her, right out of the sky.

Forces of nature and malice and death screaming at her and around her and toward her, and it was better, easier, to deal with Tucker Strong and his twin Daniel Persimmon, and their brutal father and the two mothers who loved them and the two grandmothers who hated them. The character stuff was rich. The plot was twisty enough to be intriguing but not so dense that you couldn't follow it. Karen dumped all her gothic tricks in: mood, atmosphere, thick foreshadowing, a crumbling old manor by the sea and a creepy old woman who *knows the manor's secrets.*

She had written in near-delirium, and then she had written in full-on delirium. It wouldn't do to sugar coat it. Even now she knew that the best thing for her was to get some sleep, to have a meal and go sit in a warm tub and then catch about twenty hours of shuteye before doing anything else. Her father was in his office, plucking away at his new novel; he might not be racing now, but he was just as absorbed as he always had been when he was creating at his desk, or *her* desk. Gary Luck had never even looked up when Karen, in her jeans and robe, stole out into the cold early morning and dashed away from the house.

Her fist connected with the door eight or night times before she even felt it. When it opened, it was not Henry's face that she saw. It was the woman's. *Did* she know this woman, who was a little shorter than her and a little heavier than her and whose forehead had scrunched up in a series of worry-lines.

"Karen? Karen Luck?" she asked, her voice calm.

"I want to see Henry! He stole me! Henry stole me!" This wasn't what she'd intended to say, not at all. She'd had a speech planned. Henry had stolen her *story*; had been allowed to be a lesbian before she could. Did he really think that was fair? Had he really thought that writing *Goodbye, Burger City* was something that would sit well with her?

But none of that came out. Her mouth was stuffed with something sodden and gummy. All at once, she smelled herself – rank and wet, like salt and vinegar potato chips. When had she last showered? Had she honestly forgotten how to speak? Wouldn't that be amazing? The novelist who can't say a coherent word.

"Henry. Stole. Me."

Thomas McAdams looked at her through the door, her expression alert but calm. She was trying to figure out what to do, like a smart person, like a person who does smart things all the time. Then alert changed to alarm and Karen felt herself sliding ... *sliding*...

"Oh help me," she said, and then for a good long time, everything was black.

Chapter 13: Survival

"Thomas said you wanted to see me," Henry said from the doorway. Karen fought the urge to try to throttle him. He was too far away. And anyway, she had at least three needles attached to her arms, not to mention the blooping, bleeping diodes that measured her blood pressure.

"You can come closer," she rasped. When she'd arrived, they'd intubated her at the same time they'd hooked up the liquids to her veins. Karen Luck hadn't just been dehydrated; she'd been *severely* dehydrated. Thomas had told her either yesterday or the day before that if she'd gone two days more, maybe even one, she would have died. "I can't rightly strangle you from the bed."

"You could try," Henry said, taking a few steps closer. He held a toboggan in his hands with the gloves tucked in. It was snowing out. Her shades were drawn but she'd thought it might be snowing. God, she wished she were home. At present, Karen didn't know if home meant the place in OKC or the one in Los Angeles.

"Is that a request or a prophecy?" Karen asked, trying to sit up. Her body wouldn't comply. God, had she ever felt so weak? Less than a week ago, she was running upwards of eight miles a day; now, she could barely sit up without exhausting herself.

Taking a seat by her bed, Henry said, "Why did you do this to yourself, Karen?"

She looked at him for a moment, trying to conjure up any fiery emotion – rage, fury, even righteousness. None of it came. The exhaustion was like a tide, covering everything and leaving it bare in its wake. "You did this to me," she said, hating how little conviction her voice held.

Very quietly, he said, "I didn't."

"You got to be me before I got to be me," she said. "That sucks, Henry. That really sucks."

He wanted to reach out and touch her hand. He wanted to say he was sorry. He wanted more than anything to explain himself, to tell her why he did the things he'd done and why they'd seemed necessary at the time. But he couldn't, because he honestly didn't know. At one time, he thought he'd completely understood his motivations: catharsis, moving on, letting go. Now all those reasons sounded like excuses. And he'd known it would hurt her, hadn't he? Yeah, he'd known. He just didn't know she'd wind up in the hospital. *Was* that his fault? The result of unbelievable hubris and selfishness? Henry didn't think so. Or maybe he didn't *want* to think so.

He reached for her hand and touched it tentatively. "If I say I'm sorry, would you believe me?"

Karen swallowed and there were thorns in her throat. "Thomas said you used to dress like me."

Blinking, Henry said, "Thomas told you that?"

"Thomas told me a lot of things," she said. "My Dad too. This isn't a new thing."

Fear trembled in Henry's belly, the anticipation of being caught out at his worst behavior. Only he'd already been caught. All of it was out in the open now. What was there to anticipate?

"I've been trying to be you most of my life," he said, without any foreknowledge that he was going to say it.

"That's fucked up," she said, the tonelessness of her voice more of a condemnation than shouting or screaming would be.

"You pretended to be your father for years," he murmured. "And *he* pretended to be your mother."

"I never dressed up like him," she said, knowing it was a weak, weird argument.

"But he dressed up like your mom."

Now she turned her head toward him, for the first time feeling his hand on hers. Karen's eyes locked with Henry's. "I needed you," she told him. "On 9/11, Henry, I really needed you. And you did this to me. I was in Hawaii and my world was falling apart, *the* world was falling apart. And I wanted to call you. More than anyone, you'd understand. But you betrayed me, Henry. What you did betrayed me."

Tears sprang into his eyes and he blinked them away, tightening his grip on her hand. "I didn't mean to," he said. "Please understand more than anything that I didn't mean to. And *she* needs me too. Thomas."

"Her dad," Karen said. "Your dad."

"It was all over again for her. History repeating itself, only it wasn't our fathers this time."

"Or our mothers," Karen said, quietly.

Henry closed his eyes. "There's too much death to reckon with, Karen. Too much trauma." She was silent. There didn't seem to be much more to say. Henry sat in his chair by the bed for a long while, silent and contemplative. When he spoke again, it was with some reluctance. "Are you leaving Chanler & Cushing?"

"Yes. That's what all this was about."

"Don't blame Cynthia, okay? Blame me for all this."

"There's a lot of blame to go around," she said, leaning back and looking up at the ceiling. Or maybe, she thought, there wasn't any. Maybe it wasn't as black and white as betrayal or ruin. When she thought of Cynthia, anger still wanted to crowd in; Karen didn't know why she could still summon rage for Cynthia, when this man here was the one who stole her life to write a novel.

"She's just publishing it," he said.

"It's more than the book, Henry," Karen said. Was it?

"Did you like the book?" he asked her, and immediately wished he hadn't. He envisioned her crawling out of bed and tearing the diodes off and the needles out, blood gouting everywhere, and then clawing his throat out with her bare hands. He'd deserve it, too. How do you impersonate someone for years and then write their life story from their perspective and expect to get off clean?

"Henry, you took the most intimate details of my life. All my worst traumas. My mom. The hole in my bedroom wall. The Butcher. My coming out. All of it. You took all of it and spun some fiction on it and presented it to the world. I can't forgive you. I don't think I'll ever forgive you." She paused. "It's a really fucking good book. You're a really fucking good writer. Why do you think I'm so mad?"

Now her hand twisted in his grip and she squeezed his finger. The tears that had threatened him earlier were starting to fall now. "You believed in me," he said simply. "You brought my book to Cynthia and it changed my whole life. And I'm so sorry I've repaid you like this. I didn't mean to. I don't know if I even wanted to. I just needed to get over you, Karen. I needed to stop loving you like I always loved you. It's not fair to me, or to Thomas. Or to you."

"Well," she said, thinking, *getting you a publishing contract wasn't entirely altruistic on my part, either, Henry. Do you think I would have gone to her office with your manuscript in my hand if I hadn't need to get over some of my own stuff?* But she didn't say any of this out loud. "Did it work?"

Henry sighed heavily. "I don't know."

Those three words, echoing in her brain, doubling, tripling. They carried with her over the next few days, as she worked on getting her strength back, as she got healthy enough to leave the hospital, as she found her way into her own bed in the house in OKC. Sometimes late at night she could hear her father typing in his office. He was getting faster. His block, it seemed, was over.

And just in the nick of time, too. It was time for her to rest.

At that point, she couldn't have anticipated how long the rest would last.

On the Monday after Thanksgiving, Karen bade her lawyer happy holidays and hung up the phone and wandered toward Dad's office. It was quiet in there, the kind of quiet that can unsettle if it stretches out. "Dad?"

He sat in front of his computer in the dark. "It's done," he said. "I wrote a new book."

All thoughts of the lawyer and the next few months and the other, bad thing squirming around in the back of her brain vanished. "Dad, you did it! Holy shit! Can I read it?"

Gary stood, feeling shaky, unable to take his eyes off that last sentence: *Jessica Cunningham drew her gun and kicked the door in; it was about to be a very violent day.* If he wanted to, he could end every Jessica Cunningham book with a cliffhanger. How many Jessica Cunningham books might there be? How many Sprouse and Apa books were there? What about Mike Bull? Gary Luck thought that, with a little gumption, he could match all those. His speed had picked up midway through the book and had never really wavered. For the first time in years, his brain was busting with ideas for novels. He could write them all. He was sure of it; he could write them *all*.

Standing on shaky legs, Gary silently went to the refrigerator and pulled out what was left of the turkey carcass. Skylark had prepared most of the meal, though Henry and Thomas helped. Karen and he had stood back from the chaos and watched, Karen maybe a little too intently. A little over a month ago, she had vowed never to speak to Henry Dear again in her life. Now here he was, in her kitchen with his girlfriend and mother, whipping up turkey dinner for them all to enjoy together. Maybe fainting in a guy's house had a way of putting things into perspective. Or maybe it was what led to the fainting: all that writing and the sudden release from it. For a while. For a little while.

Still, she watched him, and any time the voices in her head tried to crowd her with questions of *how could he* and *how dare he* and *he stole my life*, she ticked her eyes toward Skylark Dear, *Mrs. Dear*, older now but still lovely and perfect and … well, okay, let's admit it: sexy as hell. Sexy. As. Hell. Any lingering anger or resentment she held for Henry, whether it was justified or not, evaporated in an instant. Maybe after eating, when Henry and Thomas and her father were all in the living room watching TV, Karen would go up to her room to lie down and maybe – just maybe – call forth a few paragraphs for a new book. But the door would be open, just a little, and downstairs the faucet would turn off and then there'd be footsteps on the stairs, light and bouncy because Mrs. Dear had worn heels over but had taken them off almost immediately and had made most of the dinner in her socks. And when she reached Karen's bedroom door, she'd tap it open with tented fingers and say, "Wow, are you really working on Thanksgiving. Karen Luck, you're going to send yourself back to the hospital. Now get into bed. That's an order."

What might follow such a sally was not appropriate thinking for a family dinner, so she left that part vague while she smiled to herself and ate her third heaping of mashed potatoes. In the absence of working yourself nearly to death, your appetite returns in a real hurry.

"What did the lawyer say?"

"She thinks publishers are going to go nuts for the opportunity to publish with us," Karen said, her brow furrowing. "She's setting up an auction. Package deal, me and you. I think we might have a new publisher by Christmas."

Dad smiled shakily at her. "It's a little scary," he said. "Chanler & Cushing – your mom and I have both been there since the beginning. I've never published anywhere else."

Karen's breath stopped. "What are you saying, Dad?"

Grabbing the loaf of bread from the cabinet, he resolutely did not look at her. "Oh, I don't know if I'm *saying* anything. It's just that C&C has always been pretty good to your mom and me. You too, once upon a time. You're a millionaire, right?"

She watched as he slathered the bread with Miracle Whip, slapped a couple of slices of pre-packaged cheese on, and heaped the turkey on the bread in alternating white- and dark-meat chunks. It was revolting and Karen was considering making herself one. "Dad," she whispered. "Are you having second thoughts about moving publishers?"

Smiling – to himself? – he said, "Well, now, I'm not entirely sure I ever had first thoughts, honey."

Her mouth dry, Karen said, "Dad, I wish you had … I don't know, said something."

"The last thing I wanted was to upset you at your worst time," he said. "But it's not your worst time. Not anymore."

You sure about that, Dad?

"What are you saying? Do you want me to call the lawyer back? I can do that right now." She felt her voice rising and speeding up. Fresh emotion spilled into her from all corners, but she didn't know what the emotion was. She hoped like hell it wasn't betrayal. She was sick to death of feeling betrayed, and she was sick to death of walking back those feelings because they didn't fit into her life better.

Incredibly, Dad laughed. "Calm down, girl. I'm not looking to rock your boat. I'll go along with any plan you want. I just wish we'd talked more about it."

Karen said, "We didn't talk about it more because when it was all happening, you weren't you. *I* was you. Making your publishing decisions was making *my* publishing decisions. I didn't know you were going to write again."

Dad smiled. "*I* didn't know I was going to write again, either."

She closed her eyes. "Then what the fuck are you saying, Dad?"

He sat down at their table, this forty-five year old who had seemed older a month ago than he did now. The humor was mostly out of his eyes now. "All I'm saying is that it's the end of something for me. Something I might have thought was eternal. You have your reasons for leaving and maybe they're good reasons, but they're not *my* reasons. You see what I'm saying? I can support you, honey, and still wish that things were different." He sighed heavily. "I guess ... I guess as I get older, there's always going to be new and different ways I have to learn to say goodbye to your mother."

Karen sat down across from him. "Oh."

"It's not your fault or anything. But let me be sad, okay?"

Reaching across the table and touching his hand, she said, "I really can call the lawyer back. If you want to stay with Chanler & Cushing…"

He gripped her hand in his, and it felt like Henry doing the same thing when she was in the hospital. She gripped back. "It's been a whole bunch of years between then and now, Karen. Maybe it's okay to say goodbye to your mom." He picked up his sandwich, then dropped it back down on the plate, raising his hands to his face and letting a sob so loud and elongated it scared them both. Karen went to him, holding him from behind while he covered his face and cried into his hands. He murmured into his sobs; Karen thought he was saying, "I wrote a book, Elaine, I wrote a new book."

They remained like that for a good long while; even though it was fairly early, neither of them wrote again for the rest of the night.

Here's how it all played out:

The lawyer, a woman named Bertrice Michigan (which, in Karen's opinion, was the best name she'd ever heard, and *her* name was Karen Luck) who had worked in entertainment law for decades, placed her with Denali House, one of the few active publishers with a pedigree longer and more prestigious than Chanler & Cushing. At points in its storied history, Denali had published Faulker, Tolstoy, DuMaurier, Fitzgerald. Karen's brand of modern gothic fit in fairly well with what the company was known for, but her father's contemporary crime novels felt at odds with the company's more literary stable. Still, when there was that much potential money to be had, you found workarounds.

But the editors at Denali hadn't read a Gary Luck novel in some time, and when his newest book, *A Good Deed in a Hard World*, they were a little taken aback. This wasn't the Apa/Sprouse potboilers they'd read in their misspent youth, when all they wanted out of a book was that it carry them along with its story breathlessly and effortlessly. They hadn't witnessed the evolution of the Mike Bull novels from their spare and grimy start to their increasingly literary recent forays. A lot of that was Karen's doing, but it wasn't like Gary hadn't been paying attention to what his characters and prose could be, maybe *should* be. And honestly, hadn't he spent just as much time writing modern gothics as his daughter had? He'd just done it in his wife's office, using his wife's name.

Denali's marketing push for *A Good Deed in a Hard World* was unlike any Gary Luck had ever received. Most of his book covers had been lurid blacks and browns with shadowy faces and men in fedoras, even though no men in any of his novels wore fedoras. *Good Deed*'s cover was white, and featured an illustration of a woman at the far end of a bar. Her gun was on top of the bar, within reach. She was knocking back a cup of something – in the book, it's bourbon, but it didn't really matter. Jessica Cunningham was here to get drunk. Maybe that was a cliché – the drunken PI on the case – but it was more than that, and not just because Cunningham was a woman. The case put her in the midst of a long-buried family secret so pervasive and horrifying that it birthed ever more secrets, on and on throughout the decades, so much so that it was still poisoning the children of today. The Warther family hires Cunningham simply to help them find a missing manuscript; their great-great grandfather Jack Warther's work on the history of the family itself. It might even be apocryphal at this point, but they're willing to hire Cunningham anyway, just in case she *might* find something. The stories of Jack and his wife Eunice are cherished in the family, and what better was to preserve their memory by finding the book their beloved great-grandfather had been writing before he died?

Within a few days, she manages to find the manuscript, hidden in a hollow in the floor in the family's old beach house. But she finds something even more disturbing: the possibility that the great-great grandfather they had always loved and told stories about wasn't Jack Warther at all, but an imposter. The deeper Cunningham digs, the more she grows convinced that "Jack Warther" was really Josiah Parsons – Eunice Warther's *nee* Parsons' – *brother*. And that in order to get the real Jack Warther out of the way, Josiah and Eunice killed him, and destroyed the body slowly, feeding the remnants to the pigs at a nearby farm. And that some of their children had come before Jack Warther's death, most of them came *after*.

Denali could work with this stuff better than they could have worked with Gary Luck's shoot-em-ups (this, of course, despite the fact that he had written precisely one shoot-em-up in his life, and it was in the 70s, and it was an Apa/Sprouse experiment that he'd written in a weekend and hadn't really loved, anyway). That blinding white cover, so smartly opposing the image of Gary's prior novels, would promise to stand out on bookstore shelves. The publisher garnered quotes from literary writers like Doris Kearns Goodwin and Amy Tan; the gamble here was that the man's name will bring his old fans in, but that the literary feints will open him up to a new audience.

Before the end of 2001, Gary Luck would sign a contract with Denali: for a high six figures, Gary owed three novels. They don't have to be Jessica Cunningham books, but Gary would the idea that Denali wanted them to be. Recurring characters bring readers back, and inspire new readers to dig into the back catalog. By the time he signed the contract, he would be midway through the new Cunningham novel, *The Lonely Loons*, and just picking up steam.

His daughter Karen is having a different adventure.

Bertrice Michigan didn't have a problem with Karen Luck confiding that she was gay, and telling her that signing any contract was contingent on being allowed to be out and open about that part of herself. Michigan didn't think she would have a problem selling any publisher on that – coming out wasn't as big a deal in 2001 as it would have been in the 1990s, but the curiosity and fanfare would probably sell some books (and, she thought cynically, the protests *against* her books – and there would be – would lead to even more curiosity, rubberneckers of the literary world wanting something salacious to be either righteous or angry about). None of that was a problem. Michigan thought she could get Karen Luck a three-book contract on the controversy alone.

The problem wasn't coming out. It was *staying* out. Michigan had read all of Karen Luck's unpublished novels – what she called her banked novels. *What Happened in Alina's Room?*, *Huff*, *Beverly Hatch*, and *Not Much Left*: all good-to-great novels that should find her an extensive readership beyond any she'd previously enjoyed. The operative word in here was *should*. *Not Much Left* might be the best thing that Karen Luck ever wrote, but if it was followed with *Huff* or *Beverly Hatch*, it was going to get lumped in as a genre exercise. Her readership – both current and the potential expanded audience – might well embrace *Not Much Left* as a stunning departure, something bold and new that reflected Karen's newfound confidence and openness about her sexuality. But then? Then they'd want her to go back to what she was writing before.

"But this *is* what I was writing before," Karen told Bertrice. "Like, very literally, I wrote all these earlier. *Among* the other stuff I was writing."

"But they weren't published," Bertrice told her. "Doing all these in a row? That's risky, Karen."

Karen's eyes implored her. "But *why* is it risky?"

Thomas McAdams could have told her why. She'd read all four books and she'd liked them all – especially *Beverly Hatch* – but even though she wasn't savvy about the marketplace or particularly closed-minded, she found herself dealing with a weariness about them she didn't like feeling.

Twelve pages into the third book she picked up, *What Happened in Alina's Room?*, she put the manuscript down and looked over at Henry and said, "Another lesbian?"

Henry had rolled his eyes. "That doesn't matter once you get into it."

"Yeah, maybe, but it doesn't matter to the character either."

Laughing, Henry had said, "Well, that's the point, isn't it? Main character's gay and it's not really a big deal?"

"Sure, I get what you're saying. But isn't it *kind of* a big deal? I mean, I really like Karen, and I'm sure this book is great, but even I'm like, '*Why* is there another lesbian in this?' And if that's me, what's a regular reader going to think?"

Bertrice had come to the same conclusions, but was far more blunt. "People are going to see you as writing lesbian fiction, not fiction."

Karen's hands had balled into fists and she raised them above her head in the restaurant, wanting to scream, wanting to hurl things at the wall. "Lesbian fiction is not a *genre*! This is why I left my last publisher!"

"Karen, *I* know that. You know that. Maybe your core readership will know that. But for the rest of the world, the rest of the people buying your books? They're going to want assurances."

"This is bullshit. Assurances? What the fuck does that even mean?"

"It means that you have four brilliant books that people are going to stop reading if you publish them in a row. It means that the reading public is fickle, and as much as you and I and even they want to support you being an out and proud lesbian, what they want to read, to spend a few days with in their private alone time, doesn't always match up to their ideals. People are going to come to your back catalog after *Not Much Left* is finished and find a whole bunch of books *not* about gay women. They're going to look for more of that going forward. But if you publish *Huff* next, it's going to look to the world like you moved publishers, came out, and changed everything about your writing to reflect the fact that you're suddenly a lesbian."

"But I'm *not* suddenly a lesbian."

"Yeah, I get that. But will they?"

Karen's fists unclenched. "Why are we always thinking of the lowest common denominator? Why are we always thinking of the audience as this dumb, unwashed monoculture that's going to reject four very distinct books in very distinct styles just because the main character in each is a woman who's into women?"

"You wouldn't lose your whole audience," Bertrice said. "But you'd lose some. What's brave and courageous today is boring tomorrow."

Tears pricked Karen's eyes. Everything about this conversation sounded like echoes of conversations with Cynthia. What had that whole month of writing hell been for if it was just going to come around to this again?

"So what you're saying, Bertrice, is that it's hopeless? That writing the way I want and living the way I need to live is a pointless exercise?"

Bertrice sighed and sipped her beer. "I'm not your friend and I'm not your publisher. I'm your lawyer, and I'm a reader. I know the law and I know fiction. Is 'lesbian fiction' a genre? No. Does it feel like a genre if one person only writes lesbian main characters? Maybe. Blame the world. Blame homophobia. Blame fickle readers. You can argue until the cows come home that no one cares if Danielle Steel writes about straight white people falling in love book after book, or that John Grisham only writes about white male lawyers, unless they're played by Denzel in the movie. But the reality is, that's the standard. It's what people are comfortable reading. That might change, but it hasn't changed yet."

"So what if I want to be the change?"

Bertrice leaned in closer. "You can be. All right? This is what I'm saying. You can change everything, if you want. But you have to give a little too. It's a balance. Publish these books you're so passionate about. Get them out there. But *also* publish some other stuff, more in line with what you did before."

"Are you saying this as my lawyer or as a reader?"

"In this case, both are equally important." She swigged her beer. "And listen, maybe I'm off-base. These are my impressions. Any publisher worth their salt is going to want

Karen Luck as their client. They will publish anything you hand them. But consider the marketplace. Consider what you want in the long term verses the short term. You have a mission and that's great. But don't let it get in the way of the realities of the reading world."

One week before Gary Luck signed his contract with Denali, Karen signed her own. There was very specific language in her contract regarding her sexuality; the understanding that she was going to come out prior to the publication of *Not Much Left* was the big buzz around Denali's offices. Would it be seen as crass, "becoming" a lesbian to promote her new book and new publisher? Or could they spin actual reality into the publicity? She'd been wanting to tell her story for a long time, and now, with Denali, she finally had the freedom to do so. TV interviews would capture her palpable sense of relief. Print interviews would mention how she's all new, but also exactly the same. The cover of the book would veer only slightly from the ones on her novels at Chanler & Cushing: instead of the deep abstract browns and blacks they always used, Denali would opt for a cooler palette, royal blue featuring actual illustrations.

They weren't necessarily aiming for a new audience with their marketing blitz; anyone who knew anything about *Not Much Left* knew that the book featured a lesbian main character. They wanted to retain the *old* readership, the people who might hear *lesbian main character* and decide to skip this one. Nick Hornby, dick-lit king of *High Fidelity* and *About a Boy*, blurbed the book with a glowing "I knew Karen Luck was good, but not *this* good. *Not Much Left* may well be the best novel of the new millennium." Joyce Carol Oates, who'd written her share of gothic novels, was more succinct: "Karen Luck is the best living writer of fiction." The praise was real. The book, which had been written to ease her transition from a closeted lesbian novelist to an out and proud lesbian novelist at her old publisher, now served a different function. *Not Much Left* showed the world what Karen Luck could write if she wrote without restriction. It was exhilarating.

Did she lose some readers? Probably. Denali booked her on an extensive press tour that included bookstore signing, some lectures, and TV and radio appearances; some of these public appearances got contentious. The DJs on the *Morning Buster* radio show on WNJY were perfectly pleasant to her off the air, but once they were live morphed so completely into their shock-jock personas that they were baffled that she left halfway through the interview. The most incisive question they'd asked was, "If lesbos use a dildo, doesn't that just mean that deep down, they still want some dick?" Her novels never came up.

At a signing at a Borders in Georgia, an old woman with frizzy hair and a very small purse approached her. Karen looked up and smiled and the woman slapped her full across the face. The bookstore employees and the rest of the people in line just stood in stunned silence for a long, shocked moment. Karen, having to fight back the urge to slap this woman – who had to be in her late 70s – back, instead stared and asked why she had done it.

"I lost my little girl to homosex," this sweet woman said; Karen could picture her baking cookies in a small, cozy kitchen just a few days before Christmas, wearing a gingham apron and her hair done up in a bow. (She was unaware that she was picturing Mrs. Claus from the stop-motion animated film *Santa Claus is Coming to Town.*) "People like you. Sick. Venal. I wish you'd all die."

Later, Karen thought of plenty of responses to this horrible woman. "You touched me, now *you* have homosex," would have been where she'd start, but, "Maybe your daughter lost *you* because you're a closed-minded bitch, ever think of that?" was her favorite. In the moment, she could only stare, her mouth hanging open, and her cheek stinging, as the store security guard hauled her gently away.

And the death threats. Of course she got death threats. They generally couldn't be taken seriously – they were all written by people with way too much time and too little grammar on their hands – but she sent all of the letters to the police, just in case. The letters she dreaded the most were ones from former fans. The kinder they were, the more fragile her heart seemed.

Dear Ms. Luck,

For the past five years, it has been my honor and privilege to have been a reader of your work. Unfortunately, your decision to "come out" has ended this readership. I can't in good conscience read novels by someone I know is committing sins against God. Worst of all is that your books were honestly the only thing that helped me through my husband's death, and all the attendant pain of what both he and I went through. Now I have to throw all that away. I wish very much that you had not made such a selfish decision and had considered the readers who depend on your novels. Perhaps one day you will find God and I will be able to read your books again.

Sincerely,

Mrs. Frank Heaton

Dubuque, Iowa

Letters like that felt like X-Acto knives to her gut. Alternately, they made her want to scream and cry and find Mrs. Frank Heaton and grab her by the collar and shout, "I was a homosex when I *wrote* that shit you loved so much! I was going down on Maura McKinnon all the time when I wrote

Take With Meals. Did you like that book? Find it fucking *inspiring*? It was written by a *dyke*, you sad loser!"

Of course she did none of that. Instead, she would retreat back to her bed, worn out and wondering if Cynthia might not have been right, after all. This couldn't last forever, could it? Didn't the world have much bigger problems right now than worrying about a lesbian writer writing lesbian stories? Weren't they all supposed to be banded together now because of terrorism and presenting a united front to the world?

Over the years, she'd grown used to defending her writing when she felt it was appropriate to defend. The violent sex scenes in *I Want You To Hurt Me*, which dug into graphic, unsubtle detail that managed to be both salacious and mundane at turns. Her main character's decision to get an abortion in *Where'd She Go?* – especially the fact that she suffered no ill consequences and didn't even feel bad about terminating her pregnancy. Heck, she'd even been accused of forwarding the theory that parents and children simply couldn't have good, healthy relationships because she mostly wrote about strained family ties. Karen could defend all of that, could talk about her own good relationship with her Dad and how it was just more fun to write about fucked-up people, and how you can get desensitized to anything if you do it enough, and how abortion was a woman's right. What she couldn't seem to get a handle on was defending her sexuality. Why was she a lesbian? She just was. What made her decide to come out? It was hard living in secret and she didn't want to do it anymore. Yes, but wouldn't she be happier with a man? No, because she was a gay woman. And around and around. Fiction was about interpretation and nuance and intent. Being gay was just a fact of her life. Defending it was like defending the fact that dirt existed. But a lot of people still wanted her to do it, so she did it as best as she could.

When she went to bed every night of the book tour, she considered opening up her laptop and getting to work on the new book. On Bertrice Michigan's advice, she was working on a new novel with a straight dude at the center of it; it was called *Mike's Missing*, and it was about a group of amateur high school cyclists who go out riding on the last day of summer.

One of them doesn't come back. The rest of the book would be concerned with finding out where Mike was, and whether or not he was alive. Karen didn't know. Often when she started a novel, she had no idea how it was going to end; it was more exciting that way, finding out along with her readers where the story was going to end up.

Considering opening up her laptop was all she ever did, though. Over the course of three months, she'd gotten maybe three pages of the new book written, a far cry from three books in a single month. The entire book tour left her so drained that only when she'd been back home in Los Angeles for two weeks, staring at a computer screen night after night after night, the cursor refusing to move and her brain refusing to offer any assistance, that she realized she might be completely fucked.

Here was the thing: Karen Luck could, technically, be completely fucked for four years without anyone catching on. If she wanted to challenge Bertrice Michigan's advice, she could actually stretch that out two more years, depending on whether Denali wanted to write up some new contracts. The damned thing of it was, Karen Luck's old publisher and Karen Luck's new publisher were working together in a sort of equitable arrangement almost unheard of in the book business: Karen's big splash with *Not Much Left* would carry her through 2002; released in September, the book would probably surge again before Christmas; Chanler & Cushing had no intention of bringing out one of their last two Karen Luck novels to compete with the juggernaut of *Not Much Left*. Especially since they had their last *Gary* Luck novel, *Bullseye*, which garnered a different audience and could be promoted as *The Last Mike Bull Story*.

Summer of 2003, Chanler & Cushing released the serial killer novel *Jeremy Stain*; the lurid dark colors were back, suggestive instead of representative. C&C, Karen explained to Thomas McAdams over drinks, had to work very hard to convince their reading audiences that, while the author might be a gay woman, there weren't any gay women at all in *Jeremy Stain*. "They don't want to seem homophobic, either, so it's a tricky tightrope for them. How to put the genie back in the bottle."

"Are you sure that's what they're doing?"

"Thomas, the side of Cynthia Auburn you've always seen is the one intent on making Henry happy. You don't know what she's really like."

"Yeah, but Cynthia isn't really in charge of the publicity, is she? Or does she work in marketing, too?" Karen looked slyly over her glass at Thomas, nodding sagely but not daring to answer. She pictured Cynthia in her office, seething at the success of *Not Much Left*, and having to pretend as if it and Karen's Big Gay Book Tour had never happened.

(Cynthia Auburn, a savvy businesswoman who knew books and the bookbuying public better than Karen knew her, couldn't have been more delighted by the ambient publicity another publisher had provided. Now that the cat was out of the bag, so to speak, Cynthia was more than happy to ride the wave. And she could tell herself she'd done the right thing by keeping Karen in the closet for longer than she probably had to be, and by not letting her write the stuff she wanted to, even though it probably wouldn't have tanked her sales by a significant amount, especially in recent years. She could tell herself all that and sometimes even fall asleep normally without any sedatives. Everyone was rich and getting richer, after all. What was there to be sad about?)

Karen's new editor at Denali, a slight man with watery eyes named Benford Bramlett, advised against *What Happened in Alina's Room* as her next book. "Two serial killer novels back to back. It's going to feel samey."

"But one's a murder spree book and the other one's a mystery. They're so different." Karen didn't tell Benford that she thought *Alina* was probably the weakest of her four "lesbian novels," and that she was sort of hoping that after the splash *Not Much Left* had made and that *Jeremy Stain* seemed to be making, she thought it best to ride the wave with *Alina's Room*. The goodwill might compel people to overlook its flaws. They might be more forgiving of a third book than a fifth. "Plus, this one's a lesbian book. That's *super* different."

Benford laughed. "No one cares if it's a lesbian book or not. What the hell's a lesbian book?" Karen stared blankly at him for so long he thought she might be having a seizure. Until right now, Karen never would have considered those words could go together in that order. Was he dismissing her worry or assuring her? Was he wrong, or was he telling her that Cynthia – and Regina – had been wrong? *No one cares if it's a lesbian book or not.* Karen carried those words back to her writing studio in Los Angeles, where she sat down at her computer and put her fingers on the keyboard, fully positive that Benford had given her the key to unlock her writer's block once and for all. Whether it was true or not maybe didn't matter; people don't question placebos if they work.

But it didn't work. She sat at her computer for three hours, typing nothing, doing nothing, before closing the screen and going up to take a shower, wishing Maura was with her. That night, lying on her bed, naked with a copy of Maya Goldberg's *Bee Season* tented open next to her, she closed her eyes and dialed Maura's number from memory. She answered on the second ring.

"Karen," she said simply.

"I was just ... did we end badly, Maura?"

There was a noise on Maura's end, something loud and boisterous. Was she having a party? Or watching TV? "Karen, I don't want to go over that again. I saw you came out. Good for you. I'm honestly proud of you."

"How about you?"

"I'm already an aging actress with brown hair and no plastic surgery. I don't need to throw another iron in the no-hire fire."

Please come home, she wanted to say, unsure of why she wanted to say it. Did she miss Maura? Really miss Maura? Or did she miss someone reliably waiting for her to be done with writing, eager to feast on the scraps of attention she might receive.

Another noise on Maura's side. Not a TV. There were people in her place. Actors? Actresses? Friends? A new girlfriend?

"I miss you, Maura," she said, and that was true enough.

For a long time, Maura didn't say a word. "I don't know if we ended badly, Karen. We ended on 9/11. A lot of other bad things were happening then. But just because we were small beans in comparison ... Maybe we didn't end *badly*, honey. But we did end. You know what I'm saying?"

Karen took in breath. There wasn't much to take in.

"You have a good life, Maura."

"Write well, Karen." Then Karen hung up and after a long while, picked up her novel and dove back inside, completely unaware of how tumultuous her stomach was, how there was a throbbing ache in her chest, how tears were streaming freely down her face. Eventually she fell asleep, the hurt inside her following her down into troubled dreams she wouldn't remember the next day.

In 2004, Denali published *Huff.* Some cynical critics were quick to label it "a lesbian twist on *Take With Meals*," but most liked the book, often to a degree that Karen found a little suspect. Not at all like *Not Much Left* or *Jeremy Stain*. Completely new. Completely different. Karen Luck's post-coming out career was proving to be even more fascinating than her career in the closet. Critics were falling over themselves to praise her newfound energy and versatility.

Luck was trying all new stories now, all new characters and ways of writing. It wasn't just that there were gay women at the forefront of some of her new novels. It was that the fact of them seemed to point toward a rekindled sense of exploration, a feeling of being in love with the language in a way that some of her novels – for lack of a better term – "pre-lesbian" might have lacked. Karen wondered, on her many walks through the Hollywood Hills, what the critics might think if they knew she wrote most of her lesbian books years ago, and her non-lesbian books over the course of days, writing without thinking, writing as well as she could as fast as she could to fulfill a contract.

If Karen didn't know any better, she might have seemed as if critics were going nuts over her new stuff because she was a "lesbian voice in fiction," not just "Karen Luck, a gay woman who writes good novels." It was as if she had tried hard to carve out a new path for herself, one separate from her parents, and had wound up in a different – but no less constrictive – bounding box. Maybe all success – big and small – was a fluke. Maybe you could never get a true read on *why* people liked your work, or a pure concept of whether your work would sell and gain popularity in a bubble. Maybe it's just accident after accident and sometimes they work out.

And it *was* working out; that was the weirdest thing of all. *Not Much Left* was her biggest seller to date, and *Jeremy Stain* managed to debut at #1. Denali had wanted to rush a paperback for Christmas, but Benford Bramlett had suggested keeping the hardcover in stores. It hit the top of the bestseller list for one more week, two weeks before Christmas. Karen Luck's novels weren't just resonating with critics, but with regular readers. A good *New York Times* review could give you a boost, but only consumers got you to that number one spot. *Huff* also debuted at #1, and stuck around for awhile. People apparently needed a story about a gay chick addicted to sniffing gas for Christmas. Who was Karen Luck to argue?

The Second Tucker Strong came out in late 2005, in time to anticipate the Christmas rush. *Jeremy Stain* had hit the stores and online retailers a month before and it had included *Tucker Strong*'s first chapter, the one that ended with

"You stole my life," the second Tucker Strong said, his eyes narrowing. *"You stole it. And I aim to take it back."*

Sales soared! Benford rejoiced! A massive portion of the book-reading public found *The Second Tucker Strong* under their Christmas tree! Everyone was happy!

Except Karen Luck, who had spent most of 2005 in a full-tilt panic. The routine was so ingrained it almost didn't matter anymore. She would wake up around eleven and walk twelve miles in the Hollywood Hills. When she got back home, she fixed a bowl of cereal or some toast and eggs and brought it with her to her home office. She'd switched home offices several times – once, even into the bathroom. One morning, she decided her laptop was the problem; she found a store in the Valley that sold vintage electric typewriters. The one she selected looked exactly like the one she'd written the first draft of her first novel on. All the old sensations flooded back: spooling the paper in, adjusting it just so, hitting the Return key two or three times to bring the page down to the right level, where the first paragraph would form the first building block of a new story or a new novel. Karen found herself staring at that blank page – so tangible, so real – for as long as she had watched the cursor blink on the screen of her laptop. More than an hour. Closer to two. Then she opened up her office window and hurled the typewriter down to the decorative stones around her picture-pretty pool. It might have startled someone if anyone had been around, but the cleaning lady only came on Thursdays and there hadn't been anyone else. No one else at all.

Notebooks, she finally discovered, produced the same result as screens and keys. She didn't throw the notebooks to the pavement. Instead she simply opened her desk drawer, and slid the brand-new, unwritten-in notebooks inside, sliding it closed. Then she put her hands to her face and cried.

Her life became a series of vignettes, moments unconnected by the tether of writing. The few dates she went on were either overly enthusiastic about her fame or expressing disinterest in it so vehemently that it was either staged or insulting. There was a fine like between *I don't care that you're famous* and *I don't care about* why *you're famous.* Half the women she brought to bed were fans. Half were too busy or important to read popular fiction. It wouldn't be fair to say that she hated everyone she slept with, but she feared that she didn't much like any of them. Maybe it was hard to do when you didn't much like yourself these days.

She walked. She read. She went to movies. She dated. She didn't write. Not one sentence. Not one word. Fiction, which had once come so easily to her that she could write three coherent, well-received books in a month, was now tantalizingly, terribly, out of her grasp.

As *Tucker Strong* was starting to climb the bestseller lists, Karen Luck boarded a plane heading back home to OKC. She spent the entire flight with her eyes fixed straight ahead; her seatmate, a heavyset man named Andrew Hardy who kept accidentally banging her elbow with his, apologized the first few times but stopped when she'd said nothing. Didn't even acknowledge him. Later, he told his girlfriend that she looked like someone haunted, like a ghost had drifted inside her and had taken over. He also said that the woman looked a lot like that writer, Karen Luck. Andrew Hardy had read two of the woman's books: *Really Restless* and *I Want You to Hurt Me*, and the books had made him think of some creepy-crawly things inside his own brain that he didn't much want there. Since then, he'd laid off reading her. The woman who'd sat beside him *couldn't* be Karen Luck; someone who looked that lost and that diminished could have never written something so perverted as *I Want You to Hurt Me*. He only got up once during the flight to head into the bathroom; there, he jerked off, thinking of the scene where the one girl ties the guy to a cross and beats him until he's black and blue … then leaves him there overnight, until he screams to be set free. Only then does she know he's broken. Andrew Hardy didn't particularly want to be broken, by his girlfriend or anyone, but there was something undeniably exciting about watching it happen to someone else, even if it was just someone fictional. When he took his seat again, the woman next to him was still staring ahead. Andrew Hardy closed his eyes and tried not to think about Karen Luck anymore.

Her father picked her up at the airport and hugged her, doing that thing where he laced his hands behind her back like she was a little kid. He bundled her into the car and was only ten minutes into the drive before he asked her what was wrong.

Karen kept that staring-ahead thing that had so unnerved Andrew Hardy. When she spoke, her voice was disaffected, almost as if her speech were something separate from her body. "My newest novel is currently #1 on the *New York Times* bestseller list. My previous book is doing well on the paperback chart. I'm publishing novels with lesbian main characters, and aside from some initial blowback, the reading public doesn't much seem to care who I'm writing about, so long as it's my name on the cover. Over the last few years, I've received the best reviews of my life. I used to think it was just so the literati could congratulate themselves on reading gay woman fiction, but it's gone on long enough that I think they might actually just like my stuff. So it's a victory in the marketplace, a victory with the critics, and a victory over Cynthia, which seems less important than it used to. Everything's coming up Karen, Dad, so what could possibly be wrong?"

"Well, for one thing," he said with no preamble, "you're single."

Her eyes went wide and her mouth dropped open. The numb complacency in which she'd been stewing since LA started to drain away. "What the hell?"

"Also, you're not writing."

Karen gaped at him. "Dad—"

"It's an educated guess. I'm not aware of any deaths in our immediate circle and ... well, your tells are so obvious."

"What tells? What are you even talking about."

"'Hi Karen, how's the writing going?' 'Oh, fine. This is shaping up to be an interesting chapter.' Do you have any idea how many times you told me that a chapter is shaping up interesting?"

"Maybe my chapters *are* interesting."

"Sure, and if so, you would have told me everything about them. You're like your mother in that way. I'm quiet about my book until I'm finished. You've gotta throw every character detail, every plot twist, every motivation at me to gauge my reaction. You haven't done that in a little while."

Karen sighed. "Well, it's more than just a little while."

"Since that month?" he asked her. Slowly she nodded.

"I think maybe I burned myself out." Then, without any warning, her throat constricted and tears began to torrent from her eyes. "And I don't know what to *do*! Why couldn't Maura have been around *now*?"

Gary glanced at his distraught daughter, then turned his eyes back to the road. "Have you called her?"

Through hitching breaths, Karen recounted the night she had called her ex. How Maura had evaded the question of whether they'd ended things on a good note, how she subtly commanded Karen never to call her again. What had those noises in the background? When she and Maura had been together, she never had friends over, had never talked about going out with friends. Now, suddenly, she was part of a whole group of people? How had she done that? How does someone do that?

"And the thing is, during our whole relationship, she kept competing for my time with the writing. Now, she could have me, all of me, and she's moving on."

"Karen," Dad said. "It's me."

She looked at him, not understanding.

"She couldn't have all of you now. It's still all about the writing. It's just about the absence of it. Maybe it's even bigger than writing itself. Empty fills a lot of space."

Dragging her eyes up to the windshield, Karen could see for miles in all directions. This stretch of OKC was like that. The clouds above were weighted with dark, pregnant with precipitation. It was going to snow for Christmas. You never got snow in Los Angeles.

"How did you do it?"

Eventually, Dad said, "To tell you the truth, I'm not entirely sure. I thought about killing myself quite a lot."

Karen's heart plummeted in her chest; it felt like a bare-knuckle boxer had socked her a few in the gut. "Dad, you never—"

"Told you? Of course I didn't. I didn't want you to know." He paused. "Depression fills a lot of space, too."

Her heart still wasn't where it should be. "You still could have talked with someone, Dad. L.A. is lousy with therapists. It's actually a cliché how many therapists there are there."

"Tell me, honey," he said, "you seeing a therapist right now?"

Karen suddenly saw herself as if her actions matched her emotions; she looked like a woman who has accidentally wandered into a wasp's nest and is now flailing wildly and ineffectually to stop them from stinging. "That's not the same."

"Aren't you depressed?"

"It's not that kind of depression," she said, turning back to look at the clouds. They were so immense, dwarfing the landscape and the people in it. Crumbling a little, Karen said, "Or maybe it is. I don't know. Publishing isn't really the problem. Cynthia put this complex in me about lesbian fiction and then Bertrice didn't do much to allay that, but at this point, I think I might be okay. Maybe. I have one book left in my contract and I have two books banked. Publishing isn't the problem."

"Of course it's not."

"And I've written plenty of short stories over the years. If there's another two-book contract, I can pad it out with a collection. I've actually been thinking about that lately anyway." She laughed to herself, not without some real humor. "I was thinking of calling it *Incest and Monsters*. How's that for a new Christmas book?"

"So what you're saying is that no matter what happens, your reading public and your publisher don't have to know you've been suffering from writer's block since 2001 until sometime just before the new decade rolls around."

"It's not the publisher. It's not the public."

"It's the writing."

"What's wrong with me, Dad?"

He looked ahead. Gary Luck had followed *A Good Deed in a Hard World* with *A Tomb of Virtue and Honor*, *Coward's Deaths*, *Comfort in Despair*, and *Fair Cruelty*, the last released this July to very good sales. He'd negotiated his own contract for these latter three books after *Virtue & Honor* had done even better than *Good Deed* and with a far less extensive marketing campaign. It seemed as if Denali had done its job in announcing a new version of Gary Luck; Gary Luck had done his job on delivering on that promise. There was a new two-book contract on his desk at home right now; he'd initially meant to show it to Karen and make a big display of signing it and mailing it off. Now he thought he'd just squirrel it away until she'd flown back to Los Angeles. There was no question of not signing it; he was halfway through a new book called *The Sin of Conscience* and it was going well. The Jessica Cunningham books were getting darker and weirder and more character-driven than plot-driven the longer he stayed with them.

But he was no longer putting in ten-hour days in front of the laptop screen. He would get up in the morning, walk awhile on the treadmill and listen to an audiobook. Then a bowl of cereal and a couple hours at the book. 1,500 words was his goal in the morning – about three pages. Then the day was his. Chores. Errands. Crossword puzzles. Books to read. Shows to catch up on. And when the evening came, Skylark Dear would meet him and more often than not, they'd spend a few hours at her place with the bedroom door shut and locked.

Sometimes they'd play out his fantasies, sometimes hers, which mainly involved erotic asphyxiation. No costumes. No makeup. Usually she would just hold his head down in her lap, crushing his ears between her thighs, her hand on the back of his head, forcing his tongue to do its best work until he started feeling lightheaded, and then he'd try to yank his head up to gulp some air, but Skylark would just keep his head down for a few more seconds, just to show him that she was in charge, that she had the real power here. Then that first breath was heaven and that second breath was ecstasy and then he'd be going down again, unaided, because he wanted to please her, he wanted to make her feel good, he wanted to feel a little bit uncomfortable and a little bit powerless and sometimes he wondered how he'd managed to find two women over the course of a lifetime who managed to give him completely different experiences that exactly aligned with his sexual wants and needs.

    Of course he'd explained none of this to Karen, nor did he tell her that after a dinner he and Skylark made together, he'd go back to his writing room and spend another hour there, either rounding out his word count by another thousand or so or doing some editing, and he'd knock off in time to catch *Jeopardy!* and the nightly sitcoms and dramas and competition shows with Skylark before heading off to bed together with books and glasses of water. Sometimes it would be at his house. Sometimes hers. Aside from the fact that Gary was nominally famous and fairly wealthy (and forgiving the fact that they didn't live in the same house), it was a middle-class suburban life he'd tumbled into, the same he'd enjoyed when Elaine was alive and Karen was small. Again, more wants and needs absolutely fulfilled, and though you can never know another person entirely, he thought Skylark was similarly fulfilled. All he'd had to do to get it was pretending to be his dead wife for awhile, then drown in his own darkness for a few years before surfacing to find a good life waiting for him.

"Nothing's wrong with you, Karen," he said.

"Liar."

"Sometimes it's a matter of time. It was for me."

"I sometimes think Cynthia got into my head, and Bertrice, too. Like I *have* to write something without a lesbian lead to balance things out. And maybe I do and maybe I don't, but Dad, I tried that, too. I *totally* tried that and *still* nothing. I keep having all these great ideas, and the titles are coming to me easily, but I can't get past a single sentence."

He smiled at her. "What are the ideas?" And he watched a miracle occur: the storm clouds that had been gathering under the skin of her face and in the depths of her eyes cleared and an actual smile touched the corners of her mouth. She started talking about *Mike's Missing*, which seemed so fully formed in her mind that she could have been describing a book she'd finished. Another book, this one called *Something's Very Wrong with Margaret*, was another of her modern gothics, this one about a suburban divorced mom named Margaret who's been sleeping with the baggage girl from the local Safeway. One day, she's visited by an old woman she'd never met before who claims that this woman is her daughter.

"That's what I have so far," Karen babbled, her face now fully aglow. "I don't know if the woman really is her mother. I think it's going to be more sinister than that. And I was toying with the idea of calling it *Baggage*, but that seems kind of obvious. Don't you think that seems obvious?"

"I like the *Very* in the title," he told her, and when she turned to him, she could have been a girl again, after she had been able to weave the trauma of her mother dying into the fabric of her life, but before the stuff with Cynthia and novels and adulthood had swept in. She could have been a girl of eleven or twelve, being told they were going to go out for ice cream on a hot summer day. He was on the verge of even asking her if she wanted to stop at the Dairy Queen for a Cheesequake Frosty, but they were almost home and the snow was imminent, and besides, the DQ was closed and would be until spring.

Karen waxed rhapsodic about that *Very*, and then dove deeper into the plot, and all at once he had the idea that *he* could write it for her. That she had done so much work for him over the last few years, including writing the best Mike Bull novel of the series during her month of hell, that he practically owed her one. It was on the tip of his tongue to broach the subject, but he held back. It wasn't that he couldn't, necessarily, but maybe she needed to come to a new book on her own. Besides, it wasn't as if he was a young man anymore. He couldn't write for ten hours and then throw another three on to become Karen into the wee hours of the night. Gary Luck had a different life now, a good life. A life he'd been able to reclaim because he'd gotten his writing back and didn't want to die anymore. But maybe that was another thing he didn't have to say to his daughter while she was going through whatever she was going through. Maybe it would be enough for her to see it in action.

    The light above the garage flicked on as Gary swinging the car into the driveway. Skylark Dear stood at the window by the sink, and raised her hand to him. He raised his back, even though she couldn't possibly see him in the reflection. *Is she going to ever become Skylark Luck?* he wondered, not for the first time.

Karen (whose mind insisted that the little wave had been for her and her alone) stepped out of the car, feeling good, really good, for the first time in a long while. She glanced up. "It's going to storm, isn't it?"

Nodding, Gary said, "I hope it's not too bad. I don't want to lose power before the feast."

"Feast?"

"Thomas and Henry are on their way. Just a small celebration to welcome you back to OKC."

"You didn't have to go out of your way."

Dad shifted, a little uncomfortably. "We like getting together, the four of us. We do it at least once a week."

Karen touched the roof of the car. "You do?" Her breath made little vapor-wisps in the air. So did Dad's.

"You don't have to go back to Los Angeles when Christmas is over, kiddo," he said quietly. "I don't know if you're there because being home is hard for you, but you always have a place here."

The things she wanted to say – *yes, please, take me back, take care of me, I'm doing one fucked-up job of taking care of myself* – slid in and out of her brain so fast, she could barely credit it. "I'm just going to walk around outside a little bit," she said. "Clear my head. Cold's a novelty right now. I'm going to enjoy it before it becomes a nuisance."

Dad nodded, grabbing her suitcases. "Dinner will be ready soon. I hope you didn't become vegan out in California."

Karen grinned. "Still a filthy carnivore."

"Good. Sky's making goose."

"Extravagant."

"That's nothing. She's making a capon for Christmas dinner."

"What's a capon?"

Dad shrugged. "I don't know, it's like a penguin or something." Karen laughed and so did Dad. "See you inside, kiddo."

She hadn't done much in the way of let's remember last time she'd been home; her entire consciousness had been focused on getting the last C&C books written and off to Cynthia so she could be done with both. The two gargantuan pines that had dominated the side yard since time immemorial stood as huge and immovable and immortal as ever. Once, when Mom was still alive, they'd strung a hammock between the two trees and had spent the greater portion of a summer week taking turns sprawling in it with a soda and a book. The novelty wore off quickly as the summer heated up past the point where being outside was remotely comfortable, but Karen still recalled the memory fondly. She placed a hand on one of the pines where Mom might have tied one of the ropes. No bark was missing or rubbed away. There was nothing of her mother out here. She glanced up at the house. The light in her father's office was on; the light in the one next to it, the one they still called Mom's office, was not. Further up, her bedroom window, a dark eye on the cold world outside. She could recall, distantly, wanting to jump from that window once upon a time. Cynthia had stopped her that day. Karen wondered who might stop her today, if she decided to finally go through with it.

Then a breeze, sharp and frozen and barbed with potential, shuddered through the pines. The night was cold and getting colder, and while the weatherman hadn't predicted snow, those clouds had told a different story. Karen craned her neck further back and saw no stars above.

"Mrs. Dear, this is ... I don't have the words." Karen grinned wryly at her father. "Delicious is the only thing I can come up with."

"I can live with delicious. But Karen, you've known me literally your whole life. Don't you think you can call me Skylark?"

Henry said, "I don't know, Mom. It's a pretty weird name."

"Says Henry Dear," Thomas said.

"Says the woman named Thomas," Henry said. They had all eaten their full share of Skylark's roast goose, along with heaping piles of mashed sweet potatoes and the sweet corn on the cob. Thomas and Henry had brought competing pies ("It's not chocolate mousse pie if you just dump pudding in a graham cracker crust," Thomas argued, but on this, Karen vehemently disagreed. Then again, Thomas had baked a cherry pie from scratch and it was almost as good, so she stayed out of it.) The exhibition of the pies also marked the start of the snow, blowing in swirling, vehement gusts outside; the sound of the wind in the eaves gave the impression of lonely snow owls, crying out for a world gone cold.

Dad pushed away from the table, patting his ample gut. When had he gotten heavy? Was he like that when he was living with her and Maura in Los Angeles? "I think I have just about enough energy to get three or four pages in. What do you say, Karen? Want to give it a go?"

Deep flush rose in her cheeks. Logy from the food and wine, she didn't seriously consider shouting, even as a high voice within her quailed. Instead of speaking, she timidly shook her head. The alcohol, which had been pleasantly bubbling in her skull, now made her feel a little dizzy, a little disoriented.

"All right, no problem," he said lightly, but his eyes were on hers. *I'm trying to send you a lifeline*, his look suggested. *I can't take it yet,* she tried to tell him, looking away. *Don't you know that?* "How about you, champ?" Dad nodded his chin toward Henry, who looked surprised.

"You want to write together?"

Smiling a little sleepily, Dad said, "I don't know, I just thought it'd be fun. We've got three bestselling writers in one room. You ever hear of those stories about famous writers on a retreat and they all write together?" He shrugged.

"Thanks, Gary," Henry said. "Sincerely. I got my writing done earlier today."

"And that's why he didn't have time to make a pie from scratch," Thomas said, and everyone laughed. Karen hadn't realized how much tension had been in the room until it dissipated. Dad went into his office and shut the door. The rest of them took their coffees and headed into the living room. There was some discussion about turning on *Jeopardy!*, but no one really wanted the TV on. Skylark Dear wore a polka-dotted dress that stopped at her knees, a blue cashmere blouse whose top two buttons were open, revealing a thin gold necklace with an anchor depending from it. Her makeup was light and her hair relaxed. When she sat in the big chair, she curled her legs up under her and rested her coffee cup on her knee. Outside the wind howled and shrieked. The snow was coming down hard and fast, as if OKC had done it harm and it would have its vengeance. It was warm in here, and Skylark Dear had never looked more radiant. Los Angeles seemed a faraway city in a fairy-tale land. This was home.

"Writing any good books lately?" she asked Henry, who looked up from his cocoa with marshmallows, his eyes skittering around the room.

"I mean, I've published a few."

"I know. I read them. They're good. I liked *Lady in the Sky* the best." She hadn't. *Goodbye, Burger City* had been a masterwork. The three books that had followed – *Petals for Gretchen*, *Perforations,* and *Lady in the Sky* – had all been good, maybe very good, but none had equaled the raw power and energy of *Burger City*. It was difficult not to feel a little smug about that, but Karen managed with some effort. Smugness broke through idyll faster than screaming. "But what's in the pipeline? Thomas won't tell me."

Thomas, who talked with Karen at least once a week, smiled distractedly. "You know, that's a very interesting question that we were waiting until now to discuss with you."

Karen sat up straight. "What?" She sighed. "Goddammit, Henry, are you writing another book about my life? One time is forgivable but twice is really pushing it."

Henry set his cocoa down. "No. Just the opposite, in fact." He stood and went to his satchel, hanging off the back of his dining room chair. After a moment, he handed it to Karen, who took it with numb fingers.

Thomas leaned forward. "You tell me if I'm wrong about everything. I made a guess. I think I'd consider us pretty close by now, and you never came right out and said you were having problems, but..."

Unbuckling the satchel, Karen slid out the sheaf of paper inside. A manuscript. Of course it was. Printed out, double spaced, about six hundred pages. On the cover page, in large, welcoming font, were the words, *Full of Empty.* Below that, in much smaller font, were the words, *A new novel by Karen Luck.*

In a halting voice almost drowned out by the screeching, assailing wind, Henry said, "It's about me. It's by you."

Karen turned the page over and glanced at the first paragraph.

I was eight years old when I realized, suddenly and without much provocation, that my father was an asshole. That fact didn't stop me from trying to love him. I tried so hard for so long to make him proud of me, waiting for any indication that he cared about me. That indication never quite came. When love curdles, it becomes hate, and hating him became a hobby of mine. Murdering him was the best thing I've ever done. They still haven't found him. I'll tell you why.

She looked up. Henry explained. "It's trite to say that 9/11 fucked me up. It fucked everyone up. But after the bombing here, it was ... a lot of too much. And you coming and being so upset about the book. Justifiably, honestly, and then you left and I started writing. I don't know how much Thomas has told you about my writing process."

Skylark stood suddenly. "I'm going to clean up a little bit. You kids keep talking."

Karen watched her go, tearing her eyes away only reluctantly. Henry said, "She knows about the cross-dressing, she just doesn't like hearing about it."

"I thought you gave that up."

Thomas said, "He did. The first book was all him."

Crossing her arms, then uncrossing them, Karen said, "All his books were all him. I used to write as my Dad. I know how that works."

Henry said, "You don't. Not the way I worked. I started books by myself, tried to become you for awhile, then ended the book by myself. You don't have to understand it or condone it, but just know that that's how it worked for me."

"All right." Karen sipped her coffee and nodded for him to go on.

"What was coming out of me was this super personal book, and it's about 9/11 but I never reference that, and it's about my father but a fictionalized version of him. I never actually killed my father."

"A pity, really," Thomas interjected.

"Yeah, well, I get pretty brutal in the novel. The whole book was catharsis. All me. All mine. Except that it's yours."

"I honestly don't get...," Karen began, but she was starting to.

"He wrote your life in a novel," Thomas said. "Now it's your turn."

Karen realized she was still gripping the manuscript in her hands, and doing it so tightly that her knuckles were white. She'd turned the title page back over and those smaller words at the bottom – *A new novel by Karen Luck* – screamed off the page at her. "But I didn't write it," she said.

"But you *did* write *Goodbye, Burger City*," Henry told her. "I can't explain the alchemy of it. Or clairvoyance or whatever. If I was using you as a crutch to write all my other novels, in that book, I honestly felt like I was channeling you." He swallowed. "Maybe I psychically leeched from you. Maybe that's why you can't write now."

Henry slapped his hands to his mouth, a gesture so cartoonish that it should have been comical. Karen looked from him to Thomas and back again. "Who told you I couldn't write?"

"I had a feeling," Thomas said. "I've lived with a writer for awhile now. I know how writers talk about their books. You never talked that way about yours. They always seemed distant to you, like old friends you almost remember from sleepaway camp."

Waiting to feel offended and finding herself not, Karen said, "That's ... pretty perceptive."

"Look, I don't want to be presumptuous. And I don't ... I know I'm not part of the Luck family. But this *is* something of a tradition in this house when someone can't write. Your family rallies. You come together to make sure the books stay written. When you left home, Gary – your Dad – kind of took me under his wing. He mentored me. I think I would love him even if I didn't hate my own father. And of course I've always loved you. Just now in a different way. Please, at least read the book. And if you like it, it can be your book. No strings attached. Tit for tat."

Here are the things Karen could have done: told them all to fuck off and get a cab back to Los Angeles. Lied that she was totally writing; she had a really popular book out right now and she was going to sign another contract with Denali soon. Explained to them that the fears about having a bunch of lesbian novels in a row come out and fuck with her rep might be unfounded, and that she still had two more of those banked, *plus* maybe a short story collection, so she was doing fine without lying about a book she never wrote. But those words clanged within her: *A new novel by Karen Luck*; despite the publishing, there hadn't been a new novel by Karen Luck since 2001. And what if she got to the end of her banked books and she was still running on empty? What then?

Karen Luck said, "Thank you. Both of you. I'm going to read it and—"

Then, a massive, rending crash exploded nearby, followed by a shriek so loud that at first Karen thought it was still the wind. *No. Not the wind. My father. My father.*

Leaping from the couch, Karen shouted for him. Only that shriek, muffled by the sound of the door and the locomotive churn of the wind. She got to his office and tried the knob. It turned but the door itself refused to budge. Then Henry was next to her, his shoulder against the door. "On three," he said, and when they slammed in, the door creaked open, fighting against some unseen obstacle. Snow battled them like a solid thing, forcing itself on them like a frozen battalion. Part of the ceiling had been battered away like so much plaster under a giant's fist. The redolent stench of pine bashed their nostrils, mixing there with the icy no-scent of snow and wind. Where the window had been was now a gaping maw stuffed with tree branches; the top of the tree had hucked up against the door communicating into the living room, as if the tree had claimed this place for the outside and wanted no interference from the place of people.

And somewhere deep in the blinding morass of snow and pine was her father, Gary Luck. The ceiling light had blown out, but Gary's laptop was still glowing, casting its artificial blue-white light into the void. In the light, Karen saw two things: one, there was something wrong with his left hand, and two … two …

Dad shrieked again and Karen screamed for Thomas, screamed hard. Henry, who had for a split-second been transfixed by what he was seeing (*all the blood why so much blood*), now ran toward the office door to yank the top of the tree away. A moment later, Thomas was in with them; Karen glanced toward the opening, unable to believe that a second ago, she had been ready to accept Henry's offer to publish a book under her name. That had seemed like the craziest possible thing then. "Oh God," Thomas muttered under her breath, allowing herself that same split-second that Henry had indulged in before her training kicked in. "Okay. Okay. Henry and Karen, I need you to get whatever is on his hand off. Can you do that?"

They nodded in unison. She turned back to Skylark, who stood in the doorway, screaming inarticulately. "Sky! *Sky!* Kitchen scissors. I need them right now. *Right now.*" After a second, the woman disappeared back into the kitchen, reappearing a moment later and handing them, blade first, toward Thomas.

When the tree busted through the wall, it had taken the heavy oak bookcase with it. If the angle had been different, maybe the books would have been carried away by the gale-force winds, out into the screaming world. But the bookcase had fallen inward, and both it and the books that it housed collapsed as a single, immutable object, crushing Gary Luck's hand between itself and the desk at which he'd been working. When Karen and Henry managed to hoist the case up and off Dad's hand and the books tumbled harmlessly to the floor, Karen saw with no surprise that the books had been theirs: Elaine's, Gary's, Karen's, and Henry's. Her family's life's work. Gothics and crime stories and endless trauma. A body of tragedy.

Then Dad shrieked again, and Karen's eyes flicked from Dad's hand to the tree branch lodged in his gut. Thomas had to shout to be heard above the wind. "I'm going to cut this and we're going to have to move him out of the weather. He's going to scream. I need your help."

Karen nodded furiously, staring down at that branch puncturing her father's belly. The blood, God, the *blood*. But she'd seen gut punctures before, hadn't she? She's seen blood like this before, too. It was her father, and she suspected distantly that she was crying; some deeper part within her was trying desperately to figure out a way to assign herself blame for this, even now, even as the snow piled on her head and back and didn't melt. But most of her was simply awake and alert and aware. This was old hat now. She could do this.

Grabbing the branch to steady it, Thomas worked the kitchen shears into the wood, grimly pumping it. The tendons in her neck stood out. These shears were meant to cut through twine and supple meat, not the unforgiving bark of a tree that had always lived and, in its death throes, had tried to kill. With a final rending cry, she managed to cut it loose. The branch still connected to the tree trunk sprang back and connected with Skylark's face, knocking her to the ground. Later, a doctor would tweeze a pine needle from her eyelid. Right then she felt nothing.

Scrambling to her feet, Skylark got under his left arm as Henry got under his right. Thomas and Karen each took a leg and managed to get him through the door into the living room, spreading him out across the expansive coffee table. "Pillows," Thomas barked at Henry. He grabbed a couple of the decorative throw pillows that Skylark had added to the couch when she started coming by more frequently. Thomas got them under his legs and butt, so that Dad looked like he was kicking back with his feet up. Except for the blood. There was still way too much blood.

"Dish towels, Sky. Get as many clean ones as you can." She did, dashing into the kitchen and back in seconds. Randomly, Karen thought, *she knew exactly where they were. How often is she here?*

"Karen!" Thomas said, clapping. Had she seriously thought she was inured to stuff like this because she'd finally gotten over killing the Butcher? And, weird thought to have right now, but it seemed as if, just maybe, she *wasn't* fully over killing the Butcher. That was her father's blood. Dad might die here, in their living room. Had she spent years freaking out over *writer's block*? "I need you to apply pressure. I need you to do that right now. Don't push the branch in any farther, but get these dish towels around it and press *down*. We're trying to keep as much blood inside him as possible."

"What are you going to do?"

"I drive an ambulance. I'm going to see if it's close."

She scurried off into the kitchen to make her calls. Skylark stood astride the kitchen and the living room, glancing back and forth between Thomas and Gary. Karen kneeled on the deep-pile carpet that had lain under this coffee table since she was in high school. How many times had she done her homework like this, kneeling in front of this table, the knobby strands of carpet poking into her knees. How often had Henry been on the other side of the table, as he was now, his textbooks out, head bent, sometimes sneaking glances at her? They didn't go to the same school, and their curricula were vastly different, but Henry was always willing to help her if she needed it, always willing to come by and keep her company if she felt lonely. He did all that even after they stopped having sex. She bet he would have kept doing it even after she'd come out to him. Not because she could give him what he needed from her, but because giving everything of himself to her was a bigger part of it. Her liking him was not as important as him liking her. Had she known that then? Why was she thinking about it now?

Dad's eyes fluttered and his mouth worked. She pressed down on his wound, being careful not to stab the branch in any deeper. On the other side of the office door, the remaining branches of the tree scraped against the wood, like some feral thing wanting to be let in. Henry whispered something in his ear that she couldn't hear. Dad gasped and sobbed. "I'm not thinking ... about books ... right now." His voice sounded choked and far away. Karen wanted to hold him and offer assurances. Instead, she'd been dealt a different hand.

"You'd better be thinking about it," she said, and Henry looked up. "I didn't write all those books pretending to be you only to have you crap out on me when you're writing your own books again. I've got my own shit to write."

Dad's wan smile stuttered. "Not right now, you don't."

Her eyes went wide. "Are you seriously ... I literally have your life in my hands."

"Then Henry can write my books."

"Henry's already writing *my* books."

Henry said, "Literary historians are going to be so confused."

Unable to help it, Karen barked out a laugh. Henry did, too. Dad attempted one; it escalated into an immediate, ululating scream. "It *hurts*," he shouted.

The bluster Karen had feigned a second ago exploded. Under her hands, the dishtowels were growing scarlet blossoms, soaking the sides of her hands. Her own tears fell. "Dad. Daddy? You listen to me. Okay, just listen. I need you. I don't know if I tell you that enough. I need you in my life. And maybe Henry's better at saying that because he's always been better at emotion. But I love you just as much. And I … Daddy, I am *not* losing both of my parents to fucking *weather*."

Thomas ran into the room. "Ambulances are packed tonight, but there's one on its way. It's gotta go slowly because the roads are hellish, but your father *is* getting into a hospital tonight. How's the…?"

Skylark stepped forward. "I'll get more dishtowels. Those look all in." Her voice cracked on those last words, and she disappeared into the kitchen before anyone could see her start to cry.

"You're doing great, guys," Thomas said. "Karen, if you'd like me to take over..."

"No. I have this. Henry, could you do something for me?" The desperate look in his eyes told her everything she needed to know about wanting to be of some concrete use. "I need you to get Dad's laptop. It has his new novel on it. I don't know if he's sent it to himself or anything. Be careful but get it now, before the ambulance gets here."

He cast one glance toward Thomas, who nodded. Henry ran off and Thomas knelt across from Karen, who kept the pressure on the best she could.

"Is he going to be okay?"

Thomas bit her lip. "It's really too early to tell. We're going to do everything we can. The blizzard is going to make it hard and..."

"Thomas?"

"Yeah?"

"Tell me what I want to hear right now, okay? Truth later."

Thomas sniffed. "He will absolutely make a full recovery. OKC has some of the best doctors in the world. The snow is already lessening and this is all going to be nothing but a good story in just a few months."

"Okay."

"Okay?"

"Thank you."

Then, distantly, the sound of the ambulance siren carried on the wind, wafting and winding its way toward the house, traveling on frigid breezes. The next hour blurred by, too many people in her house, in her living room, barking orders, crouched over her father, relaying messages to Thomas in jargon she couldn't understand. In the midst of it all, Karen found herself backed into the corner by the painting with the deer on it. Henry was next to her, the laptop tucked under his arm, his face as white as the snow piling up on Dad's desk and on the books they'd all written over all these years.

When he clutched for Karen's hand, she took it, and held it tight. She didn't think. She didn't pray. She just stared, transfixed. Had she thought she couldn't be made numb by all this? Now that she didn't have to be brave, didn't have to be useful, numbness just came.

Thomas approached them. "We're taking him to Our Lady," she told them. "I'm going to be blunt here. You can't come. You can't follow behind. The roads are too bad and none of us want to worry about you two – or Skylark – when we should be spending all our time trying to save your father." Thomas said this looking at both of them; if she knew that she was speaking in error, she didn't correct herself.

"But I want—"

"I know what you want, Karen. This time you don't get it. I will call with every update. I will keep you informed. It's serious but it may not be deadly. That's the truth. The actual truth. Let us help him."

After a hesitation, Karen nodded, and then her father (*their* father?) was gone, and the house was once again silent.

Skylark, who had yet to move from her place between the kitchen and the living room, leaning against the wide doorway as if she was holding it up with her back, forced a smile. "Well, I guess I'll start in on the dishes," she said, and then fell to the floor, heavy sobs racking her body. Karen went to her at once, getting her arms around the woman, who grabbed blindly back. "It's not *fair*," she screamed. "I had a shitty husband. I've done my penance. I paid for loving him. I'm sick of paying. Gary was supposed to be a reward. Why is this my *life*?"

Henry got her around the other side, and they led her to the couch. There, she sprawled out, closing her eyes and almost immediately falling asleep. Karen could think of no better refuge, but she was as keyed up and jittery as she had ever been.

"Karen." She looked at Henry, who had opened the laptop; his face glowed in the blue-white light. She came around to look into the screen. The last words her father wrote were

Cunningham slammed his face into the wall as hard as she could. She felt his nose crunch. It didn't matter how tough and roided-out you were; if someone broke your nose, you were diminished. The man crumpled to the floor and wjdfplkf:Ewu['

Karen almost couldn't look at it. She could envision her father in his cozy, safe, familiar office, buzzing on the high only good writing can offer. Had he even heard the initial crash, or was he fully engaged in that awesome fragment, *if someone broke your nose, you were diminished*. It was so specific and universal. That word, *diminished*: had it come to him after some rumination. Had he considered *reduced*? Or even *fucked*?

"Do you know what the rest of the novel is about?" Henry asked her.

"Jessica Cunningham fucks up the bad guys," she said. "Nothing specific."

"Okay," he said. "Then we go off vague." Henry retreated to the kitchen table, setting the laptop down on a trivet and starting to move all the food and dishes to the sink and the counters and the fridge. After a moment, Karen pitched in, pulling off the paper tablecloth and wiping the table down with the rag hung over the faucet. She sat and he sat. Henry opened up the laptop and said, "The man crumpled to the floor and. And what?"

Karen said, "He's ... he's um. Screaming. Convulsing. Holding his nose."

"What's Jessica doing?"

"What *was* she doing?"

Henry pressed the PAGE UP button and glanced at what Gary had written. "Investigating something." He looked Karen in the eyes. She looked back. "Vague."

"Okay. There's a back room. There's a ... oh, damn, what if there's a kid being held in there. She didn't expect that. It's not the same mystery. It comes in out of nowhere."

"Good," Henry said. "Now shut up for awhile." Henry hunched over the laptop, poised his fingers over the home keys, and began to type. Karen watched him without moving. Distantly, she was aware that she was thirsty, but she'd written through thirst before. She had never seen Henry work; he stuck his lower jaw out and furrowed his brow, the heat of his concentration baking off of him in radiation waves. By the time he'd finished, an hour had passed. With a grunt, he stood and turned the laptop her way. "Go," he said.

If it occurred to her to remind him that she *couldn't* write, that he had written a whole novel for her to publish as her own because she knew that, she didn't mention it. She didn't bother mentioning it to herself. Those long walks in the Hollywood Hills, those unproductive staring sessions with her own laptop, those days of waking up and wanting to die – those moments all seemed so distant now. Silly, even. Who had that woman been?

"Mirabelle," the girl told her, and then promptly burst into tears. "I want my Daddy. I want my Daddy!"

That last sentence socked her one in the gut. Maybe Henry had known that. Probably Henry had known that. He was at the sink, filling up two glasses of water. Karen took a long gulp and without thinking this a momentous moment, she started typing.

Jessica closed her eyes and held the girl closer. "We'll find your Daddy," she said. "But first things first. Let's get out of here, huh?"

Karen wrote for an hour, then flipped the laptop back around to Henry. She barely glanced at the phone on the way to the bathroom; when she came back, she refilled both glasses and sat across from Henry, watching him work.

Neither of them noticed when Skylark woke up and went back to her place in the doorway between the kitchen and the living room, watching them. If they *had* noticed, they might have said that her look was somewhat indulgent, as if she were watching on, admiring the kids for doing whatever they could to get through this long night. She wasn't.

They have this. They have their writing. Thomas is right in it. My ex-husband might as well be dead, I've always kept my colleagues at a distance, and I never tried that hard to make friends. So now I'm here, all alone while the man I love is in critical condition, all alone in a house that isn't my own. All alone even though my son is here, all alone even though this girl I've known since she was a baby is here, all alone because I didn't think I needed defense mechanisms anymore after Welton. I gave them up and now I'm here, alone and vulnerable and sick with dread. Goddammit, Gary. I didn't know I'd need protection from you.

She cried silently, unaware that she was doing it, as Karen and Henry swapped Gary's laptop back and forth between each other until dawn. They were heading toward the book's denouement when the phone finally rang. All three of them started out of their haze. Karen left Jessica Cunningham midway through the gun fight to leap toward the phone hanging on the wall. She listened. She muttered assent. She hung up.

"He's alive," Karen told them, her whole body numb. "More than alive, actually. Stable. The branch didn't actually pierce his stomach. It came close and he had to go into surgery but … he's okay. That part didn't…"

"Karen," Skylark said, touching her shoulder. Under any other circumstance, the touch would have sent little thrills throughout Karen's body. Not now. Not this time. "How's his hand?"

"Oh, that," she said. "Well, he's going to lose that. They had to amputate. It was unsalvageable. Thomas used the word *necrotic*. I don't really know what… So they cut off his *hand*. That's what happened while we wrote his book. They saved his life and cut off his hand."

"Can we go there now?" Henry asked.

"When the roads are passible, we can. Probably later today. The snow stopped but the roads…"

"Karen."

"He lost his hand, Henry."

"Let's finish the book."

"Fuck the book."

"Fuck *you*. Sit down and finish your goddamned turn."

"It doesn't matter anymore. Aren't you listening to me? He lost his *hand*."

"And so he might not be able to finish it himself. Sit down. Write."

Karen turned to Skylark, whose tears streamed down her placid, almost robotic face. "He's alive," she said. "You keep glossing over that but it's the most important part. He's alive and he's going to stay alive. Write your book, Karen. He's alive, so write your book."

They finished the new book just after four. They had been writing almost straight through for twenty hours. Karen hadn't written like that since her month of hell, one-third of which was spent in Dad's ruined office. Henry had the last turn, finishing the book with this short paragraph:

Damage was inevitable, Jessica thought. You could try to avoid hurt and pain, but those things have a way of finding you. But sometimes, just sometimes, you find ways to live with damage. You incorporate it into your life, and though it fits uneasily with your unhurt parts, it does *fit. Survival was underrated. They were going to survive. Today, that was going to have to be enough.*

Karen read the paragraph three times before flicking her eyes up over the rim of the keyboard to Henry's face. "Okay."

"Yes?"

Karen typed the words THE END at the bottom, hesitated, then, impulsively, wrote *a novel by Gary Luck* underneath that. She showed it Henry, and to Skylark, who both nodded. Twenty minutes later, they were in a cab. Thirty minutes after that, they were at the hospital. The sun was already going down by the time the three of them approached the front desk; technically, visiting hours would be over soon, but they were giving some leniency due to the storm.

Gary was groggily awake by the time the three of them arrived, sitting up in his bed and feeling the occasional lightning-streaks of emanating from his hand and his belly. Even medicated, he knew that he didn't want to seek out either locus of pain. Whenever he thought about looking down at his gut or over at his hand, he heard the crash and the shattering of glass; heard the sound of the bookcase tumbling; felt himself turning to face what was happening at exactly the wrong time, leaving his belly prone and his hand vulnerable. He didn't need to see to know what happened. Gary Luck understood what it meant to be diminished.

Then his daughter was in the room with him, holding him, tears streaming from her face, wetting his. He held her back as best as he could, not wanting to hug her because when he hugged her, he always laced his hands behind her back and squeezed tight. It was the way he'd hugged her the day her mother went missing, and all the days after. He wanted to comfort her as he'd done back then, to assure her that things were going to be okay. Not great, sure, not perfect, but okay. They would live. How could he do that when he couldn't even hug her right? Tears swam into his eyes and pooled there.

"Daddy, I…"

Then Henry was there. "We saved your laptop," he said at once, almost shouting. "We saved it. Now you can write more books. It's going to be fine, Gary, because we saved your laptop."

Gary murmured, "I can write more books."

A brilliant, terrible smile appeared on Henry's face. "Yeah! Isn't that something?"

Skylark, his love, appeared, and for the first time since coming awake, Gary felt himself relax against his pillow. The drugs were there to help him handle the pain better, and for the most part they were working, but they seemed to be working better now. He wanted to tell Henry that he was like a son to him, and he wanted to tell Karen he loved her more than anything else in this whole world, but that right now, right this second, all he wanted was this good woman by his side.

Somehow, someway, Skylark Dear read his mind.

"Kids, why don't you wait outside for a little bit. I want to talk with your father alone." *Your father*, she'd said, including both of them. A small smile appeared on Gary's face, despite everything. Ever since becoming aware of his injuries, images had been flashing through Gary's mind: men on islands, their clothes tattered, foraging for fruits and hunting if they could. Men in makeshift huts, staring out the misshapen doors at storms raging outside. Men crossing deserts, parched, unable to keep going but going anyway. Survival. Images of survival. He clung to these thoughts and others like them. The days ahead were going to be hard, but maybe not impossible. And maybe not without their pleasures. Maybe it wasn't simply a matter of mere survival.

Skylark approached his bed and touched his forehead. "Warm," she said.

"Hot?" The grogginess, the druggy lightheadedness, seemed to dissipate at her touch.

"Not really. Not a fever."

"Is that Mom instinct?"

"Everything's Mom instinct," she said. Then: "I want to cry for you. I think I'm going to wait until later for that. I've already cried for myself and that seems selfish now."

He smiled. "It's not."

She said, "Do you want to know what the kids did all night?"

Gary's smile faltered a tiny bit. "Please don't tell me they had sex."

Skylark's eyes went wide. "My son is about as close to married as you can get and your daughter's a lesbian."

Trying to shrug, Gary said, "Well, they've done it before."

"They wrote," Skylark said, meeting his eyes. "They wrote *your* book. They think they finished it."

Gary found himself laughing, which hurt his belly but he did it anyway. "Of course they did. That's what they do. But they didn't finish it."

"No?"

"No. Even if it's brilliant, they didn't. I was Doreen Daley and then I was Elaine Luck. It took me a long time to figure myself out as a writer and I'm going to keep doing that."

Sky put her hand on his arm, the one that ended abruptly at the wrist. "You know…"

"I know," Gary said. "I'm going to figure it out. But if that book and the one after it are going to be written, I'm going to write them."

"Good," she said. "And you're going to do it in my house."

Gary raised his eyebrows, feeling sleepy again, and safe. "Am I?"

"Yeah. Yours is going to need some renovations. There's a little hole in your wall."

"So I'm going to be staying with you for awhile?"

"Maybe for more than awhile. If that doesn't cramp your swinging bachelor lifestyle."

Swallowing back tears, Gary said, "Skylark, we should have done this so long ago. I love you. You know that, right? I've loved you for years and I…"

"Shh. I know. I love you too."

"We're going to move in together."

"Yes."

"It's not mere survival. I will live through this but it's not just living through it. It's being with you. It's us."

"Well thank God," she said, and found tears springing to her own eyes. "I thought you were just into me for my body."

He smiled, close to sleep. "Well it's not the smallest consideration."

Skylark returned his smile, and kissed him on the forehead. "Sleep well, Gary Luck. I'll see you when you wake up."

Then he drifted, and the pillow was soft and the beeping sounds of the monitors lulled him, and she could feel the gentle pressure her lips left on his forehead. It was 2006 before he was able to go home, and by then, home was a different place. His writing studio was new, slightly more modern, with a throw rug under the big oak desk and books set into recessed shelves. The lone window looked out on the Dears' backyard, sloping down to the woods far back. There had been trees closer to his window, but Skylark had ordered them cut down. She hadn't had to that, but he thanked her for it anyway.

He'd read the kids' version of *The Sin of Conscience*, which was ... disjointed and weird at best. There was good writing in there, but it absolutely didn't connect to the story he'd been telling and often didn't connect to the story *they* were telling. According to Skylark, they hadn't read anything that he, Gary, had written ... nor were they too keen on reading what each other had written. Writing itself was the important thing. Getting through by writing.

Gary Luck woke up his laptop, put the stump of his left wrist on the desk, and opened his document. With his one hand, he slowly – so slowly – began to type. That night, he managed a single page, and by the end of his session, he was crying hard.

The next night he got out two pages. Then two and a half. It took him six months to finish the novel that his daughter and almost-son had written in a night, but it was his. It was his.

Not mere survival. Not by a long shot.

Chapter 14: Hello, Burger City

"If you're here to renegotiate a contract, I'm listening. If not, I'm gone."

Cynthia picked up her glass and looked into it. It was a good line that she absolutely didn't intend to follow up on. Over the rim of her glass, Karen was still absorbed in the menu. "Can you recommend anything here?"

"The steak Diane," Cynthia said, wanting to be furious, not knowing if furious was the right reaction. She'd gone to see Gary Luck the moment she'd heard about his accident, but Karen had already gone home to Los Angeles by then. She'd spent a lot of time over the last few years considering the things she had told Karen, the restriction she'd put on her writing and publishing. At the time it had seemed like the absolute right thing to do; in the moment, it seemed eminently defensible. Just lately, she wondered. Absolutely she had wanted to push a new and untested writer into her greatest mainstream success ... but she'd remained a mainstream success. At some point, Karen Luck had been a tested name and pretty much nothing – even being gay, especially in the early 2000s – was going to really knock her off that perch. So why, Cynthia had asked herself over and over in the intervening years, had it been so important to keep Karen writing the type of novel she'd always written?

Karen rolled her eyes, and for the barest moment, Cynthia could have sworn she was sitting across from Elaine Luck, as she had been all those years ago. In that moment, Cynthia could actually smell Elaine's perfume. What had it been called? Something fantastic, something … Cloud Dreams! That was it! Only Elaine could get away with wearing something so Young Miss friendly as Cloud Dreams; there was always that whimsy in her that Karen never entirely approached. She could be funny, and she could be sweet, and she could sure as hell be talented. But she could never be Elaine.

"Kind of a vintage choice, don't you think?" Karen asked.

"If I recall correctly, you were always fond of vintage choices."

Karen smiled. "You weren't mocking my affection for older women when it was directed your way."

"Well, my mouth was full a lot of the time."

"Dirty old woman."

"Right back at you."

Karen signed and surveyed her old lover. And nemesis? Maybe. After all this time, it was sort of hard to get worked up over that stuff anymore. When you've literally held your father's life in your hands, when you see firsthand – pun definitely not intended – how fragile people are, all the little trials and arguments just don't seem to matter as much. Was this a lesson Karen might have learned after seeing her mother carried away by a tornado? Or after accidentally killing a man, and seeing his spread of carnage out before her as she did it? Or even, for God's sake, after watching that woman jump from that window over and over again? Life is precious. Life is a gift. Besides, Karen thought she might have figured out Cynthia's whole deal by this point. Which was sort of the point of this.

"I think we need to talk," Karen said. "Frankly, openly. About real stuff. About us. About your place in my life, and in my Dad's. You're our history, Cynthia. And I know I was the one that left but not having you around has kind of sucked."

Cynthia, suddenly on edge, waited for the other shoe to drop. There would be a *but* here. Or some cruel twist of the knife. "Oh yeah?" Her hackles rose. She'd been alive for nearly sixty years without her hackles rising. Karen Luck was many things, but boring wasn't one of them.

"Yeah. I don't think you treated me as fairly as you could have when we were working together, but ... hell, Cyn. Maybe I didn't treat you fairly, either."

"Karen, whatever this is..."

"It's a peace offering. And I think you're going to want the peace."

Karen rummaged in her satchel and pulled out a thick sheaf of paper. Forcibly, Cynthia was reminded of that day, so long ago, when Gary Luck had done the exact same thing, producing the first of Elaine Luck's lost manuscripts. *Chaos Logic* had kicked off a long, fertile period, both for Elaine's posthumous career but also for Gary's midcareer trajectory. He had never done Tom Clancy numbers, but he'd been widely read and mostly loved. Then, just as Elaine's last book was making its way to the market, this girl shows up with her fresh voice and demands and is more popular than either of her folks ever were.

This felt like déjà vu. This felt like repetition.

"I won't say that Dad's accident had an upside. It didn't. He lost his hand. He could have died. There's probably no upside to that." Cynthia patiently waited. Karen was holding what was clearly a manuscript in her hands but refusing to present it. This was meant to be theatrical. Okay. She could play along.

"But...?"

"But. Due to the damage of the house, we had to move a bunch of stuff from Dad's old office and put it in Mom's. Lots of renovations to the house now. Trying to make it tree-proof, you know."

Cynthia smiled tightly ... then felt that smile loosen. She sighed, hating that she was loving this. This was Elaine.

Gary could never tease her like this. Karen really did take after her mother. "I see," Cynthia said.

"Well, when we were moving stuff around in Mom's office to accommodate Dad's, we accidentally stumbled across this."

Now Karen presented the pages. They were clearly a printout. On the top were the words *And Now Come the Fires*. Underneath, in smaller type, were these words: *a novel by Elaine Luck*.

"Karen," Cynthia said, laying her hand on the top of the stack, unable to help the thrill that ran through her, unable to stop herself from the overwhelming giddiness of seeing that name after all this time on something that was as-yet unpublished.

"I know what you're going to say. This is clearly from a computer. My Mom obviously only ever wrote on a typewriter."

"That was one of the things I was going to say."

"The manuscript wasn't doing as well as it could have. There'd been some water damage, even before the big blizzard. We brought it to a place that scanned in the old pages and converted them to pixels. Then I went through and did copyediting, fixing some of the typos and stuff the scanners created. Then Dad went in and did a full edit to make sure it all flowed.

"And does it? Flow?"

"It flows. It's really good. Imagine publishing an unearthed Elaine Luck novel. It'd be like when they found that missing James M. Cain book, but even more mainstream. First, I think you'd want to do it because it would probably sell pretty well. Second, I think you'd want to do it because it'd mean you got to do one last favor for my Mom."

Questions stacked up in Cynthia's mind – *what's it about?* chief among them – but she dismissed them all. "Let me run a little scenario by you, Karen," she said. "There's a popular novelist who can't write. She keeps publishing, but they're all old books she wrote when she was with her old publisher and never released. Then one day, perhaps spurred by a traumatic event, this author sits down and decides to try her hand at a, quote, missing manuscript by her dead mother. How am I doing so far?"

Karen grinned. "Please continue. It's a fascinating story."

Warming up to it, Cynthia said, "No stakes. No win or lose. She can't write as herself but maybe this goes well. And maybe it's just an exercise at first, but then it grows and becomes something bigger. Better, even. Good enough to publish. So this writer, maybe wanting to mend fences or get back at her old publisher in some way that makes sense only to her, decides to offer the manuscript up for publication as a 'lost' novel. Because maybe she's writing again on her own and she can afford to do it. Sound right?"

"I don't know," Karen said. "Like I said, it's a good story."

"But is it true?"

"Truth is subjective," Karen said, sipping more of her wine. "Now let me run a scenario by you."

"I'm all ears."

"There's a woman who's in love with another woman. She's been in love with her for years, but it took her a long, long time to figure it out. The woman she's in love with is straight, you see, and can never love her back the way she wants and maybe needs. Maybe she gets used to the setup, the pining without resolution. At first the pining was torture. Then it was exquisite. And then it was impossible. Because then the straight woman is taken away, before he gay woman can ever profess her love. How am *I* doing?"

"It's a little clichéd," Cynthia said, not taking her eyes off of Karen's.

"Isn't it, though? The twist comes when you find out the straight woman had a daughter, and the daughter, against all odds, turns out gay. But this presents a problem for the gay woman, who is still in love with the mother. Being intimate with the daughter of the woman you're still in love with is maybe good. Her not actually *being* her mother is bad. So maybe this woman tries to mold her into the image of her mother. Presenting as straight as she can, because that's how she loved the woman who left her. The pining could happen again. And that works. That works for a hell of a long time. Sound familiar?"

Cynthia sucked in breath, closing her eyes. "If I say fuck you, Karen, does it prove or disprove?"

Karen reached across the table, over the manuscript, and took Cynthia's hand. "I don't want to hurt you anymore. I don't want to hurt anymore."

Her eyes opened, and locked with Karen's. They weren't Elaine's, but they were close. And they were earnest. "All right."

"There's been a whole conspiracy of keeping my mother alive, Cyn. Me and you and Dad. She didn't deserve to die so we've been making sure she didn't."

Cynthia nodded toward *And Now Come the Fires*. "Did you write this, or did she?"

Karen watched her for a long moment. "I found a manuscript that has my mother's name on it. Do you want to publish it?"

"Of course I want to publish it."

"Then you have to agree to terms."

"I'm listening."

"One more Mike Bull book from my father. One book from me. And my main character is…"

"A lesbian. Yes, I assumed."

Karen laughed. "Nope. Wrong again. My main character is just a missing kid. His name is Mike. He's not even gay." She paused. "And all the proceeds from my book are to go to the Johns Hopkins Transplant Center."

Cynthia wasn't aware that she was in a reverie until Karen startled her out of it. "Oh!" she said, then let it filter down into the marrow of her thoughts. "Oh."

"So," Karen said. "The steak Diane?"

Cynthia picked up the manuscript and found the first chapter. This is how the book started:

When we are in pain, we always think we've reached our threshold long before we have. If it escalates incrementally enough, we have a chance to build a tolerance. Only when the source of the pain is finally gone do we realize just how awful it was. I almost died summer I lived with my grandmother, but I didn't know that until much, much later.

"You know," Karen said. "Weird thing. The main character in *Mom's* book is a lesbian."

Cynthia's lips curled into a knowing smile. "Is she, now?"

"Weird, isn't it? She was always just a little bit ahead of her time."

The food eventually came. Conversation turned to other matters. Wine was drunk, then drunk some more. And before Cynthia could take the check away – "Chanler & Cushing is paying for this, and I'm letting them." – Karen leaned in conspiratorially. "You know, as much as I kind of want to be weirded out by you being into my Mom and dating me, it's not that far off from what I was doing."

"Oh no?" Cynthia's head swam and she let loose a giggle.

"I was in love with someone else, too. Before I was in love with you." She considered. "After, too. Still, actually."

"Okay, I'll bite. Who was it?"

"My best friend's mom."

Cynthia's eyes went wide. "*Henry's* Mom?" Karen nodded deeply. "Well. It's not that she's not a knockout."

"She's *still* a knockout." They clinked glasses and Karen drank deeply.

"But you know. Your best friend's mom? Now that really *is* a cliché."

"Look, I might be a lesbian, but I'm still a suburban kid from Oklahoma. I've got a rep to live up to."

"You have no rep."

At this, they both laughed. Did they sleep together that night? Like the question of whether the latest Elaine Luck discovery was *really* an Elaine Luck discovery, maybe it's best not to know.

The sign was in the window when Karen drove up. She nearly crashed the rental when she saw it. It was almost too shocking to believe.

Henry was sitting in the booth when she came inside and slid across from him. His face was one longview stare, his mouth agape, his eyes wide.

"You saw," she said.

"They can't be closing. This is Burger City. It's an institution."

"Maybe it's not really closing. Maybe we read the sign wrong and it's just closing for renovations."

"Karen, I read the sign eight times and I asked the waitress. It's closing. In like two months."

Karen looked around hopelessly, as if the answer might be under the table, or over near the pie carousel. "I mean … we have money, right? And I've probably been selfish with mine. I could give money. Save the diner. It'd be like those movies we used to watch on TV when we were kids, but we don't have to ride BMX bikes in order to save the rec center."

"We just throw money at it," Henry said.

"That's right. What's wrong with that?"

The voice behind her answered. "Because the owner doesn't want to keep it open." Karen turned and found herself looking into a face she thought she knew, but only barely remembered. "It was his father's, and it's been his for forty years. He's just done with it. He wants to retire."

Henry said, "But surely someone…"

"No one wants the diner," the waitress, cute in her striped yellow-and-white skirt and matching blouse, informed them. Her speech had the cadence of a truth told over and over, like a mantra or a prophecy. "The land, on the other hand…"

Karen asked, her heart sinking, "What are they building?"

The waitress shrugged. "Condos, I think. The way of progress."

Both Henry and Karen laughed at that, but the sound was bitter. Karen tilted her head. "I know you, don't I?"

The waitress' weary façade dropped and a smile lit her face up. "I was positive you wouldn't remember."

Karen's eyes widened. "From Sears! You liked *Really Restless*."

"Oh, so you're the one," Henry laughed, then shut up as they both looked at him.

"You made good on your promise," the waitress said, still grinning. "You wrote more characters like that."

Karen, who had been both pressed for time and also maybe borderline insane when she'd last seen this girl, had never noticed that she was kind of beautiful. Not older, sure, but then again, *she* was older, wasn't she? In her thirties now, and this girl – stop saying *girl*, Karen – this *woman* was probably not that far behind. Her eyes were hazel and her body had some intriguing curves and Karen liked the way her hair frizzed up and couldn't entirely be held down by the pins she'd set into it. *Is this how the midlife crisis begins?* Karen wondered, and wanted to laugh. *I throw my lifelong predilections overboard for the new model, is that it?* Maybe it was a cynical thought, but this woman was looking at her and she was looking right back, and Karen thought if there was gas in the air, the spark between them might set off an explosion.

"I did. I'm going to keep doing it, too."

"You are?"

"I am. When the story warrants it."

"That's good."

Karen felt herself starting to bite her lip, then stopped herself. "You have me at a disadvantage. You know who I am, but here I am, looking for a name tag and coming up short."

The waitress' face turned bright scarlet. "Oh, wow. Hi, sorry. My name's Dorothy."

Karen reached out and shook hands ... then let her hand linger a moment. Their eyes met. Dorothy's hand was surprisingly soft and Karen didn't want to let go. She thought, *I'm no one's prize, Dorothy. I'm obsessive. I put my writing above everything else, and I'm starting to wonder if that might not be the best strategy for life. I mean, that's sort of how my dad lost his hand. Then again, learning to write with one hand was one of the things that saved him after the absence, so I don't know what lesson I'm supposed to take here. All I know is that you are so pretty, and I would be so lucky.*

"I'm Henry," came the voice from the other side of the booth.

Karen let go of Dorothy's hand and turned back toward her oldest friend. "Are you not aware that I'm flirting right now?"

"Oh wow, this is you flirting?"

Dorothy couldn't stop grinning. "Okay, this *is* you flirting. I was like 70% sure."

"Be 100% sure. And ignore Henry. We used to date in high school, back before everything."

Not needing to be told what *everything* meant, Dorothy grinned and nodded. "Nice to meet you, Henry."

"But it's nicer to meet her."

"I'm not sorry to say that that's true."

After a small, slightly awkward pause, Dorothy took their orders and scurried off. When the bill came, Dorothy's number would be written on the back. Karen would call it that night and the two of them would talk deep into the night. When Karen flew back to Los Angeles three months later, Dorothy would be on the plane with her. And the future opened wide.

Now, alone in the booth again, Karen said, "I spoke to Cynthia."

"I know. I still say you didn't owe her anything."

"Maybe not. But my Mom did. And it's going to help my Dad, too. Everyone wins."

"What about Karen Luck? Does she win?"

Karen Luck, whose life had once been interrupted by a tornado, let the question settle into her. Her books were selling well, but that was only part of the point. She was writing again. *Mike's Missing* was only the first of what she was calling the "new Karen Luck books." She had already written another and was working on a third. Her output would slow a little bit as Dorothy moved in, but over the course of their first year, they would work out the sort of rhythm that Karen could never muster with Maura. Her Dad had always said that writing was the most important thing, and for a long while, that was true. But even now, sitting in Burger City with her best friend, she was starting to believe that that might be true only when you're on the fringes. When you're desperate. When you're alone and need a lifeline, when it's the only thing that helps you get up in the morning, when you need some sort of structure in your life to stop you from feeling so lonesome you want to die. Writing is the most important thing when it has to be the most important thing. But it doesn't always have to be.

"Yeah," she said, raising her glass of orange juice. "I think I do win."

Henry picked up his own glass. Early this year, he had published *Full of Empty*, the book Karen had opted not to publish as her own. It had garnered him the best reviews of his career and his biggest sales since *Goodbye, Burger City*. You didn't have to be Karen Luck to be lucky. That was a lesson he'd learned almost too late. Almost. "What are we toasting to?"

"What do you think?" she asked. "Burger City, and the sad march of progress."

"Not all progress is sad," he said.

"You got me there," Karen said.

"To Burger City."

"To Burger City." Karen looked around the old diner, which would soon be pushed aside to make room for new things. Off by the dessert carousel, she thought she could almost see her mother as she was right before she died, smiling and waving. Near the jukebox, a much younger version of her father, the way she remembered him from her childhood. He gave her a thumbs-up and winked at her. As she cast her gaze around Burger City, it seemed to fill with the ghosts of her memory, echoes of people she'd known and maybe loved. Maura in a waitress uniform, playing another role. Skylark Dear, rushing in through the front door, looking exactly as she had the day she and Henry had gotten kinky for the first time. Thomas McAdams, the most recent echo here, looking as she had the night she had saved her father's life, collapsed into a chair, looking harried and hung-out, but with a smile on her face. She'd earned that smile. She'd earned every smile.

Soon enough, this place would no longer be here, and the people who had determined her life would similarly move on. Karen, who had been born in Oklahoma City but who would not die there, would be moving on, too.

Karen Luck touched her glass with Henry Dear's. "Goodbye," she said.

Kevin Quigley

July 31, 2019

Cambridge, Massachusetts